THE PURSUIT OF BEING NOTICED

ROBERT GADKEY

The Pursuit of Being Noticed by Robert Gadkey

This is a work of fiction. Names, characters, organizations, places, events, and incidents are either products of the author's imagination or are used factiously. Any resemblance to actual persons, living or dead, or actual events is purely coincidental.

Copyright © 2021 by Robert Gadkey

All rights reserved.

No part of this book may be reproduced, or stored in a retrieval system, or transmitted in any form or by any means, electronic, mechanical, photocopying, recording, or otherwise, without express written permission of the publisher.

Published by RAWC Publishing

www.rawcpublishing.com

ISBN: 979-8-9850038-1-9 (paperback)

To Angela, as always.

JOIN MY VIP CLUB

To thank you for buying this book, I invite you to join my exclusive VIP Club where you'll be the first to hear about my new books and get two of my short stories – absolutely free.

There's no obligation. You'll never be spammed, and you can opt-out at any time.

To join, go to the back of the book to sign up.

Robert Gadkey

Everybody acts out a myth, but very few people know what their myth is. And you should know what your myth is because it might be a tragedy and maybe you don't want it to be.

—Carl Jung

1

Kate Becker struggled to hide her smile as she peeked at her sister.

The view of downtown Austin from the seventeenth floor of the Wilshire Professional Building was everything she had expected an office at Susan Wilson Law to be. More, actually. The other firms where she had worked offered only bland cityscape views, but Susan demanded the very best. Which was why every office at the firm had a view of the city and the river and the horizon beyond. On that sunny afternoon, it felt like you could see all the way across the world.

"So, what do you think?" Kate asked.

It wasn't much of a question. Anyone with half a brain could have heard her sister's jealous grunts.

"It's not bad, but—"

"But what?"

"I don't know," Jessica said, turning away from the wall of windows and walking back towards the center of the office. "I guess, I just thought it would be... bigger."

Bigger? Was she serious? The office was twice the size of Jessica's tiny broom closet at Goldman & Simmons. Kate knew this for a fact because before she accepted the new job, her sister had teased her about being older but having a smaller office.

"They're a standard size."

Jessica shrugged. "If you say so."

Kate's eyes narrowed. "I do say so. And you'd know so too, if Susan ever let you back here before."

Her sister ignored the jab and glanced down at Kate's ultra-modern black desk. She grabbed a business card from a plastic holder.

"Is this real cotton?"

"Of course, it's real cotton," Kate said. "Do you think Susan would accept synthetic?"

Jessica held up the card up to the light, examined both sides, then ran a finger across the debossed lettering on the front. "I heard a rumor Ms. Wilson printed special cards for VIP clients, but I've never seen one before. It's even got your name on it. After only a week."

"What can I say? Susan needs her star player in the game."

"Uh-huh."

Jessica tried to hand the card back to her, but Kate refused to take it.

"Keep it. To remember your visit. Susan ordered me to hand out a hundred this month."

"You'd better be careful with all that 'Susan' talk, sis. Word on the street is she forces even her childhood friends to call her Ms. Wilson."

Kate wrinkled her nose. "Word on the street? Please tell me Goldman doesn't have you walking the streets now."

"Haha," Jessica said, her face turning serious. "I'm glad you're having so much fun, but you'd better not lose sight of our deal. Or screw it up by doing something stupid. Like calling her Susan to her face."

Kate rolled her eyes. "Relax. Everything is under control. Susan treats us like family. I'll get you a job. You just have to be patient."

"Right."

"What? You don't believe me?" Kate said.

"I believe you should stop calling her Susan."

"Listen, I'll prove it to you. Tell me the one thing Susan values above all else?"

Jessica glanced away, thought for a moment. "Loyalty."

"Okay, sure. That's a good guess. But I'm talking about the other thing."

"Respect."

Kate sighed. "Yes, respect. Who doesn't value respect? But I'm talking about the thing that keeps this place alive?"

"Money?"

Kate flashed her sister an annoyed look. "And how does a law firm make money, Einstein?"

"By winning cases."

"Right. Susan cares about winning. First, foremost, only."

"That's true," Jessica said. "Even when you think she can't win, she always does."

"You wouldn't keep a picture of her on your nightstand otherwise."

Jessica blushed. "I had to move it. A guy who stayed over thought she was my mother. He got all weird when I tried to explain."

Kate shook her head. "Didn't I say it was weird?"

"Well," Jessica said defensively, "Napoleon Hill says you're supposed to wake up to your object of desire."

"Napoleon Hill's an idiot."

Kate grabbed a sheet of paper from the inbox on the desk, handed it to Jessica. She waited for her sister to scan it before continuing.

"That, sis, is your ticket to the Susan Wilson fast track to success."

Jessica raised an eyebrow. "A resume for someone called Riley Anderson?"

"Yes," Kate said proudly. "Riley is the way you're getting hired. And the way we can get even with Tina. Once and for all."

Jessica's eyes went wide.

Tina Black was the most pretentious, shady, cut-throat, social climbing, backstabbing whore in all of Texas. And she was smart too, which also made her dangerous.

"Tell me everything, sensei," Jessica said.

They sat at the desk. Kate in a black, mid-century modern office chair. Jessica in a simple straight chair across from her. Kate hoped it was the first of many strategy sessions held there.

"Remember last week when I told you Susan took me to dinner at the Austin Club?"

"Do I remember?" Jessica said curtly. "Please, woman. Have some respect."

Kate wanted to take it slow, rub it in a little, but when she glanced at her watch, she saw there wasn't time.

"As I'm leaving the Club, guess who I see."

Jessica gasped. "No, I don't believe you." Kate nodded. "I thought they banned her for life after she dumped her drink on that special needs waiter."

Kate shrugged. "Apparently, she's appealing. She claims the waiter dumped the drink on himself because he was ashamed for mixing up her order."

Jessica shook her head. "That woman has no shame."

"It would seem not. Anyway, as we're passing each other on the stairs, she stops, looks back at me, and starts bragging about this new associate they're hiring. Says the woman is the next RBG."

"What?"

"She called her RBG 2.0!"

"A baby lawyer? Better than Ruth?"

"She's clueless," Kate said.

"I heard a rumor she made an ignorant comment about the new RBG statute too."

Kate shook her head, then took a deep breath, tried to calm herself. Retelling the story was causing her blood pressure to spike. "I called her an idiot. But she just stood there, smirking. Then, get this, she says I wouldn't recognize talent if it hit me in the face."

"My God," Jessica said, in disbelief. "Why does anyone like her?"

"Few do. But I zinged her back, hard. I asked her why, if this woman was such a catch, she didn't have a job already? I mean, even the dimwit grads have jobs this late in the year."

"Touché," Jessica said. "I bet she huffed and puffed and scurried back to her little hole."

Kate shook her head. "She stood her ground, droning on about how law firm data metrics suck. She said the algorithms firms use can't spot originality."

Jessica looked away. Kate could tell her sister was debating whether to say what she thought.

"You know," Jessica said cautiously, a moment later, "she isn't wrong on that part. Take Goldman, for example. You know we hire only the best. Top of the class. Order of the Coif. Still, most of them turn out to be duds."

Kate nodded. "That's what I was thinking as I drove home. What if Tina found the next RBG? Can you imagine what Susan would say if she heard I knew but didn't act?"

"Stop. I'm getting heartburn already."

"So, you understand I didn't have a choice," Kate said. "I had to act."

"Act? What do you mean?"

"I offered the woman a job. For more money than Tina's firm can afford to pay."

Jessica's mouth fell open. "Please tell me you talked to Ms. Wilson first. Got her approval."

"No, there wasn't time. And don't give me that look. You're acting like I'm nuts."

"I didn't think so before, but now I'm not sure."

Kate scoffed. "This isn't even the important part. Susan said I could hire a staff person."

"A lawyer is not a staff person, Katie."

"They could be. They can be. Whatever. The point is I sent her an offer by email, without meeting her."

This revelation caused Jessica to sit back in the chair.

"Okay."

"And now, the little diva is playing hardball. She claims she isn't sure she wants to work here. Have you ever heard such nonsense?"

"I see."

"Do you? Because it doesn't seem like you do. The woman's demanded to 'meet people' and 'understand the culture' before she accepts my offer. What kind of idiot doesn't jump at working for Susan Wilson Law?"

"Maybe," Jessica said, her voice building as she spoke, "a person who didn't apply for a job!"

"Don't put this back on me."

"I—"

Kate waved a hand at her. "Can we argue about this later? Right now, I need your help. If Riley turns us down, goes to work for Tina, we're in big trouble."

"We? There's no we. I had nothing to do with it."

"Come on, Jess. Don't be a fool. Do you think Susan will ever hire you, if I mess this up?"

Her sister's eyes narrowed. She glared at Kate.

All things considered, Kate thought the conversation had gone well. Jessica had exploded more over less.

After a moment, her sister let out a long exhale.

"What do you want me to do?"

2

"I take it back. You are nuts," Jessica said.

They were in a conference room at the end of the hallway, past Kate's office.

In the week since Kate started at the firm, she hadn't seen one person venture past her door. It was as if her office served as some informal edge of civilization, a point beyond which no rational person dared go.

It made little sense to her because the other conference rooms were in constant use. Still, this one, a masterpiece of futuristic design, was always empty. White table, white leather chairs, white walls. It was precisely her style. And she had resolved to use it as her own until someone pushed her out.

"Seriously, tell me you're joking," Jessica said. "Because this is your most screwball idea yet. And I'm including the time you said we should pretend to be foreign exchange students who didn't speak English."

Kate pressed her lips together. For screwball ideas, there was no contest. Jessica was the master. She had notebooks chock full of them. And the thing about pretending not to speak English had landed them an all-expenses-paid weekend at a four-star hotel courtesy of two guys who thought French women were more skilled in the art of love.

"It will work," Kate said. "I saw it once on TV."

Jessica's mouth fell open. "Oh, well, if you saw it once on TV."

Kate rolled her eyes. "Let's go over it again. Tell me what you're going to say when Riley enters the room."

"Fine." Jessica sat up straight and contorted her face into a goofy, cartoon-like character. "Hello, Ms. Anderson. I'm Sarah. Kate's paralegal. Kate is *so* amazing. She's like a real superstar. If you want to be a superstar too someday, take the job. What's that I hear? Is someone knocking at the door? Oh, my, it's Ms. Becker herself."

"Stop joking around," Kate said. "This affects you too."

Jessica scoffed. "You don't think I know my entire future is riding on this middle school warm-up act routine."

Kate knew it was childish, but if she had learned anything over the years, it was that people wanted to be a part of something special, something important. A job at Susan Wilson Law might not be saving the world, but it was a chance to be on the top team, to be close to the best. That wasn't nothing.

"If she doesn't buy it," Kate said, "just tell her why you want to work here. It convinced me."

This seemed to relax Jessica. "All right. I guess I could do that."

There was a knock at the door.

Kate glanced back over her shoulder to see the firm's receptionist standing in the doorway. The woman looked annoyed.

"I've been searching all over for you," the woman said.

"Is Riley Anderson here?" Kate asked.

"Do you think I came down here to chat?"

Kate ignored the jab. It was best not to provoke the help.

"Could you bring Ms. Anderson back here, please?"

The receptionist raised an eyebrow, looked as if she didn't understand. Kate felt sorry for the woman.

On her first day at the firm, some secretary, Kate couldn't remember which one, told her the receptionist was a *special* hire.

When she heard it, Kate had secretly cheered her boss's commitment to inclusive hiring. But now, as she stared at the woman, she wondered if maybe a public-facing position wasn't a bit of an overreach.

Kate tried again, this time speaking louder, slower. "Could you bring Riley Anderson back to the conference room, please?"

The receptionist's face switched from confusion to anger.

"Why are talking like I'm an idiot? I heard you fine. I was just trying to figure out who said you could use this room?"

Kate felt her sister's eyes bore into her.

"Well, I, um..."

Maybe she didn't have explicit permission to use the room, but where did a pea-brained receptionist get off putting her on the spot? She was a senior associate. She answered only to Susan. And the firm administrator. And a couple of other senior lawyers. But not staff. And never a receptionist.

"Susan told me I could use it," Kate said. "Whenever I want."

"Is that so?"

The women didn't believe her.

"Yes. If you have questions, stop by Susan's office. Ask her yourself."

The woman hummed.

They both knew she wasn't going to be asking Susan anything.

"Now," Kate said, "if you would please get Riley. We need to start our interview."

As the receptionist turned and walked away, Kate felt a twinge of guilt. She hadn't wanted to lie, but she couldn't afford to lose face. Law firms were like high schools with gossip. She didn't want people whispering about her during her first month at the firm.

3

Riley Anderson crossed one leg over his knee, then uncrossed his legs, and pressed both feet flat against the floor. He was trying to seem relaxed, but the eagle-eyed woman behind the big cherry reception desk was staring at him.

He understood why. No man had ever interviewed for a job at the firm before. In fact, if forced to guess, he'd say he was the first man to ever even sit in the lobby.

When he first received the email from Kate Becker offering him a job, a job which he neither applied nor interviewed to get, he assumed it was a prank. A buddy razzing him for being unemployed still. Or maybe a phishing scheme trying to steal his identity. Whatever it was, he knew it wasn't real.

Susan Wilson Law was an all-woman firm, an elite ball-busting operation focused on shattering the glass ceiling. It had no interest in a guy like him.

He was about to delete the message from his phone when he showed it to a former classmate sitting beside him in the law school's career services office. He thought it might get a laugh.

The classmate scoffed and shook his head. "It doesn't make you special. They have to take the next person on the List."

The List was the law school's answer to the law of supply and demand. With too many graduates chasing too few jobs, the List gave the illusion of full employment. Jobs on the List were crappy, temporary, and involved lots of document review, which a trained monkey could do, and a computer soon would do. No reputable firm hired people off the List.

"It's a joke, big guy," Riley said. "Susan Wilson doesn't hire off the List. She does on-campus interviews. Don't you remember that day all those women showed up carrying designer handbags? It was like a scene from The Devil Wears Prada."

The classmate flashed him a confused look. "I don't know what that is, but if you don't want the job, just tell Darla."

This was not a real option.

At just under five feet tall and over three hundred pounds, Darla was a tyrant who cared nothing about graduate job satisfaction. Her singular focus in life was stretching the definition of law-related employment to include demeaning, low-wage work, hoping to nudge graduates into declining her offer, which, under the school's placement rules, would render them ineligible for future help and erase them from her life. It was like when an unemployed person stopped looking for work and disappeared from the statistics.

Riley couldn't afford to let that happen to him. He had ninety thousand dollars in student loans and a mother who depended on him for support. So, he went to the interview, hoping it wasn't a joke.

A woman's voice called out from a doorway near the front of the room.

"Mr. Anderson, Kate Becker will see you now."

4

Kate peeked out her office door, staring down the long hallway back towards the lobby. She was hoping to catch sight of Riley. The more information she had on the woman, the easier it would be to feign a connection.

She heard voices and laser printers but didn't see anyone.

Where are they? she thought. A normal person could have walked back and forth six times already.

As she stared off at nothing, her mind drifted away. She imagined herself in Susan's office, on the bright white couch in the conversation space, holding a half-full glass of whiskey. Susan sat across from her, on a pastel armchair, exhaling in relief.

"I can't thank you enough," Susan said. "Snagging the next RBG is a real game changer. You probably saved the firm."

Kate raised an eyebrow. "Probably?"

"All right, all right. You saved us, Kate. You did. I shudder to think what would have happened if that whore, Tina Black, had landed Riley." Susan glanced up at the ceiling, shook her head, then looked back at Kate. "I know you've only been here a week, but my gut says you're special. How about becoming my business partner? Equal, of course. With profit sharing."

"Hmm." Kate tried to sound unimpressed, as a warm, tingly sensation spread across her body and dollar signs danced in her eyes. "I appreciate the offer, Ms. Wilson—"

"Call me, Susan."

"Of course, Susan. But I need to think about it. When look into the future, I've always imagined my name on the letterhead."

Susan leaned forward, rested her elbows on her knees. "Is that all? Because I don't care about the name. Let's change it. We could put yours first. How does Becker & Wilson sound?"

Kate glanced away, trying to suppress a smile. She looked past the conversation space towards the back of the room, where a dark wooden conference table had eight chairs around it. Altogether, she guessed the office was two, maybe three times bigger than hers.

"Would people believe it?" Kate said, looking back at Susan. "Us being equal partners? Since your office is so much bigger than mine."

"You want this office? Take it. Just promise me you'll stay."

"Well—"

"Listen, I need you, Kate. I'll do anything to keep you. We could even hire your sister. Make her partner too."

Kate sucked in a breath through her teeth. "I don't know. Jessica isn't really partnership material."

Susan laughed. "I was thinking the same thing. We could make her a mascot, though. You know, hire her, but keep her an associate forever. Like charity."

"It would be charity, wouldn't it?"

Susan nodded.

She was about to agree when the woman's voice suddenly changed. It morphed into a horrible, screeching troll. She felt a pinch on her arm and was snapped back to reality.

The receptionist snapped a finger in her face.

"Earth to Kate Becker. Come in rescue rider."

Kate took a step back.

"What are you doing? Stop it!"

She noticed a man standing beside the woman. He was dressed

in a blue suit with a white button-down shirt and tie. Clean-shaven with short hair, he had a ruggedness that reminded her of an actor from a hiking boot commercial. Her heart raced.

"Don't snap at me, missy," the receptionist said. "I thought you had gone insane, swaying and mumbling like a homeless person."

"I was not," Kate said.

The receptionist glanced at the man beside her. "Tell her."

The man hesitated for a second. "You seemed to be thinking very hard."

Thinking hard? What did that mean?

"Whatever," Kate said in a huff. "I'm fine now. Where is Riley Anderson? You're supposed to be taking her to the conference room."

"He's right here."

Kate's eyes went wide. "What?"

The receptionist grinned. "Mr. Riley Anderson tells me you've offered him a job."

5

On Friday afternoon, Kate couldn't leave work fast enough. Since word spread she hired a man, rumors of her impending termination had swirled like a hurricane gaining strength over warm water. Susan Wilson hadn't confronted her yet, but it was coming. She knew it. Whether in weeks, days, or hours, her life would soon be over. Her dreams were dead, gone forever.

And it was all because of Tina Black. If that whore hadn't lied about Riley being the next RBG, she never would have hired her or him or whatever it was.

This time, Tina had gone too far.

The two had a history dating back to their first week at Harvard Law. It was an election year. Tina was campaigning for votes outside their contracts class, trying to con undecideds into believing Republicans cared about ordinary people. This was back before all the Republicans went crazy, so it was conceivable an intelligent person might vote red. Except Tina wasn't good at persuading people.

When an Asian girl said she was voting Democrat because "we all do better when we all do better," Tina lost it. She began yelling about the dangers of Socialism. Obviously, Kate couldn't let a sweet girl get torn to bits by a savage beast. For a moment, it looked like they might actually wrestle. Thankfully, they didn't.

But over the next three years, things continued to spiral. Tina hid books in the library. Criticized Kate's comments in class.

Kate would have been forced to act if graduation hadn't come over the horizon. Boston was sixteen hundred miles from Austin, a distance undoubtedly far enough to keep the peace.

Except it wasn't.

On the first day of the Texas Bar Examination, when Kate came out of a bathroom during a break, she saw Tina standing near the wall.

"The real question," Tina said smugly when Kate went over to ask why she was there, "is why you're here. You know Texas is a red state, right?"

Kate clenched her jaw and walked away, not explaining that she had grown up in Austin, that the city was her hometown.

From there, Tina Black became a shadow she couldn't shake. When Kate joined the litigation section of the Bar Association, Tina joined too. Ditto for the Women's Lawyer's Guild. Every place Kate went, Tina followed.

So, when she got the job at Susan Wilson Law, a position they had both applied for, it was only natural she'd rub it in Tina's face a little. She expected some retaliation, of course. But not this. This was too much.

Kate pushed open the door to the high-rise condo she shared with her mother, quickly changed clothes, and then filled a water goblet with wine before collapsing onto the living room couch. She was in the middle of a long swallow when the doorbell rang.

She didn't move.

"Stay put," her mother said twenty seconds later, crossing the living room holding a dishtowel. "It's not like I was doing anything."

Kate wished her mother had stayed in the kitchen and continued chopping peppers. She had a pretty good idea who was at the door, and she had no interest in talking to her.

"Jessica," Barbara said, smiling widely after opening the door. "Katie didn't tell me you were coming by."

"She didn't know. I wanted to surprise her. She's been so down lately."

"Oh, that's nice." Her mother glanced back at her. "Isn't that nice, Katie? Your sister came to cheer you up."

"She didn't come to cheer me up, Mother. She came to gloat."

"Gloat?" Jessica came into the condo and walked over to where Kate sat on the couch. "Why would I gloat?"

"Because it's your nature."

Jessica put a hand to her heart, feigned hurt. "Maybe it's your nature, but it isn't mine. I care about you, deeply."

"Right," Kate said. "If you care so much, why'd you convince Riley to take the job when I was trying to get him to pass."

"Girls, please," Barbara said. "Stop arguing. I can't take any more tonight."

"Sorry, Mom," Jessica said. "But this is important. I did it to help you, Kate."

"Help me?" Kate forced a laugh. "Do you know how ridiculous that sounds?"

"It's true. Everyone could see you had lost your mind that day. I had to save us."

Kate shook her head, muttered under her breath.

"Look," Jessica said, "people already heard you offered the guy a job. I figured our best play was to own it."

Kate's eyes went wide. "Own it? You're saying I should pretend I *intentionally* hired the first man at an all-woman firm?"

Jessica nodded.

"That's absurd."

"No, Katie. What's absurd is that you hired the first man at an all-woman firm *unintentionally*."

"Enough," Barbara said sternly, shooting both of them hard looks. "Katie, if you don't want this man working for you, just say you made a mistake. I'm sure he'll understand. He can't be too excited to work at an all-woman firm."

Kate and Jessica exchanged puzzled looks.

"What? Did I say something wrong?" Barbara said.

Kate shook her head. "You just don't understand, Mother. Susan has fifty associates working for her. In a good year, maybe one or two make partner. The rest get pink slips. She's got lawyers lined up to take your place before you even leave. She doesn't give people second chances."

"Kate's right," Jessica said. "It was lucky for her to get the job the first time."

"Haha," Kate said, rolling her eyes.

"What I don't get," Barbara said, "is why you two want to work for someone like that. She sounds like a horrible person."

"It doesn't matter what kind of person she is, Mother," Kate said. "She's the best."

"She's not the best," Jessica said. "RBG was the best."

Kate sighed. "Of course, RBG was the best, you idiot. But RBG isn't hiring anymore, is she?" Jessica looked away. "Working for Susan opens doors that are locked to everyone else."

"Which is why," Jessica said, rejoining the conversation, "that you need to do whatever it takes to keep your job."

"And you think owning it could work?"

"You don't have another choice," Jessica said.

Kate paused, thinking it over. "All right. Let's talk through what we're going to do."

Barbara scoffed.

"What?" Kate said.

Barbara didn't answer. Instead, she made her way back to the kitchen. It was her standard approach to conflict. Avoid, avoid, avoid.

Kate called out to her. "If you have something to say, say it."

"Why would I have anything to say, honey?"

Back behind the counter, Barbara grabbed the chef's knife off the counter, raised it high into the air, and slammed it down onto a wooden cutting board so hard neighbors two doors down could have heard it.

"Careful, Mom," Jessica said. "You could whack off a finger."

"Don't be silly," Barbara said, raising the knife again and slamming it down harder. "I've done it this way for years."

"You obviously want to say something," Kate said. "And we want to hear it."

"Oh, really?"

"Yes."

Barbara sighed. "Fine." She set down the knife, hastily wiped her hands on a towel, then glared at Kate. "Here it is, honey. You're thirty-four years old. When are you going to grow up? Stop seeking approval from a woman like this Susan Wilson character?"

6

Kate sat in the third row of the stadium-style auditorium at the Texas Bar Association's Austin campus, nervously glancing back over her shoulder, looking for her sister. She was trying to save Jessica a seat, but if she didn't show up soon, Kate would be forced to let one of the snarky lawyers at the back of the room have it.

"My God," Jessica said, plopping down beside her. "The new barista in my building is terrible."

Jessica had come in through a side door without Kate noticing.

"You think every barista is terrible," Kate said.

"No, I don't. But, come on. If you don't drink coffee, maybe don't work in a coffee shop."

"I suppose."

Jessica raised an eyebrow. "You suppose? You'd have slung this frothy mess back at the girl. You're the biggest coffee snob I know. Of course, I mean that in the nicest possible way."

"Of course," Kate said, exhaling.

"What's wrong?"

"It's this Riley situation. It's got me twisted up. I owned it like you said."

"So?"

"So I didn't know having an associate could be so much work. It's like babysitting a toddler. I spend half my day just trying to make up things for him to do. Do you know how tiring that is?"

"You're the one who hired him. Maybe, you should give him a real chance."

Kate clenched her jaw, fought the urge to lash out. "I did give him a chance. Look what happened. Do you think I'm interested in a fertility law seminar? He said it was the only full-day CLE available."

"That doesn't sound right," Jessica said.

"It isn't right. Which is why I can't trust him to do actual work."

A man walked to the podium, tapped the microphone twice. He told everyone to take their seats and then introduced Dr. Raul Agarwal of the Minnesota Fertility Clinic.

Jessica leaned over, whispered in Kate's ear. "Next time, I'll have my people register us."

"Your people? You don't have people."

"I do." Jessica motioned towards the back of the room. "See the woman with the clipboard?"

Kate scanned the group that had been luring at her earlier. "You mean the high school girl?"

Jessica frowned. "Willa's no high school girl. She's number one in her class at UT. And she's my new protégé."

Kate scoffed, then studied the girl more closely. She was the short straw in a line of lumpy, middle-aged men. Dressed in skinny jeans, a suede camisole, and black boots, the girl had her hair tied high in a bun and wore heart-shaped glasses.

"Since when do you have a protégé?" Kate asked.

Jessica dismissed the question with a wave, but Kate already knew the answer. Willa was her sister's reaction to Kate having hired Riley. Of course, the fact that hiring Riley was the biggest mistake of her career didn't matter. If Kate had an associate, then Jessica needed one, too.

Kate said, "How did you convince Goldman to give you the budget?"

Goldman was Jessica's boss, and Kate's too before she accepted the job at Susan Wilson Law. His generosity made Ebenezer Scrooge seem like a bleeding heart.

"Wake up, Katie. No one pays law student interns. And she knows your man, Riley. From back when he was in school."

"Good for her. He's not my man."

"Isn't he?"

"I'm only his boss."

"What a shame."

"A shame? Do you remember a thing called Me Too?"

Jessica shook her head. "Not remotely similar. First, Riley doesn't deserve to work at SWL. If he quits, no one can say you hindered his career. Second, he's a man. You can't take advantage of a man. If he rises up, he consents."

"You're terrible."

"Does that mean I have your blessing to take a run at him?"

"What?" Kate's eyes went wide. "No! Stay away from him."

The words came out louder than she intended, causing the people around her to turn and look. Even Dr. Agarwal stopped talking.

"If you two are done," Dr. Agarwal said in accented English, "maybe we start now, yes?"

Kate swallowed hard, then slid down low in her chair. For the next forty-five minutes, she tried to hide her face.

7

During the morning break after Doctor Agarwal's lecture, Kate stood in the lobby waiting for popcorn. She couldn't stop her mind from spinning over what she had heard.

She was scrolling a website on her phone when she heard her sister's voice. She looked up to see Jessica coming towards her, with her new protégé in tow.

"Kate," Jessica said dramatically. "I want you to meet one of my people. Kate, this is Willa. Willa, this is Kate."

The two shook hands.

"Nice to meet you, Willa."

She wanted to tell the girl to run. Whatever experience Jessica was promising was not worth the cost. Big picture, the girl was better off working at a fast-food joint. At least there, the tyrant in charge had to pay you minimum wage.

Willa smiled. "It's an honor to meet you, Ms. Becker. I read your profile in The Austin Lawyer. Your closing argument in the Blackwell case was exquisite."

Her argument in that case was exquisite, wasn't it? She had always thought it was good, but now, reflecting on it, she thought exquisite was a better word. Maybe the girl wasn't a lost cause.

"Thank you," Kate said. "Several people have said similar things."

"Ha," Jessica scoffed. "I wouldn't get too big a head, if I were you. The other side is appealing. You might be rebuffed before it's over."

"I'm not worried," Kate said.

Willa nodded.

"Well, you should be," Jessica shot back. "Goldman gave me the case after you left. And just between us, he's not happy. We can't understand half of your strategy decisions."

"I believe it," Kate said. "That's why Susan hired me and not you."

Jessica huffed, then glanced at Willa. "Tell Kate what you did. Her protégé said it was impossible."

"Okay," Willa said. "During Dr. Agarwal's talk, I made a few calls. Blah, blah, blah. Now you're both registered for this afternoon's employment discrimination seminar."

Kate raised an eyebrow. "I thought that seminar was sold out months ago."

"It was," Jessica said. "First rate protégés make things happen."

Kate resisted the urge to fire back at her sister.

"How'd you do it, Willa?"

"I called my father. He knows everybody. It was no big deal, really."

"Who's your father?"

"Michael Katzman," Willa said.

Kate's eyes went wide. Her mouth fell open. She glanced at Jessica, who smiled back knowingly.

"As in Chief Judge Michael Katzman?" Kate said. "Of the Fifth Circuit Court of Appeals?"

"Yeah, that's him," Willa said.

Jessica reached out, gently touched her protégé's arm. "You ought to run along now, Willa. It might take some time to find the conference coordinator. I don't want us stuck in the middle of a row again. Like Kate did this morning."

Willa nodded, then faded into the crowd of lawyers around them.

When she was gone, Kate said, "Have you lost your mind? You can't use Katzman's daughter as a personal assistant."

"She's my protégé. I'm giving her experience."

"Katzman's going to kill you."

"No, he won't."

Kate squeezed her eyes shut, pinched the bridge of her nose. "Do you know why people call him the Frogfish?"

"Who calls him that?"

"Everyone," Kate said, exasperated. "It's because he lures you in, acting all nice and sweet, then Bam! His jaws snap shut, and he eats you like a tasty treat."

Jessica rolled her eyes. "Fake news."

"Fake news?"

"Willa says his temper's an act. He's really a big softy at heart. When I talked to him on the phone, he seemed appreciative I even took Willa under my wing."

"Is that right," Kate said sarcastically.

"This attitude, is it because you're still pouting about Riley? Because I don't think it's reasonable to expect him to be better than Willa."

Kate sighed. "It is not about that."

"Then what now?"

They took several steps forward but stopped ten feet short of the popcorn stand.

Kate glanced away, debated whether to say anything. After a moment, she looked back at her sister.

"Do you ever worry we'll end up alone? Living together in a rundown senior high rise. Telling stories about our cats like they're our kids."

"God, no," Jessica said, shaking her head. "Cats are environmental disasters. They kill more songbirds every year than wind turbines. It's a fact. All serious environmentalists support banning domestic felines."

Kate flashed Jessica a hard look. "I'm being serious. When did we become the sort of women who didn't want children?"

Jessica shrugged. "I don't know. I think it's genetic."

"Yeah, I'm not sure."

Kate moved to the popcorn stand and began filling a bowl with caramel and cheese popcorn.

"I wanted to become a lawyer to expand my opportunities," Kate said, "not to limit them. I didn't realize that by pursuing a career, I might be making another non-choice."

Jessica scrunched up her face. "A non-choice? What are you saying? You want to have kids now?"

"Yes, no, I mean, I don't know," Kate said defensively. "Don't you think it's outrageous no one talks about the fertility cliff? I mean, we can say we're the same as men all we want, and in most ways we are, but in this way, this most fundamental way, we're not."

Jessica made a gagging sound. "I knew this would happen. The second I heard that misogynist start talking about women's bodies, I wanted to hurl my cup at him. Open your eyes, Kate! The man's got an agenda. He's trying to control our bodies. I bet he makes his wife wear a burka. If he even has one."

Kate knew nothing about Dr. Agarwal's private life, but she knew her sister's raging wasn't helping.

"I don't think his political opinions effect my egg availability," she said.

"Maybe not. But they affect your emotional availability. What he said was that the fertility cliff starts at thirty-five, Kate. Starts. You're only thirty-four. You could have kids tomorrow, if you wanted to. Not that you should."

They walked to the corner of the room and picked at their popcorn like birds, people watching as lawyers passed by the table.

"Who would impregnate me?" Kate asked a while later.

"Is that a real question?"

"Yes. I'm not getting knocked up by some frat boy who jacks-off in a cup."

Jessica laughed. "That'd be wild. Listen, if you're serious about this, why not do what Monica Longshore did? She froze her eggs. I guess they put them in a deep-freeze, next to the severed heads. She says she can have kids at eighty, if she wants."

"I doubt that's true."

"When we get back inside, I'll text Monica and get you the doctor's number. She raves about her. And trust me, she's no misogynist."

8

On Friday afternoon, Kate stood beside a wooden podium at the front of the Susan Wilson Law staff break room, watching as the firm's IT specialist, a tank-like woman called Luda, tried to force a round cable into a square port on the side of her laptop.

"It doesn't fit," Luda said, growing more frustrated by the second.

"Obviously, it doesn't fit," Kate said. "That's why we called you."

"You need a connector. Do you have a connector?"

Was that supposed to be a joke? No reasonable person could think Kate might have a connector for a cable that ran down the podium, under the carpet, up the drywall, through the ceiling, and to a projector mounted high on the wall of the firm break room.

"I can't be the first person who's had this problem," Kate said. "There must be an adapter around here somewhere."

Luda shook her head. "You're the only problem."

Kate took a deep breath, glanced off towards the rows of empty folding tables. There were still a few more minutes before people would arrive.

"Is there another laptop I could use?"

Luda shrugged. "Just pass around the computer. Show people your pictures."

Kate stared at the woman incredulously. It was the worst IT solution she had ever heard. Not only did it render her multimedia presentation useless, but it would take way too long.

When Susan's office administrator asked her to give a get-to-know-you talk at the firm's weekly luncheon, she had told Kate to fill an entire hour. *An hour?* she thought. I can't entertain a group of high-powered lawyers for an hour. Five minutes, okay. Ten minutes, maybe. But sixty? No way. What did the woman think she was? Some sort of professional jester?

Still, Kate agreed because it's what good lawyers at great firms did. They accepted assignments with a smile.

She spent a weekend splicing clips together, funny, law-related videos she stole from YouTube. It would not win an Emmy, but it was passable.

However, without a cable to hook up her computer to the projector, it was all pointless.

Before Kate could think of another option, Luda walked to the food table at the back of the room, piled three sandwiches onto a paper plate beside a mountain of chips, then disappeared out a side door.

"I don't think she's coming back," Riley said.

"Crap. We're screwed."

"Relax. It's not a big deal. Like I've been trying to tell you, no one is coming anyway."

Kate turned up her nose. "Stop saying that. Of course, people are coming. And don't ever tell me to relax again."

"They're not, Kate."

A middle-aged woman entered the back of the room and went straight for the food table. Wearing jeans and a faded gray sweatshirt that bordered on inappropriate even for staff on casual Fridays, the woman filled a plate with food, then sat down at a table.

"See," Kate said, whispering. "I told you people would come."

"I'd give it another second before I declared victory."

The woman reached into her purse and pulled out a worn paperback. She cracked it open and held it up in front of her face.

"That proves nothing," Kate said defensively. "I haven't even started talking yet."

Riley glanced at his watch. "Come on, Kate. Let's grab sandwiches. You can bring me up to speed on the Portman case. If anyone does show up, you can stand up and take questions."

Never, she thought. First, she wasn't eating lunch with Riley like a colleague. Second, she had no plans of ever reading him in on the Portman case.

"Step back, Riley. I need to start."

"Start? You're not seriously going to talk to an empty room, are you?"

"It's not empty."

"What are you going to say? You don't even have your videos."

"I can wing it. I'm an accomplished lawyer. Now, sit down, Mr. Anderson."

She waited for him to take a seat in the front row before introducing herself. Talking when no one was listening felt weird, but Susan had asked her to talk, so talk she would. The last thing she needed was for Susan to pop in and find no one at the podium.

It was not the best extemporaneous speech of her life. Although, in fairness, she had never tried to fill an hour before without notes. That she was still talking at the thirty-minute mark, she figured was an achievement.

She was in the middle of explaining why she founded a Latin club at her high school, when the book-reading woman raised her hand.

Kate stopped mid-sentence.

"Do you have a question?"

"How much longer do you think you'll be? Because I could read at my desk."

Kate's heart fell. Of course, she knew the woman wasn't listening, but she had hoped at least a little of what she was saying penetrated the woman's thick skull, if only by osmosis.

"Maybe another twenty minutes. Susan asked me to fill the entire hour."

"Oh, yeah, right."

The look on the woman's face said she knew something.

"Did you hear something about my talk?" Kate asked.

"What? No."

She was lying. Kate was sure of it.

She left the podium and went to the table where the woman sat. Riley joined her a moment later.

"What did you hear?" Kate asked.

The woman looked at Riley. "I'm not getting involved. You tell her. You were there. You heard it too."

"What did you hear, Riley?"

"Let's go back to your office, Kate," Riley said. "It's better if we talk there."

Kate shook her head. "No, we're talking about it here. It's because I hired him, right? People are pissed because he's a man."

The woman didn't answer. She kept her eyes on Riley.

"Tell me, Riley. It's not a request."

He hesitated. "Okay, but you need to stay calm. And remember, it's only a rumor. It might not even be true."

"Spit it out."

"People are saying that... Ms. Wilson doesn't like you."

Kate forced a laugh. "Doesn't like me? That's it? That's your big secret? Wow. This place is like high school. Obviously, Susan isn't my biggest fan right now. I'm not a big fan of me either. But it will all blow over. Once she sees me in action, she'll love me again."

The book-reading woman raised an eyebrow. "Again? She never liked you."

"Excuse me?"

"Stop," Riley said. "I'm handling it."

The woman continued. "Ms. Wilson hired you by mistake. She

mixed up your name. She thought your sister was you, and you were your sister."

Kate's chest tightened. It felt like an elephant had stepped on it. She struggled to catch her breath, wondering if she was having a heart attack.

9

The news hit her like a ten-foot wave crashing onto a rocky shore. She held it together long enough to make it back to her office and close the door, but then the feelings bubbled over. Tears. Sobs.

When her breathing stabilized, she tried to carry on the only way she knew how: by throwing herself into work. Yet, no matter how hard she focused on the tiny black marks on the paper, her mind refused to translate them into sentences. She kept hearing the woman's words in her head. "She thought you were your sister and your sister was you."

She covered her mouth and screamed, careful not to let any of the sound escape.

At six o'clock, she quit for the weekend, powering off her laptop and zipping it inside a brown leather satchel. When she stood up to leave, vertigo overcame her. She sat back down. Squeezing her eyes shut, she focused on counting her breath. *You need to get control of yourself, Kate Becker*, she thought. Otherwise, you'll end up in a padded room where people talk to you like a toddler.

With her eyes closed, she lost all sense of time, counting one, two, three. At the number forty, she caught a whiff of a man's aftershave.

Her eyes flicked open.

Standing in front of her, leaning over the desk, Riley's face was two feet from hers. His head was tilted to the side, and he was saying her name, asking if she was okay.

She scooted her chair back.

"Were you just trying to kiss me?"

He forced a laugh. "Kiss you? In your dreams. I was worried. You were in a trance again."

"No, I wasn't," she said.

"Trust me, it's better if you were. When I opened the door, you were moaning my name."

"I was meditating, you idiot."

"With my name?"

"You must have heard me wrong. What are you doing here? I didn't say you could come inside."

He moved back and sat down in a straight chair across from her.

"I knocked for like five minutes, but you didn't answer."

"So you just broke in?"

"Yeah, that's what I did," Riley said sarcastically. "Anyway, I spoke to Veronica at T & J about the Portman case."

"What? Who said you could do that?"

"No one. I tried to dodge her, but Margie said your phone was on DND, and your voice mailbox was full."

Kate started to yell at him, but stopped when she remembered hitting the do not disturb button after the break room fiasco.

"Well, get on with it. What did she want?"

"Their client is refusing to drive to Austin for depositions. They want to do them at their home office instead."

"In San Antonio?" Riley nodded. "What a load of crap. Their client is an insurance company. They have reps everywhere. They're just trying to waste my time."

"I figured."

"So, you told her no."

Riley shook his head. "I told her yes."

"You told her yes?"

Kate's voice was loud, bordering on yelling.

Riley nodded. "You're always going on about how a defendant's testimony needs to be pinned down before you can assess a case's value. So, I figured the inconvenience was better than a delay."

Kate wanted to lash out at him, tear him apart for acting without her permission. Susan wouldn't have tolerated such insubordination. First year associates who think are dangerous people.

But she didn't. Her phone shouldn't have been on DND, and Riley's instincts were correct. She would have ridden a cargo ship to China to pin down Portman's testimony if need be. Anything for a win. A win was her only hope of changing Susan's opinion.

Kate sighed. "Listen carefully, Riley. If you ever do that sort of thing again, I will kill you. Got it?"

"Got it."

Her chest loosened a bit.

"Have a good weekend," she said, expecting him to get the hint and to stand up and leave.

But he didn't move.

"Was there something else?" she asked.

He hesitated. "If you ever need to talk, you know I'm here for you, right? People say I'm a good listener."

She rolled her eyes. Cut the guy one break, and he thinks we're BFFs.

"Thanks, Riley. But I'm fine."

"Okay. . . but it would be normal, if you weren't. Hearing you landed your dream job by mistake would rattle most people."

Kate hummed. "Yes, I suppose it would. Good thing I'm not most people." She stood up and headed for the door, motioned for him to follow. "And for the record, I don't believe Susan hired me by mistake. People like her don't make mistakes."

He nodded, although Kate could tell he didn't believe her.

10

The fertility specialist that Monica Longshore recommended had an office in an upscale medical building on the west side of Austin. Rows of red flowers lined a concrete path to the door. The parking lot was smooth and black and looked like they repaved it once a month.

Kate wasn't sure why she had made the appointment. Jessica was right about her not wanting kids. Most of the time, the idea never crossed her mind. But occasionally, just for an instant, she'd get a flash of maternalism. Not the old-fashioned do the laundry, make birthday cakes, and drive carpool kind. The more modern, hip version. The sort of mother who took her children to museums and theaters and performances.

Over the years, these spells of maternal instinct came more frequently. Never close enough together to threaten her life plans, however. Not until that morning at the reproductive law seminar. Hearing her body was barreling towards a fertility cliff had caused an awakening of sorts. It nudged her to make the appointment, submit to a battery of blood work, and spread her legs in the cold metal stirrups of the exam room.

"But you want to get pregnant, yes?" Dr. Lotus asked.

They had moved from the exam room to Dr. Lotus's private office. Kate had her pants back on, but the intensity of the doctor's stare made her feel just as vulnerable as before.

Everything about Dr. Lotus seemed intense. She was a short, compact, sixtyish woman with chin-length brown hair that parted down the middle. She wore small round glasses and spoke with the hint of a Russian accent.

"Well, I don't know for sure," Kate said. She didn't know what to say, because she never thought anyone would pressure her to decide today. "Do people usually do inseminations on the first visit?"

Dr. Lotus nodded. "My patients are serious people, Ms. Becker. And these are serious matters."

"Of course."

Kate glanced away, trying to make space to think. While the exam rooms were the comfortable sheik you'd expect from a high-end specialty practice, Dr. Lotus's office was plain and bare. There were half-packed cardboard boxes open on the floor and empty bookshelves.

"Are you coming or going?" Kate asked.

"A little of both. Next month will be thirty years in practice. Medicine isn't what it used to be anymore."

Kate nodded. The week before, she had read an article in The Austin Lawyer about a group of freshman state senators trying to ban what they believed were immoral research practices.

"Is it because of the new stem cell regulations?" Kate asked.

Dr. Lotus waved a hand at her. "It's everything, dear. Ever since those fools in Scotland cloned the sheep, I have to fill-out five different forms just to have lunch. If a person didn't know better, they'd think I was making Frankenstein's baby, instead of helping women have healthy children."

"Sometimes, I wonder if we're making progress."

Dr. Lotus shrugged. "For now, I am here. For how long, I cannot say."

Kate swallowed hard. As far as doctors went, the woman

seemed fine. But not so great to make her want to get impregnated today.

"Back in the exam room, I asked about freezing my eggs. Is that something we could consider?"

"No," Dr. Lotus said curtly.

"No? You mean not a great idea or not a possibility?"

"Not possible," Dr. Lotus said. "Your condition affects both egg quality and quantity. Even if we harvested all your eggs, which we could not do without severe pain," Kate flinched at the mention of pain, "they would not survive implantation. Your only option is to have a baby now. Even still, the odds of a live birth are less than fifty-fifty."

Less than fifty-fifty? This version of the story was even worse than the one the misogynist told at the fertility lecture. There had to be more options. She was only thirty-four years old.

Dr. Lotus must have sensed what she was thinking because she grabbed a notepad, scribbled out a name, then tore off the sheet and handed it to her.

"You want a second opinion, yes? Call Dr. Diver. He's faculty at UT. He will tell you the same thing. Although it will take you eight months to hear it, and he won't be able to help you because of–"

"Regulations?"

Dr. Lotus nodded.

"Let's say I needed to wait a little while. A year at most. What would my odds be then?"

"One percent. You need to inseminate today, Ms. Becker."

No way was that happening.

Kate shifted in her chair. "Even if I wanted to, I couldn't. I don't have a partner, and I haven't found a donor yet."

"There is no time for bespoke donors, Ms. Becker. Your only hope is a charged injection."

"A what?"

"It's a technique I pioneered. I combine specimens for optimum potency and motility. I've had reasonable success in geriatric patients like you."

Kate hummed. She didn't appreciate being called geriatric.

"When you say combined, does that mean from more than one person?"

Dr. Lotus sighed, glanced down at her watch. "Ms. Becker, do you want a baby or do you want a medical school education? Because there isn't time for both."

I don't want either of those things, she thought. What I want is to be normal. To have another year or two or ten to find a man or donor before plunging over the fertility cliff.

Dr. Lotus reached into her coat pocket, handed Kate a business card.

"When you get serious about a baby, call me. My cell number is at the bottom. If I'm here, I'll help."

11

The following Saturday, Kate spent the afternoon on the patio behind Café Noir, a trendy coffeehouse two blocks from her condo. Camped out at a wrought-iron table beneath a wooden pergola, she had just finished setting up her chessboard when Jessica's protégé, Willa, came strolling up.

"Hi, Ms. Becker," Willa said, pulling out a chair and plopping down across from her.

Willa's face was full of a kind of boundless enthusiasm usually seen only in college freshmen who still believe anything is possible. She wore a casual pink dress that looked like it cost five hundred dollars and had her hair tied high in a bun.

"Hello, Willa," Kate said disappointedly. "What brings you here?"

"Ms. Becker sent me."

Kate sighed. "I figured. Is she cancelling?"

Willa shook her head. "Just a little delayed."

"Delayed? What is she? An airline?"

"It's a matter outside of her control. She couldn't help it, Ms. Becker."

Kate hummed. "She didn't tell you, did she?"

Willa looked away for a moment, shifted in her chair. "Ms. Becker sent me as her proxy."

"I see."

"She wants you to talk to me as if I were her. Then, when she arrives, I'll summarize the conversation, bring her up to speed quickly."

Kate forced a laugh. "Yeah, I don't think so."

"It's a very common arrangement, Ms. Becker. People all over the world use proxies in their most important affairs. In some places, you can even get married by proxy."

"Not anymore," Kate said, shaking her head.

"Yes, even today. My roommate in college was from Gambia. Our junior year, she married a farmer by proxy in a letter. There were lots of tears, but we told her they might be tears of joy."

Kate flashed Willa a puzzled look. "Well, we don't proxy marriages in Texas—"

"Actually—"

"—and I'm not doing coffee by proxy either."

She waited for Willa to stand up and leave, but the girl stayed planted in the chair.

"Willa?"

"Yes, Ms. Becker."

"That was your cue to leave."

"I'm sorry. I can't. Not until the other Ms. Becker arrives."

Kate sighed. It was one thing for Jessica to risk the wrath of Judge Katzman by using Willa for quasi-work-related tasks. But to send her as a proxy to weekend coffee? That was a bridge too far.

"Do you play chess, Willa?"

"Not anymore, Ms. Becker. Too many terrible memories."

"How so?"

"When I was a kid, my father used chess as a punishment. Whenever my GPA dipped below 4.0, he'd force me to play."

Kate fought the urge to smile. She could imagine herself parenting that way.

"A little misguided perhaps," Kate said, "but not wrong. You know that chess improves children's reading and math scores."

"I've heard. About five hundred times."

"Well, you mustn't let him take the game from you. Once you eke out a few victories, you'll see the beauty of it."

"I don't think so. To me, it's ... boring."

Kate gasped. "Boring? No, no, no. Now, we must play."

"I'd rather not."

Kate hummed for a moment. Suddenly, an idea came to her.

"You know, as Jessica's proxy, you're obligated to do what she'd do. And she'd play me in chess."

"I think you were right before, Ms. Becker. I should go."

"Nonsense," Kate said. "We're playing. And I'm afraid I can't go easy on you."

Willa sighed. "One game."

"Splendid. I'll be white."

Kate pushed a pawn on the right side of the board up one square to f3.

"What did you make of the fertility seminar?" Kate asked. "Pretty crazy, huh?"

Willa nudged the pawn in front of her king ahead two spaces. She did it quickly, without seeming to reflect on the significance of an opening move. Kate frowned. She expected better from Judge Katzman's daughter.

"I thought it was super depressing," Willa said. "I mean, how can educated women be so clueless? Obviously, spinsters can't have babies."

Kate coughed, nearly choking on her own spit. Where did the perky little co-ed get off calling thirtyish women spinsters?

"Spinsters is a pejorative word, Willa."

"Sorry, Ms. Becker. I only meant that if a person is self-partnered—"

"This isn't about self-partnering," Kate said gruffly, although she wasn't exactly sure what the term even meant. "This is about society misleading women. Telling us we have all the time in the world. Saying we can freeze our eggs or do in vitro. All while the fertility cliff sneaks up and pounces."

Willa tilted her head to the side. "I'm not sure the cliff actually pounces, Ms. Becker. To me, it has always seemed more like a lazy river. You know, the kind you're hoping ends long before it does."

Kate clenched her jaw, pushed a pawn ahead two squares. "You're not understanding what I'm saying. Women need to hear the truth. Before it's too late."

"Are you sure you want to go there, Ms. Becker?"

"Yes, I'm sure, Willa. I'm going to ask the progressive women's lawyers guild to host a speaker on the topic."

"If you want to take back your move, I won't tell the other Ms. Becker."

Kate huffed. "What? No, I don't need a mulligan."

"Okay."

Willa grabbed her queen and slid it diagonally across the board to h4. Kate's king stood in its path, unguarded, boxed in, unable to getaway.

"Checkmate."

"I hardly think—"

Kate leaned forward, studied the board closer. There had to be a move she wasn't seeing.

Out of the corner of her eye, Kate saw a person approach the table, clapping.

"Bravo, Willa," Jessica said, admiring the board. "You Fool's Mated her. That's a bucket list item for me, which, since you're my proxy, I'm counting as my own."

Willa stood up, offered Jessica the chair.

"Sorry, Ms. Becker," Willa said. "I was going to let you win, but then I thought maybe it was a test."

Kate took a deep breath and leaned back in the chair. "Yes, of course, it was a test. And you did just fine, Willa."

12

Losing to Willa zapped Kate of any further interest in chess. Looking down at the board, she began repacking the game pieces into a leather travel case. As she did so, her sister, who was seated across the table, began breathing noisily. She was trying to get Kate's attention without saying it.

"Good God, woman," Jessica said a minute later. "Could you move any slower?"

Jessica grabbed the remaining pieces off the board and shoved them into Kate's bag.

"I take it you have something to share," Kate said.

"Guess who's been nominated for the Austin Pro Bono Service Award?"

"I don't know. Me?"

Jessica frowned. "You? Why would you be nominated? You never do pro bono work."

"Okay. Is it Goldman?"

"Haha. Hilarious."

"Well, congratulations, sis," Kate said. "I suppose this means you patched things up with Scott Stevens."

"Indeed I did. You know, he's not really such a terrible person. We both apologized. It was all very civil."

Jessica's feud with Scott Stevens dated back years. It was the product of too much drinking and grinding and sucking face at a public fundraiser, which, the next morning, morphed from shame into hatred.

For a moment, Kate didn't understand how they had made up. Jessica never apologized. Then it hit her.

"Please tell me Judge Katzman wasn't involved," Kate said.

"Michael? Of course he wasn't involved. All he did was facilitate a conversation."

Kate shook her head.

"You're acting like I didn't deserve to be nominated," Jessica said. "Even Scott says I do. No big firm lawyer logs more pro bono hours than me."

"This isn't about pro bono hours, Jess."

"Actually, it is. That's why they call it the Pro Bono Service Award."

Kate leaned forward, rested her elbows on the table. "You understand Katzman isn't doing you all these favors out of kindness. Someday, he's going to call in his chips. And you'll have to repay him."

Jessica waved a hand at her. "You're crazy."

Kate sighed, then looked away. Usually, she would have persisted until her sister saw reason. But not today. Today, she didn't have the energy. If her sister wanted to tangle with the Frogfish, so be it.

Jessica sensed the different rhythm and grew concerned.

"Are you planning on telling me what the doctor said?" Jessica asked.

"There's nothing to tell."

"Come on, Kate. I can see the hurt all over your face."

Kate sighed. She didn't want to talk about it, but her sister wasn't the type who let things go once something piqued her interest.

"The short story," Kate said, "is my reproductive organs are collecting Social Security, and your girl, Willa, thinks I'm a spinster."

"You're not a spinster, Kate. You're—"

"Self-partnered."

Jessica turned up her nose, shook her head. "I was going to say barren."

"Oh, great. That's makes me feel a lot better."

"It should," Jessica said. "Before, you were all, should I? Shouldn't I? Now you know you can't. So, you can move on without second guessing."

"You can't say that sort of thing to a woman who finds out she's infertile. It's insensitive."

"I would never say it to a woman. I said it to you. My sister. A person who, until last week, never expressed a scintilla of interest in kids."

"Yes, I did."

"No, you didn't. We've always been on the same page. Remember that time at the symphony when the boy wouldn't sit down. We all had to wear phony smiles and pretend we didn't care because he had autism." Jessica made air quotes with her fingers at the word autism. "I still don't think he actually did."

Kate rolled her eyes. "I'm not barren. Not yet anyway. I just have a very, very small chance of conceiving."

"A small chance? Then what are you whining about? Everyone has a small chance of conceiving."

Kate explained what Dr. Lotus had told her. When she finished, Jessica's eyes went wide. Her mouth fell open.

"This combined injection business sounds a lot like a medical gang bang."

"Gross," Kate said, although she had a similar thought when she first heard it.

"Break it down. The woman's a doctor. She swirls a gang of samples together. Then she bangs it into you. Medical. Gang. Bang."

Kate's face turned red. She regretted telling her sister anything.

"I can't believe it," Jessica said. "You're actually thinking of doing it."

"No, I'm not," Kate said quickly. "I mean, I don't know. I haven't decided. My window is closing fast, forever. It's not like I have other options."

"These guys in Lotus's sample, do you even know their IQs?" Kate shook her head. "Maybe they're below average. Maybe they have three eyeballs and four nipples."

Kate's heart raced. Tears pooled in the corner of her eyes.

"Relax," Jessica said. "I'm only joking."

"This isn't a joke to me," Kate said, wiping away a tear with the back of her hand.

Jessica's face softened. "Forget I said anything. Listen, if you really want to get knocked up, let me help. I'll get you pregnant. And it won't be by some ninetieth percentile baby daddy. I'll find you the real deal."

Kate smiled.

"Hell, maybe, we'll even do it together," Jessica said, trying to lighten the mood. "I think I'd make a pretty hot mama. Don't you?"

Kate laughed. The idea was preposterous. Nobody in the world wanted kids less than Jessica. Still, the joke had worked its magic. A wave of relief washed over Kate.

As much as they competed, argued, and fought, when it mattered most, they were sisters. Sisters who showed up for each other.

13

A few days later, Kate pushed open her front door to the sound of laughter. Even before stepping inside, she recognized the familiar, high-pitched cackles of her mother's card club ladies.

The wily seniors were camped out at the dining room table, surrounded by paper plates and half-drunk glasses of cheap wine.

At least this time they're not smoking, Kate thought. Three weeks earlier, she had come home from work to find the condo board president standing in her living room, his fists balled at his side, threatening to call the police.

"Smoking has been illegal in this building for twenty years," he said indignantly.

"This is America, tootsie," Carol shot back in her baritone, chain-smoker voice. "Last I checked, people can smoke outside."

"You're in the dining room!"

Carol waved a dismissive hand. "We opened the patio door. What else do you want from us?"

It had taken Kate three weeks and two bottles of wine to convince the man not to ban Carol from the building. She had made the effort only because her mother begged for her help. Now, seeing Carol back at the dining room table, sitting smugly in the same chair, she regretted it.

Kate closed the door as her mother called out to her.

"Hi, Katie."

"Hello all," Kate replied in her cheeriest, most upbeat tone.

It was an act. Kate couldn't stand five minutes in the same room with the card club crew. Yet, over the years, she had learned the best way to handle these women was by faking happiness. Cheerful people weren't fun to talk to. Not even for people as bored as the card club ladies.

As if triggered by the tone of her voice, Carol glanced over at her. "What are you so happy about?"

"No reason," Kate said. "Just glad to see you all."

Carol hummed.

For a moment, Kate wondered if she had gone too far. Her mother might have told them about the Riley fiasco. If so, they'd never buy her happiness routine.

Before she could say more, Carol glanced back down at the cards in her hand, seeming to lose interest. Kate exhaled in relief.

Barbara said, "Your sister is on her way over."

Kate raised an eyebrow. "Did she say why?"

"Only that she had exciting news."

When the doorbell rang a moment later, Kate answered it.

"Hello, Jessica."

Without a word, her sister smiled and twisted around a three-ring binder so Kate could see the cover. It was black with gold script monogrammed on the front.

Kate gasped. "Is that?"

"Yes."

"I thought–"

"It was lost, but I asked Willa to reconstruct it using our old notebooks."

From the table, Barbara said, "Please tell me that's not what I think it is."

"What are y'all talking about?" Carol said.

They went over to the table. Jessica held the book out in front of her like a pastor at a church carrying the gospel.

"Meet Manscape," Jessica said, her eyes full of passion.

"What's that?" Carol set down her cards to give Jessica her full attention.

This was another wonderful thing about the card club ladies. They treated Jessica like a golden child.

"Let me tell you a story," Jessica said. "Transport yourself back to 2006. Pluto has just lost planetary status. And only a few first adopters are calling the pound sign a hashtag."

Kate rolled her eyes. "You're wrong about the hashtag thing."

Jessica silenced her with a hard look. "Anyway, Katie and I are away at school. Different colleges, of course. Academics were always a struggle for her."

"I was top of my class at Harvard."

"Yes, we know," Jessica said somberly, before looking down at the floor and observing a moment of silence. A second later, she continued with gusto. "It's a Friday night. Kate calls me after another online dating disaster. And remember, in 2006, online dating isn't cool yet."

"You're saying she was a loser even back then, huh?" Carol said.

"Carol, hush," Barbara said.

Kate sighed. "That's not how it happened. Let me tell it. So, it's a Friday night. I called Jessica because she was supposed to call me, but I hadn't heard from her. When she picks up the phone, I can tell she's been crying." Kate looked at her sister. "Do I need to tell them why?"

Jessica pressed her lips into a fine line, shook her head.

"I didn't think so," Kate said. "Anyway, after I got her calmed down, we agreed the conventional approach to dating wasn't right for us. So, we decided to solve the love/dating conundrum by searching the globe for successful relationship patterns."

"Wait," Carol said. "I thought you were in college."

"They were in college," Barbara said. "Kate's version of searching the globe means going to the basement of the library."

"It's not safe to linger there, Mom," Jessica said. "Plus, we also used the internet."

Kate nodded. "Once we understood the dynamics of true love, we modeled it, then converted it to a formula. The formula produced a series of questions we called Manscape. Thanks to the hard work of Jessica's protégé, it has now been resurrected."

Jessica bowed slightly. "Three days I had to get my own coffee to make it happen."

Carol wrinkled her nose. "Smells fishy to me."

"What?" Kate said.

"If those questions were so great, why didn't either of you recreate it before now? Lord knows, you both need help finding a man."

"Carol!" Barbara said.

"What? I'm only saying what we're all thinking."

Jessica reached out, touched Kate's arm. "Let me answer."

14

"We never reconstructed it," Jessica said, "because after law school, Kate and I resolved not to marry."

"I wouldn't say resolved." Kate said.

"Yes, Kate. Resolved. Don't you remember signing the white paper on the patriarchy of marriage? I have a copy at home, if you've lost yours."

Early in Jessica's legal career, the woman obsessed over white papers. Every week when they met for coffee, she'd produce a new one for them to discuss.

"I don't see why I need to sign them," Kate said a few weeks later when her sister handed her a pen.

"You need to sign because your comments have become eerily conservative."

Kate scribbled her name at the bottom without reading to make her sister shut up. She hadn't given the matter a moment's thought since.

"The only thing I remember about that patriarchy white paper is it made me laugh," Kate said.

Jessica's eyes went wide. "Laugh? What's funny about women

losing their identity? Being forced to give up careers for their husbands?"

"I don't think it's that way anymore."

"What are you saying? You want to get married now, too?"

Kate forced a laugh. "Married? Who would I marry? All I said was that I'm not resolved against it."

Jessica put a hand over her heart. "Well, I have to say, that's a rather distressing change."

Kate frowned at her. It wasn't distressing. And it wasn't a change.

"You never answered my question," Carol said. "Why did you recreate the questionnaire now?"

"Because Kate's infertility–"

"Jessica!" Kate said, her face turning bright red.

She hadn't told anyone else about her doctor visit, not even her mother.

Barbara stood up from the table and came over to her. She put an arm around Kate's shoulder in a consoling gesture. In the Becker family, this level of physical intimacy constituted a considerable display of emotion. Kate glared at her sister.

"Oh, Katie," Barbara said. "I'm so sorry. Why didn't you tell me?"

"It's fine." Kate fought back the emotion building inside of her. "I'm not infertile. At least, not yet anyway. I just have a very low chance of conceiving."

"Which is why I resurrected Manscape," Jessica said. "To find Kate a sperm donor."

Barbara's face lit up. "You've decided to get pregnant?"

"No, no, no," Kate said. "I'm just gathering information. I haven't decided anything for sure."

Jessica tilted her head to the side. "What do you mean you haven't decided? I thought it was resolved, on the patio at Café Noir."

"It wasn't."

Jessica's eyes narrowed. "Then why did I force Willa to recreate the questionnaire?"

"I don't know why you do half the crazy things you do."

Jessica gasped.

"Girls, please," Barbara said.

"No, Mom!" Jessica's voice rose. "This is classic Kate. She cries on your shoulder. Begs for your help. Then after you spend hours finding a solution, she claims she doesn't want it."

"The girl's got a point, Barbie," Carol said, joining the conversation. "It sure seems like Jessica went to a lot of trouble. Kate ought to at least try it."

Kate glared at Carol. Give it a try? Was the woman serious? Did she actually believe Kate ought to dip a toe in the pregnancy waters because her sister spent a few hours recreating a questionnaire? She imagined talking to her future child. "I'm sorry were not that close, kid. I never expected to conceive. I only did it because your aunt's protégé spent twenty hours on a questionnaire."

Barbara's voice pulled her back to reality.

"Don't listen to them, Katie. Follow your heart. Do what you think is beset. You know I'll always support you, even if I never have a grandchild, not in my whole life."

Great, Kate thought. First anger, then guilt.

"I'm not saying I don't want a child," Kate said. "I need time to think about it."

Carol cleared her throat. "If you want my opinion, I say—"

"Shut up, Carol," Barbara said.

The room went quiet. None of the card club ladies ever talked to Carol that way. Kate appreciated her mother standing up for her.

"Mom's right," Jessica said. "No one should have a baby unless they're sure. Fortunately, I am. I'm going to use the Manscape formula to find myself the perfect father."

Kate's chest tightened, and her vision began to blur. From somewhere far away, she heard Carol hooting and hollering praise on the golden child.

15

The next morning, Kate awoke feeling groggier and more hungover than three glasses of wine typically left her.

After Jessica's big announcement, Kate had retreated to her bedroom and stayed there with the door closed until morning. She knew her mother would want to talk about what happened, but she wasn't ready. Not yet.

To avoid an awkward confrontation, she rose early, showered quickly, and was tip-toeing across the living room towards the front door, when her mother called her name.

"Katie, is that you?"

She didn't answer. She just kept moving, faster.

"Katie, stop. Let's talk for a minute."

"I'm fine, Mother. There's nothing to talk about."

"Please."

Kate turned around.

Barbara was standing on the far side of the living room. She was dressed in a white terry cloth bathrobe tied at the front. Her hair was matted down, and her eyes were red and bloodshot.

She walked over to Kate.

"Have you decided if you're going to get pregnant?"

Kate forced a laugh. "Was I supposed to work it out in one night?"

"It's not something you work out, honey. It's something you feel, inside."

Kate didn't know what she felt inside. Since her visit with Dr. Lotus, she had gone back and forth a thousand times on whether to have a baby. At the moment, she was in camp no. But that could change any minute.

"What I feel is I'm going to be late for work."

Her mother crossed her arms, flashed her a disappointed look. "You're deflecting. I think you know what you want, but you're afraid to admit it."

Kate scoffed. "Gee, great pep talk, Mother. It's always great to be called a coward first thing in the morning."

"No one's calling you a coward, honey. Trusting your feelings is hard."

"Do you think Jessica is trusting her feelings?" Kate said.

"What? Why would you say that? We're not talking about her."

"Of course," Kate said sarcastically. "She's probably planning for ten kids by now. Look, you don't need to worry about me. I'll figure it out. I always do."

Barbara frowned. "It's not a problem to be figured out. Just ask yourself. When you're old and gray, will you look back and regret not having kids?"

"You don't think I've tried that? If I knew the answer, we wouldn't be talking."

"But you do know the answer, Katie. You just need to find the courage to admit it to yourself."

Kate scoffed. "I have to go."

Barbara stepped closer.

"Will you regret not having kids, Katie?"

"What I regret is letting you watch all those intervention shows on TV."

Barbara reached out, took her hand. She looked Kate squarely in the eye. It felt like the woman was peering into her soul.

"Will you regret not having kids?"

Kate's bottom lip began to quiver.

"It doesn't matter what I regret," Kate said, tears filling her eyes. "I won't give up my career. I've worked too hard."

"No one's asking you to stop working, honey."

"But I'd have to," Kate said, sobbing. "I can't do it alone. I can't be a single mom."

"You wouldn't have to be. I'll be here for you. The same way I'm going to be here for your sister's baby."

Kate fought the urge to tell her mother that Jessica was never going to have a baby, that she was only pretending to steal the spotlight. The same way she had hired Willa to outshine Riley.

They stood together a moment longer before Kate pulled back and wiped away a tear. Waving a hand in front of her face, she tried to clear her eyes in hopes no one at work would know she'd been crying.

"How would I find a father?" Kate said.

"You could try that Manscape thingy? Your sister seems to think it's pretty good."

16

It was a little after nine o'clock in the evening when Jessica sat up in the dining room chair and hit the period key on her laptop.

"There," she said, her voice marred with tiredness and relief. "It's done. Anyone under five foot ten is now officially out."

They were at Kate's condo tweaking the Manscape questionnaire. Kate stood across the table from her sister, holding a glass of red wine. She had been nursing the same six ounces all evening, careful not to let the alcohol cloud her judgment. She needed all of her facilities if this crazy idea were to have any chance of success.

Using Jessica's Manscape questionnaire to find a sperm donor was not her first choice. Or even her third. After admitting to herself that she might want a baby, she called Dr. Lotus's office. While the thought of being injected with a combined sample still gave her the willies, the woman was a medical doctor. She spent her career solving these sorts of problems. If she thought a combined specimen was Kate's best shot, then maybe it was.

But when Kate got through to the scheduling clerk, the woman told her there were no openings for two months. Two months! She couldn't wait that long.

Begging and pleading, Kate pressed the woman to find her an appointment. Eventually, the scheduler relented and agreed to add Kate to a special "priority cancelation list." Although after the call ended, Kate was sure pretty no such list actually existed.

She next toured the city's most reputable sperm bank, an offshoot of a big, national group. She quickly soured on them, however, when the director admitted to her that they were, in fact, only a franchise. A franchise medical clinic? No, thank you. Franchises were reserved for fast-food joints, gas stations, and fitness studios. Not sperm banks.

Out of options, Kate called her sister and agreed to explore using Manscape. At least until her appointment with Dr. Lotus. There was no harm in having more options.

"I think you'll come to see it was a smart change," Kate said, setting down her glass of wine and retying her ponytail for the third time in two hours. "No one wants a kid with a Napoleon complex."

"Right." Jessica was unconvinced. "So, that's it then? I can close the document? Because if I shutdown my computer, I'm not restarting it again."

Her sister was being a bit of a drama queen. Kate had only asked her to restart the computer once, to change the college eligibility language to limit the pool to Ivy League graduates.

Kate hummed. "We're close. I just feel like there's still something missing."

"Are you serious? The questionnaire is fifteen pages long! What else could you possibly add? You've already insisted on perfect pitch, tongue rolling, and a preference for former fighter pilots."

"Don't act like you didn't appreciate my Naval preference. You've always had a thing for the top-gun types."

"We've got more than enough."

Kate shook her head. She went to the living room and began to pace near the coffee table. A moment later, she stopped.

"My, God! We almost forgot the most important thing."

"Which is?"

"Political affiliation."

Jessica wrinkled her nose. "Political affiliation? I don't think that's a genetic trait."

"Are you sure? Because I don't want a gun-toting, big-government hating, snot-nosed religious fanatic running around my house."

Jessica rolled her eyes. "Fine. I'll add another disqualifier. Are we excluding only militia types? Or are all Republicans out too?"

Kate frowned.

"Okay, okay," Jessica said. "All Republicans are toast. Are we done?"

"Not quite. That reminded me. How are we handling reliability? I don't want a flake baby."

"I don't think babies can be flakes, Kate."

"Sure, they can. And don't forget about kindness or conscientiousness. They're important too."

"We're not adding those things."

"Yes, we are."

Jessica studied her for a moment. "Do you know what I think? I think this is all pretext. I think you don't really want a baby. I think you're adding these criteria to make sure we find no one."

Kate scoffed. "Me? You're the great pretender. Everyone knows you only claimed to want a baby to upstage me in front of the card club ladies."

Jessica's eyes narrowed. "How dare you!"

At that moment, the front door burst open. In came Barbara, sopping wet, hair matted flat against her head, water running down the side of her face.

Kate gasped. "Oh, no."

She hurried to the door and tried to help her mother wiggle out of a wet sweatshirt.

"Get back," Barbara said, twisting away from Kate. "I made it this far on my own. I can do the rest."

Kate watched as her mother yanked the heavy cloth up over her head and struggled to pull her arms out of the sleeves.

"How could you forget to pick me up?" Barbara said. "You're the one who drove me to the movie."

"I don't know," Kate said. "It slipped my mind. We were fixing the questionnaire and–"

While Kate was watching her mother peel off the sweatshirt, Jessica ran to the bathroom and grabbed a hand towel. She came back, handed it to Barbara.

"Thank you, honey," Barbara said. "At least one of my daughters cares about me."

17

A half-hour later, Barbara returned to the living room. She was freshly showered, dressed in a white terry cloth bathrobe, and smelled of lavender. The instant Kate saw her in the hallway, she rushed to the kitchen and poured her a mug of chamomile tea.

"Okay, okay," Barbara said, begrudgingly accepting the tea as a peace offering. "I forgive you. This once. But next time, it will take more than tea."

"There won't be a next time," Kate said. "I only forgot because Jessica and I were caught up in the Manscape questionnaire."

"Don't bring me into this," Jessica said. "I didn't know you were supposed to pick her up."

"It's fine," Barbara said. "As long as you two finished the project, my little stroll in the rain will be well worth it."

Kate smiled sheepishly. "We're almost done. Just a little more tweaking."

"No, no more tweaking," Jessica said. "Fifteen pages is enough."

Barbara's eyes went wide. "Fifteen pages! How do you plan to get anyone to fill it out?"

"We're going to pay them," Jessica said.

"Pay them?" Barbara's voice was thick with disbelief. "You can't pay people just to fill out a form. You'll end up with a bunch of hobos and weirdos."

"I'm not thrilled about it either," Kate said. "But Asha says it's standard procedure."

"Who's Asha?" Barbara asked.

"She's the VA I hired in India," Jessica said.

"The V what?"

"VA. You know, virtual assistant. Think online secretary."

"I see," Barbara said. "And she lives in India?"

"Yes," Jessica said.

Barbara hummed. "Are you sure this is a good idea?"

"Of course," Jessica said. "Everyone's hiring Indian VAs these days. It saves lots of money."

"I'm sure it does, honey," Barbara said. "But I thought you girls fought against exploiting vulnerable people."

"We do," Kate added. "But this isn't that. We're hiring a personal assistant, not starting a factory. Plus, there are no qualified Americans."

"Really?"

"Find us one. We'll interview them," Jessica said. "But, just so you know, to be competitive, the American would need a four-star VA rating, extensive experience coordinating sperm donor searches, be willing to work nights, and do it all for less than two hundred dollars."

Barbara raised an eyebrow. "I don't think that's realistic, honey."

"It's a bit of a gray area, I'll admit," Kate said. "But you know I don't have a lot of time. And Jessica says Asha has won several awards for her concierge sperm work."

Barbara stared blankly at them for a moment, then shrugged. "If you think it's okay, I'll support you."

Kate winced at her mother's polite rebuke, then gathered herself and refused to let it darken her mood. She didn't have another option.

She looked at Jessica. "Can you forward me Asha's email

address? I'd like to send her an email. Make sure she's clear on how our preferences differ."

"Sorry," Jessica said, shaking her head. "Can't. The VA package I bought allows only one contact person. Apparently, she's had problems in the past with people abusing the program. But if you send me the message, I can pass along whatever she needs to know."

Kate pressed her lips together, nodded slightly. She didn't like that idea at all.

18

The morning after the marathon Manscape session, Kate opened her bedroom door to the smell of freshly baked cinnamon rolls.

This was unusual for a weekday. Typically, her mother stayed behind a locked door until Kate left for work, a sort of unspoken detente the women had reached to live in the same space.

"Why are you up so early?" Kate asked, stopping at the dining room table to survey the large spread of food. Besides cinnamon rolls, there was coffee, orange juice, fresh fruit, and an empty place setting across from her mother.

Barbara looked up from the newspaper. "It's Robert Frost Day, honey."

Kate's eyes narrowed. Robert Frost Day? Again? No way. She was almost certain they had just celebrated it two months ago.

She poured herself a cup of coffee and waited for the caffeine to clear her mind before responding.

"It can't be RFD," Kate said, pulling out a chair across from her mother and sitting down. "We went to the fair on RFD, remember? Jessica ate the wonky vegan hot dog and threw up all over Carol's Chinese flower dress."

"Oh, yes," Barbara said, smiling. "I remember."

Carol's freak out was the only good memory Kate had from that sun-drenched afternoon. Otherwise, the day was carnies and pigs.

"So, it can't be RFD for at least another nine months."

Barbara shook her head. "Carol found out we've been doing the wrong day. I guess you're supposed to celebrate the day he published the poem, not the day he wrote it. So, to get back on track, we're celebrating twice this year. Better than missing a time, right?"

No, Kate thought. Not better. Worse. Much worse.

Of all the made-up, self-serving, revenue-inspired holidays that existed in the world, RFD was by far the worst. Not that Kate had anything against the man or his poems. Restricted to their proper context, a high school classroom or library talk, Kate might have even been a Robert Frost fan. She enjoyed the road less traveled as much as the next person. But Carol had weaponized the poem into a holiday to torment her and her sister.

Carol got the idea from an interview she saw on local TV news. A disabled veteran had written a pamphlet, called it a book, self-published it online, then began selling it out of the trunk of his car. For a mere $26.95, cash only, a person could read about the road less traveled and discover the magic of Robert Frost's poetry for themselves.

Never much of a reader, Carol opted not to buy the book. Instead, she made up her own set of rules and called it a holiday.

At first, the card club ladies seemed unimpressed. No one liked doing things outside their comfort zone. So Carol pivoted.

"Girls, I've had a vision," Carol said one evening. "Robert Frost Day wasn't meant for us. It was meant for them: Kate and Jessica. We can use it to fix them."

The card club ladies liked this delusion. RFD was exciting again. Barbara put enormous pressure on Kate and Jessica to play along, which was how they ended up at the county fair last summer.

But she'd be damned if she'd do it twice in one year.

"Well," Kate said, grabbing a cinnamon roll from the plate in the center of the table, "you can tell Carol I'm out. Once a year is plenty for me."

Barbara inhaled sharply, cradling her coffee cup with both hands. "I see. . . If you feel that strongly about it, it's probably best you tell Carol yourself."

You want me to tell her because you're scared to do it, Kate thought.

"She's your friend. It should come from you."

"But Carol created this holiday for *you*. She's bound to have questions only you can answer."

Kate forced a laugh, then took a bite of her cinnamon roll.

"Mother, please tell me you don't actually believe any of that nonsense. Otherwise, I'll have to redouble my efforts to find you an old folk's home."

"That's not funny, Katie."

Kate sighed. She hated talking about Carol so early in the morning.

"Hand me the front section of the paper," Kate said. "I need to scan it for stories about Susan. She's got two big cases marching to trial soon."

Barbara reached past the front section and grabbed the Metro pages, handed it to Kate instead.

She flashed her mother a confused look.

"I heard you. I heard you," Barbara said. "I thought you'd want to see this first. There's a nice story about your friend, Tina Black."

Kate tensed up. "Tina Black is not my friend."

"Really?" Barbara sounded surprised. "Is that new? Because I hear her name around here all the time."

"It is not new," Kate said sharply. If her mother had spent even a quarter as much time worrying about her feelings as she did about Carol's, she would know the two were enemies, not friends. "Tina Black is a horrible person. She cares only for herself and her career. She's a disgrace to everyone."

Barbara raised an eyebrow. "A disgrace? How so?"

"How so?" Kate felt defensive. It was like someone had asked her to explain why two plus two equals four. The fact was so obvious she didn't know what to say. "Because she's terrible. That's how so."

Barbara hummed. "I think that's what they call a conclusory argument, honey."

Kate's face turned red. "No, it's not a conclusory argument, Mother. It's a summary argument. My opinion is founded on hundreds of complex legal reasons you can't possibly understand. All you need to know is that Tina Black is a backstabbing skank."

"That doesn't sound like the woman in the article."

Kate looked down at the paper and saw a two-inch photo of Tina smiling back at her. She was standing on stage beside a man wearing an ill-fitting sport coat. The two were at a banquet. Tina was holding a plaque.

The plaque was the Bar Association's annual Difference Maker Award. According to the story, Tina had won it by wasting her Saturday mornings volunteering to help people who couldn't afford a lawyer. Her current pet project was a guy called Damion, who claimed his ex-girlfriend had abused their baby. Using her super-hero-like legal powers, Tina had crushed the woman and convinced a judge to withhold all visitation rights from her.

"Interesting," Kate said.

"See, I told you she wasn't all bad."

Kate shook her head. "No, mother. It's even worse than I thought. Tina railroaded that poor woman because she didn't have an attorney."

"I doubt that's true, honey. The judge is the one who decided the case. He wouldn't have taken away the baby without a good reason."

Kate forced a laugh. "Maybe in theory. In real life, it doesn't work that way. Crazy things happen when people don't have lawyers. That's why public defenders exist. Only they don't in family court."

"Huh." Her mother seemed interested, which didn't happen much when they talked about the law. She mulled it over for a second, then her eyes lit up. "I figured out what your Robert Frost Day project could be."

"No," Kate said. "There is no RFD project."

"You could volunteer to help someone who can't afford a lawyer. It's perfect. Not too far outside your comfort zone, but far enough Carol couldn't complain. Everyone knows you hate volunteering."

"I don't hate volunteering," Kate said defensively. "It's just, with my new job, I don't have time."

"There's another reason you should do it. For the publicity." Her mother pointed at Tina's the picture. "I bet she gets lots of new clients because of that photo."

Kate turned up her nose. "I doubt it. And even if she did, Susan wouldn't want any of those losers."

Kate wiped her face with a napkin, then pushed back her chair.

"I think you're looking for an excuse not to do it," Barbara said.

"I don't need an excuse," Kate said. "I have to go. Susan's called a quarterly meeting this morning for all the lawyers."

When Kate reached the door, her mother called out to her.

"Don't forget to call Carol."

19

The all-attorney meeting took place in the staff break room at Susan Wilson Law.

When Kate arrived at two minutes before nine, it was standing room only. Female lawyers dressed in all shades of grays and blacks sat in rows at rectangular folding tables. Strange energy hung in the air. Something had zapped these fire-breathing dragons of all their spirit.

She found Riley at a table in the back. As the only man in the crowd, he stuck out like a sore thumb.

"Thanks for saving me a seat," she said, sliding into the chair beside him.

"No problem."

His voice was edgy, sending the message that saving the seat hadn't been easy. She glanced around at the other lawyers in the room, looking at everyone and no one in particular.

"My old firm didn't invite associates to quarterlies. Not that anyone would have wanted to go. I mean, who cares about profits if you're not getting any. On the other hand, if the firm's losing money—"

"The rumor is that these can get quite intense," Riley said.

Kate rolled her eyes. "The only thing intense about a quarterly is the boredom. If it weren't for the face time I'll get with Susan, I wouldn't have walked down the hall."

A shrill voice broke over the chatter.

"Ms. Wilson doesn't attend quarterlies."

Kate leaned forward and glanced to her right, down the table, and across the aisle. The correction had come from a heavy-set, forty-something woman dressed in a black pants suit so tight it looked painful.

"Okay, thanks," Kate said coldly.

Behind her, another woman spoke up.

"Did anyone see this morning's paper? Such a wonderful story about Tina Black."

"I saw it," another woman added. "I forwarded it to Ms. Wilson. Does anyone know why Tina doesn't work here? She'd be a fantastic addition."

Great, Kate thought. *One person starts talking and suddenly we're all friends.*

Riley nodded. "I agree. Tina is a class act. I'm glad she's finally getting some recognition. She deserves it."

Kate scoffed. "I wouldn't believe everything you read in the paper, Riley."

Riley flashed her a strange look, then turned towards the front of the room. She followed his gaze and watched as three women entered through a side door.

"Who the hell is that?" Kate asked.

The women moved towards the podium in a triangle formation, a leader and two minion-like bodyguards.

The woman in charge was a giant. Six feet tall, broad-shouldered, and as pretty as a guy named Hank. She seemed to love the color black. Black hair, black trench coat, black turtleneck, black slacks. Even the mole on her cheek was black.

"My God," Riley said. "She is scary."

"Who is she?"

"It's The Hatchet," a woman behind them hissed. "Be quiet. She'll hear you."

Kate pulled her eyebrows together. She didn't know what to make of the scene.

"It must be a skit to scare the newbies," Kate said.

Riley shook his head. "I told you about her. The day we discussed Marsha's new knitting hobby."

Kate stared at him blankly. As a rule, she didn't listen to stories about hobbies. Especially when the stories involved people she didn't know. But she did have a hazy recollection of Riley saying Susan was unhappy. It was something to do with lawyers not pulling their weight.

But this didn't strike her as particularly important because partners always complained about associate billing. Nothing was ever enough. During her first year in practice, she actually knew a woman who gave birth at five o'clock in the morning and got wheeled into a mediation later the same day. When the partner was asked about it later, he said he didn't see a problem since "both mom and baby were healthy."

The Hatchet stepped to the podium.

"Good morning, people." The woman's voice purred like she was sitting behind a desk stroking a fat cat. "Unfortunately, the dismal performance we discussed during my last visit has metastasized. And Ms. Wilson has ordered me to cut it out, before it chokes us all to death."

20

The Hatchet's words spiked the tension in the room. Two rows ahead, a pencil-thin woman sobbed. All around Kate, whispers and wide-eyed people were trying to figure out what the threat meant for them.

She couldn't understand why everyone was so frazzled. Clearly, this comic book villain had her facts wrong. There was nothing dismal about the firm's performance. A month before, Susan had sat for an interview with The Austin Lawyer Magazine, where she bragged about the firm's year-over-year profit growth. Last quarter's results were something to be celebrated, not derided.

The Hatchet reached inside her trench coat, pulled a sheet of paper from her breast pocket.

"Let's start with the A's again. Where is Abrams, Lacey?"

Two tables ahead, a woman Kate didn't recognize inched up her hand like it might get chopped off.

"Stand up, woman," The Hatchet barked. "The meek may inherit the Earth, but they shan't keep a job here."

The woman slowly got to her feet. Her hands shook at her side. Kate winced at the display. No one wanted a lawyer who got frightened at the first sign of conflict.

"Please don't cry, Abrams, Lacey," The Hatchet said. "Your part will be done soon enough."

Kate tried to remember if she had ever seen Lacey around the office before. She didn't think so.

She leaned over and whispered in Riley's ear. "Are you sure that woman works here? She doesn't seem the type."

"Yes. Be quiet."

Kate turned up her nose. "I don't think so. I think she's a plant. Like I said, this is all part of a skit."

"Her office is three doors down from yours."

The answer made Kate pause. That couldn't be true, could it? She would have noticed a woman whose office was so close to her own.

Kate wondered if the stress of the moment was overwhelming Riley's senses. It happened in eyewitness testimony. People confused even the most obvious details.

The Hatchet continued, "Please tell us, Abrams, Lacey, how much money in new business did you generate for the firm this year?"

Kate hummed to herself. It was an odd question to ask in a group, especially in a firm like Susan Wilson Law where Susan controlled everything.

"Um... none."

The Hatchet nodded. "Very good. And how much did the firm pay you?"

Okay, now that was out of bounds. Lawyers weren't like the silicon valley oversharers who pretended businesses were mini-republics where everyone got one vote, and everyone deserved to know everything. Lawyers kept stuff private. It was their nature.

Abrams, Lacey swallowed hard. "$120,000, ma'am."

The answer drew gasps from the crowd.

The Hatchet nodded. "Good girl. Now pay close attention. This next question is trickier. How much should Ms. Wilson cut your salary to make up for your leeching?"

The woman tensed.

"Leaching? I only started here six months ago." The Hatchet stared at her blankly. "Plus, last month, I billed more hours than anyone in the firm."

"I want a number," The Hatchet said.

Tears streamed down the woman's face. Although, to her credit, she didn't sob or make any other embarrassing noises.

"But I—"

The Hatchet sighed. "Time's up, Abrams, Lacey. You're fired. Be gone."

The Hatchet swatted Lacey away like a fly, and the bodyguard minions swooped in, carrying her off before she could even mount a protest.

The Hatchet glanced at her paper. "Azure, Sonia. Stand up, please. You're the next contestant on Termination Nation."

Kate watched a pretty blonde get to her feet. She looked to be mid-twenties, athletic, and to have an aura of confidence the last woman lacked.

"I'm Sonia."

"Wonderful," The Hatchet said. "You saw what happened to our last friend. Can we save time? Agree that you're a leech too?"

The woman shook her head. "I've brought in new business."

The Hatchet rolled her eyes. "Be serious, Ms. Azure. Do you think Ms. Wilson wants to draft wills for your family? Personally, I think these kind of clients are worse than no business at all. Just give me a number, okay? A number to make up for your leeching."

Unlike the last woman, Sonia hid her fear well. "Thirty percent."

Kate choked when she heard the answer. Grabbing Riley's water bottle, she tried to cover her cough with a slow sip of water but couldn't stop herself. The Hatchet glared in her direction.

The question was absurd. No firm in its right mind would cut the salary of a young lawyer who actually generated business. The type of business didn't matter. It was the effort that showed promise. But to her credit, Sonia was smart enough to realize she needed to offer The Hatchet something, if she wanted to keep her job.

Sonia's offer seemed to surprise The Hatchet. The woman tilted her head to the side and paused a moment. "Let me be sure I understand. As a reparation, you're willing to work for thirty percent of your old wage?"

Sonia shook her head. "No. I meant I'd accept a thirty percent pay reduction."

"Oh." The Hatchet's voice sounded disappointed, but her face didn't match the tone. "Wrong answer. Goodbye, Ms. Azure."

The goons swept in and carried Sonia away. In one big swoop, they grabbed her and all her possessions, quickly erasing any trace of her existence.

The Hatchet moved down her list. "Becker, Kate. Please rise. It's your turn to spin the wheel." Kate stood up. "No new business, right?"

Kate's mind churned through possible answers. If she wanted to keep her job, she needed to do something drastic. She had give up too many holidays and weekends to quit on her dream now.

"Actually," Kate said, "that's not right."

The Hatchet stared at her blankly, waiting for an explanation.

"I signed a big case," Kate said. "One that's been in the news. By chance, did you see today's Metro section?"

21

"You're sure this is the place?" Barbara asked.

She was in the passenger seat of Carol's sedan, a white Buick Lucerne, her body leaning forward, straining against the seatbelt, her eyes focused across the parking lot at the unusual-looking office building in front of them.

The building was on stilts. At least, that's how it looked to Barbara. Steel posts held an aging structure twenty feet above rows of parking spaces. The neighborhood wasn't dangerous exactly, but she hadn't felt comfortable since they left the freeway.

"The name's right there," Carol said, pointing at a monument sign by the road.

Indeed, it was. Barbara had seen it when they first pulled into the lot.

"Maybe I should wait and talk to the girls first," Barbara said.

"No way, Barbie. I didn't drive all the way out here for nothing. You're getting out of this car. One way or the other. Capisce?"

"What if I have to quit because Kate gets pregnant?"

Carol laughed from her belly, leaving no doubt what she thought of that possibility.

"It could happen," Barbara said.

"Oh, get real, woman." Barbara frowned at her. "Listen, you know I adore Kate. She's smart, pretty, successful. But a mother? No, I just don't see it."

Barbara's blood pressure rose. "I think Kate would make a great mom."

"No one is saying Kate couldn't do it. Lord knows, when the girl sets her mind to something, she conquers it like Attila the Hun. What I'm saying is she doesn't want to do it. And if you wait around until she admits it, you'll be twisting in the wind for years."

Barbara sighed, trying her best to believe Carol didn't know what she was talking about.

"Even if I did volunteer," Barbara said, a moment later, "it's not like they'd actually be my grandkid."

"Oh, baloney. No one believes that."

"You do. You said it when I showed you the flyer."

Carol shrugged. "But you don't. And that's what matters. Now get inside before you miss the meeting. I can't handle listening to you whine for another month."

The second floor of the stilts building had thin industrial carpet, old wallpaper, and a strong musty smell. A line of people stood outside the door of Grannies R Us. Barbara took a place at the back.

When she called the organization a week before, she understood the meeting to be a one-on-one informational session with a staff person. Not a large group event. If she had known it would be this way, she wouldn't have come.

A woman's voice called out from behind her.

"Barbara? Is that you?"

Barbara turned to see Yata Miller coming up behind her. Yata was a tall, thin, sixtyish former hippie with long silver hair that hung down past her elbows. She was dressed in black jeans and a gray duster and had a large canvass tote bag slung over her shoulder.

Yata lived in the penthouse of Barbara's building. Officially, she was a semi-retired novelist who had struck it rich writing a series of science fiction novels about vampires in space. But the consensus around the building was she got her money the old-fashioned way: by marrying into it. Kate and Jessica subscribed to this view. Both of them had read one of Yata's books and said it wouldn't buy a latte, let alone a penthouse. Barbara didn't know because she didn't read novels about silly things.

"Hello, Yata."

"Why didn't you tell me you were coming?" Yata's voice was so overdramatic it made Barbara's ears hurt. "You could have ridden in the Subaru."

Barbara pretended to be disappointed. "Darn. You know how much I wanted to."

Yata waved a hand at her. "It's fine. Why don't we go tonight? That way, we could spend the entire evening in the car."

Barbara winced. Yata was nuts for Subaru. It started when her nephew bought a dealership. Ever since then, the woman was hawking them on the street like a religious fanatic. Kate believes Yata gets a commission for every car she sells because there's no other way to explain her bizarre behavior.

"Tonight's no good. I have to help Kate."

Yata nodded, immediately accepting the explanation. Yata didn't like Kate. She thought Kate was cold, hard, self-centered, uncaring, and generally needed a lot of help.

"Are you nervous?" Yata said. "You seem nervous."

Barbara caught herself wringing her hands and stopped. "Maybe a little. I'm just not sure I can keep up with a kid today. All this technology. It might be too much for me."

Yata shrugged. "I think technology makes them dumber."

"A woman in my card club has a grandson who's obsessed with video games. It's all he talks about. She ordered a book to learn the lingo, but before it even arrived, he quit the game and moved on to a new one. How do you handle that?"

Yata shook her head. "Grandparenting rule number one. Never care about what interests them."

Barbara raised an eyebrow. "What?"

"I'm serious, Barbie. You need to take charge from the beginning. Our job isn't to bond with these kids. Or even to like them. It's to plug the holes caused by marginal parenting."

"I didn't see that in the brochure."

Yata leaned in close, whispered in Barbara's ear. "These kids are generational losers. For most, their best hope is delivery work. That's if they don't end-up in prison. Now, don't give me that look. It's nature. Every species has losers. Lucky for them, we don't eat ours."

Barbara's mouth fell open. "If you feel that way, why are you here?"

"To help, of course. As much as genetics allow. The ten-year-old girl I picked off the website said she likes to read. It's something, I suppose. Assuming she even can."

"They have kids on a website? No one told me."

"It figures," Yata said. "The woman who runs this place could have been a client, if you get what I mean."

While they were talking, Yata had scooted ahead of her in line. Barbara didn't care, though, because she hadn't decided if she was going inside yet.

22

The woman working the door at Grannies R Us looked like she was born at a non-profit. Or if not there, then at public radio for sure. She had spikey gray hair, rectangular glasses, and wore a black leather jacket with a scarf tied around her neck.

"Name?" the woman asked as Yata approached her.

"Yata Miller."

The woman glanced down at her clipboard. "Can you spell the last name for me?"

"Seriously?" Yata said, her eyes narrowing. "You want me to spell Miller?"

"If you could, ma'am."

"M-I-L-L-E-R."

The woman ran her pen down the left-hand column of the roster, touching the names as she went, dotting each one with black ink like a battle scar. "I'm sorry, but I don't have a Yata Miller."

"If you don't have Yata Miller, then you've got the wrong list. I've been working with Veronica, you know, the lady who runs this place."

The woman's eyes got big. "Are you the one who wrote the book?"

Yata frowned. "Not a book. Five books. All which have been optioned."

"Optioned?" The woman seemed intrigued. "Tell me how."

"It doesn't matter how," Yata said curtly. "Just add my name to the list, so Veronica knows I was here."

The woman nodded, and Yata pushed forward. She disappeared inside before the lady had even finished writing her name.

"Hello," Barbara said a moment later when it was her turn. "My name's Barbara Becker."

The woman consulted her roster again. "Gosh. Your name isn't here either. Were you also working with Veronica?"

Barbara shrugged. "Maybe. I don't remember the name."

"But you were told to come today?"

"Yes. But if there isn't room, I could come back another time. I don't want to put anyone out."

The woman waved her off. "Nonsense. We have plenty of room. I'll add your name to the list. Go on ahead."

The inside of Grannies R Us was a large, bullpen-like workspace. Offices ran along the windows on the left. In the center, the metal desks normally used by administrative staff were pushed aside and replaced by rows of folding chairs facing a podium at the back.

Barbara made her way down the center aisle, searching for a place to sit. There was only one open spot. It was in the front row beside Yata Miller.

She picked up a small electronic keypad that was on the chair seat and sat down.

"See the little redhead," Yata said, looking back towards the door. There two girls near the back wall, both about age twelve, one with red hair, one with black. They were standing beside an older boy, maybe sixteen or seventeen, who was playing with a cell phone. "She's mine. But I could get you the black-haired one. Veronica owes me."

Barbara laughed uncomfortably. "Thanks, but I'm not ready to commit just yet."

"Well, I'd be careful if I were you. If Veronica senses even a hint of openness, she'll match you with that teenage stink bomb."

"I don't think so," Barbara said.

Yata raised an eyebrow. "You don't think so?"

A middle-aged woman with chin-length dirty blonde hair, a tight smile, and tired eyes stepped to the podium. She wore a blue cardigan over a blue blouse with black slacks and a pearl necklace that was too big to be real.

She introduced herself as Veronica, the group's founder, then did a brief presentation on the Do's and Don'ts of volunteer grannying before asking the three kids to join her up front. Using a projector on a wheelie cart, she emceed an audience participation trivia game where people used the keypads to vote answers to questions about the children's likes and dislikes. Much to Barbara's surprise, she got every question about the girls right. Apparently, she still had good parenting instincts.

"One last question," Veronica said. "And I'm not giving much away to say it's our only one about Garrett. He's been such a good sport, coming back year after year."

Yata scoffed. They were sitting less than ten feet from the boy. Surely, he had heard her. Barbara shot Yata a hard look.

"What? From what I hear, the kid's a-"

"Be quiet. He can hear you."

"So?"

Barbara shook her head and made clear she wasn't interested in further side-talk, then looked back up towards the screen. The question was still open for voting. It read: Slate Rock is a popular video game. The main character has a friend whose name is:

1. Heath Herbs
2. Zach Zumac
3. Freddie Fredricks
4. Mickie the Moose

Barbara pressed the answer on her keypad. She didn't need to think about it. She knew it. Slate Rock was the video game Carol's grandson had obsessed over before declaring it boring. If she had a nickel for every inappropriate comment Mickie the Moose made, she'd be living in the penthouse next to Yata.

The results flashed on the screen. The guesses were split between the first three choices. There was only one vote for number four.

"Interesting," Veronica said. "You'd think random chance would have gotten us more fours. But maybe it's a sign. Who said four? Raise your hand. You got it right."

Barbara did not raise her hand. Instead, she kept her hands folded in her lap. If she had known she'd be the only person to pick number four, she would have chosen a different answer.

Veronica looked down at the podium, then pressed a button. A moment later, the keypad in Barbara's hand began flashing like a restaurant pager.

"It's Barbara," Yata said, pointing at her. "She's the winner."

Barbara cringed.

"Wonderful," Veronica said. "Please come up to the podium so everyone can meet you."

23

At six o'clock that evening, Kate rolled to a stop beside the curb on a suburban street ten miles from Susan Wilson Law. The road was in a planned community called Uncommon Heights, which usually would have drawn a series of sarcastic comments from her about the irony of jamming cookie-cutter houses together on land as flat as the Texas prairie, but that night, she was too busy fending off Riley's accusatory questions to feel very witty.

"What was I supposed to do?" Kate said, looking over at him. Riley was in the passenger seat of her car, judging her. "Should I have let her fire me?"

"I never said that."

"You realize that if I'm gone, you're next, right? I mean, like literally following me out the door. No chance Susan keeps you without me." He nodded, and she took a breath. "Wait. Why didn't she call your name? You start with A."

Riley shrugged. "Maybe I'm not on the problem list."

Kate scoffed. "Trust me, if that pretty blonde who had only just started at the firm was on the list, you're on the list."

"Well," Riley said, "she didn't call my name, did she?"

Sometimes, Kate wanted to smack him.

"Not yet. Which is why you need to help me sign up Ruth Jacobs ASAP. Once we represent the girl, I won't have lied to The Hatchet."

Riley flashed her a puzzled look. "I'm pretty sure the truth doesn't work that way, Kate. It's a lie if it's false when you tell it. It doesn't matter what happens later."

"Can you stop being so black and white? Once the girl signs her name, everything changes."

"Even if that's true, and it isn't, we still can't just show up at her house uninvited and beg to be her lawyers. It violates ethics rules. We'll get in trouble."

"Riley, Riley, Riley." Kate said, sounding disappointed. "If you're going to be a rule monger, at least be a good one. Read the rule again."

He glanced down at a softcover book containing the Texas rules of court, which was open on his lap. She looked past him out the window and up the front yard towards a two-story house with yellow siding. Black house numbers screwed into a wooden pillar on the front porch matched the address she had taken from court records.

"Except?"

He looked up at her. "Except what? You don't qualify for any of the exceptions, Kate. Unless you're her cousin. Are you secretly her family?"

"Don't be ridiculous."

"Then showing up uninvited and asking to be her lawyer is against the rules."

"Come on, Riley. You can do better."

She pushed open the car door and stepped out onto the street.

The grass on both sides of the blacktop driveway was thick and lush, the perfect only achieved by a lawn service that sprayed chemicals. For a moment, when the wind changed directions, she thought she heard the comforting sound of traffic noise, but it disappeared so quickly she wondered if she had imagined it. The suburbs gave her the willies.

Riley jogged up beside her as she stepped onto the concrete walk that led to the front door.

"Please tell me I'm missing something, because the only other exception deals with volunteer lawyers."

"Bingo, Red Rider. You've got it."

"Volunteering?" His eyes went wide. "The Hatchet isn't going to count volunteer lawyering as bringing in new business. In fact, I'll wager it pisses her off even more than the lie."

He was right. It was a problem. But volunteering was the only way she could be sure to sign Ruth as a client. The article in the paper about Tina Black mentioned both parties being unemployed and on medical assistance. Kate figured the house belonged to Ruth's parents.

"One problem at a time," Kate said. "If we can flip the story, convince people Ruth is a victim of Tina Black's abusive tactics, we'll generate media coverage. And to Susan, good press is worth more than a little cash."

"Except, there's no evidence Tina Black is abusing the legal system."

Kate rolled her eyes. "Oh, she's abusing the system, Riley. No doubt about it. It's her nature. Now be quiet, unless you have something helpful to say."

She knocked on the plastic shell of a flimsy screen door and waited. From inside the house, she smelled chicken soup and heard running water.

A hallway in front of them ran the length of the house. A moment later, a sixtyish woman rounded the corner at the back and began hobbling towards them, walking with a clutch like she had knee problems.

As she approached, Kate thought the woman looked out of place for a cookie-cutter subdivision. She was dressed in a loose-fitting paisley shirt with a navy denim skirt that stretched down past her ankles. Her hair was short and curly, and she had a gold cross around her neck. She could have been a farmer's wife or a Sunday school teacher.

"May I help you?" the woman asked.

Kate flashed her a disarming smile. "Hello. I'm Kate Becker. This is my associate Riley Anderson. We're lawyers from the Susan Wilson Law Firm. Is Ruth here? We were hoping to talk to her."

The word lawyer caused the woman's face to turn dark. Her eyes narrowed.

"She doesn't live her anymore."

"Are you her mother?" Kate asked.

"What's this all about?"

"Do you know how we could reach her?"

The woman shook her head. "This is because of that article in the paper, isn't it? I told David not to talk to that reporter. Even an idiot could see she had an agenda. But do you think he listens to me?"

"We don't have an agenda, Ms. Jacobs," Kate said. "We just want to talk to Ruth. Help her get her daughter back."

The woman laughed, then looked at Riley. "Is she crazy? Because she sounds crazy to me."

Riley smiled. "It sometimes seems that way, ma'am." Kate shot him a hard look. "But usually, there's a method to her madness."

The woman pushed open the screen door.

"You've got ten minutes."

24

They sat at an oak table in a no-frills kitchen that made Kate feel like she was in Eastern Europe, where the people had nothing extra. No nicknacks or clutter. The only decoration was a small wooden cross on the wall. The inside of the home did not match the manicured lawn out front.

Ruth's mother handed them mustard-colored mugs filled with hot tea, then sat down across the table. Kate cupped hers with both hands, inhaling the warmth of the plain black tea. She intended to let the woman speak first.

In the brief silence, she tried to make sense of what was happening. It was her first voyage into the bizarro world of offering people free legal services, and it wasn't what she expected. She never thought Ruth (or her family) might refuse help. What sort of idiot didn't want a free lawyer? Especially one who worked at the best firm in town.

"Now, tell me why you're really here," the woman said. "And don't give me that altruistic bull—"

Kate studied Ruth's mother for a moment, trying to determine the best angle to play, then opted for a version of the truth.

"You're right, Ms. Jacobs," Kate said. "I don't know the first thing about your daughter. But I know the other side's lawyer, Tina Black. She's a snake. The woman will do anything for publicity. Including stealing a baby out of her mother's arms."

The woman nodded. "I don't doubt that's true. When I called Damion after Ruth got served the papers, he said his lawyer was the toughest lady in town."

Kate smiled. "She thinks she is. Tina Black and I both interviewed for the same job. Guess who my boss picked?"

"I'm sure you're very capable Ms.—"

"Kate. Call me, Kate."

"Okay, Kate," the woman said. "I'm sure you're very capable. Which is why you shouldn't be wasting your time on my daughter. The judge already heard her side. He took the baby anyway."

Kate shook her head. "Without a lawyer, Tina Black likely twisted the facts so hard your daughter didn't stand a chance."

The woman sipped her tea and studied Kate for a moment.

"Maybe sometimes that's true, but not here. Here, nothing would have mattered."

"You can't know that for sure," Kate said. "Trust me. I've won hundreds of cases people said were losers."

Okay, maybe not hundreds, she thought. But three didn't sound as impressive to non-lawyers who didn't know how hard it was to get in front of a jury these days.

"My daughter deserved to lose, Ms. Becker. She has problems."

Kate held her face steady, tried not to react. She knew little about family court, but she knew enough to understand it wasn't good when your client's parents were against you. It tended to make judges sit up, pay attention.

Riley jumped in, tried to fill the awkward silence. "What makes her unfit?"

The woman looked past Riley towards a clock on the stove.

"I have to leave in a minute. My bible study group starts soon. The short story is Ruth rejected our faith. She gave in to the sensual pleasures. It's a miracle my grandbaby was even born healthy."

"So Ruth is an alcoholic?" Kate asked.

In the newspaper, Tina Black had called Ruth "a drunk who couldn't walk a straight line at eight o'clock in the morning." She claimed Ruth hid liquor bottles throughout the trailer where she lived with Damion and drove drunk with the baby in the car. Kate had dismissed this as hyperbole because there wasn't any proof apart from Damion's own self-serving testimony.

The woman nodded. "Ruth drinks too much. Amongst other things."

Riley asked, "Has she ever been to treatment?"

"No. We asked her to see our pastor, but she refused."

Kate sipped her tea and mulled it over as Riley continued to ask a series of meaningless questions. After a minute, she remembered something she had learned in law school that made her doubt the mother's story.

"Let me make sure I understand," Kate said, "You're concerned about Ruth. I get that. But what about the father? Aren't you worried about him, too?"

The woman stiffened. "I don't know the boy. My daughter isn't the type who brings dates home for dinner."

Kate nodded. "Of course. Yet you still think your grandchild is better off with him. A guy you don't even know."

The woman's face turned red. "I didn't say that. The judge is the one who awarded him custody, not me."

"Right," Kate said.

The anger receded from the woman's face and was quickly replaced by a thick layer of politeness. She pushed back the chair and stood up.

"I must now ask you to leave. Pastor Montgomery has a kind heart for all things except those who come late to bible study."

When they were standing on the front porch, Kate said, "I'd still like to talk to Ruth. Do you have a number where we could reach her?"

The woman shook her head, then closed the heavy wooden door and was gone.

25

When they reached the car, the sun was already below the horizon. The last of the orange twilight about to give way to a cloudless, black night. All along the street, house lights blazed like some overeager steward had gone door to door, switching them on early to avoid even a hint of darkness.

Riley glanced at Kate from the passenger seat.

"So, we're done, right? Moving on from this extraordinary plan?"

Kate turned up her nose. "Um, no. Why would you think that?"

Riley hummed.

It was the first time he had made that noise to her, and she didn't like it. It meant he was too comfortable with their relationship.

"She said Ruth has problems," Riley said.

"I don't buy it."

He raised an eyebrow at her. "You don't buy it?"

"No, I don't buy it. My gut says there's more to the story."

"I'm sure there is more to the story, Kate. Probably lots more. Maybe the girl also snorts coke."

She shook her head. "There's something about the mother that gives me the willies. What did you think of the inside of the house? Too spartan, right? It reminded me of a Puritan settlement. I thought she might brand me with a scarlet letter."

Riley shook his head. "It's a simpler life, Kate."

"Come on. There were more crosses than furniture."

"I wanted this to work out, too, Kate. But the case is a loser. When a girl's own mother doesn't support her—"

"I know, Riley. That's what makes it so suspicious."

"No, it doesn't. You're trying to latch on to anything you can to keep this case alive. A mother being against her own daughter is a red flag. It's like a flashing neon sign saying, 'Danger! Keep away.'"

This time, Kate hummed for a moment. "What if the mother is the one who's crazy?"

Riley sighed, then closed his eyes. "Okay, Kate. I'll bite. Give me one reason that's plausible."

"I'll do better. Here's two. First, the mother tried to take her daughter to a pastor for treatment. If that's not—"

"Nope," Riley said. "Doesn't count. Many people visit their pastor for help."

"Not for addiction problems, they don't. But whatever. It doesn't matter. Answer me this: What normal woman believes her granddaughter is better off being raised by some rando she didn't even know?"

The question made him pause, which told her she was on the right track.

"Maybe he's clean," Riley said a moment later. "He might be nothing like the girl."

Kate flashed him a disappointed look. "I expected more from you."

"Fine. I admit, it's weird. But ones don't marry tens is just a saying. It proves nothing."

The phrase "ones don't marry tens" was the sum of the family law knowledge Kate had learned in law school. It stood for the idea that educated, upstanding people rarely impregnate junkies.

"On the contrary," Kate said, "it proves everything. Either this guy is just as screwed up as Ruth, which means we could still turn the case around, or Ruth's not as bad as her mother claims, which is interesting too."

Riley hawed. "You're reaching. It could be a lightening strike."

"A what?"

"A lightening strike. You know, something that's rare but happens all the time."

"That's not a real phrase, Riley."

"Yes, it is. There are a million reasons why a decent guy might have impregnated Ruth."

"Perhaps, but like you said, it'd be a lightening strike. The smart money is still on ones and tens."

"In theory, but not here. The judge has looked at the evidence and—"

"Please, Riley—"

His hand went up like a shot. "Don't give me that line about Tina Black twisting the facts. I'm not an idiot. The judge has already ruled, Kate. He's not going to reverse himself unless we show overwhelming evidence of fraud. Something you'll never be able to do."

"I was worried about the same thing. But it turns out that family court procedures are different than our normal civil cases. I checked. The judge who signed the first order was only hearing emergency filings. Court Admin is going to assign us a new judge to handle the case. Nothing is precedential. Ruth gets a do-over."

"Still, it would be almost impossible."

"Only almost."

Riley shook his head. "None of this matters if we can't find Ruth."

"Do you always give up so easily? Finding Ruth will be a snap. Susan has like twenty PI's on the payroll. All it will take is one phone call."

"Oh, okay." His voice was thick with sarcasm. "I'm sure Ms. Wilson won't mind us using firm resources to find an alcoholic woman who lost her baby so we can represent her for free."

Kate ignored him, started the car.

There were three quick raps on the driver's side window. The noise startled her. She looked over to see a young woman standing outside the window. The girl couldn't have been more than twenty. She had a gray hoodie pulled up over her head like she was trying to hide her face. If they hadn't been in a cookie-cutter subdivision, Kate never would have rolled down her window.

"You're here about Ruth?" the girl asked.

Kate wondered how she knew. "Yes. Do you know her?"

"You're lawyers?" The girl must have seen the surprise on Kate's face because she said, "I saw the Harvard sticker in the back window."

"Oh, right," Kate said. "Yes, we want to help Ruth, but we can't find her."

The girl studied them for a moment, as if deciding whether to trust them.

"I could get her a message," she said. "Tell me your number."

Kate looked down at the center console and grabbed a business card from a cup holder. After she handed it to the girl, she glanced at Riley and flashed him a cocky smile.

26

Two weeks after Kate paid her share of Asha's fees, the Indian VA provided the first set of potential sperm donors. Jessica was over the moon about her matches.

"Isn't Asha the best?" Jessica said, in a tone that sounded a lot like, "Without me you never would have found such an amazing VA."

Kate had no basis to opine because she still hadn't been allowed to see the names of the men who matched her criteria. When she asked Jessica to forward her the list, her sister got defensive. "It violates the terms of service," Jessica said, acting as if Kate didn't understand legal lingo. "Let's meet for lunch on Thursday. We'll talk it through together. In the meantime, keep your fingers crossed. I'm working on a little present that might solve all your problems."

Kate had a bad feeling in the pit of her stomach. The fact that Jessica was refusing to share the list could only mean one thing. The matches were terrible.

This was how Kate came to be in a parking lot outside a four-star hotel near the Austin International Airport. She switched off the car's ignition and waited for a plane to pass overhead before turning to look at Jessica. The aircraft had come so close it felt like she could reach up and touch it.

"Tell me why we're really here," Kate said. "And don't give me a line about the hotel's food. This place is deserted."

Jessica twisted in her seat. A huge smile crossed her face.

"Of course, we're not here for the food," Jessica said. She paused to build dramatic tension. "Remember how I said I was working on something special for you? Well, he's inside."

"What?"

Her sister was always doing this sort of thing. Changing the rules of a game after it started.

"I only agreed that you could be Asha's point of contact because you promised not to do anything without talking to me first."

"I know," Jessica said, not sounding even remotely apologetic. "And I didn't want to. I didn't. But when I saw Michael's profile, I knew he was perfect for you. And I was worried you might get scared. Not agree to meet him."

Kate pulled her eyebrows together. "Why wouldn't I agree to meet the perfect man?"

Jessica reached into a bag at her feet, pulled out a manila folder, and handed it to Kate.

"Because he's international."

Kate opened the folder and saw a wallet-sized picture clipped inside. The man's name was Michael Patel. He looked about her age, had fair skin, wavy black hair, and a three-day beard. The small picture had a professional flair to it that made her wonder if he was an actor. A Bollywood star, perhaps?

She didn't want to admit it, but her sister was right. She never would have pursued an international donor. Not because she disliked foreign men. No ovulating woman would turn down a night with Michael Patel. It was the cultural component that worried her. Being a single mom seemed hard enough. Add to that the prospect of educating a child in another culture and it seemed too much.

She scanned the rest of the resume. Michael Patel seemed to check all the boxes.

Am I being too hesitant? she wondered. A little gun shy? People from different cultures have children together all the time. There's no reason I couldn't learn Indian traditions. Plus, I do like curry. And yoga. And I took a mediation class once.

She closed the folder, handed it back to her sister.

"I'll meet with him," Kate said, doing her best to sound put off, "but only because I don't want to be rude."

Jessica nodded.

They got out of the car and headed to the hotel. After passing through a lobby, they stopped in an enormous open-air atrium with a glass-paneled ceiling four stories above the ground. Someone designed it to feel like a tropical oasis. There was a waterfall, palm trees, and secluded conversation spaces separated by fake rocks.

Jessica pointed at a sign for Canyon Restaurant, and they followed a stone path around to the right.

"I'm still mad at you," Kate said. "When you get back to the office, you need to forward me the email with all my matches."

"I can't. It violates—"

Kate glared at her sister.

"Okay," Jessica said. "I will. And just so you know, you might have also agreed to pay travel expenses."

Kate stopped walking. "Why might I have done that?"

"Because it will save you time. Come on, Katie. Two grand is nothing, if it nets you a baby. Think of all the memories you'll make as a mother. Plus, it was the only way he'd come."

"I see."

At the entrance to Canyon Restaurant, a sea of unoccupied tables filled the open-air space. The place was so deserted it felt closed.

"He's here," Jessica said. "I know he is. I was texting him in the car."

Kate followed her sister into the center of the restaurant, where they stopped and looked around. Off in the corner, she saw a man at a table, his head tilted down towards a phone. He hadn't seemed to notice them.

She nudged her sister. "That better not be him, Jess."

27

"Ew," Jessica said after spotting the man at the table. "So, his picture might be a few years old."

A few years old? The man at the table resembled the man in the picture the way a tenured university professor sometimes resembles a photograph in the student directory. Both were male, had similarly shaped faces, and shared Indian ancestry. Beyond that, there was about thirty years of difference.

"What was Asha thinking?" Kate said. "This guy is ancient."

"To be fair, we didn't give her an upper age limit."

Kate's eyes went wide. "I didn't realize we needed to exclude senior citizens. I suppose I'm lucky he's not a hundred-year-old guy with an oxygen tube clipped in his nose."

"Come on, Kate. Be reasonable. It's a miracle she found anyone at all for you."

The man looked up, waved at them.

Kate put on a fake smile and headed towards the table. Out of the side of her mouth, she whispered to her sister. "Don't say a word. I'm ending this."

Up close, the man seemed even less desirable than she first thought. He was bald except for a patch of stringy white hair on the top of his head. Where his hair did grow thick was in a place it didn't belong: on his chest, sticking out the top of an unbuttoned yellow sports shirt.

They sat down in straight chairs across the table from him.

Kate hadn't even said hello when her nose was assaulted by the most terrible smell of her life. At first, she didn't realize where it was coming from. But then, as the man leaned forward to shake her hand, she realized it was his armpits.

She jerked her chair back a foot, desperate for cleaner air. The extra space didn't help. She would have needed to go clear across the atrium to escape the vinegary, garlic smell.

"Expenses are now five thousand," the man said. "Maybe more. The bus to my village runs only Tuesdays."

"No problem," Jessica said, squirming in her seat.

Of the two of them, Jessica had always been the more scent sensitive. She was on sensory overload, which Kate thought served her right.

"Did you come directly from the airport?" Jessica asked. "Because if you need to freshen up, we can wait."

"No," the man said. "I am good."

Kate flashed Jessica a tight smile.

"Please," the man continued. "Ask your questions. I will tell you why Michael Patel should make you in the family way."

Jessica hummed, then pulled out the manila folder Kate had reviewed in the car.

"Tell me about your work history," Jessica said. "I see nothing after MIT. That's a pretty big gap."

For a second, the man looked confused. Or maybe ashamed. Kate couldn't tell which.

"Michael Patel made bad choices at university," the man said in a heavy, sorrowful voice. "Terrible choices."

Kate tried not to smile. The perfect ten Asha had found was now talking about himself in the third person. What a nut.

"Tell us what happened," Kate said.

The man looked away for a moment, then back at them.

"Michael Patel came to America to become a doctor. But then he lied. He majored in. . . theater. And he never sent money home to his family."

"Well," Jessica said, sounding a bit relieved, "that's not the worst thing now, is it?"

The man's eyes narrowed. He gave them a look that would have sent Kate running for the car if it hadn't been midday in an upscale hotel atrium.

He reached into the front pocket of his jeans, pulled out a small plastic bottle. A three-ounce travel size a person can carry on an airplane. He plunked it down in the middle of the table.

Kate flinched when she saw the milky liquid.

"A sample," the man said. "From Michael Patel. Good motility. Bad morphology."

Kate sat on her hands to make sure there was no way she could touch it.

"Go ahead," the man said, nudging the bottle towards Jessica. "Take it."

"Um, no, thanks," Jessica said. "Please, take it back."

The man looked hurt. "But we agreed. You said to bring a sample to speed up the process."

"I did not."

Anyone watching would have known Jessica was lying. Kate knew it from the way her sister's eye twitched. Kate had a similar tell. So did their mother. It was genetic.

"I'm sorry," Kate said. "My sister made promises she shouldn't have made. I'm the one looking for a baby. And I'm only interested in a father my own age."

The man tilted his head to the side. "But Michael Patel is thirty-six. That is close to your age, yes?"

It took Kate a second to connect the dots.

"Michael Patel is your son?" Kate asked.

The man nodded.

"And he sent you here on his behalf?"

The man took a deep breath, crossed his arms, and appeared to think about his answer. In the end, he choose truth, which made him look very unhappy.

"No. My son did not send me."

"Oh, that's too bad," Jessica said quickly, sensing a way out. "Unfortunately, we can't accept a sample without donor consent. Have a nice trip home."

"Why did you come?" Kate asked.

The man shrugged. "My family owes people a lot of money for Michael's education. And that," he pointed at the bottle, "is the least he can do to help. My boy is very smart, Ms. Kate. Everything on the paper is true."

Neither Kate nor Jessica spoke again until they were back in the car, driving out of the parking lot.

"I threw up in my mouth when he pulled out the bottle," Jessica said. "As soon as I get back to the office, I'm sending Asha an email. No more old men, third-party applications, or samples."

Kate squeezed the steering wheel. She spoke slowly, deliberately, with her eyes focused on the road. "I want Asha's email address."

"I already told you. That's—"

"It's not a request."

Jessica huffed. "Even if I did, she wouldn't respond to you."

"Oh, she's going to respond to me. From now on, I'm the contact person."

28

On the Saturday after her trip to Grannies R Us, Barbara got up extra early. She couldn't sleep despite it still being dark outside. Her brain was working too fast, mulling over why Veronica had wanted to see her and why she had foolishly agreed to meet the woman at the condo on a weekend.

A meeting during the week wouldn't have posed a problem. Kate left for work early. But on weekends, her daughter dithered around the condo, lounging on the couch, sipping coffee, and pretending to enjoy old books like *Moby Dick* and *War and Peace* because smart people liked them.

She was in the kitchen, mixing a box of muffins she had hidden in the pantry, when she heard a door open. She turned to see Kate, who was wearing a hot pink t-shirt and black yoga pants.

"Do I smell lemon poppy seed muffins?"

"Oh, yes," Barbara said. "But don't get too excited, because I had to use real milk. You finished the last of the almond milk yesterday."

"I did?"

Barbara nodded.

In fact, Kate had not finished the last of the almond milk yesterday. Before Barbara began mixing the batter, she dumped the carton down the sink, hoping that the smell of muffins her lactose intolerant daughter couldn't eat might nudge her to leave the condo.

"Don't worry, honey," Barbara said. "I'll get more at the store today. But if you want a muffin, I bet you could get some at that chess club of yours. Don't they do dairy free on weekends?"

"Usually."

"You should go there. Call your sister. You girls always have fun playing on Saturday mornings."

"It's a good idea, Mother. And I'd do it too, except for one thing. The club's closed this weekend. I've told you that four times this week. They're waxing the floors for Fabiano's visit."

Barbara pulled her eyebrows together. The name sounded familiar, although she couldn't place it because she zoned out when her girls talked chess. It was such a dull, dull game.

"Oh, right. Fabio. Well, call your sister anyway. She can meet you at Cafe Noir. They have dairy-free muffins."

Kate shook her head, then walked over to the couch and plopped down in a corner. She pulled her bare feet up underneath her.

"Maybe tomorrow. This morning, I'm all about self care. I'm drinking coffee and reading the newspaper. Say, can you grab it for me from the hall?"

"Of course," Barbara said, smiling tightly. "It's not like I'm getting ready for company."

Kate gave her a funny look as she passed by the couch. When she pulled open the front door and saw the newspaper on the mat in the hallway, she got an idea.

"Oh, no," Barbara said dramatically.

"What?"

"Hold on a sec, honey. I need to check something."

She stepped out into the hall and let the door close behind her. After glancing over both shoulders to make sure she was alone, she bent down and grabbed the newspaper off the floor, then took off down the hall like a shot. Within ten steps, she was out of breath, gasping for air, but she didn't slow. She kept moving.

When she reached the elevator bank, she tossed the newspaper into a tiny wastebasket under the call buttons. Then she retraced her steps back to the condo. She was still breathing hard when she pushed open the front door.

"What happened," Kate asked, sitting up on the couch.

"He did it again."

"No!" Kate's voice rose in disgust. "Tell me you're joking."

"I wish I were, honey."

A tiny part of Barbara felt bad for framing the boy. He had actually done his job, this time. But if he had always done his job like a paperboy should, one mistake wouldn't amount to anything, would it?

"It's the third time this week," Kate said. "I'm calling customer service. Someone needs to report him."

"If you think that's the right thing, honey."

"I don't want to do it, Mother. But on-time delivery is the core function of a paperboy. No one reads day old papers."

"That's true."

"This the last thing I needed this morning. Do you realize how much pressure I'm under at work? I need time for self-care."

"I know, dear," Barbara said. "Do you want me to call his mother? She might have an extra paper."

"The guy's twenty-six-years-old!" Kate said. "We shouldn't have to call his mother every time he screws up."

"Quite right. I suppose he ought to face the music. Although—" Barbara reached into her pocket and pulled out a five-dollar bill. "It might be less stressful for you if instead of reporting him you went to Cafe Noir and got yourself a crisp copy of The New York Times. You know how good writing helps you breathe. It'd be my treat."

"Well—"

The doorbell rang behind her.

Barbara glanced at her watch, hoping it was too early for Veronica, then went over and opened the door. Jessica breezed past her, heading straight to where Kate sat on the couch. She tossed a newspaper into her sister's lap.

"Look what I found. In the trash," Jessica said.

Kate gasped. "In the trash?"

"Yes. It was in the little can by the elevator."

"Dear Lord!"

Barbara closed the door and joined the girls.

"It's probably not yours," Barbara said.

"No, it's definitely hers." Jessica pointed at a small mailing label stuck to the back of the paper. "See. Kate's address is right there."

Barbara hummed. How had she never seen that sticker before? She had recycled hundreds of Kate's old newspapers.

"What were you doing digging around in the trash?" Barbara asked.

The question caused Kate to raise an eyebrow. For a second, she thought her distraction might work. Neither of her girls ever touched things in the trash.

"Don't give me that look," Jessica said. "I saw a corner of it sticking out of the basket. I believe what you want to say is thank you."

Kate nodded. "Quite right. Thanks, Jessica."

"My pleasure."

Kate opened the newspaper and pulled out the arts section, handed it to Jessica. "Grab some coffee. Then come join me on the couch."

Jessica did a little half-bow. "Why, thank you, kind sister. I shall."

"Whoa, whoa, whoa," Barbara said, holding up her hands. "I've got a better idea. Why don't you two go play chess in the park? Who's that man you're always talking about challenging?"

"You mean Homeless Harry?" Jessica asked.

"I think so," Barbara said, pretending to remember the name.

"Homeless Harry doesn't play on Saturdays, Mother." Kate spoke with her face hidden behind the newspaper. "I'm starting to think you don't listen when I talk."

"Although," Jessica said, "you know who might be there?"

"Who?"

"Marbles."

Kate lowered the paper, looked at her sister. "You think so?"

Jessica nodded. "I do. They released him, you know. Something about him being fixed now."

Kate laughed. "Fixed now? Ha. That's funny."

"It is. But someone told me that if you play him early enough in the morning, he's still lucid. Or lucidish anyway."

Kate closed the paper. "I'll get dressed."

A moment later, when Kate was in the bedroom, the doorbell rang again.

Barbara looked uneasily at Jessica.

"Are you going to get that, Mom? Or should I?"

"Oh, I'll get it, honey," Barbara said, her feet still planted on the floor. "I'm just trying to think who it might be."

"You know, you don't have to guess. You can just open it and find out."

"Right, right. Silly me."

Barbara went to the door and pressed her eye against the peephole. Her heart skipped a beat when she saw Veronica on the other side.

"Well," Jessica said, "do I need to call building security?"

Barbara glanced back at her daughter. "I have a confession to make."

29

With a red face, Barbara stood inside Kate's bedroom, her back to the closed door, acting like a guard whose job was to prevent people from coming or going. She had whisked Jessica back to Kate's room after saying a quick hello to Veronica, intent on keeping them from talking.

"Okay," Barbara said, exhaling a long breath. "I have to say something. And I don't want any comments from either of you."

"Who was that woman, Mom?" Jessica asked.

"What woman?" Kate came out of a walk-in closet slipping on a pair of flat shoes. "Is she the reason you two are watching me get dressed?"

Barbara said, "Last week, Carol, drove me to a meeting about volunteering."

Kate and Jessica exchanged glances.

"Well, that's nothing to be ashamed of, Mother," Kate said. "I think volunteering is a great idea. You've been spending far too much time with those card club crazies."

"I agree," Jessica said. "A little birdy happened to tell me that the Blanton Museum is looking for new people."

Kate pulled her eyebrows together. "What? No, you idiot. I'm the one who told you that. It was six months ago. After that church lady spanked the boy who scratched the Pellegrini."

"Oh, yeah," Jessica said, a flash of recognition in her eyes. "I remember now. The little brat got off easy, if you ask me. I would have caned him, like they do to criminals in Singapore. The Pellegrini is priceless."

"It's not priceless."

Barbara waved a hand at both of them. "Museums aren't really my thing."

Kate put a hand over her heart. "As much as it pains me to hear that, Mother, I can't say I'm surprised. Follow your heart. Volunteer wherever you feel needed."

"Yeah, blaze your own trail, Mom," Jessica said.

"Just promise me," Kate said, "that you'll be careful. A lot of shady organizations prey on old people."

"Old people?" Barbara said. "I'm not old people. And do you know how crazy that sounds?"

"No, she's right, Mom," Jessica said. "Some of these organizations are really sketchy."

"You girls are being paranoid."

"I wish we were," Jessica said. "Just last week, Willa told me about a questionable group of volunteer grandparents."

Kate forced a laugh. "Volunteer grandparents? Who knew such a stupid thing existed? Personally, I think anyone who volunteers to be a grandparent deserves to be scammed."

Barbara pressed her lips together. "No one deserves to be scammed, Katie. And what's so bad about volunteer grandparenting?"

"It's nuts. I bet it's a haven for molesters. Creepy old men with greasy hair and mustaches. Guys who drive El Caminos with mattresses in the back."

"You've lost your mind, honey," Barbara said. "I happen to know that most volunteer grandparents are women. And science shows people live longer when they spend time around kids. Plus, the kids benefit from our life experience."

Jessica smiled. "Sounds like someone's heard the radio jingle."

"I haven't heard any jingles," Barbara said defensively.

Jessica studied her for a moment, then glanced around the room as if to make sure they were still alone before speaking. "What I'm about to tell you is highly confidential. Can you keep a secret, Mom? Never to be repeated to anyone. Especially not Carol."

Barbara rolled her eyes. "Of course."

Jessica continued. "You know how I said Willa told me about that questionable grandparents group? Well, she knows about it because she overheard a meeting in her father's study. Her dad is a federal judge. This meeting was with two clean cut guys, who wore dark suits, carried guns, and drove a black suburban. She specifically heard the words volunteer and grandparents and fraud."

Kate's eyes went wide. "Really?"

"Mm-hmm." Jessica looked proud of herself.

Barbara frowned. "That means nothing."

"Oh, but it does," Jessica said. "Willa said the investigation is very serious. And Willa is never wrong."

"Jess is right, Mother," Kate said. "Willa is amazing."

"Well, I don't believe a word of it," Barbara said.

Kate tilted her head to the side, looked confused. "Why are you so upset? It's not like you're going to be one of those losers. Soon enough, I'll be pregnant and give you a real grandkid."

"Me too," Jessica added. "And unlike Kate's babies, mine will be emotionally stable."

Kate flashed Jessica a hard look.

"You're right, girls," Barbara said. "I shouldn't care, should I?"

"So, who's the woman?" Kate asked.

Barbara hesitated, then blurted out the first organization that came to mind.

"That's Veronica. She's with TAR."

Kate's eyes got big, her mouth fell open. "TAR? We had an agreement, Mother!"

Barbara wondered if Kate would have taken the news better if she had simply told her the truth. Kate really, really disliked animals.

"Our agreement," Barbara said, "was that I wouldn't bring any pets into the condo. I never said I wouldn't volunteer at the shelter."

"You can't be serious." Kate's voice bordered on yelling. "As soon as one of those mutts makes eyes at you, you'll turn into Dr. Doolittle. We'll have ten living here by morning."

"That's not fair," Barbara said.

"I agree with Mom," Jessica said. "You're being very judgmental, Kate."

"Oh really?"

"Yes, we ought to trust Mom's judgment. If she says her animal addiction is under control, we should believe her."

Kate scoffed. "You're only saying that because your building doesn't allow pets."

"Not true. The boy at the end of the hall has a fish. And let me assure you, madam, we notice when he forgets to change its water."

Kate rolled her eyes.

"Listen," Barbara said, "we can talk about it again later. Right now, you two should get to the park. Play chess with Mr. Marbles. I promise not to make any commitments."

Kate hummed.

Before her daughters could answer, Barbara opened the door and hurried out of the room.

30

Barbara raised a finger in Veronica's direction as she hurried through the living room, breezing past the woman as if an extra second might be the difference between golden brown muffins and charred black hockey pucks.

She pulled the tin from the oven, arranged the muffins on a white dinner plate, then rushed back into the living room carrying the plate, a pot of coffee, and two mugs with her pinkie. She set everything down on the coffee table just as Kate and Jessica emerged from the back bedroom.

"Veronica," Barbara said, brushing her hair back, trying to catch her breath. "These are my daughters. Kate and Jessica."

Kate stepped forward, tentatively extended a hand. "Hello."

"Nice to meet you," Veronica said, shaking both girls' hands.

"You two had better get going." Barbara looked at Veronica. "They're off to play chess in the park against someone called Marbles."

"Mother—"

"This Marbles person is quite a character," Barbara said.

"Mom, stop—"

Barbara twirled a finger at her temple. "Apparently, he gets a little cuckoo if you don't play him early enough in the day. Isn't that right, girls?"

Veronica's eyes narrowed. "You're not talking about Charlie Bradford, are you?"

Barbara shrugged. She looked at her daughters for support, but neither of them would meet her eye. Both were staring down at the floor.

"Charlie lost his eye in 9-11," Veronica said curtly. "And he's worked very hard to overcome the PTSD."

Barbara shot the girls a hard look. She should have known this was another of their nasty nicknames.

"I'm disappointed in you two." Barbara used a stern voice hoping a public rebuke would help soothe things over with Veronica. It seemed to work. The woman's face relaxed. "All right, now, off you go. Veronica needs to talk to me alone."

Kate and Jessica started towards the door.

"Actually," Veronica said, "if it's not too much trouble, maybe they could stick around for a few minutes. It's important everybody in the family be on board. This is a big commitment, after all."

Kate raised an eyebrow. "A big commitment?"

"Not from you, honey," Barbara said. "Go play chess. We'll talk about it later. Like I promised."

Jessica looked at Kate. "If she thinks we should stay—"

"Then we should stay," Kate said. "I don't want PETA saying we're insensitive."

Kate leaned in close to Jessica and whispered something in her ear that made her laugh.

They sat on the living room couch, no one touching the muffins, no one drinking the coffee. Veronica had a portfolio open on her lap.

"Barbara, you made quite an impression on Garrett last week."

"Last week?" Kate said. "When was this?"

"At our orientation session. Your mother was the first person Garrett ever responded to."

"Wow," Jessica said sarcastically. "So exciting."

"It was nothing," Barbara said.

"Maybe to you," Veronica said. "But to us, it was special. It gets tough to match a volunteer to someone Garrett's age."

"How old is this, Garrett?" Kate asked.

"Sixteen."

Jessica turned up her nose. "Sixteen? What's that in people years? Like a hundred?"

"One hundred twelve," Kate said.

"People years?"

Jessica ignored Veronica. "I suppose it's not that old, if he's a parrot. Parrots live a long time, right?"

Kate nodded. "Longer than you want them to."

Jessica laughed. "Good one."

"Girls, quit it," Barbara said. "Garrett isn't a parrot."

"Actually, a parrot wouldn't be the worst thing," Jessica said.

"No?" Kate asked.

"Look at it this way. If Mom brings home a parrot, that animal will say in the cage. This animal will drag his butt all over the furniture. Leave you little treats in places you won't find until they stink."

Kate's eyes went wide.

Barbara cut in before either of her daughters could say more.

"Veronica, what did you want to talk about?"

Veronica appeared unsettled by the conversation. She took a moment to compose herself, then spoke to Barbara. "I was hoping to convince you to be Garrett's grandmother."

Kate scoffed. "Grandmother? That's what you call them now?"

"Do you have a problem with that word?" Veronica asked.

"No, not when it's used correctly," Kate said. "I mean, come on. If you're going to anthropomorphize, why not just call her his mother?"

Veronica stared at Kate, blinked once. "Because he already has a mother."

"Of course," Kate said. "Obviously."

"Am I missing something? Because I don't understand what's going on here."

"I'll tell you what's going on," Kate said, getting to her feet. "Calling her a grandmother is the last straw for me."

"Katie—"

"No, Mother," Kate said. "I'm not holding my tongue any longer. You can waste your time with this group if you want, but that mutt is never stepping foot inside this condo. I've worked too hard for too long to have him destroy the place."

"Katie!"

"Kate's right," Jessica said. "Imagine what would happen if Garrett got loose and mounted one of Ms. Tuttle's little dogs. We'd have to move out of state."

The idea that Garrett might impregnate a dog pushed Veronica over the edge. She slammed her portfolio shut and stood up.

"Obviously, this was a mistake," Veronica said.

"Don't act like I'm the bad guy because I don't want some stray in my house, licking his butt, climbing in my bed."

Veronica huffed, then hurried out of the condo. Barbara chased after her.

31

For the second time in an hour, Barbara found herself running down the hallway towards the elevators. She caught up to Veronica just as the woman pressed the down call button.

"I want to apologize," Barbara said. "Kate was out of line."

"Only Kate?" Veronica said.

"Okay, Jessica, too."

Veronica glanced at her, shot Barbara a hard look.

"All right, all right. I could have handled it better, too. But in my defense, I didn't know his name wasn't Marbles."

Veronica turned back towards the closed elevator doors.

"We're not those type of people," Barbara said. "We're not. It's just, I shouldn't say anything. Oh, what does it matter now. Kate is infertile. The word grandparent is a trigger for her."

Veronica sighed. "I'm sorry. I'm sure it's a very challenging time for her. But—"

"I'm learning," Barbara said. "It'll never happen again."

The elevator dinged. The doors slid open. Veronica stepped inside and pressed the button for the lobby.

"Have a nice weekend, Barbara," Veronica said.

When the rubber seals on the doors were a foot apart, Barbara stuck out her hand and forced them to rebound. She used an arm to keep them open.

"Did you say the boy was already attached to me?"

Veronica shook her head. "No, I didn't use those words."

"I think you did."

"What are you saying, Barbara? That you still want to volunteer?"

"Oh, goodness, no. How could I?"

"Good. Then please remove your arm so I may go."

Barbara kept her arm in place. "But if the boy were attached to me, it wouldn't seem fair to punish him because of our little misunderstanding."

"He's not attached to you, Barbara. In fact, I'm not even sure he wants a grandmother."

"What? Who doesn't want a grandmother? Does he have brain damage or something?"

Veronica's eyes narrowed.

"I was joking. What I meant is that everyone wants a grandmother. They're the best. They buy you gifts, take you places, get you ice cream when your parents say no."

"That's not what our grandmothers do."

"Listen, you said I was the only one he responded to, right?"

Veronica hesitated. "Yes."

"Well, that's how attachment begins, isn't it? I need to meet him. See if there's a spark."

"A spark? This isn't a date, Barbara."

"I understand."

"What about your daughters? Are they going to behave?"

It was a fair question. It would take time and finessing and a little luck to bring them around. For now, however, it didn't matter because she wasn't going to tell them anything about it. Or bring the boy to the condo.

"They'll be fine," Barbara said. "You'll see."

Veronica hummed. "Okay. I'll set up a meeting. But this is a big deal, Barbara. You need to take it seriously."

32

The day after Kate visited Ruth's mother's house, she was back at her desk, fingers hovering over the keyboard, struggling to find the right number to include in a settlement demand on one of her other cases. Earlier that morning, she had gotten an email from opposing counsel begging for a reasonable settlement offer.

The phrase reasonable settlement offer was technical attorney speak. In plain English, it meant something like, "Seriously, woman, give us the lowest possible number you'll ever accept. If it fits within our nuisance budget, we might pay you."

Attorneys made these sorts of requests to either: (1) seem like a reasonable person who cared about settling, or (2) screw with your head. Sometimes, it was both.

No matter how brilliant a lawyer was, formulating a reasonable settlement offer always shook a person's confidence. This was because it required you to pick apart your own case and zero out any questionable claims. After you laid yourself bare before them, they'd grab a magnifying glass and a scalpel and start poking around until there was nothing left but bone. Then, they'd call your first offer ridiculous and suggest a figure about half as much.

It was because this process inflicted heavy psychological

damage that Kate used it on other but rebuffed those who asked it of her. Except when she couldn't. Like now.

The two-faced lawyer on the other side had copied Susan on his email requesting a reasonable settlement offer. As a boss who loved money but didn't personally work on cases, Susan responded immediately with a curt "offer to follow." This put Kate in the position of having to divine a number that wasn't too big or too small, and that looked good to a boss from thirty thousand feet. It was like tap-dancing through a mind field.

She glanced away from the computer and rubbed her throat. It felt like it was on fire. The letter was giving her indigestion. Or maybe that was the vegan chili she had eaten for lunch from the sketchy food truck on the street.

There was a knock at her door. She looked over as Riley poked his head inside her office.

"If it's a bad time, I can come back."

"No, it's fine. What do you need?"

He sat down across from her, holding a yellow legal pad in his left hand.

"Ruth Jacobs called this morning. She's coming in tomorrow at ten."

Kate flashed him an annoyed look. "I know. Gretchen copied me on the email, too."

"Right. So, you saw the attachment, then?"

"I scanned it. Can we do this tomorrow? I need to finish this thing."

Riley flipped open the legal pad and pulled out a loose sheet of paper from the back. He handed it to her. "This was the last page of the pdf."

It was a print-out of the Notice of Case Assignment for Ruth Jacobs's case, paper confirmation of what she explained to him that night in the car. When a new case is filed with the court, a clerk assigns a judge to handle it. The notice tells you the lucky judge's name.

Kate gagged when she read it.

"Walter Isaacs? Good Lord! I thought that pompous windbag retired." Riley shook his head. She handed the paper back to him. "Have I told you the story about him? The guy literally hates my guts. Two years ago, I had him on a case. He kept asking me to repeat myself. After about the thousandth time, I lost it. I offered to buy him hearing aids. He wasn't amused."

"I wouldn't think so."

"Yeah, well, guess what he wears now?"

Riley waited for her enthusiasm to die before continuing.

"Today's day ten, Kate," Riley said.

"Crap."

The rules of family court procedure gave litigants the absolute right to strike one judge on a case within the first ten days of assignment. After that, a person needed to show bias to get a new judge.

"Then Ruth needs to hire us today so we can strike him by COB."

"I've been calling her," Riley said. "The number we got goes straight to voicemail. I can't even leave a message because her mailbox is full."

Kate squeezed her eyes shut and pinched the bridge of her nose. "I assume that's our only number?"

"Correct," Riley said. "Maybe this isn't a bad thing. You know, if Isaacs really is that terrible, Ms. Wilson must know it. She'd understand if we dropped the case."

It was a hopeful thought, but not at all how Susan would react. As a woman who had kicked, scratched, and clawed her way to the top, Susan wasn't keen on excuses, quitting, or failure.

Kate opened her eyes. "Draft a Removal Notice for me to sign."

"What? You can't do that. She hasn't hired us yet."

"Thanks for the advice, professor."

"Kate, you'll get in trouble."

She shook her head. "Give me one reason anyone would say Isaacs is a good draw for her."

"It doesn't matter."

"Sure, it does. Our job is to protect people. Help the Ruths of the world get a fair shake. Hell, she'd strike the man herself, if she were smart enough to do it."

Riley shook his head. "Don't act like you're doing this for her."

"I am doing it for her."

"And for you."

"And for us, yes. Why can't both be true?"

"You're going to get in trouble with the Bar Association."

"Only if they find out," Kate said. "Which they won't. Tomorrow, when she comes in, we'll backdate the retainer agreement one day. In a week, no one will remember when she signed what."

"What if she blows off the meeting? Never hires us?"

Kate smiled. The guy was so green it was hard to even talk cases with him.

"Then we quit," Kate said. "Attorneys come and go all the time. The people at the courthouse will assume she couldn't raise the money for the retainer. It's simple."

"I don't know, Kate."

"You don't have to know, Riley. That's why I'm the boss. Now get drafting, okay?"

Riley left her office without saying another word. An hour later, he sent her an empty email with the notice attached.

33

The Michael Patel disaster proved two things to Kate. The first was that Asha was unqualified, untrained, and generally ill-equipped to handle important work. Her career trajectory seemed destined for inward-facing, clerical roles. Kate told Asha these things during a short exit interview she conducted the day after Jessica forked over the woman's email address.

To her credit, Asha accepted the constructive criticism with a smile. In an upbeat tone, she told Kate there were "many, many ways a VA could earn money in this world." Kate nodded, hoping, but doubting, the woman might someday make something of herself.

The second thing Kate learned was that Jessica was a terrible leader. "I'm worried about you," she said the following Saturday when they met for coffee at Cafe Noir. "If Susan ever saw this, we'd have issues."

Jessica scoffed. "I agree with you, sis. Let's hope she never finds out you wasted so much time creating an AAR for a personal matter."

AAR stood for After Action Review. Susan was a big fan of

them. She had learned about the concept from a podcast hosted by a retired Navy Seal. Kate snatched the paper back from Jessica's hand.

"Don't be such a baby," Kate said.

Jessica stood up and stormed out of the coffee shop.

That was four days ago, and they hadn't spoken since.

Typically, four days without talking to her sister would have bothered Kate. But not now. Now, she was too busy fixing Asha's mess to care.

The woman's organizational system for tracking applicants was the electronic equivalent of a set of Russian nesting dolls, folders within folders within folders. It was going to take her forever to sort it out.

She was about to give up when she saw that a new person had applied. It was well past the deadline Asha set, but Kate figured scanning the resume couldn't hurt. And boy, she was glad that she did.

The man was perfect.

And tonight she was going to meet him.

"I know, I know," Barbara said, coming out of the kitchen carrying a large stainless steel bowl filled with popcorn. "I'm staying in my room until after your meeting ends."

Kate looked up from where she sat the dining room table.

"I didn't say anything."

"Not in the last five minutes."

Okay, maybe she had gone a little bit overboard emphasizing the need for privacy, but this video conference could literally change her life. If things went well, she'd have a father for her child.

She glanced back at her laptop. Three blinking dots filled the screen, along with the phrase, "Waiting for host to start meeting." She checked the clock at the bottom of the screen. Still fifteen minutes until she'd get to see the man's face.

The doorbell rang. She looked over to see her mother welcome Jessica inside.

"What are you doing here?" Kate said gruffly.

"What do you mean?" Jessica was acting as if Kate's question didn't make sense. "Can't a daughter visit her aging mother? No one knows how much time Mom has left."

Barbara's eyes narrowed. "Don't talk about me dying."

Kate said, "You expect me to believe it's just a coincidence that you show up at my condo a few minutes before my video conference?"

Jessica shrugged. "How would I know about any video conference? You fired me, remember?"

Barbara sighed. "Girls, stop it. This silliness has gone on long enough. Apologize to each other. Then shake hands."

Kate glared at Jessica a moment longer, then reached out and took her hand. Since they were little, their mother had always insisted they end arguments with a handshake. It was like living in a 1950s sitcom.

"Sorry," Kate muttered.

"Yeah, me too," Jessica said. "Maybe I could have been more diligent with Asha."

Kate waved her off. "No worries. I've got us back on track. After tonight, I'll have my donor locked-up, and I'll be able to focus on your search."

Jessica winced. "Great. I can't wait."

"You underestimated me, sis."

Jessica hummed.

"Is that the new Surface Pro?"

Kate nodded. "Susan insists we have the very best technology. Can you believe this thing has all the firm's client data on it and yet it still takes up only a tiny fraction of the memory?"

"Wow," Jessica said.

"Tell us about this guy, Katie," Barbara said. "Who is he?"

"Well, his name is Leonard Slaterberry. He works for an NGO in Africa."

Jessica raised an eyebrow. "Leonard Slaterberry? Is that a joke? It's like the fakest sounding name I've ever heard."

"Nice," Kate said tersely. "He's not originally from Africa. He's there because he's trying to pay forward all the advantages he's gotten in life. In fact, he doesn't even want any money from me."

Jessica made a gagging sound. "I hate it when people pay it forward. Every time it happens to me, I get screwed. Take this morning. I'm in line at Cafe Noir. This Santa Claus in front of me buys my coffee, then tells me to 'pay it forward' to the next person. Guess who's behind me? Three teenage girls who want extra large whipped cream lattes. His kindness cost me thirty-five bucks."

"It's nothing like that," Kate said.

Jessica pointed at the computer screen.

"Your meeting is starting."

Kate slid the cursor over the green join meeting icon and clicked. The laptop beeped at her, but the meeting didn't start.

"Why isn't this working?" Kate said.

"Here, let me do it," Jessica said.

"No."

Kate reclicked the icon. Again, nothing happened. A second later, the webpage reloaded. It said the meeting had ended.

Her phone vibrated in her pocket. She pulled it out and saw a text message from a number she didn't recognize. She read it and breathed a sigh of relief.

"It's Leonard. Apparently, the internet's spotty where he is. He's going to try again in a few minutes. He said he emailed me a list of references to review."

Kate opened her email, clicked on the message, then double-clicked on a pdf attachment.

Suddenly, her screen went black.

She tapped the spacebar twice, but the computer didn't respond.

A moment later, a series of color bars filled the screen. The kind they used in the 1960s when a TV channel went off the air for the evening. An annoying tone blared out of the speakers.

Ten seconds later, the test pattern was replaced by a skull and crossbones with the following message:

This computer now belongs to the Free Nigerian People's Army. You have forty-eight hours to transfer one hundred thousand dollars in bitcoin to the address below. If you do not, we will publish all your files online.

Kate gasped. "Oh. My. God. What just happened?"

34

"I'll tell you what happened, Einstein," Jessica said. "You downloaded ransomware."

Kate felt her chest tighten. Darkness closed in at the edge of her vision.

"No, I—"

"Yes, you did," Jessica said in a huff. "You violated one of the basic rules of computer security. Don't open a file from someone you don't know."

"I, I...."

While Kate struggled to find words, her mother came over and put a hand on her shoulder.

"Breathe, Katie. It's fine."

Jessica scoffed. "No, Katie. It's not fine." Her sister seemed to grow angrier by the second. "Do you realize what you've done? You screwed me!"

"Jessica, please," Barbara said. "Kate feels bad enough already."

"Oh, I'm sorry," Jessica said sarcastically. "We don't want Kate to feel bad. I'm sure Susan Wilson will still be open to hiring me after the dust settles. Oh, wait. No, she won't, because Kate bankrupted her firm."

Barbara shot Jessica a hard look.

"Don't tell me to settle down, Mom," Jessica said, continuing to spiral. "Outrage is a normal reaction when someone destroys your life!"

"Enough," Barbara yelled.

Kate reached up, touched her mother's hand. "No, Jess is right. I should have never have used my work computer. I wasn't thinking."

She felt her mother's hand flinch. Apparently, she hadn't grasped the seriousness of what had happened until that moment.

"I'm sure your boss has a plan in place, honey."

Kate was sure she did too. The first part would involve firing Kate and holding her up for public ridicule. Her name would now be discussed at attorney ethics seminars for decades.

"I'll resign tomorrow," Kate said. "Not that it will fix anything."

"You can't quit," Barbara said. "You've worked too hard."

"I don't have a choice. As soon as someone finds out, they'll report me to the Bar. I'll be lucky if I only get suspended."

While Kate and Barbara were talking, Jessica walked across the room and appeared lost in thought. When the conversation lulled, she looked at Kate.

"Mom's right. You can't quit."

"What? Why not?"

"Because I'm not letting you take me down this way," Jessica said. "I saw a documentary on ransomware once. A guy in it had a similar thing happen to him. But instead of crying about it, he fought back."

"How?"

"I don't remember exactly, but I think he hired a hacker to hack the criminal. Steal back all his data"

Kate's eyes lit up. "Is that possible?"

"I think so, yes."

"Come on, Katie," Barbara said. "Don't make it worse. You need to report it. You know the cover up is always worse than the crime."

Jessica raised a finger. "Maybe not here. In the documentary, they said that close to fifty percent of all data breaches go undetected. And even when they are discovered, it usually takes three to six months to find them. You'd definitely be safe if you tried to hack back for a week or two."

"It's wrong," Barbara said.

Kate knew her mother was right. Reporting the incident was what she should do. It was also what her duty as a lawyer required. By covering it up, she was exposing her clients to further potential harm.

But keeping it secret was also the only way she might keep her job and her reputation.

"How would we find such a hacker?" Kate asked.

"I'll call Willa," Jessica said. "She knows everyone."

Jessica went out onto the balcony and closed the door behind her.

"I know you don't approve, Mother," Kate said. "I don't like it much either. But you heard Jessica. It's our only shot to make things right for the clients."

"And for you," Barbara said.

35

On the morning of Ruth's appointment, Kate was back at her desk, playing chess against the computer because she couldn't concentrate on work.

At three minutes before ten, there was a knock at the door. Riley poked his head inside.

"She's here."

Kate studied his face, trying to determine if he was still mad at her. He looked okay, but she thought she detected a hint of irritation in his voice. It seemed flatter, more robotic than usual.

She sighed to herself, then got upset for doing so. Why did she care if Riley was angry at her? She was the boss. He was the worker. Susan didn't care if her associates were mad at her. Plus, no one could seriously argue striking Judge Isaacs was the wrong thing to do now that Ruth had shown up. Still, his disapproval weighed on her.

She motioned him inside and waited until he was across the desk to speak.

"Are we good?" she asked.

"Of course."

She knew he was lying.

"Listen, Riley. You don't have to like all my decisions, but you do need to respect them. So either get onboard or start looking for a new job, okay? Because I don't want you in that conference room if your head is not in the game."

He hesitated, appearing to think it over for a moment. Kate thought there was a chance he might leave. The only thing more embarrassing than hiring the first man at the firm would be having him quit on her. Still, she needed to keep him in line, office gossip being what it was.

"I'm on board," Riley said. "I made my case. You overruled me. It's done."

Kate breathed a sigh of relief.

"For the record, I didn't overrule you. I made a judgment call. Which proved right."

He looked down at a legal pad in his hand, not buying her explanation.

"We got a new judge assignment," Riley said. "A guy named Terrance W. Eide. Ever heard of him? A few of the paralegals said he's new. The firm doesn't have a file on him yet."

"Did you say Terry Eide?"

Kate could hardly stop herself from smiling. If Riley hadn't been there, she would have leaped into the air and done a little celebratory dance. Of all the judges on Earth, there was no one she'd rather have than Terry Eide. But until that moment, the possibility had never crossed her mind.

It didn't seem possible because as the newest member of the Travis County bench, Terry was supposed to be in traffic court for two years, twiddling his thumbs, learning to zip and unzip his robe, and generally becoming more honorable, which was something he needed.

She had first met Terry at The Austin Chess Club a year earlier. He had come as the guest of a bobble-headed insurance agent, who showed up sometimes to pass out business cards. Whenever Kate or Jessica heard the bobblehead's salesman-like voice, they ran the other way because neither he nor his guests were serious players.

All they wanted to do was talk. Or sell you something. Or explain how much money you could save by bundling policies. The worst of the bobblehead's guests was a funeral director who tried to convince everyone to buy adjoining burial plots.

"It's not fair," Jessica said, looking up at a tournament bracket drawn on a piece of butcher block paper taped to a wall by the chess club's front entrance.

Kate frowned. "Usually, people don't smile when they're trying to be sympathetic."

"Maybe this Terry Eide is a good player."

"Then, maybe you want to switch with me."

"I wish I could," Jessica said, "but you know it's against the rules. Good luck."

When Kate found Terry Eide sitting behind a chessboard at a table near the back of the room, he was not what she expected. About forty, he had close-cropped brown hair, a strong jaw, and an athletic build. He was dressed in dark blue jeans and a white button-down shirt open at the collar, with his sleeves rolled up to his forearms.

He took to her immediately, which she didn't mind because he was good-looking and because he made her laugh, neither of which happened very often at the Club.

Later that night, she recounted the story for her sister over a glass of red wine at her condo.

"Please tell me you're joking," Jessica said.

Kate smiled, shook her head. "No, I beat him with a pawn. You'd have been proud."

"Not if it really took you eight moves. I could have beaten him in four. Bobble-head's guests are always pathetic."

Kate rolled her eyes. "Not this one."

"Do you think I win all the tournaments by luck? I know how to beat guys like him."

"I think you won tonight because you had easy draws."

Jessica forced a laughed. "Funny. So, when are you and Mr. Pawn going out on a date?"

Kate shrugged. "I don't know. I thought we connected, but he just disappeared after reporting our score to Ted."

"Figures. Most guys can't handle being beaten by a woman."

But Terry Eide was not most guys. Two weeks later, he was back at the Club for another Friday night mixer. This time, he was the guest of an awkward patent lawyer. They smiled when they saw each other across the room but did not speak.

He came back again the following week and the week after that and the week after that. She would have called him a stalker if he hadn't made her heart flutter. He popped up in empty chairs beside her and got matched to her during every open chess session.

Once, she told him she preferred men who wore bow ties. The next time she saw him, he wore a blue one. Then a gray one. Then a polka dot one that made her laugh because he looked so silly. She was going to tell him she was joking, but then she didn't see him again.

Now she understood why. Terry Eide had fallen in with the judicial crowd and got himself appointed to the bench.

Riley's voice pulled her back to the present. "So you have heard of him?"

"I think maybe we played chess once at the Club."

Riley nodded, accepting the explanation.

"So, here's a random question," he said as they headed down the hall towards the lobby. "When we spoke to Ruth's mother, did you get the sense she was from New England?"

"No. Why?"

"Me neither. But, when she checked in at the front desk, the receptionist she had this over-the-top Boston accent. Like ridiculously bad. You know, 'pahk the cah in Hahvud Yahd' stuff."

Kate felt her stomach tighten.

"Weird," she said.

36

Kate pulled open a locked door and stepped into the public lobby at Susan Wilson Law. She stopped beside the reception desk and scanned the two rectangular seating areas. There was one on each side of a marble aisle that bisected the room and ran all the way back to the elevators.

Susan had intended the space to impress and intimidate. And even after a few weeks at the firm, the lobby still gave Kate goosebumps every time she saw it, which wasn't very often because Susan required employees to use a back door.

Kate's eyes focused on the room's only visitor. A twenty-something Southern belle sitting with her knees close together in an armchair on the right side. The woman was dressed in a faded yellow sundress that was probably fashionable before she had washed it thirty times. At first glance, Kate thought the woman was pretty. Her wavy blond hair, busty chest, and tiny waist were Hollywood style. But as she got closer, she saw that the woman's face was hard and weathered. It reminded her of someone she had seen once at a truck stop. A woman who had aged twenty years because of coffee and cigarettes.

Kate stopped a few feet short.

"Ruth?"

The woman stood up, flashed her a warm smile.

"Yes."

"I'm Kate Becker. This is my associate, Riley Anderson."

"Thank you so much for seeing me. I had almost given up hope. Damion's lawyer, Tina, Tina—"

"Black. Tina Black," Kate said.

"Yes. Tina Black. She's evil."

Kate nodded. "She can be. Follow me. Let's talk someplace more private."

Kate spun on the balls of her feet and started towards the reception desk, intending to lead Ruth back down the same interior hallway from which she had come, when she saw The Hatchet blocking her path.

"Ruth Jacobs?" The Hatchet said, coming over to them. "Is this *the* Ruth Jacobs? Why didn't you tell me she was coming?"

Kate kept her face neutral. "I didn't realize you wanted to meet her."

"Why wouldn't I want to meet her? You know I meet all the firm's special clients." The Hatchet extended a gloved hand towards Ruth. "Patricia Vulcan. I'm Katie's boss."

Kate clenched her jaw. In no sense was The Hatchet her boss. In fact, Bar Association rules specifically forbid non-lawyers from supervising attorneys. Susan was the only person she reported to.

"Nice to meet you, Ms. Vulcan," Ruth said.

"Please, call me Patty."

"Okay, Patty."

Kate stepped forward, hoping to break up the conversation before it took a turn for the worse.

"If it's all right with you Patty, we need to get started," Kate said. "We have a lot of ground to cover."

The Hatchet flashed her a hard look but quickly recovered her phony demeanor.

"Of course, of course," she said. "I wouldn't dream of interrupting." The Hatchet looked at Ruth. "Can I just say you're an inspiration to women everywhere. All across America, women are rooting for you."

Ruth perked up. "They are?"

"Yes," The Hatchet purred. "Your poise. Your strength. It's remarkable. I'd be a puddle of tears if a patriarchal system stole my daughter."

Ruth smiled. "I am pretty remarkable, aren't I?"

"Yes," The Hatchet said, nodding. "I probably shouldn't tell you this, but Kate says you're going to be famous when this is over."

Ruth glanced at Kate. "You think so? You really think I'm going to be famous?"

Kate shifted uncomfortably. "I'm not sure about famous."

"Don't be modest," The Hatchet said. "Tell her what you told everyone at the quarterly meeting. How you think her case is going to get national media coverage."

Kate cleared her throat. "Um, well, we have to win in court first."

The Hatchet smiled. "Such classic, Kate. Always trying to lower expectations. Don't worry, Ms. Jacobs. Kate assured me your case is a slam dunk. In fact, she told me she'd quit if you didn't win."

"I didn't say that."

The Hatchet reached into the breast pocket of her trench coat and pulled out a business card. She pressed it into Ruth's hand as if it were a valuable coin.

"Take this," The Hatchet said. "My personal cell number is on the back. If you ever need anything, and I mean anything at all, call me first. All right? There's nothing more important to this firm than our VIP clients."

When Ruth heard the words VIP, her shoulders shot back. She suddenly seemed an inch taller, as if The Hatchet's false praise had jolted her alive.

The Hatchet glanced at Kate. "May I have a word in private, Katie?"

Kate asked Riley to take Ruth to the conference room by her office, then followed The Hatchet to the elevator bank.

"How long must this charade persist?" The Hatchet asked. "Even your boy toy knows she's nuts. I think she got off easy only losing the baby. If it were up to me, I'd have locked her in the loony bin."

Kate held her face steady. "I don't know what you're talking about."

The Hatchet snorted. "Please. You look silly. All I'm trying to do is help. If you get down on your knees, right now, and beg for my forgiveness, I'll get you a severance. Maybe even a reference. I'm not an unreasonable person. I'm really not."

"Thanks, but I'm good."

"Being tough isn't about never quitting, Katie. It's about having the courage to quit when you have a bad hand."

"Obviously, we see the case differently."

The Hatchet shook her head. "No, we disagree on whether you'll admit you're wrong. I know you will, eventually."

"Time will tell."

The Hatchet shrugged. "I suppose. But don't say I didn't try to help you."

The elevator dinged, and the doors slid open. The Hatchet stepped inside, pressed a button, then turned to face Kate.

"Do what you want, Ms. Becker. But heed this warning. If you or that whack job client of yours causes any embarrassment to this firm, I will make it my life's work to ensure you never have another job in Texas. Do we understand each other?"

Kate swallowed hard but continued to stand tall. When the elevator doors closed, she brought her hands to her face and cried.

37

When The Hatchet was gone, Kate dashed into a bathroom near the elevator and ran the water in the sink until all the red was out of her eyes. She dried her face with a paper towel monogrammed with Susan's initials, then practiced her fake smile in the mirror, curling her lips more, then less, trying to replicate the easy-going look clients expected from a top-flight lawyer.

She must have gotten it right because neither Ruth nor Riley commented on her puffy eyes when she sat down at the conference room table. Kate listened as Ruth rambled on for the next forty minutes, telling an unbelievable tale of woe.

"It feels like you don't believe me," Ruth said, stopping to take a breath after a fifteen-minute monologue.

It feels that way because we don't, Kate thought.

Ruth's basic story was that none of this would have happened if her mother hadn't joined a cult-like church in west Austin. As Ruth told it, her mother had clicked on a social media ad for a mega-church, streamed twenty minutes of sermon highlights, then decided her only shot at salvation was to move to Texas to "join the flock."

Ruth insisted she only ended things with her boyfriend, Damion, because she caught him having sex with her mother.

Kate choked on her coffee when she heard it. It took a moment for her to compose herself.

"Of course, we believe you," Kate said, still trying to clear the tickle in her throat. "It's just— It's a lot to take in all at once. Tell me again why you think Damion's lying about your alcoholism."

Ruth sighed. The woman had already told it twice, but Kate hoped a third time might help her believe it.

"Because it's the only way he can get full custody."

"Right," Kate said. "And he wants that because?"

Ruth looked annoyed. "Shouldn't you know? You're the lawyer."

"Of course I know," Kate said. "I just need you to say it again. It's part of my process."

Ruth rolled her eyes. "If Damion gets full custody, he gets to make all the decisions. Including having it baptized in that cult church."

"It?" Riley said. "Don't you mean her. You're baby isn't a thing, right?"

"Is he supposed to talk?" Ruth asked.

Riley picked up a stack of court papers Ruth had set on the table and flipped to the pictures at the back.

"How do you explain these photos of empty liquor bottles?" Riley asked. "The ones he claims you hid in the ceiling. Under the bed. All over the trailer."

"I already told you. He planted them," Ruth said.

Kate leaned forward. "Why would he do that, Ruth?"

"Why?" Ruth's voice was full of disbelief. "Is this your twos first case? He made it up because I told him he's never seeing the baby again after I caught him with Mother."

Kate sighed. "Ruth, we're trying to help you. But unless you have evidence—"

"I saw it with my own eyes. What other evidence do I need?"

"He'll deny it," Kate said. "Without proof it's actually happening, if you suggest it, you'll come off looking crazy. It will only reinforce his theory that you're a drunk."

"But it's true."

"Winning in court isn't about truth," Kate said. "It's about telling a story that fits a judge's belief system. Damion filed pictures of the empty bottles because another judge already labeled you a drunk. If we want to flip the narrative, we need to tell a story that will make sense to Judge Eide. A story that uses all the pieces of the puzzle and explains why Damion lied."

Ruth stared at her blankly.

Kate continued, "For example, what if Damion lied about your drinking because he's an abuser. Abusers try to control women. They use kids as weapons. It would make sense that an abuser might lie about your drinking, right?"

"I guess."

Kate nodded. "Abuse is actually a perfect explanation. It explains everything. Plus, it'd give the judge cover for not buying the chemical dependency claims. Do you follow?"

"So, you're saying it'd be good if he abused me?" Ruth asked.

"It'd be better than good. It'd be great. In fact, I'd say your odds of winning would improve to like ninety percent."

"But," Riley said, jumping in, "you can't say it, if it's not true."

Kate flashed him an annoyed look. "I said 'for example'."

"Oh, I heard you," Riley said. "But I'm not sure Ruth did."

"I heard her just fine."

"So," Kate said, eager to move on, "if we find the right facts, we can create a believable story. That's why I'm pressing you so hard. You never know what could be important."

Ruth looked down at the table, bit her bottom lip.

"You can be honest with us, Ruth," Kate said. "We never judge people."

Ruth glanced up at Kate. "It's like you said, Ms. Becker. Damion's been abusing me. He's been abusing me real bad."

38

When Kate got back to her office after walking Ruth to the elevator, she found Riley standing near the windows, staring out at the Austin skyline. His arms were crossed, and his tie was loosened. It was only a few minutes before noon, but he looked like it was quitting time.

"She's a fuc—"

"Stop!" Kate said. "Take a breath."

"The woman's crazy."

Kate started for her chair but stopped when she realized how close it was to him.

"You don't know for sure," Kate said.

"Yes, I do."

"We're lawyers, Riley. Not psychiatrists."

He scoffed at her. "Come on, Kate. If you really can't see it, I'm going to start worrying about you."

"Maybe the woman is a little off. Who isn't sometimes? We don't get to choose our clients, Riley."

"Are you serious? Because you literally just chose her."

Kate ignored the jab, partly because it was true and partly

because she didn't enjoy defending Ruth's sanity. She had only done what was necessary to save them both.

Riley went over to the desk and plopped down in her chair. She pressed her lips together. She hadn't told him he could sit there. In fact, she hadn't invited him back to her office at all.

"We can't help her lie, Kate."

"For the last time, you don't know she's lying."

"You spoon-fed her the abuse idea. Basically told her what to say."

Kate felt her blood pressure rise. "No. I merely gave an example of a compelling narrative."

"And told her it'd be great if she were abused. That she'd win her case."

Kate cringed. It sounded bad when he said it that way.

"I was very clear when I walked her to the elevator. Lying isn't an option. I told her that if Tina Black catches her in a lie, she'll have zero chance of winning."

"So?"

"So what?"

"Did she agree to drop the abuse nonsense?"

Kate hesitated. "She said she'd think about it."

"Think about it? What's there to think about?"

Kate shook her head. "There's always something to think about, Riley. Whatever she decides, it's our job to support her."

"It isn't."

"Yes, it is." Kate took a deep breath. She wasn't going to let a first year associate tell her how to handle a case. "We've done our duty. We advised her not to lie. We warned her about potential consequences. Now, unless you have clear proof she's lying, we follow her lead. As the client, she sets the direction."

Riley sighed but didn't respond, conceding that she was right. It wasn't a close call. Lawyers weren't allowed to override client wishes.

He got up and went back to the windows. Kate quickly moved behind the desk, reclaiming her place of authority.

"So what do we do now?" Riley asked.

"We wait," Kate said. "Ruth promised to decide by morning. When she does, we need to start to drafting her affidavit. I want to file it with the court ASAP. We need to give Judge Eide plenty of time to read it before the hearing."

39

Matt Simpson wandered across the busy newsroom, weaving past cubicles occupied by real journalists. It was late on Thursday night. Fifteen minutes before press time. The bullpen work area was buzzing with energy. The scrappy reporters of The Austin Free Press banged away at their keyboards, making the stale air sound like it was full of typewriters.

At least, that's how Matt imagined a room full of typewriters would have sounded.

In truth, he knew very little about the past. At twenty-two and fresh out of Harvard, his eyes were focused straight ahead. This was his one shot to prove his grandfather wrong. He didn't intend to waste it on some lame history tour.

He stopped outside Tim Bowers's cubicle, poked his head inside.

"Busy night, huh?"

The man's fingers raced across the keyboard. "Leave me alone, kid. I'm almost done."

Bowers was slouched in a cheap office chair, staring at a computer screen like it had mystical, mesmerizing powers. Matt had watched him pull marathon sessions to finish a story before.

Once, the man had sat at his desk for fourteen straight hours, alternating between chugging diet soda and peeing back into the same bottle from which it came, to meet a deadline. He did it because a group of reporters abandoned a story after the paper laid them off.

Bowers slammed the enter key. "Finished. Ten minutes to spare." He swiveled the chair towards Matt.

"You look like hell," Matt said.

Bowers nodded. "I keep telling you, kid, I'm the ghost of Christmas future. But still you come back."

"Was that the follow-up on the pharmaceutical story?"

"Yeah," Bowers said. "And before you go spouting off, let me say I don't think the people deserved to lose their life savings. But who believes a cheerleader develops a cure for cancer in her garage? I mean, please. Use a little common-sense."

"They were desperate for hope."

"No, they were stupid. And afraid. You can't skirt fate, kid. It comes for us all. And it's always bad."

"Thanks for the life lesson, Bowers."

Normally, Matt wouldn't have befriended a person like Bowers. But Bowers was the closest thing there was to a celebrity in Austin journalism. He had won the Pulitzer Prize twice and been named Texas Journalist of the Year four of the last five years. Bowers called the awards a noose around his neck. Every time he won one, the judge in his divorce case increased his ex-wife's alimony by another five hundred a month.

The awards might have cost him a little money, but they were also the only reason he still had a job. Bowers's short temper, aversion to rules, and knack for offending people made him hard to employ. He was the only person at the paper with the courage to speak to Matt.

"So," Matt crossed his arms and leaned against the side of Bower's cubicle. "I was hoping you might give me a lead. Something so good they'd have to publish it."

"Really?" Bowers reached forward and switched off his desk lamp. "Only one? Why not two? How about ten?"

"Come on. You've got like twenty right there." Matt pointed towards Bowers's computer monitor. There were yellow sticky notes taped around the edges with names and telephone numbers written on them.

Bowers rose, grabbed his leather trucker jacket off the back of his chair, and slung it over his shoulder.

"Maybe they don't teach this part in school, but finding a story is the whole game, kid. Even my ex could do this job, if you gave her a good lead."

Matt sighed.

Bowers slid past him and began walking towards the elevators. Matt jogged to catch up to him.

"You know I'm almost out of time," Matt said.

"Seriously? Because I had given up hope you were ever leaving."

At the elevator bank, Bowers pressed the down call button. The doors slid open. He stepped inside, and Matt followed.

"If you won't do it for me," Matt said, "then do it to screw with Arthur."

Arthur was the paper's publisher. He was the picture of a corporate yes-man. Matt's grandfather had installed him as a puppet ten years earlier when he needed to fire an editorial board who had taken to writing negative commentary about the parent company. Because Arthur had no experience or interest in journalism, Bowers enjoyed making the man's life difficult.

Bowers hummed. "Tempting, but I'll pass."

"Pass? You never pass on screwing with Arthur."

"I do when you're involved."

"Is this because of Diane?" Matt asked.

Bowers scoffed. "Yeah, it's because of Diane."

"I said I was sorry."

"Sorry? What am I supposed to do with sorry? Tell the plaintiff's lawyer, 'Sorry, you can't sue us for defamation because Matt Simpson apologized for not running down the story.'"

"They didn't sue us, Bowers. They only threatened."

Bowers looked down at the floor, shook his head in disgust.

The elevator jerked to a stop at the underground parking garage one floor below street level. Like everything else in the old building, the elevator worked, sort of. It took a moment to catch its breath before the doors opened.

Bowers stepped out onto the concrete floor. "There's a reason people start in obituaries, kid. It takes years to get a feel for the job." He paused. "I'm sorry your grandfather is dicking you around and not giving you a real shot to keep this job, but me giving you lead won't help things. In fact, it'll only make things worse. Trust me."

Matt swallowed hard.

There was no point in pushing it further. Bowers wasn't a man who caved under pressure.

"Right," Matt said.

"Now, if you'll excuse me," Bowers said. "I have to go throw up. All this mentoring has made me queasy."

40

Matt knew Bowers was probably right. Not only about him being inexperienced but also about a lead making things worse. It had almost happened with the Diane story. Bowers had only asked him to do a little due diligence, and he screwed it up. Handling a full investigation by himself would be much, much harder.

Still, he wasn't ready to give up. Not yet.

Later, when he looked back on that moment, he would tell people he should have quit right then. If he had returned to New York before the year was up, he could have spun it. People in his world understood a person not wanting to work for less than high-six figures. In fact, the toughest question he'd likely face was why it took him so long to wise up.

His mother probably would have thrown him a party. An elegant affair with all the right society people. She would have laughed, sipped her third martini, and told everyone how great it was to have her Mattie back.

Her smile would have been more relief than happiness.

Ever since she brokered the one-year peace deal with his grandfather that landed him the job at the paper, she had been pressing him to quit.

"Congratulations, Mattie," she said on the Friday afternoon after his first week. She called at precisely five o'clock eastern, not realizing Austin was an hour behind. "I hope you're proud of yourself. You've broken your grandfather's heart."

The statement was absurd. William P. Simpson's heart was harder than a diamond. At seventy-two, the man ran marathons, skied the Alps, and exercised by throwing axes. This was when he wasn't working seventy hours per week running Simpson Holdings, the nation's largest privately held company.

"I'm sure grandpa will manage," Matt said.

"Not this time." He could hear his mother slurping a martini in the background. "He's depressed."

"Grandpa doesn't get depressed, Mom. He's too stubborn."

"Make jokes, Mattie. But this is real. Armando said he hasn't worked in a week. All he's done is sit in his study reading."

Not working was unusual, Matt thought. Although, it didn't mean the man was depressed.

"Grandpa reads all the time, Mother."

"Novels, Mattie! He's reading novels!"

"All right. So, maybe it's a little weird."

His mother scoffed. "No, it's not a little weird. It's a catastrophe."

Matt frowned. "I don't think Grandpa taking a week of vacation to read a novel is a catastrophe."

"Are you paying attention? If your grandfather isn't working, no one's running the company. And if no one's running the company, then no one has any money!"

Ah. It clicked. He finally understood. His grandfather was playing dirty pool. While the old man had publicly agreed to give Matt a year to prove himself as a reporter, privately he was scheming against him. By acting depressed and refusing to work, his grandfather was stirring the family into hysterics, which he unleashed on Matt.

"I'm not sure what you want me to do, Mom."

"I want you to grow up, Mattie. Stop all this foolishness. Come home and work for your grandfather."

"We have a deal."

"Oh, sweet Jesus! Enough with the deal already. Do you know how lucky you are? Your cousins would kill to be your grandfather's protege."

"Really? Then why don't any of them work at the company?"

"Stop fighting your destiny, Mattie. One way or another, you're becoming CEO. I'm texting Armando right now. He's sending the jet."

Matt forced a laugh. "Good luck with that."

His mother scoffed. "When did you become so obstinate?"

"Obstinate? I'm not sure that's the word you want. Generally, it's considered a good thing when a child wants to earn their own money."

"Don't take that tone with me. Everyone has a job, Mattie. We all pull our weight in this family."

That was a whopper of a lie. Matt's grandfather was the only living Simpson who ever worked for a living. Possibly Matt could squeeze in that category too, if you counted his time at paper. Although, the paper was a subsidiary of Simpson Holdings.

"I need to go, Mom. Tell Grandpa to put away the books. I'm not coming home until the AP picks up one of my stories."

Or until a year passes and I fly home a failure, he thought.

The elevator doors opened to the tenth-floor newsroom, and he retraced his steps back to Bowers's cubicle. After glancing around to make sure no one was watching, he slipped inside and sat down in the chair. The padding was worn thin, and the metal shell felt hard beneath his bottom.

The computer on the desk in front of him was the dark. Around the edges of the monitor, there were post-it notes filled with Bowers's tough to read handwriting.

Matt knew from his time hanging around the cubicle that the post-it notes were Bowers's best leads. Because of the man's celebrity, he had become the default contact for half the whistle-blowers in Texas. Tips came in so often that Bowers usually didn't write them down. When he did, it meant something.

Any of the post-it notes would have been enough to launch Matt's career. The trouble was, Bowers spent twelve hours a day staring at the screen. He'd notice if one vanished. And Matt couldn't risk leaving a note in place once he started running down a story. Bowers was too unpredictable. He might wake up tomorrow and decide to rescreen the entire batch of tips. It had happened before.

Matt leaned back in Bowers's chair and sighed. His eyes drifted off towards the ceiling.

Why did everything have to be so hard? He only needed one lead. One. Uno. Ein. It wasn't like Bowers would miss it. The guy had more leads than he could investigate in five lifetimes.

The phone on Bowers's desk rang.

Matt flinched.

He leaned forward and checked the caller id.

Private number.

Bowers had told him once that most tips came in late at night when an actual person is unlikely to answer the phone. This had never made sense to Matt. Why go to the trouble of tipping a reporter if they're not even around to take the call? Still, at that moment, he hoped Bowers was right.

He lifted the handset. "Austin Free Press. Matt Simpson speaking."

The caller hesitated. "Is this Tim Bowers's phone?"

"Yes. I'm part of his team. Can I help you?"

"Ah..."

"Do you have a tip for a story, sir? Because if so, you'll want to talk to me. I do all the preliminary screening."

The man hummed. "I was told only talk to Bowers."

"Mr. Bowers is very busy, sir. He's won two Pulitzers. Did you think he'd answer his own phone?"

"I guess not."

The man's voice softened a little.

"Like I said, I handle all the tips. Is there something you want to report?"

"Okay, but not over the phone. Do you know Driscols? The bar on Seventh and El Dorado?"

"I can find it," Matt said.

"Good boy. Go to the bar. Ask for Lenny. He'll point you in my direction."

41

Driscoll's was a single-story flatiron brick building in a rundown industrial area west of downtown. Roughly the shape of a triangle with a smooshed tip, the building had no windows and a green front door lit by a pair of old-fashioned globe lights. The entrance was on the sidewalk, set back ten paces from where El Dorado intersected Seventh Street. A yellowed lightbox sign bolted to the side of the building proclaimed it to have been established in 1956.

The instant Matt stepped inside, he felt heads turn. The boisterous crowd, packed together like sardines in a can, began sizing him up. It was obvious he didn't belong. His wrinkled brown sport coat, white button-down shirt, and khakis stood out like an orange hunting vest amongst the dive bar's t-shirt and jeans crowd.

In one sense, the bar didn't differ from a thousand other working-class joints whose patrons had been left behind by progress. A classic, saloon-style bar with a mirror ran the length of the right side of the room. The center was high-topped tables with studded red vinyl barstools. On the left, tiny booths were under vintage tin metal signs for old beers that no longer existed. The air was hazy. The place smelled of popcorn.

But in another sense, it was nothing like the neighborhood bars Matt had staggered through while on pub crawls at Harvard. People wearing costume party masks dotted the crowd like blotches of red in a sea of yellow. Not the flimsy plastic masks held in place by rubber bands. But helmet masks. The kind worn by mascots at D-1 football games.

Matt squeezed his way to the edge of the bar, where there were no stools. He stopped beside a pair of middle-aged men with beer bellies and red noses. The men eyed him for a moment before deciding he wasn't worth the effort. Matt raised his hand, tried to get the bartender's attention.

After what felt like forever, a bartender wearing a white unicorn helmet with a pink horn came over to him.

"What will it be?" the bartender said.

"I'm meeting—"

"The eagle." He raised his arm and pointed across the room towards the back corner.

Matt leaned to the side and looked past the two men. Near the back of the room, close to the emergency exit sign and a pair of old pinball machines, there was a man wearing an eagle mask sitting alone in a booth.

"Thanks," Matt said.

As the bartender turned and walked away, Matt spoke to the man beside him. "These masks, they're not normal here, right?"

The man raised an eyebrow. "Nothing gets by you, does it, kid?"

Matt ignored the jab and weaved past the high-top tables on his way to the booth. As he walked, he tried to get a read on the man calling himself Lenny. But with a mask covering his face, all Matt knew for sure was that the guy liked his shirts starched and that he looked fit. Athletic, not muscular.

"Are you Lenny?"

The man invited Matt to sit, then held two fingers in the air until the bartender acknowledged his request for a refill.

When the man's hand was up, Matt noticed a black Rolex

Daytona on his wrist. It was a forty thousand dollar watch. Matt knew because his grandfather wore the same one.

"I assume Chivas is good for you," the Eagle said.

Matt shrugged. "It's fine."

The Eagle raised an eyebrow. "What? You don't like scotch?"

"Not really."

"I thought all reporters liked scotch."

Matt shook his head.

The Eagle hummed.

"What's with the masks?" Matt asked.

"I prefer to remain anonymous."

The unicorn bartender trudged over and clanked two glass tumblers down onto the table. He glared at the Eagle, then spun around and went back to the bar.

Matt said, "You can't be that anonymous. He obviously knows who you are."

"Oh, Hank? He's a good boy. He'd never talk. He's just upset because he didn't want to be a unicorn. But what was I supposed to do? He refused to be a banana or a bear or a cat or a goat. So unicorn it was."

Matt brought the glass to his lips and took a sip. He tried to imagine what Bowers would do in this situation. The one thing he knew for sure was that the masks wouldn't have bothered him. At least, not as much as it was bothering Matt. One of Bowers's Pulitzer prizes had come from anonymous source reporting. Matt asked him about it once. Bowers shrugged and said he still didn't know who the guy really was.

Matt tried not to wince at the scotch's strong, turpentiney taste.

"Good isn't it?" The Eagle asked.

Matt set the glass back on the table, nudged it forward with the back of his hand.

"Personally, I'm more of a beer guy."

"Try it again. It gets better with time."

"No, thanks," Matt said. "What information do you have for me?"

"Me? Don't you mean us? As in you and Bowers."

"Yeah, that's what I said." Matt's patience for this guy was running thin.

The man pulled a folded sheet of paper out of his shirt pocket and handed it across the table. Matt opened it. The paper was blank, except for a nine-digit number written in black ink.

"What is this?" Matt asked.

"Your tip."

"I gathered," Matt said.

"It's the number of a Travis County Family Court case. Go read it. You're welcome."

"Family court? As in divorce and stuff?"

"Yeah," The Eagle said, nodding.

Matt sighed. He should never have agreed to come to the bar without making the guy give him at least a thumb nail sketch of the lead first. If he had known the tip was about family court, he'd never have come.

"Let me guess," Matt said. "You know a guy who got screwed by the system. And you want me to write a story about how it's biased."

The Austin Free Press got twenty "leads" a month like that on its general tip line. If Matt had wanted to waste time chasing his tail, he didn't need to steal a lead from Bowers to do it.

"You got it," The Eagle said. "Except this case involves a pretty young lady. Not a short-tempered construction worker."

The Eagle apparently thought this distinction mattered because he looked as if Matt ought to be excited. He wasn't.

Matt tossed the paper back onto the table. "I wish you would have said it was a divorce. You could have avoided the trouble of all the masks. We don't do family court stories."

"But you haven't read the file?"

Matt slid out of the booth, stood up. "I don't need to read the file, Lenny. Or whatever your name is. I've seen it a hundred times. But I'll tell you what. Call me when you find a story about a couple that loved getting divorced. We never see those."

"Look at the file, kid."

There was a directness in the man's voice that sent chills down Matt's spine.

He grabbed the paper off the table, then turned and left.

42

The woman at Grannies R Us strongly suggested that Barbara meet the boy at his home.

The address she gave led to a single-family housein a blue-collar neighborhood in west Austin, a green and tan 1940s craftsman, with painted wood siding, a low-pitched roof, exposed beams, and a covered porch with a white bench. A single exterior light was beside the dark wood front door. It shined bright yellow even though it was ten o'clock in the morning.

Barbara climbed three wooden steps to the front porch, knocked on the door, then glanced back towards the tree-lined street. Carol was in the driver's seat of her Buick Lucerne, craning her head, trying to get a look at "the woman."

Barbara hadn't wanted Carol to drive her, but none of her other friends would do it. They all had "doctor's appointments" or other questionable conflicts.

For a moment, Barbara considered driving herself, but she feared Kate might have canceled her car insurance already since she promised not to drive again after the incident with the police car. *I should never have agreed to it*, she thought. It wasn't my fault.

The cop was parked in a loading zone. No one can park in a loading zone. Not even the police.

She heard the deadbolt snap back and waited for the door to open inward.

A woman smiled at her weakly. She was about five-four, thin, with shoulder-length brown hair that looked like she had just gotten out of bed. She was dressed in jeans and a white cotton T-shirt that let you see her black bra beneath it. Barbara guessed the woman was about forty, although she could have been younger because the bags under her eyes made her look old.

"Hello," Barbara said. "My name's Barbara Becker. I'm from Grannies R Us."

The woman extended a hand. "Heather Daniels. I'm Garrett's mom. Come in, please."

She led Barbara to a cozy living room with painted yellow walls, a brick fireplace, and so much dark-stained wood, on the floor, around the windows, and in the exposed beams in the ceiling, that it felt masculine.

Barbara sat on the edge of a chocolate brown leather sofa; the woman sat on a matching armchair next to her.

"Let's talk for a minute. Before you see Garrett," Heather said.

"Sure," Barbara said.

"I want to thank you for agreeing to be Garrett's grandmother. It means the world to us."

Barbara struggled to make her grimace look like a smile.

"It's my pleasure."

Someone at Grannies R Us had miscommunicated. She had not yet agreed to be Garrett's grandmother. She was only meeting with him to see if there was chemistry. But she let the comment go.

Heather said, "I'm sure you've heard we've had trouble finding a grandmother."

"Oh, really?"

Heather nodded. "It's my fault. It's always been just us. Garrett and me. Even though I've always wanted him to have a grandparent, a part of me thought no one was good enough. But, obviously, we can't be choosy now."

Can't be choosy? Barbara wasn't sure exactly what the woman meant, but she didn't like how it sounded.

"Oh, I'm sorry," Heather said. "That came out wrong. My brain isn't working these days. Garrett's condition has me all mixed up."

"Condition? What condition?"

Heather paused, tilted her head to the side. "They didn't tell you?"

"No."

"Garrett has cancer."

The words caused Barbara to recoil. Instinctively, her hand went to her neck, to the place behind her ear. She traced the outline of an enlarged lymph node she had been touching for the past week, debating whether it was getting bigger, and if so, how much bigger, and if so, was it big enough to warrant a trip to the emergency room. Suddenly, her lymph node felt like it was on fire, pulsating with every heartbeat.

"I'm so sorry," Barbara said.

"Thank you. It's been rough. But I'm grateful Veronica found you. Not everyone is comfortable around sick kids."

Barbara swallowed hard. "I try to see Jesus in everyone."

Heather nodded. "Do you have questions about his condition?"

The irrational part of her brain wanted reassurance his cancer wasn't contagious, which, of course, she knew it wasn't and could never be. Even so, she was afraid to ask anything for fear the question might slip out of her lips. Instead, she avoided the subject, told herself the boy was normal.

"How do you envision this working?" Barbara asked. "You know, since he's a teenager."

Heather shrugged. "Whatever you and Garrett decide is fine. He can still do most things. Only not for as long. Do you have medical training, Barbara?"

She perked up, sensing a way out. "I'm afraid I don't. If that's necessary, I can ask Veronica to send over someone else."

Heather waved a hand at her. "Don't be silly. I knew nothing when Garrett got sick. We can teach you."

Barbara smiled curtly. "Wonderful."

Heather stood up. "Wait here. I'll see if Garrett is ready to meet you."

43

Ten minutes later, Barbara was in the passenger seat of Carol's Buick, clutching the hand grip on the door panel, while her friend raced down the freeway, weaving back and forth across the lanes of traffic, skirting between cars like they were part of an action movie.

"Slow down," Barbara said, digging her fingernails into the plastic. "You're going to kill us."

Carol shook her head. "Staying here is what will kill us. The faster we get away from these nuts, the better."

Staring straight ahead, Barbara saw cars dotting the horizon.

"So," Carol said, glancing over at her, "she didn't even let you see the boy?"

When Carol turned her head, she drifted her hands right, swerving the car and almost colliding with a truck beside them. The man blared his horn. The vehicles got so close Barbara could have reached out and shook his hand. At the last second, Carol yanked the wheel back left and pressed the gas pedal to the floor, sending them hurling down the freeway even faster.

Barbara's heart raced. She didn't think she could take much more of this.

When they were free of the pack, she relaxed her grip and took a deep breath.

"He's sick," Barbara said. "Cancer."

Carol shook her head. "That's terrible. A lady in my building. Her grandson got the cancer. Drove the entire family mad."

"I don't see how it could be another way."

Carol peeked over at her again, this time careful to keep the car pointed straight ahead. "I guess it's lucky then. If he didn't meet you, he won't be disappointed when you quit."

Barbara pulled her eyebrows together. "Quit? Who said anything about quitting?"

"Come on, Barbie. We both know you're gonna quit. You're not much of a caregiver. In fact, truth be told, I don't know how you past got the prescreen."

"You think I can't do it?"

"I know you can't do it."

"Why would say such a horrible thing?"

"Two words. Katie's flu."

Barbara scoffed. A few years earlier, when Kate was sick, she had spent a couple of nights sleeping on Carol's couch. She did it to be responsible. Everyone knows the flu is dangerous for seniors.

"This isn't like that," Barbara said. "Cancer isn't contagious."

"Maybe, but you still freak out every time someone talks about the doctor."

Carol veered to the right, whizzing past a convoy of military trucks. When they were clear again, she eased back on the throttle, returning to her normal cruising speed in the low eighties.

"Don't get me wrong," Carol said. "I don't care that you're a germaphobe. But the kid is dying and—"

"You don't know he's dying."

"What I'm saying is you can't bail when things get tough."

Barbara was trying her best not to think about doctors. Or sickness. Or death.

"I appreciate your concern, but his mother said she'd teach me everything I need to know."

"So, you're really going to do this?"

"Of course."

Carol hummed. "All right. Then I'm holding you to it. Going to make sure you don't get a sudden urge to run."

The idea of Carol hovering over her shoulder, second-guessing her every move, sounded less than appealing.

"That's a kind offer, Carol," Barbara said. "But it would never work. Not with all the medical privacy issues."

Carol waved a hand at her. "I'll stay in the car. Be your chauffeur."

"I don't think–"

"I'm not going away, Barbie. You owe it to this boy. Plus, you don't drive."

Barbara let it go. There was no use arguing further. Carol would never back down. And she was going to need a ride. Lots of them.

"Fine," Barbara said. "You can be my chauffeur. We're going over again tomorrow morning. His mother says he should be less tired then."

"Tomorrow morning? What's the rush?"

From the look on her face, it was clear Carol hadn't considered the possibility that she'd be pressed into service so soon.

"He's dying, Carol."

"I guess."

In the distance, a sign overhanging the freeway said, "Grove Square Mall – ¾ mile." Barbara pointed at it.

"Get off here. I need to stop at the grocery store."

Carol shook her head. "No. Judge Paula starts in half an hour. She's new this week. Remember the used car salesman I told you about. The guy with the handlebar mustache. Well, he's back again. I'll never understand why people keep buying cars from that cheat."

Judge Paula was part of the first sentence Carol ever spoke to Barbara. It was at Cafe Noir. Barbara was having coffee with Kate out on the patio. Carol was part of a group listening to a free talk on the joys of knitting. Abruptly, she stood up, walked over to Barbara, and demanded to know if Barbara had ever heard of Judge Paula. Barbara nodded, assuming everyone on earth had heard of the TV judge. Apparently, everyone did not include the woman sitting beside Carol because Carol went back over to the group and grabbed a bag of yarn off the woman's lap. She then laughed loudly and winked at Barbara. The rest was history. A part of Barbara assumed Judge Paula might be part of the last sentence Carol uttered to her, too.

"Don't you record that show?" Barbara asked.

"So, what if I do?"

"I need to get something for the boy."

Carol scoffed, then hit the brakes, slowing the car to forty miles per hour while waiting for space to Frogger across two lanes of traffic. They made it only by crossing two solid white lines.

"What does he need?" Carol asked, speeding up the exit ramp and across the parking lot towards the grocery store's front door.

"Pomegranate molasses."

Carol turned up her nose. "Is that some fancy syrup?"

"I don't know."

"Well, you'd better go straight to the counter and ask the lady. Because if it takes you more than ten minutes, you're thumbing your way home."

Barbara didn't think Carol would actually leave her, but she went straight to the counter anyway, not wanting to tempt fate.

44

The address Willa gave for the ransomware hacker led to a rundown apartment community of squat, two-story brick buildings on the east side of town. From the overgrown shrubs and cracks in the cement, it looked like the maintenance man had quit back in the 1970s and never been replaced. Trash spilled over the top of a dumpster, and near the front door of one building, a bicycle without tires leaned up against a wall.

Apartment No. 214 belonged to a man called Wayne, who apparently didn't have a last name. "He's that good, Ms. Becker," Willa said. "You know, like Cher or Madonna."

Kate accepted the explanation because she had no idea how to find anyone else qualified to "hack back." But as she sat on the metal folding chair in Wayne's living/office room, she was beginning to have serious doubts.

"You did the right thing by calling me," Wayne said. "These things can be tricky. You don't want to risk going with the big box boys."

Kate wondered if the big box boys actually did this sort of thing, because if so, she would rather hire them instead.

"You came recommended," Kate said. "Remind me again how you know Willa?"

The man did not look like someone who knew Willa. He was too old, late thirties, too grungy, he had a mullet haircut, and dressed too poorly, his black T-shirt and jeans made him look like a homeless person. The only connection that made sense was if he sold Willa drugs.

"Good try, Ms. Becker," Wayne said. "But you know how the law works. Privileged information."

Kate flashed him a puzzled look. She didn't know if he was joking or if he seriously believed some form of confidentiality covered his work.

"Have you always worked out of your home?" Jessica asked.

Jessica seemed to have no problem with Wayne or his apartment or the fact that their entire future depended on him.

"Not always," Wayne said. "I used to have an office. Before the thing with the woman. It was a misunderstanding, though. She wasn't even that pretty."

Kate closed her eyes, pinched the bridge of her nose.

"Wayne, could you give us a minute? I'd like to talk to my sister for a second."

"Sure thing, Ms. Becker. Need to drain the snake, anyway."

He pushed back his gaming chair, stood up, and grabbed an empty soda bottle off the desk.

"Either of you ladies care for something to drink? I've got Mountain Dew and, well, water."

Kate shook her head and waited for him to close the bathroom door before leaning in close and whispering to Jessica.

"We need to go. Now. If I had driven, we'd be gone, already."

"Relax," Jessica said. "So, he's a little unconventional."

"Unconventional? The guy's an idiot. And what was that thing about the misunderstanding with the woman?"

Jessica shrugged. "I don't know. But he said she wasn't pretty."

Kate stared at her sister, blinked once.

"Okay, I admit it. He's a moron. But look, they don't give out hack back diplomas at Harvard, do they? Willa says he's good enough. I think we should show some tolerance."

"Well, if Willa says he's good enough, maybe he should see if he'll cut us a package deal? Hack back and impregnation."

Jessica frowned. "None of this is Willa's fault."

Kate sighed. "I know. I'm sorry. I'm just having second thoughts. Maybe Mom was right. Maybe I should fess up."

"That would be a terrible idea," Wayne said. He had slipped out of the bathroom and made his way to the kitchen without either of them noticing. He walked over to the desk, clutching a fresh bottle of Mountain Dew. "What you need to do, Ms. Becker, is let me catch the jungle rat. I'll grab him by the tail and shoot napalm straight up his ass."

Kate's mouth fell open. "Napalm?"

Wayne nodded. "It's scary to think about, isn't it? But don't worry. As a Fellow in the American Academy of Certified Online Internet Protectors, I'm only allowed to use my powers for good."

When he finished talking, he winked at her.

"Thanks for the consult," Kate said, having heard enough. "But we're going to need to think about it."

Wayne's eyes narrowed. "Is it because of the price?"

"I don't think—"

"What's the price?" Jessica asked.

Wayne lowered his voice.

"Normally, a napalm injection retails for $499. But I like you two gals. So, I'll do it for $475. If you sign-up now."

"Wow," Jessica said, looking at Kate. "That's a sweet deal. I think we should do it."

"No way," Kate said quickly. "I mean, is it even legal?"

Wayne shrugged. "Who knows what's legal anymore, Ms. Becker. In Denver, you can order weed with your fries, but not here in Texas."

Kate stared at him blankly, not sure how to respond.

Jessica jumped in and tried to salvage things. "I'm sorry about my sister. She doesn't always recognize a deal when she sees one."

"It's okay. My brother's a bit of a dud, too. But it is a fair question. Technically, it's a legal gray area. It depends on where I inject the napalm. It would be best if I did it in Panama. Which I could do, for another fifteen hundred dollars. Let's call it an even two grand."

"You could wipe all the data for two grand?" Jessica asked.

"For you, honey, yes."

Jessica stood up like a shot and extended a hand across the desk.

"Deal," she said. "Pack your bags, Wayne. You've got a plane to catch."

45

On the morning of Ruth's court hearing, Kate arrived at the Travis County Courthouse thirty minutes before their case was scheduled to be called. She had asked Ruth to meet her in the hallway outside Judge Eide's courtroom so they could go over again what was likely to happen. She had explained it three times already, but Ruth still didn't understand why they couldn't cross-examine Damion about all of his lies.

It was a problem she faced in many cases. When people heard the word court, they assumed trial. But real life wasn't like those free-wheeling TV judge shows. Today's hearing would be paper-driven. There would be no live testimony. The attorneys would reargue what they had written in briefs and answer questions the judge had, but that was it. In a few weeks, she'd get an email telling her who won and the rules they'd have to follow until a trial could be held, months or years in the future.

Kate glanced down at her watch. Ruth was late. If she didn't show up soon, they wouldn't have time to talk before a bailiff ushered them into the courtroom.

At the end of the hall, the elevator dinged. The doors slid open. Tina Black strolled out, accompanied by her client.

When Tina saw her, she flashed Kate a big grin, then came over to her.

Tina was dressed in a cream-colored blouse and black pantsuit that fit her like a glove. It was tailored to show off her skinny legs and tiny waist.

"Hello, Katie," Tina Black said in her usual, condescending voice. "Couldn't resist the urge to champion another lost cause I see."

Tina smelled of excess hair spray and perfume.

"I actually feel pretty good about our chances," Kate said.

Tina raised an eyebrow. "Tell me you're not drinking the Kool-Aid."

Drinking the Kool-Aid was a common affliction amongst trial lawyers. Kate's old boss called it The Drafter's Paradox. The theory was that a lawyer's belief in his/her chances of success was directly proportional to (1) the lawyer's personal investment in a case; and (2) the time remaining before court. The more invested a lawyer was, the more they thought they could win.

"The pictures are compelling," Kate said.

Tina forced laughed. "Compelling? In what way? For a psych hold?"

Kate had similar thoughts when Ruth showed her the stack of pictures proving Damion had abused her the day after their first meeting. The photos were ink-jet printouts of selfies showing Ruth with a terrible-looking shoe-polished black eye. When Kate asked if she had any other evidence, Ruth got huffy and threatened to text The Hatchet.

"We'll see."

"Indeed, we will," Tina said. "If it had been me, I would have just claimed abuse and not filed the pictures. I mean, who says it didn't happen? My guy isn't an angel."

"Thanks for the advice," Kate said tersely.

Tina shrugged. "It's not our problem, though, right? We just work here. But still, the pictures do make your woman look silly."

Kate ignored the jab. "Does your guy have any interest in settling?"

"I don't know. Is she willing to terminate her parental rights? Because if so, I could probably swing a few grand for your attorney fees. That'd help you out with Ms. Wilson."

"Don't be ridiculous. I'd never agree to terminate rights."

"You mean your client would never agree to terminate rights."

"Yeah, that's what I said."

"Uh-huh," Tina said. "I assume you've shown her the numbers?"

Kate hesitated. Numbers? What numbers? There were no numbers in the pleadings.

"Yes," Kate said.

Tina studied her for a moment. "Oh my, God. You don't even know what numbers I'm talking about, do you?"

"I'm done playing games, Tina."

"Listen, I'm not being difficult. I'm talking about child support, okay? My guy hasn't asked for it yet, but he will. You need to do the math. Five hundred a month times twelve months times eighteen years. A hundred grand, minimum."

Kate swallowed hard. Why hadn't Riley mentioned child support? She made a mental note to yell at him the next time she saw him.

"My associate briefed it," Kate lied. "Ruth isn't motivated by money."

Tina shook her head. "That just proves she's nuts. How is Riley working out, anyway? I was bummed you stole him from me."

"Yes," Kate said. "I'm sure you were heartbroken."

"I was. He's a real catch."

The courtroom door swung open. A burly sheriff's deputy with a bald head and a handlebar mustache pointed at the two of them.

"Judge wants to see both of you in chambers."

Kate glanced over her shoulder, scanned the hallway for Ruth. "My client isn't here yet."

The deputy shrugged as if he didn't care.

They followed the man through a locked door, then weaved past a maze of empty cubicles to an office on the side of the building. The deputy stopped outside an open door. He motioned for them to go in.

Tina Black cut in front of Kate, stepped into the room first.

46

As the newest judge in Travis County, Kate expected Judge Eide's chambers to be small and unimpressive.

Judges were part of a hierarchal world where seniority decided everything from case assignments to vacation priority. Even still, Kate wasn't prepared for what she saw.

Judge Eide's chambers was a small, empty room. A gunmetal desk, fluorescent ceiling lights, and two hard-backed guest chairs. The drywall was bare, and the carpet was worn thin.

The Judge was on his feet. He shook Tina's hand first, then hers. He told them to sit, then took his place behind the desk.

"Ms. Black, I saw the article in The Austin Times. Real good coverage. Alan must be pleased."

Alan was Alan W. Weitzman. The founder of the firm where Tina Black worked. Kate had only met the man once, years earlier. Even back then, the guy looked like he was a hundred years old. Kate figured Alan didn't know Tina existed.

Tina smiled. "Thank you, Your Honor. If it's not inappropriate for me to say, I was so glad when the Governor appointed you to the bench. There's no one more deserving."

Kate wanted to gag. The phony politeness was making her

queasy. It was always this way back in chambers. Judges and lawyers acting buddy-buddy like they were friends who cared about each other. But they weren't, and they didn't.

Judge Eide said, "I'd offer you coffee, but I lost my machine."

"Oh, no," Tina said. "What happened?"

"The Chief. He's turning the screws on me. He's pissed I jumped traffic court and got myself assigned to the family block straight away."

Tina raised an eyebrow. Judges didn't just "jump traffic court."

"How did you manage that?" she asked. "I thought all new judges had to spend two years in the suburbs."

Judge Eide smiled, shook his head. "A magician never reveals his secrets, Ms. Black."

Translation: Be careful counselor, we're acting friendly, but we're not really friends.

Tina gave a slight, submissive nod.

Judge Eide rocked back in the chair and laced his fingers behind his head. "So, where are we on this one? Are we going to get it done today?"

By "get it done," Eide did not mean will there be enough time for both lawyers to make thorough arguments so I can render a fair and just decision. Instead, he was asking if either of the clients was being unreasonable so he'd know which one to hammer into settling so he could get the case off his desk. Many people forget that when they have a court hearing, a judge must write a decision. This takes time and effort. Time which a guy like Judge Eide could spend elsewhere.

The confused look on Tina face made clear she didn't speak Eide. Or at least, not fluently, anyway.

Judge Eide continued, "Counselors, I'm sure I don't need to tell you how much happier people are when they settle a case themselves. The research is clear."

"Yes, Your Honor," Tina said. "But that research doesn't apply here. If you look at Judge McDaniels's prior order—"

Judge Eide's hand went up like a shot. "I'm going to stop you there, Ms. Black. Are you saying Judge McDaniels's Order is precedential? That I am obligated to follow it?"

It was a trap.

"No, of course not," Tina Black said, shaking her head. "I'm just saying that if you read Judge—"

"Then let's stick to the facts, all right?" Judge Eide said. "Because I believe my duty requires me to be fair, impartial, and open-minded. Don't you agree, Ms. Becker?" Kate nodded but did not speak. It was best not to interrupt a judge when they were doing your job for you. "Good, good. Ms. Becker, do you think there's a chance of settling today?"

Obviously, the answer was no. Ruth's and Damion's motions both asked for sole custody. Both had accused the other of being an unfit parent. But that wasn't the answer Judge Eide was looking for. He wanted hope.

"Of course," Kate said. "Settlement is always possible."

Eide clapped his hands. "Excellent. How about this? Since both your people want the kid a hundred percent of the time, why don't we split the baby? Pardon the pun. Given them each half. Mom gets fifty percent. Dad gets fifty percent. That'd be fair, right?"

Fair? For whom? Even if Ruth and Damion were lying about the unfitness stuff, they still couldn't cooperate enough to get lunch, much less raise a human being.

At that moment, however, Ruth had no parenting rights, and she had made some pretty flimsy abuse allegations, so Kate thought fifty-fifty sounded pretty good.

"Sounds fair to me," Kate said quickly, heaping even more pressure on Tina.

"Ms. Black?" Judge Eide asked.

"Your Honor, respectfully, no." Tina Black sounded like a whiny teenager. "My client would never agree. And I couldn't in good conscious recommend it to him. There are safety issues at play."

Judge Eide reached for a manila folder on his desk. He pulled out two pictures Kate had filed with Ruth's motion, waved them in the air.

"Have you seen these, Ms. Black? Because these worry me. I'm concerned your guy might be a domestic terrorist."

"A domestic terrorist? Come on, Your Honor, please! They're fakes."

"Fakes?" Judge Eide's face turned red. A vein throbbed on his forehead. "Show me the evidence, Ms. Black. Right now. Because I'm not letting you put the victim on trial. Not in my courtroom."

"We've hired experts. A forensic medical examiner, and a computer expert in California."

"West Coast experts, huh?" Judge Eide said. "To me, that's code for you got nothing."

"Ms. Becker dropped these pictures on us only three days ago, and she won't give us access to the digital file. I had planned to ask for a continuance today so we can investigate."

"Denied," Judge Eide said. "Your guy brought the motion. He's not skirting justice because he got exposed."

Even to Kate, who was enjoying every second of the show, Judge Eide's comments seemed wildly unfair. There was no way Tina Black should have expected Ruth to offer phony pictures. But this was what happened when you told a judge there was no hope of settlement.

Tina huffed. "Then I make a motion for the pictures to be stricken from the record. Ms. Becker submitted them late."

"Denied. I will not close my eyes to domestic assault because of a procedural rule."

"Your Honor, procedural rules exist so people have a chance to meet the evidence offered against them."

Judge Eide motioned towards Tina. "Go ahead, Ms. Black. This is your chance. Meet the evidence offered against your client."

"I can't. My experts were just retained."

Judge Eide shrugged.

Tina looked on the verge of losing control. Somehow, she reached down deep inside herself and found one last ounce of courage.

"Since you're forcing us forward today," Tina said, "I request permission to call witnesses at the hearing. I need to cross examine Ruth about the pictures."

Judge Eide hesitated.

For a moment, Kate worried Tina had finally found an argument to beat her, but then Eide answered in a loud, booming voice.

"Denied! Any other extraordinary requests, Ms. Black? Because you're on quite a roll today."

Tina's shoulders fell. She slumped in the chair.

Ninety-nine percent of all judges in America would have sided with Tina. But in that courthouse, on that day, Eide was a unassailable, divine-right king. His opinion was the only one that mattered. If he believed Ruth, if he found her pictures credible, no appeals court in the world would second-guess him. Mostly, this was because appellate judges hated family law and did anything they could to avoid getting entangled with it.

Tina knew these things, of course, which was why she looked distraught.

Judge Eide rubbed the vein on his forehead.

"This is what I wanted to avoid," Eide said. "This is what I don't like." He looked squarely at Tina. "I don't want to hurt your client, Ms. Black. Maybe he is a good guy. But if you force me to have a hearing, I'm afraid he's going to lose. I might be forced to deny him all contact with his child."

Translation: Give up. Resistance is futile.

"I don't want that to happen," Tina said.

"Good, good," Eide pointed at both lawyers. "So, go figure it out. If you two agree, it'll be like this discussion never happened. For what it's worth, fifty-fifty still seems fair to me."

Tina sighed. "How am I supposed to sell it to my guy? He's convinced he's going to win."

Judge Eide nodded. "I don't envy you, Ms. Black. Managing client expectations is the hardest part of the job. Maybe tell him I wanted to throw him in jail. Explain that you convinced me not to do it, if he settled for fifty-fifty."

Tina's eyes went wide. "You can't throw him in jail."

Eide shrugged. "Who knows what I can do, Ms. Black? I have a lot of power. Plus, he doesn't know it. Remind him it's only temporary. He can make whatever arguments he wants at trial. If he's right, I'll rule for him."

When Tina Black left the room and disappeared down the hall, Kate stopped in the doorway. She looked back at Eide. He smiled and winked.

47

Two days after Matt met The Eagle in a bar, he found Bowers hiding in the employee break room at The Austin Free Press. It was three o'clock in the afternoon, and the smell of microwaved curry lingered in the air.

Bowers was at a big round table in the back corner, hunched over, head down, reading the sports section of a newspaper and eating jelly donuts. He used a napkin to wipe his mouth, then reached inside a white cardboard box for another round. Matt walked over, sat down across from him.

Bowers sighed, not bothering to look up. "Kid, if you ask me for a lead again, I swear, I'm going to kill you."

"I said nothing."

Bowers hummed in disbelief, then resumed reading the sports section of the paper.

"Can you believe Calonge? The bum blew another save."

"He's a rookie."

"So? I'll tell you what'd I do if I were the GM. I'd rent him the smallest compact car they make and force him to drive all the way back to single A ball in Oregon. Not give him a dime for a motel either."

"Why a small car? Because he's so tall?"

Bowers flashed him a look that said he was an idiot.

Matt said, "You don't punish the number two prospect in baseball because he has a few bad outings."

"A few bad outings? Kid, you should have been a lawyer. You're a real champ at twisting the facts."

Matt shook his head. "The guy's dominated at every level. You know he was triple-A Player of The Year last year, right?"

Bowers stared at him.

"It takes time to adjust to the big leagues," Matt said, feeling defensive. "The speed of play is faster."

Bowers frowned. "Says every busted prospect ever. If a guy's got talent, he figures it out. Quick. If not, it's best to cut him loose before he gangrenes."

"Well, I think he's going to be good."

"Do you think that will happen before or after you get fired?"

"Cute," Matt said.

"What can I say? I'm a sucker for tough love mentoring."

"Uh-huh." Matt paused for a moment, letting the conversation drift away. "Speaking of mentoring, I wanted to ask you about a lead."

Bowers scoffed, squeezed his eyes shut, and pinched the bridge of his nose. "Jesus, kid."

"I'm not asking you for a lead, Bowers. I want to ask you *about* a lead."

Bowers shook his head. "I'm starting to think this is another of Arthur's schemes to get me to quit. He can't fire me so he recruits a kid to drive me insane."

"That's not fair."

"Really? How many times in the last ten months have you seen me in this break room?"

Zero, Matt thought. Bowers hated small talk, work celebrations, and the smell of reheated leftovers.

"I don't know," Matt said.

"Use those investigative skills, big boy. Ask yourself: Hmm, I wonder if it's a good time to talk to Bowers about leads when he's eating a whole box of jelly donuts at three in the afternoon."

Matt had sensed something was off with Bowers, but their relationship wasn't the type where you shared feelings.

"Do you want to talk about it?" Matt said.

Bowers turned up his nose. "No, I don't want to talk about it. I want to eat donuts. Lots of 'em. Until I forget about the story I lost. And I never, ever, want to hear you say the word 'lead' again."

Bowers reached back into the donut box and jerked his hand out. It was empty.

"Crap," Bowers said.

They rode the elevator down and went out the main entrance of the newspaper building. The sidewalk was calm, but that would change soon when people finished the first shift and began cuing for buses that would whisk them out to the suburbs.

They jaywalked across a street and went inside a mirrored glass skyscraper with a sundial on the plaza out front.

The donut shop was in a group of takeout restaurants down a small corridor off the right side of the lobby. It was impossible to see unless you knew where to look, wedged between a taco stand and a hot dog joint. The display case in the front was dark. The only light in the stall came from behind a swinging door, back where they made the donuts.

Bowers knew the lady on duty. She frowned, then disappeared in the back, returning with a box of a half-dozen. She charged him the day-old rate, and they ate in a common area with no one else around.

Matt waited to speak until after finishing a jelly donut and licking the sugar off his fingers. He didn't love the taste. The lemon filling was too tart.

"It must have been some story, if it rattled you like this," Matt said.

Bowers nodded. "It was. It was going to be my third Pulitzer."

"What was it about?"

"Let it go, kid. I don't want to think about it anymore."

"Come on, Bowers. You can't say it was Pulitzer worthy, then leave me hanging."

Bowers hummed. "Fine. It involved corruption in the courts. Happy now?"

Corruption in the judicial branch was always a good story. It hit all the conventions to win an award. Abuse of power, secrecy, and, if you were lucky, sex, too.

"Who'd they go with?" Matt asked.

"What?"

"You said you lost the story, so I assumed the source went with someone else."

Bowers scoffed. "Don't be ridiculous, kid. Why would they go with someone else?"

"Then how did you lose the story?"

"I violated the golden rule of journalism. Never give a source time to think. Get them on the record before they change their mind."

"Ah, I see."

"Oh, do you? Here's another tip. Never let the guy call back. He'll just get scared. Flake out. They always do. It doesn't matter how much of big shot he is."

Matt felt his heart race in his chest.

"He was supposed to call back?"

Bowers raised an eyebrow. "Isn't that what I just said? Whatever. He'll probably call back around Halloween. He was so paranoid about not being in the middle of the story he insisted on wearing a mask to our meeting."

48

Kate brought the ceramic mug up close to her nose, closed her eyes, and inhaled the cinnamony aroma of Cafe Noir's trademark black tea.

She was on the private patio behind the coffee shop. She had come straight from court, intent on savoring her tiny victory before anybody could ruin her day. For the moment, even the sun was cooperating. It had broken through the clouds and warmed her face after the chilly air drove all the other customers inside.

For the first time in a while, she felt like she could breathe again. A real breath. The kind you didn't even know was gone until it came back and sent a wave of relaxation coursing through your body.

The instant the tea touched her lips, she heard the patio door squeak open. She opened her eyes to see Riley coming towards her.

She sighed. "How did you find me?"

"Your sister. She called to find out what happened at Ruth's hearing. When I said you weren't back yet, she gave me this address."

"Of course she did."

He pulled out a wrought-iron chair across the table from her and sat down.

"So, what happened?" Riley asked.

She told him everything, except for the part about Eide's winking.

"Jesus," he said, shaking his head when she had finished. "I mean, wow. I believe you, but I don't believe you."

Kate shrugged. "What can I say? I'm that good."

"I guess. Why do you think he bought her story? The pictures are so bad."

Kate turned up her nose at him. "They're not that bad."

"Yes, they're terrible, Kate. When you didn't come back right away, I thought maybe he threw you in jail for suborning perjury."

Kate rolled her eyes. The guy could be so dramatic. It was no wonder he fit in better at the firm than she did.

"What matters is that Eide believed it, and Tina Black forced her guy to settle. So, thanks to me, Ruth has her baby back. Fifty percent of the time anyway."

Riley continued to shake his head in disbelief. "I can't say this increases my confidence in our justice system."

"Like I said, you have a lot to learn about how law works."

The statement had come off a little smugger than she intended, but she had earned this little victory lap, and he was raining on her parade.

She was about to tell him to go back to the office and do some work when he said, "I guess the one good thing is Ruth's happy. She won't be calling The Hatchet soon."

Kate sighed. "You'd think, but no. After we put the deal on the record, she started pressing me for details. She wanted to know why Damion agreed to settle. I screwed up and told her the truth."

"Why is that bad?"

"Because when she heard Eide had threatened to give her sole custody, she lost it. Accused me of selling her down the river."

"Seriously?"

"Yep. She said the blood was on my hands. She said an abuser should never have fifty-fifty custody of a baby."

Riley hummed. "She has a point."

"No," Kate said, sounding annoyed, "she doesn't have a point. Eide only said those things to make him settle."

"What? Why would he do that?"

She didn't answer. There was nothing she could tell him that would make sense except for the truth. And under no circumstances was she going to admit that she only won because Eide was crushing on her.

"I can't explain everything to you, Riley," Kate said. "I'm not a law school. If you want to keep working here, you need to keep up. Start figuring stuff out for yourself."

He nodded.

She felt a ping of regret inside for making him feel dumb. Back when she had been a new lawyer, people used this trick on her all the time. When she figured out what they were doing, she swore she'd never use it on someone else. She still believed that. Starting again, now.

"So, what happens next?" Riley asked.

"Judge Eide ordered us to mediate with a guy called Shanti."

"Is he any good?"

Kate hadn't heard of the guy before, so she figured probably not.

"It doesn't matter because Ruth believes she has the judge on her side now and is refusing to settle for less than one hundred percent custody."

"Sounds tough to get."

"Try impossible. No judge in Texas is going to write the words one hundred percent custody in an order. Which brings us to your next assignment. I need you to draft the most wide-ranging, scorched earth discovery imaginable. Focus on sensitive, embarrassing issues. We need to find Damion's weak spot. Exploit the secret he's hiding."

Riley raised an eyebrow. "What makes you think he's hiding a secret?"

"Everyone's hiding a secret, Riley. If we tug on the right thread, it will come out. Then we can leverage him into giving up the kid."

He looked uneasy.

"Man up," Kate said. "This is the job. We took an oath to use every dirty trick in the book to fight for our client."

"Is blackmailing the guy into giving up his kid really what's best for Ruth?"

"We've talked about this, Riley. Ruth sets the goals. We execute."

"I know, I know. I'm just. . . it doesn't solve our problems with The Hatchet. We have to do more than just win Ruth's case. You promised the woman a media bonanza."

Kate knew what she promised. Every time things slowed down, her brain ruminated on it.

But there was nothing she could do about that at the moment.

She put her faith in an article she once read about Susan. Apparently, Susan faced a similar situation after starting her own firm. To rally staff, she told them to ignore the end result. Focus instead on winning every day. If you do that, Susan claimed, the result will take care of itself.

Kate hoped her boss was right.

49

"Mother!" Kate yelled down the hallway towards her mother's bedroom. "You need to go. The car's downstairs."

"Stop yelling." Barbara shuffled out of her room with her head down, rummaging through a big black purse. "You're always yelling. I can't find my wallet. I'm not leaving until I find my wallet."

Kate sighed, then reached into the front pocket of her slacks and pulled out a wad of folded bills. She peeled off two twenties, held them out for her mother.

"Take this. We'll find your wallet later."

"It's not about the money," Barbara said. "Carol forget her wallet last time, and the tween at the concession stand wouldn't serve her wine."

Kate glanced down at her watch. There were still fifteen minutes until Wayne was supposed to call with an update.

Barbara laughed loudly. "Would you look at that? It was in the bottom of my purse."

"Unbelievable," Kate said dryly.

The doorbell rang. As Kate started across the living room to answer it, Barbara reached out and snatched the money from her hand.

"I'll take this, too," Barbara said. "Just to be safe."

"Of course."

Kate pulled open the door. It was her sister, Jessica.

"I'm not late, am I?"

Kate shook her head. "Say goodbye to Mother. She's on her way out."

"Bye, Mom," Jessica said, walking into the condo and shucking off her coat. "Off for another night on the town with the card club ladies?"

"I wish," Barbara said. "Your sister is kicking me out. For privacy reasons."

Kate rolled her eyes. "I would hardly call VIP theater tickets and a private car to the show kicking you out."

"For me," Jessica said, "it would depend on what I'm seeing."

"Me, too," Barbara said. "Your sister tried to kill me by getting tickets for that French movie. You know, the one that's so long the woman died from it."

Kate squeezed her eyes shut. "For the hundredth time, Mother. The woman died at the movie. Not from it."

Jessica glanced at her. "You're not talking about the La Roue remake are you? Because it's almost seven hours long."

"I thought she could make a day of it. And it got decent reviews online."

Barbara waved a hand at her, then looked toward Jessica. "Don't worry about me, honey. I swapped out the tickets. We're seeing Flying Trains."

Jessica winced. "Is that the comic book movie about the family who turns into flying freight trains?"

"Agh," Barbara put her fingers in her ears. "Don't spoil it for me. I haven't seen the previews."

Kate shook her head. When Barbara was gone, she went to the kitchen and poured two glasses of wine, then sat down next to Jessica at the dining room table.

Jessica said, "Have you given any thought to what you'll do if it's bad news?"

Kate took a long breath. "Tomorrow will be a full week. I think I'd have to report it."

"Of course..." Jessica took a sip of wine. "Did I tell you I've been doing a little pleasure reading about computers? They're quite fascinating machines. Did you know that most data breaches are never solved?"

"I did not know that."

"It's true. So, I was thinking. And hear me out before you say no. What if you said your computer was stolen? Claim someone grabbed your bag at Cafe Noir. No one could blame you for that. I'd be willing to punch you in the eye, if it'd help your story."

Kate flashed a little half-smile. "Thanks."

"Or you could go with the shoe polish look like your client."

"Yeah, I don't think I'm going to add filing a false police report to my resume. If Wayne hasn't sorted it out, I'll take my lumps."

Jessica swallowed hard. "Even if it means losing everything?"

Kate shrugged.

"Promise me," Jessica said, "you won't self-detonate until after you talk to a lawyer. I can set something up for you."

Kate's phone chirped, and the video chat icon flashed on the screen. She ran her finger across the glass and answered it.

"Hi, Wayne," Kate said.

Her eyes were drawn to the beachside resort in the background. Of course, she knew Wayne was in Panama. She had paid for his airfare and hotel and food. Apparently, also his drinks at a Tiki bar. A pair of women dressed in skimpy bikinis danced on the beach behind him.

"Hi, Jessica," Wayne said, leaning in close to the phone. His cheeks were red, and his voice was too loud, even for a bar. He was winking at her in a way that suggested either an eye injury or bad flirting.

"It's Kate," she said, correcting him. "What have you found?"

"Oh." He sounded disappointed. "Is Jessica there, too?"

Her sister leaned over, waved at him. "Hi, Wayne. Are you surviving down there?"

"Just barely," he said. His eyes darted away, and Kate heard him ask the bartender for a refill. "The women here aren't like you gals in the states. They're insatiable. I have to keep them away with a stick."

Kate shook her head. Why had she hired this man?

"Please give us the update," Kate said firmly.

"We're on track. This morning, I worked a little magic on old Leonard Slatterberry. I convinced him to give us a week's extension. He balked at first, but when I told him you'd pay double, he came around. They always do."

50

Kate's eyes went wide. It took all her composure not to fire him on the spot.

"Who gave you permission to pay double?"

Wayne waved a hand at her. "Don't get worked up, Ms. Becker. You're not gonna pay. He knows it. It's only part of the game."

"I don't understand."

"It's better not to try." Wayne glanced away again, thanked the bartender. "This dance we're doing... it's some high-level shit."

"That much I do understand"

"It's stage four, Ms. Becker. Does that help? Imagine playing 3D chess in the middle of a hurricane. Than turn out the lights."

"So," Jessica said, leaning over and getting her face on camera, "it's more like 5D chess? Or even 6D?"

Wayne nodded, not seeming to grasp Jessica was making fun of him.

"I can't say more here. There's a guy who's been eying me for two hours. But, I can tell you this: Leonard Slatterberry isn't his real name."

"No way," Jessica said in mock surprise.

"Yep. His real name is Viper314."

Wayne looked at them as if the name should mean something. Like he was a pop star or the world's richest person.

"Is that good or bad?" Kate asked.

Wayne sighed. "Viper314 is the world's most famous hacker. Some people think he's a myth. A combination of ten or fifteen hackers working together. Personally, I don't believe either. I've never been all that impressed with his work, and hackers couldn't tie a shoe together without sniping at each other."

"Wait," Jessica said. "Is this the guy The Times wrote the article about? The one who hacked into the investment bank and published all those emails about fraudulent foreclosures?"

"Sounds like him," Wayne said. "The webheads love him because he's a modern-day Robin Hood. Steals from the rich, gives to the poor."

"It doesn't make sense," Kate said. "Why would a guy like that target someone like me? I'm not rich or famous."

Wayne shrugged. "Who knows what you did to irk him, Ms. Becker."

"I did nothing to irk him. Perhaps you made a mistake."

"Doubtful," Wayne said, shaking his head. "I don't make mistakes. And computers don't lie. The root search I ran turned up an odd file extension. I took it to a chatroom for longtime pros. The verdict was unanimous. It's Viper314."

"Where do we go from here?" Jessica asked. "I mean, we can't hack back the world's best hacker, right?"

Obviously not, Kate thought. She doubted whether Wayne could go toe-to-toe with a middle school novice. There was no chance he'd stand up against the world's best.

"I wouldn't give up just yet," Wayne said. "The reason I negotiated an extra week is because I've got a lead on the snake. I can't go into it now, but, if things play out right, I might have a straight shot to his hard drive. He won't even see me coming until he's swimming in napalm. I just need a little more money."

Kate raised an eyebrow. "How much more money?"

Wayne hummed and hawed and acted as if he felt uncomfortable talking about money. "If I had to estimate, I'd say two more."

"Two grand!" Kate yelled. "I've already sent to you to Panama. What else could you need?"

Wayne shook his head. "Panama is the problem, Ms. Becker. Well, not Panama, but this resort. It's crawling with distractions. I need privacy. A place where I can think without getting, you know, distracted."

"You picked the resort, Wayne," Kate said.

"What was I supposed to do, Ms. Becker? You were pinching pennies."

Kate threw up her hands, looked at her sister. "I can't take this anymore."

"Let me try," Jessica said.

Kate stood up and walked away. She went to the kitchen and poured herself a large glass of wine, then eavesdropped on them.

"Here's what I don't understand," Jessica said. "If Viper314 knows Kate isn't going to pay, why would he give her extra time?"

"Good question," Wayne said. "I think it's because he's rattled. Most criminals won't buy data when a Certified Online Internet Protector is in the game."

Kate laughed, causing wine to go up her nose.

"Listen," Jessica said, "Kate's skeptical. I believe in you, of course. One hundred percent. But you have to give me something I can use to keep the money flowing."

There was a pause. Kate assumed Wayne's little brain was scheming another lie.

"Okay," Wayne said. "I'll tell you this. The ransomware email. It came from India."

Kate felt her throat tighten. India? No, he must be mistaken. He probably meant Indonesia. Or Indiana. Weren't Dan Quayle and Mike Pence from Indiana? Maybe they did it together?

She took a deep breath, then two quick gulps of wine. Even if he was right, even if the email did come from India, it didn't necessary mean anything. India was full of computer nerds. Half the world's hackers probably live there.

"Do you know where in India?" Jessica asked.

"I could narrow it down," Wayne said.

"I'll call you back."

A moment later, Jessica stood across from Kate in the kitchen. Her arms were crossed, and her lips pressed into a fine line.

"What did you say to Asha?" Jessica said.

"Asha? I said nothing to her."

"You're lying. You think it's a coincidence that a few days after you fired our Indian VA, you're targeted by ransomware from the same place?"

"Wayne said it was Viper314."

Jessica scoffed. "Wayne is an idiot. You and I both know it's Asha. You pissed her off, and she created this Leonard Slatterberry character to get even."

"That's ridiculous."

"What did you say to her in the exit interview?"

"Nothing."

"You gave her career advice, didn't you?"

"Why would I do that?"

"Because you can't resist being the smartest person in the room."

Kate huffed. She had only said those things to help Asha. To help her. But further argument would get her nowhere.

"Let's say you're right," Kate said. "Let's say it is Asha."

"It is Asha."

"Wouldn't that be better for us?"

"How do you figure?"

"Wayne's a moron. There's no chance he could napalm the real Viper314. But Asha's no pro, either. Maybe he could napalm her."

Jessica's face lit up. "I see where you're going."

"So, we're in agreement then? I'll give him another week. Pay the extra two grand."

Jessica nodded. "I don't think you have a choice. Ethically, you need to get your clients' data back."

51

Matt had to wait a full week after his talk with Bowers before The Eagle agreed to meet again.

At first, he thought it might not happen. He had sent the man three text messages, all of which went unanswered. Then, out of the blue, on day six, The Eagle texted him a time and location to meet. Three o'clock on Saturday afternoon.

While waiting to hear from The Eagle, Matt had gone to the courthouse and leafed through the public file. It was four hundred pages of motions and affidavits and pictures. Even after reading it, though, he still wasn't sure what the story was.

Not that the case was boring.

The parties had slung some big arrows at each other. Abuse. Chemical dependency. There was even a Hollywood-like reversal of the custody order. But there wasn't a Pulitzer-winning story.

What little story existed had already been told by The Austin Times in Tina Black's community service profile. And even that wasn't a good story anymore since Black's client agreed to share joint custody with the baby's mother. He hoped that Bowers's instincts about The Eagle were right and that it was his own inexperience that was keeping him from seeing a big story.

Matt turned right onto Lee Street, then slowed and glanced at his phone, which was clipped to the car's dashboard. According to the map, his destination was two blocks up on the right.

He continued down a wide residential street lined with multi-million dollar estates and big front yards. Up ahead, he saw cars parked on both sides of the road. They seemed to link like long trains stretching off towards the horizon.

He stopped in the middle of the road across from the address The Eagle had given him. It was a huge Spanish-style mansion with a Terra cotta roof and arched windows. People were coming and going up and down the driveway like it was a party.

Matt shook his head. The Eagle was playing games again.

He parked in the first open spot he found, then followed a pair of millennial hipsters dressed like Indie folk singers up the mansion's driveway.

To the right of the grand house was a porte cochere that led to a detached garage in the back. People were streaming through it like fans arriving for a ball game. He tagged along, figuring the crowd knew where it was going.

When he reached the backyard, he stopped and gazed in wonder. The formal English garden behind the house, lush with trees and trimmed shrubs, had been transformed into a 1960s hippie-style theme party. The hedges were painted psychedelic yellows and reds. Retro paper fans with peace symbols hung down from the trees. A lime green Volkswagen Beetle with loopy flowers was parked sideways on the grass.

There was a red sign on a wooden stake pounded into the ground in front of him. The white lettering mimicked handwriting, but the spacing was too perfect for a hand to have done it. It said, "Welcome to Austinstock. Three Hours of Peace & Music." An asterisk appeared after the last word. Matt had to lean in close to read the small printing at the bottom. "Nudity and sex prohibited. This isn't 1969, people!"

Matt laughed, then went onto the grass, feeling just as out of place as he had that night at Driscoll's Bar. Once again, his button-down shirt and khaki pants stood out like a sore thumb against the long-haired, free love crowd dressed in hippie garb.

He wandered towards what he assumed was the bar. A yellow VW bus with the word groovy painted on the side and two women hanging out the windows passing out drinks. He stopped at the back of the line and scanned faces, looking for The Eagle.

Even if he had known what he looked like, he wouldn't have been able to spot him in the sea of costume-wearing party-goers. He resolved to wait for the man to come to him.

"You in line for hippie juice?" a man said behind him.

Matt turned and saw a middle-aged man with shoulder-length brown hair, a mustache, and John Lennon style glasses. The man had a tie-dye bandanna across his forehead and wore a sleeveless suede vest, a v-neck t-shirt, and jeans.

"I don't know," Matt said, not caring either way.

"You don't know? It's only the best thing about this party. Watermelon vodka, coconut rum, lemonade, and strawberries. Absolutely delectable."

"Okay. Maybe I'll try it."

"You must. The other thing you must try," the man stepped forward and leaned in so close Matt could smell the stale coffee on his breath, "are the easy lays. Give it an hour or two. The women get very frisky."

The drink line moved forward, and Matt took a step back to regain his personal space.

"I saw the sign."

The hippie waved a hand at him. "PR. All PR. The city made Alexandra put it up after last year. I mean," the man spoke out of the side of his mouth, "can you defend an orgy in a family neighborhood?"

"Thanks for the tip," Matt said. "Maybe I'll check it out."

He turned back towards the front and hoped the man would get the hint that their conversation was over. It didn't work.

"We could party together," the hippie said. "I have nothing against you Establishment types."

"I'll let you know," Matt responded, not looking back.

A woman in a maid's uniform hustled out of the mansion carrying an enormous bowl of reddish-pink liquid. She set it on a folding table in front of the VW bus. A minute later, the line was gone, and he ladled himself a little hippie juice into a plastic cup.

He went towards the back of the property, where a group of brightly colored tables and chairs waited empty. The hippies weren't interested in idle conversation. They were gathered around booths along the sides of the property, getting their faces painted or tarot cards read.

"You're not much fun, Mr. Simpson," the hippie from the drink line said as he pulled out a chair across the table and sat down. "Ask your questions so we can get this over with. I don't want you ruining my mojo."

Matt shook his head. "You're really putting in the effort to stay anonymous."

The hippie didn't answer.

"So, I went to the courthouse and read the file you suggested. There's nothing newsworthy there."

"You're missing it," the hippie said.

"Missing what?"

The hippie frowned. "I thought you and Bowers were good at connecting dots."

"We are. But we can't solve a puzzle if we don't know the picture."

"I'll point in you the right direction, Mr. Simpson. But then it's up to you. I can't risk putting myself in the story."

Matt nodded.

"I assume you saw custody changed after Judge Eide took over the case."

"It was a big flip to go from Dad to fifty-fifty."

"Not as big as it could have been. The rumor around the courthouse is Eide threatened to go even bigger. Give mom sole custody."

Matt shrugged. "So?"

The hippie looked put out. "So?"

"Look," Matt said, "I'm sure this is all very exciting in an inside baseball sort of way, but it's not news."

"Did you read The Austin Times story? The piece about the father's lawyer, Tina Black?"

"Yes," Matt lied.

"Then you know about the reporter."

"What about her?"

"You know she's dating Judge McDaniel's law clerk."

"Why do I care who she's dating?"

"Because it explains everything."

Matt squeezed his eyes shut. He felt like he was in the middle of the Costello brothers' "Who's on first?" routine.

"Concentrate, Mr. Simpson," the hippie implored. "Before the mother hired a lawyer, Judge McDaniel ruled for the father, who is represented by Tina Black. Then, a second later, McDaniel's clerk's girlfriend writes a story about who? Yep, you guessed it. Tina Black. Smells fishy, don't it?"

Fishy? Matt thought. Um, no. Try normal. People without lawyers lose cases all the time. And reporters write puff pieces about people they know. The only thing that smelled fishy was the hippie's convoluted logic.

However, he didn't say these things out loud because of Bowers's instinct that a Pulitzer was lurking around somewhere, and he didn't want to risk losing it.

"You're saying these things are related?"

"Think hard, Mr. Simpson. Surely, you must be familiar with stories of powerful men behaving badly. You can't believe the legal field is different, do you?"

Matt's eyes narrowed. "I'm still not following. Are you saying Judge McDaniel is exploiting female lawyers or that he's having an affair with Tina Black?"

The Hippie held up his palms, acted coy. "Maybe both. Or neither. You're the reporter, Mr. Simpson. Investigate. Tell the world what's happening."

Matt scoffed. "You're not giving me anything."

The Hippie took a long slow drink of his hippie juice. "Maybe I need to speak to Mr. Bowers. I'm sure he'd understand."

"No," Matt blurted. "I'll figure it out."

The Hippie smiled.

Matt stood up to leave.

"Here's a tip, Mr. Simpson. Start with the mother. And her lawyer, Kate Becker. Tug on that thread, and you never know what might unravel."

52

The following day, Barbara stood in the hallway outside Garrett's bedroom and waited to be invited inside. Her stomach was filled with butterflies. She took a deep breath, then switched the little paper shopping bag she held from one hand to the other, wiping her clammy palm against her pant leg.

Why am I so nervous? she thought. If he doesn't like me, it will be for the best. Not even Carol could blame her for quitting if the boy asked her to go. "I wanted to help," she imagined herself telling Veronica at the Grannies R Us office. "I was even ready to do the medical stuff, but he wouldn't let me."

She opened the door and peeked inside the room. It was smaller than she imagined. Tiny, actually. A twin bed was pushed tight against the far wall. Beside it, under the window, was a wooden nightstand with a lamp. On the wall close to the door, there was a three-drawer dresser. And that was it. No pictures or posters or anything else on the pale yellow walls that made it look like the room of a sixteen-year-old boy.

The boy was on the bed, lying on his back on top of the covers, his head propped up with pillows, his ankles crossed. His face was hidden behind a yellowed paperback. He was dressed in a t-shirt and jeans.

"Garrett," the boy's mother said. "This is Grandma Becker."

The boy lowered the book, studied Barbara for a moment. Hearing the woman call her Grandma Becker made her feel ridiculous. She should have told her not to say it. They weren't fooling anyone.

Garrett raised an eyebrow. "Grandma who?"

Barbara stepped forward. "You don't need to call me that. It's a stupid thing they do to try to make it seem special."

Garrett held a straight face for another second, then smiled. "I'm just joking. Of course, I know you. Come closer. But not that close, I'm contagious."

The mother waved a hand at him. "Stop it. Can't you see she's already nervous."

"I'm not nervous," Barbara said.

"Let me get you a chair so you two can talk for a bit."

The mother left and returned a moment later, carrying a wooden chair from the kitchen. She plopped it down close to the bed. On her way out of the room, she closed the door.

Since learning Garrett had cancer, Barbara had imagined all kinds of grotesque horribleness that could be his appearance. Pale face, ashen eyes, saggy skin. She even wondered if he might be hooked up to an IV or one of those machines that emitted a constant beeping sound. But the boy she saw was none of those things. If his mother hadn't told her he was sick, she wouldn't have guessed it.

He had short blonde hair, brilliant blue eyes, and a baby face that was a good year away from shaving. He was thinner than the teens she saw at Café Noir, the ones who ordered sundaes with whipped cream and chocolate syrup and called it coffee, but not overly so. He reminded her of the boys she went to school with, the lanky, skinny ones who seemed to no longer exist.

She reached into the paper bag on her lap, pulled out the bottle of pomegranate molasses. She held it out so he could see it.

"I got the one you wanted," she said.

"No way."

He took the bottle from her and turned it in his hands so he could read the label. "You really did. I can't believe it."

Barbara smiled. She could get used to this kind of Santa Claus grandmothering.

"It wasn't easy," she said. "My friend and I drove around for hours, stopping at all these little Turkish shops. Eventually, we got the address of a woman who lived above a laundry mat. She has a cousin in Ankara. She wasn't going to sell me her extra bottle until I told her about you."

He shook his head in disbelief, handed the bottle back to her. "Amazing."

"Should I ask your mom if she has crackers so we can try it?"

"No, not now. I'm not feeling so great."

His color still looked good to her, so she figured it must have been something inside, something you couldn't see. Cancer was always sneaking up on you like that.

"Can you put it in my special place for me?" he asked.

He pointed towards the bottom drawer of the dresser. Barbara went over to it, crouched down, and tugged on the handle. It was an old wooden box where the drawers slid directly against the base. She glanced inside and saw unopened DVDs, soda bottles, and canned goods coated with a fine layer of dust. It looked like someone had cleared out a gas station store shelf five years ago and never opened it again.

She looked back at him. He was lying on the pillow again, staring up towards the ceiling.

"Are you sure you want it in here? I don't want you to forget about it."

"Oh, I'd never forget about it. I keep all my treasures in there."

Her heart sank. She felt sorry for the kid. If these things were his life's treasures, he didn't have a clue about what really mattered. Real treasures couldn't fit in a dresser drawer. She decided to teach him.

"Let's stop here for today," she said. "I don't want to push you too far."

Garrett sat up like a shot. "For today? Does that mean you're coming back again?"

"Of course, I'm coming back again, Garrett. Does that surprise you?"

He pressed his lips together, hummed for a moment.

"I'm just so happy," he said. "People rarely come more than once."

"Well, I'm not most people."

"Clearly."

He laid back down, stared up at the ceiling again.

"Is there anything else you need," she asked.

He hesitated, not looking at her. "I'll be fine. You've done enough already."

She could tell from his voice that there was more. He wanted to ask for something but was afraid.

"You can tell me, Garrett. Helping is what grandmothers do."

He turned to look at her. She felt like she could see inside his soul. The sadness nearly broke her heart.

"Do you know what a Mexican Fire Opal is?" he asked.

She shook her head.

"It's a gemstone that some people believe has magical healing powers. I don't believe it, though. I saw one once at an art fair. I wanted to buy it, but my Mom said no. Oh, never mind. It doesn't matter. I'm sure the doctors will find something to help me."

Barbara swallowed hard, fought back tears.

"These gems, are they expensive?"

He shrugged. "I don't know. Not very."

"I'm going to get one for you, Garrett," she said.

"No. Don't. It's too much trouble."

She waved him off. "Hush. The next time you see me, you'll have a Mexican fire rock."

"Mexican fire opal," he corrected.

It was as she closed the door to his room that she heard him say it.

53

Carol glanced over at Barbara, her eyes wide, her face full of disbelief. The vein on Carol's forehead had gotten so big Barbara worried she might have a stroke.

"He said what?"

They were back in Carol's Buick. Barbara was in the passenger seat, relieved the freeway wasn't busy, and Carol was behind the wheel, driving with only one hand.

"You heard me," Barbara said.

Carol shook her head. "I couldn't have, because it sounded like the kid said, 'I love you, Grandma Becker.'"

"So what if he did?"

"So what? Lord help me, Barbara Becker, please don't say you think that's normal."

"Normal? Who's to say what's normal anymore?"

"Don't give me that PC crap. A sixteen-year-old boy doesn't tell an old woman he loves her the first time he meets her."

"Who are you calling old?" Barbara paused for a moment, hoping the attempt at levity would lower the temperature in the car. It didn't work. "Listen, of course, it's strange. But my point is it's understandable."

Carol raised an eyebrow. "Understandable? Does he know you're not really related? That you're only a fake grandmother?"

"Thanks," Barbara said. "Your support means everything to me."

"I am supporting you, Barbara. I'm trying to keep you off the crazy train."

Barbara huffed, then shifted her body, angling it away from Carol and towards the passenger side window. She stared off towards an undeveloped right of way beyond the road and buildings in the distance. She pretended not to hear as Carol huffed her own frustration.

A few miles later, without warning, Carol yanked the steering wheel to the left, sending them hurling across both middle lanes of the freeway to the far left side. Then she pressed the gas pedal to the floor, whizzing past a pickup truck.

"Aren't you worried about getting into an accident?" Barbara asked.

Carol shook her head. "No. I have excellent reflexes."

They passed two more exit ramps before either of them spoke again.

"Tell me why you think he's not crazy?" Carol said.

Barbara sighed. She didn't want to have this conversation again. There was nothing she could say that would change Carol's mind. When Carol decided something was true, she didn't listen to contrary facts. She might pretend to listen, nod occasionally, even ask a follow-up question or two, but her mind wasn't in it. Her mind was off planning her counter-attack. But they were still fifteen miles from home, so waiting it out wasn't an option either.

"Maybe he's getting attached to me. Maybe that's why he said it."

"On the first visit?"

"Come on, Carol. Open your eyes. The kid's dying. He sits alone in that room all day reading those old books. Then I come along, show him a little compassion. It's normal he gets attached quickly."

Carol flashed her a skeptical look. "You don't know any of that's true."

"Really? That's what you're going with? That this is all a big lie? Well, you should know that Garrett teared up when I offered to get him that rock thingy he thinks could save his life."

"What?"

"See, I told you the whole love-you comment wasn't a big deal."

"Wait, wait, wait," Carol said. "Back up. Before, when you first told the story, you said the kid didn't believe in the rock thingy."

Barbara let out a long breath. "No, I didn't say that. Well, okay, fine, maybe. But it doesn't matter. You're focusing on the wrong thing."

"I don't think so."

"Well, I do. And I'm the only opinion that matters. I'm his grandmother."

"You know, you're not, right?"

"I don't have the energy to deal with your drama, Carol. I'll have Kate or Jessica give me a ride to get the rock. You can take a few days off. Maybe the break will give you some perspective."

Carol grumbled, then shook her head. "Fine. We'll do it your way. Happy now, Barbie?"

Barbara smiled. She was indeed happy at winning the concession. She pulled out her cell phone and ran a quick internet search for Mexican Fire Opals and Austin Art Fair. She found an address for an artist who had had a booth at the fair for the last ten years.

"This has to be the guy," she said, pushing the little directions icon. "Look at that, his studio is only forty minutes away."

54

Two weeks after Ruth's court hearing, Kate waited in her car outside a run-down strip mall ten miles west of downtown Austin. The parking spaces around her were empty. A couple of late-model imports occupied spots close to a weight loss center at the far end of the complex.

Kate had resolved to stay in her car until Ruth showed up. The last thing she wanted was to make awkward small talk with Tina Black or the mediator.

The guy was a fruitcake.

Bhagavan Om Shanti, born Nathanial Elmer Anderson, grew up a WASP in Omaha, Nebraska. On his eighteenth birthday, he ran from the farm and didn't stop until he reached the Pacific Ocean. In San Francisco, he bounced from couch to couch until the beauty of Zen exploded in his heart "like a firework over the nighttime sky." Then he shaved his head, changed his name, and ran to a monastery in Japan to become a Buddhist priest. Shanti said these things on his website like he was proud of them.

Kate had rolled her eyes when she read it that morning while standing in line for coffee at Cafe Noir. What were the odds of a guy like Eide had a friend named Bhagavan? She figured they were pretty remote. She made a mental note to ask him about it the next time they were alone. There had to be more to the story.

A white pickup entered the parking lot down by the weight loss center. Kate couldn't tell for sure because of the distance, but she thought the woman behind the wheel looked a lot like Ruth. A man sat beside her in the passenger seat.

Kate cursed under her breath.

Since that day in court, she had left Ruth three voicemail messages trying to arrange a time to meet to prepare for mediation. Ruth had returned none of her calls. In the last message, Kate left the mediator's address and reminded Ruth to come alone. The court order only allowed the two parents and their lawyers to attend the session.

The pickup made a wide turn and stopped directly in front of Shanti's storefront office.

Kate grabbed her leather satchel off the floor of the backseat, then pushed open her car door and stepped out onto the blacktop. She crossed the parking lot and reached Ruth's truck just as the woman closed her door.

"Ruth," Kate said. "Did you get my messages?"

Ruth turned to face her. "Yeah, I got em'. So what?"

"So," Kate motioned towards the man coming around the front of the pickup, "I told you not to bring anyone."

"You said only lawyers could come. Well, he's my new lawyer."

"What?"

"Ms. Becker, meet Mr. Elwood Lincoln. He's here to protect my interests on account of you selling me out all the time."

The man stopped beside Ruth and extended a hand towards Kate.

Mr. Elwood Lincoln was a string bean with a baby face and a fuzzy adolescent beard. He was dressed in a white button-down shirt and black slacks that looked like they were first worn to a church confirmation. In his left hand, he held a hardshell briefcase.

Kate shook the boy's hand. It was cold and clammy.

"Nice to meet you, Mrs. Becker," the kid said.

"Elwood, is it?" Kate asked.

"Yes, ma'am."

"You ought to stick to using miz. Not all of us girls are married."

Elwood blushed. "Yes, ma'am. Sorry, ma'am. Didn't mean any disrespect, ma'am."

Ruth struck the kid on the arm. "Stop all the 'yes ma'am', 'sorry, ma'am' nonsense. She ain't your boss. She works for you."

"What are you doing, Ruth?" Kate asked. "You have an entire firm behind you. You don't need some newbie." She glanced toward Elwood. "No offense, kid."

"None taken, ma'am."

Ruth scoffed. "If y'all are so great, why are you working for free?"

Kate hated this argument. Versions of it got tossed around by clients all the time. If you ever tried to be friendly and cut a person's bill, half the clients would turn around and accuse you of misconduct or overcharging them.

"I'm handling your case pro bono because I believe in you, Ruth."

"Ha. That's funny. Because I don't believe in you. If you want to stay on my team, Kate, this is how it's going to work. Elwood is in charge. You do what he says. If you've got a question, you ask him. If he thinks it's pertinent, he'll ask me. Got it?"

"Come on, Ruth. You can't be serious."

Ruth looked at Elwood. "Is your worker talkin', Elwood? Because I'm hearing a lot of jabbering."

"Ruth, Judge Eide will never allow this sort of telephone game."

Ruth squinted at Elwood. "You'd better get control of your people, Wood. Otherwise, I'll hire a new lawyer. Someone to manage you."

"Yes, ma'am," Elwood said, nodding. "Right away, ma'am. I'll get her under control."

Ruth shuttered, then took a deep breath and exhaled slowly. "You know I can't handle all this stress, Wood." She ran a hand down the front of her faded sundress, pretending to smooth out the wrinkles. "I'm going inside to mingle. If your worker wants to join us, she'd better get on board. Otherwise, send her home. No one will miss her."

Kate watched as Ruth held her head high and swung her hips on her way into Shanti's office. When the door closed behind her, Kate looked at Elwood.

"Where do you work?"

"Right now?"

His voice was hesitant like he didn't want to say.

"Of course, right now," Kate said.

"Um. Mostly at the TireMart on 24th and El Dorado."

Kate's eyes went wide. "What?"

"It's only part-time, ma'am. I'm still in school."

"You're still in law school?"

"No, ma'am," Elwood said, shaking his head. "I hope to go to law school someday, though."

Kate stared at him, blinked once.

"Right now, I go to Barton Creek Community College. You know, home of the fighting ferrets. But I am pre-law. And I'm taking family law this semester."

Kate squeezed her eyes shut, began rubbing her temples.

"I have experience, ma'am. My parents are divorced. Twice. Not from each other. That'd be kind of weird, right? Actually, I've been through four divorces. Five, if you count my aunt. I usually don't count my aunt. Do you think I should count my aunt?"

Kate sighed. "How old are you, Elwood?"

"Nineteen, ma'am. But I'll be twenty in eight months."

Kate opened her eyes and hummed. "Here's the thing, Elwood. You seem like a good kid. And since you're pre-law, I assume you know you can't represent Ruth since you haven't gone to law school and passed the bar exam."

He nodded. "Yes, ma'am. We learned about this. It's called the unauthorized practice of law. It's a felony. A person could go to prison for it. Although, it's rare."

"Right," Kate said. "So, you know why you can't go inside. Because if you did, I'd be obligated to call the police on you."

She wasn't actually obligated to do anything, but she was serious about calling the police.

"I told Miss Ruth the same thing," Elwood said. "But she wouldn't listen. She thinks you're only in this for yourself. I told her that since you work for Susan Wilson, you have to be good. We studied Mrs. Wilson in school. She's an amazing lady."

"That's true," Kate said.

"The only way I could stop her from firing you was by agreeing to be the middle man. She made me be your boss, but I thought maybe we could be more like colleagues."

55

Barbara stood on the sidewalk out in front of her condo building, scanning the street in both directions, searching for any sign of Carol's Buick. She glanced down at her watch, then checked her cell phone for missed calls and text messages. There were none.

That Carol was late was neither unusual nor unexpected. The woman deemed herself on time if she arrived wherever she was going without missing anything important. This posed problems if Carol drove you somewhere without a firm appointment time or someplace that was open all day. She could arrive ten, twenty, thirty minutes after she promised to pick you up and shrug it off with a wave. "Relax, Barbie," Carol would say. "We're not late."

But the woman was always late, which upset whoever they were meeting, which spiked Barbara's blood pressure, which changed the dynamics, which ruined the entire experience. And all she could do was "relax," since Kate had conned her into not driving anymore.

She sensed movement to her right. She turned and saw a Subaru Wagon fishtail around the corner. The car was going way too fast for a city street. It seemed out of control, engine revving, tires squealing and smoking the pavement. It raced down the lane near the curb and skidded to a stop in front of her.

She bent over a little, trying to look inside, but the tinted windows were too dark. A moment later, the driver's side window rolled down. She saw Carol smiling up at her.

"Sweet ride, huh?" Carol said.

"Carol! What are you doing? You could have killed someone," Barbara said.

"I told you it was fast," a woman's voice said from inside the car.

Barbara looked past Carol to the passenger seat. At first, she couldn't believe her eyes. Then it all made sense. Of course, Yata Miller was involved with Carol test driving a Subaru.

"This thing's a beast," Carol said. "It's got more pick up than I did in my twenties."

Barbara hummed. "Yes, well, that's nice, but we need to get going. We're late already."

"Relax, Barbie," Carol said with a dismissive wave. "We're not late."

Barbara pressed her lips together. "Where's your car, Carol?"

"In Yata's space. Under your building. She's letting me park there while we cruise around in style."

"Then get out, so we can get it," Barbara said.

Carol shook her head. "Nope. We're taking Yata's car today."

"No, we're not."

"We are if you want me to drive you," Carol said. "Plus, Yata's going to the kid's house anyway, so it only makes sense we ride together."

Barbara's eyes got big. "Why is Yata going to Garrett's house?"

"Get in," Carol said. "We'll explain on the way."

Barbara hesitated, then pulled open the door to the back seat. She was certain she wasn't going to like Carol's explanation.

The inside of the Subaru was classier, more sophisticated than she expected for a car whose TV commercials emphasized driving off-road or on a rocky beach by the ocean. The light brown leather interior contrasted with the shiny black console. And although she'd rather choke on her own tongue than admit it, a part of her understood why Yata liked the car.

The instant she closed the door, they were off. Carol had them racing out of town, running as many red lights as she did green.

When they were on the freeway with the tall buildings behind them, Barbara said, "Why are you here, Yata?"

Yata twisted in the seat, looked back at her. "Jeez, Barbie—"

"Don't call me that."

"Veronica asked me to lend a hand. Since you're struggling to find your way."

"I'm not struggling to find my way. And from what I remember, we both started on the same day."

Yata shrugged. "Some people learn faster. Don't take it personally. I've always been a savant. Maybe that's why people say my books are so realistic."

"Aren't your books about vampires in space?" Barbara said.

"Yes." Yata did not appear to catch the sarcasm. "Are you a fan, Barbie?"

She shook her head, rejecting the idea.

"Well, you ought to try them," Yata said. "People swear they've changed their—"

"I can't remember the last book I read," Carol said. "I think it was in high school. Probably that *War and Peace*."

"*War and Peace*?" Barbara said skeptically. "You've never read *War and Peace*."

"Oh, I'm sure I did," Carol said. "It's a wonderful book, ain't it, Yata?"

Yata hummed. "It's very long, Carol. I'm not sure anyone has read the entire book."

"Well, I did," Carol said. "And I'll tell you what. It moved me. You know, because of the all the war and then the peace."

"Uh-huh," Barbara said. "Carol, I'll bet you a hundred dollars you haven't read a thousand pages in your whole life, let alone one book."

The comment made Yata chuckle, which caused Carol's face to

turn red. Carol enjoyed poking fun at others, but she wasn't a good sport when people poked back.

"Oh, you think that's funny, do you?" Carol said, glancing at Barbara through the rear-view mirror.

"I think it's a little funny," Barbara said. "Especially since you refused to get readers last year because you said reading was for chumps."

Carol's eyes narrowed. "Well, just keep on laughing, Barbara Becker. That's the attitude that got Yata appointed as your supervisor."

"Supervisor?" Barbara looked at Yata. "Since when are you my supervisor?"

"Since yesterday," Yata said. "I'm not thrilled either. You know these kids are a lost cause. So I'm here, but not here, if you know what I mean."

Carol scoffed. "That's not what Veronica said. She told you to ride Barbara hard. Make sure the boy wasn't up to no good."

Yata pulled her eyebrows together. "No, she didn't. You're the one who said that."

Barbara met Carol's gaze again in the rear-view mirror. "What's she talking about, Carol? Why were you meeting with Veronica?"

Carol shook her head, sighed in frustration. "Way to go Yata. You weren't supposed to tell her I was there."

"Oh. . . right," Yata said. For a woman who claimed to be a savant, she was slow at connecting the dots. "This doesn't change your interest in a Subaru, does it? Because my nephew can get you a great deal."

"Why did you go behind my back, Carol?" Barbara said.

"To help you." Carol's eyes were alternating between the road and the rear-view mirror as they came up fast on a group of cars packed close together. "I told you there's something off about that boy. He shouldn't be sending us on wild goose chases. Hunting for syrup and Mexican rocks.

"There is no us," Barbara said, "Only me. I'm the grandmother. If you don't want to drive me anymore, I'll find someone else."

Carol hit the brakes, stopping them from colliding with the back of a slow-moving, late model sedan. "Good luck finding somebody. Maybe ask around a truck stop. See if there's an old guy who misses the road."

"Now, you're being absurd," Barbara said. "Garrett didn't make us drive to Houston. We did it. And it was a good thing, too, because the artist had the opal."

"Which you should never have paid five hundred dollars to get."

Yata perked up at the cost. "You paid five hundred dollars for the boy's gift?"

It sounded bad when Yata said it that way.

Barbara said, "Actually, it was a deal. The man said Mexican Fire Opals this red can go for upwards of five grand. So, technically, I made a profit."

Carol laughed. "Okay, genius. We'll all believe the man sold it for five hundred out of the goodness of his heart and not because he was trying to screw you."

"Barbie," Yata said, "you know you're not supposed to buy the children gifts. It violates the handbook."

"I never got a handbook," Barbara said.

"See, I told you she needed to be ridden hard," Carol said.

"And anyway," Barbara said, "it's not a normal gift. The boy has cancer. Some people believe the opal has magical healing qualities."

"Do you believe it heals the sick?" Yata asked.

"What?" Barbara shook her head. "No, of course, not, that's crazy."

Yata hummed. Her eyes narrowed. "I'm going to keep my eye on you, Barbie. I think Carol might have a valid concern."

56

Bhagavan Om Shanti's conference room was what Kate expected from a Buddhist priest turned family court mediator. Which was to say there was nothing conventional about it. No hardwood table. No faux leather chairs. Instead, there were a series of bizarre lounge chairs (if an exercise ball on a moving dolly counted as a chair) arranged in a circle around an octagon-shaped coffee table inlaid with gold leaf. On top of the table, there was a bronzed Buddha statue with two flickering candles. The room lights were dimmed, the shades drawn, and the place smelled of Sandlewood incense.

Yet, the atmosphere was the opposite of calm.

Shanti held out a wooden spoon and flashed Ruth a stern look. Kate wondered how often the Buddhist priest was forced to glare at people during sessions.

"It is because I want to hear you," Shanti said, "that only the person with the spoon may talk."

Since Shanti had invited them into the room, Ruth had been interrupting whoever held the spoon. Whether by design or sheer luck, Ruth hadn't gotten to touch it yet.

"I ain't gonna sit here and let him lie," Ruth said, glaring back at Shanti. "Not when I have proof he's hurting my baby."

Damion scoffed from across the circle.

"I told you this was a waste of time," Damion said to Tina Black, who was on a plastic stool beside him. "The woman's crazy."

Ruth's eyes narrowed. She leaned forward on a clamshell-shaped stool and coiled herself like a snake preparing to strike.

"You think that's nuts?" Ruth said. "Come closer. I'll show you nuts."

Tina Black said, "Ms. Becker, you need to control your client."

"Ruth, calm down," Kate said.

Ruth shook her head, glared at Kate. "I told you never to talk to me again. If you got something to say, say it to Elwood."

Tina Black flashed Kate a confused look.

"Let's try again," Shanti said, reaching deep for patience. "Damion, a moment ago, you expressed a willingness to make the current schedule permanent. Is that something you're still willing to do?"

"I don't know," Damion said.

"Damion, we've been over this," Tina Black said. "If we don't settle today, Judge Eide will schedule a trial. And trials carry risks."

Everyone knew the risk Tina was talking about was Judge Eide's threat to give Ruth sole custody. A part of Kate almost felt sorry for him. Eide had flipped his world upside down for no logical reason.

Damion grumbled, then nodded. "As long as our daughter is safe."

"Safe?" Ruth's voice exploded again. "Safe from who? You?"

"How could anyone be expected to co-parent with her?"

"Ms. Jacobs, please," Shanti said. "Wait for the spoon."

"He doesn't have the spoon," Ruth shot back.

Shanti looked to be nearing the end of his rope. Apparently, even a Zen master has limits. He thanked Damion for being flexible, then reluctantly handed Ruth the spoon. She hesitated for a moment, acting like she might not take it.

"Me? You're going to let me talk?" Ruth said.

Shanti flashed her a tight smile. "Would you be willing to continue a joint schedule, Ruth?"

Ruth glanced past Kate down towards where Elwood sat. She waited for him to pull out a stack of photographs from his briefcase and hand them to her.

Kate glanced at the top picture as it passed by. It was another of Ruth's shoe polish black eyes. Only this time from a new angle.

The room went silent as everyone watched Shanti review the photographs.

"So now you understand," Ruth said, "why I'm so concerned."

"Ruth," Shanti's voice was calm, "it's difficult for a parent to be away from their child."

"Don't patronize me, Om Shanti. If you've got something to say, just say it."

Shanti looked down at his hands. "I think shared custody, fifty-fifty, is a good outcome for you."

"Excuse me?"

"Ruth, we've already seen these pictures. Judge Eide has already seen these pictures."

Ruth shook her head. "No. These are new ones. I took 'em last weekend."

Kate held her breath, hoping no one was actually listening to Ruth. Because if they were, they'd have realized the pictures were fake. Ruth hadn't been alone with Damion in months. There was no way she could have taken new pictures last weekend.

"What I meant," Shanti said, pressing on, his voice beginning to waver under strain, "is that the abuse occurred before you agreed to share custody with Damion. Once you agreed to a joint schedule, you can't use old evidence to say the schedule isn't safe. Do you understand?"

Ruth shook her head. "It don't make no sense. I only agreed because my lawyer made me do it."

Shanti frowned. "Come on, Ruth. You don't believe that."

"Yes, I do. Why do you think I hired a new lawyer?" Ruth glanced down at Elwood. "Tell 'em Elwood. Tell 'em what happened."

A silence fell over the room as all eyes turned to Elwood. The kid struggled to sit up straight in the chair.

Elwood cleared his throat. "Ms. Jacobs feels her options. . . weren't fully explained."

Tina Black's mouth fell open. "Are you saying Kate botched the hearing?"

"I wouldn't say botched," Elwood said.

"I would," Ruth shot back. "She screwed me big time. If Kate had done her job, I never would have settled."

Kate clenched her jaw. It was one thing for Ruth to disrespect her in private, but to call her incompetent at a mediation was too much.

"You work for Kate, right?" Tina asked. "I mean, aren't you basically saying your firm screwed your client?"

"He doesn't work for me," Kate said. "Or Susan."

"What?"

"He's his own man," Ruth said. "It's why I hired him to keep tabs on Kate."

"Is this some sort of joke?" Tina said.

Kate shook her head. "The only reason I'm still here is because Mr. Elwood Lincoln isn't—"

She stopped herself mid-sentence. She wanted to call Elwood out, tell everyone how her screwball client had hired a community college student as her new lawyer. But all it would do was get her fired. Prove The Hatchet right.

If she wanted any chance of keeping her job, she needed to endure this humiliation like it meant nothing.

"What if I had new evidence?" Ruth said to Shanti, eager to be heard. "Evidence that proved Damion was a sexual deviant."

Damion scoffed. "Jesus, she's making it up as she goes now."

Ruth wagged the spoon at Damion. "Wait for the spoon! Wait for the spoon!"

Kate squeezed her eyes shut. She didn't know how much more crazy she could take. You're too close to your dream to give up now, she told herself. Hang in there a little longer. You've been through worse things.

Ruth yelped.

Kate opened her eyes to see Shanti sitting back down in his chair. He was breathing hard, clutching the spoon in his right hand.

"Please," Shanti said, sounding as pained as he looked. "Everyone, take a breath. Calm down." He looked at Ruth. "Unless this new evidence is—"

"It is," Ruth said.

"serious and shows Damion has engaged in criminal-"

"It does," Ruth said.

"conduct." Shanti sighed. "If it's so serious, why didn't you mention it before?"

Ruth paused.

Kate had to give the woman credit. She was like a crocodile. Once her jaws snapped shut, she never let go.

"Because I was afraid no one would believe me. And because Kate silenced me." *Nice touch*, Kate thought. Keep on blaming the lawyer. "But I refuse to be silent anymore."

"Then spit it out, Ruth," Shanti said, sounding annoyed.

"Damion belongs to a secret cult church." Ruth paused as if waiting for people to gasp. "Full of pedophiles."

Damion pushed his chair back, stood up. "That's it. I'm done. I'm not listening to anymore of her crazy."

"Sit down, Damion!" Ruth yelled.

Damion ignored her, looked at Shanti. "Thank you for trying to help us, sir. You seem like a decent guy. But there's no way I'm ever agreeing to give her custody. If the judge does it, fine. But I won't."

"Sit down, Damion!" Ruth yelled.

Damion walked out the door of the conference room. Tina Black followed a step behind.

Ruth's face was bright red. She looked to be on the verge of losing her mind. "If you're not back by the time I count to five, I'm telling him everything. Including the stuff you don't want him to hear!"

Damion didn't come back. And Ruth didn't tell anyone anything.

57

The three women huddled close together on the front porch of the 1940s craftsman-style house, waiting for someone to answer the door. Barbara had tried to convince Carol and Yata to stay in the car, but neither woman would have it.

Carol looked over at Yata. "What should I say when the mother answers?"

"You should say nothing," Barbara said, jumping in to answer. "You're not even supposed to be here."

"Yata!" Carol whined.

Yata shook her head. "No, Barbie's right. You haven't been trained, Carol."

Barbara resisted the urge to ask what sort of training Yata was talking about since she had no training either.

"Don't worry, though," Yata said, "I'll work you in."

"Okay," Carol said, sounding dejected. "But make sure Barbie doesn't talk the whole time. She's a monopolizer."

Barbara raised an eyebrow. "You realize I'm the grandmother, right?"

"Fake grandmother," Carol shot back. "You should say it every time so you don't forget."

"Ladies, please," Yata said. "We're all professionals here. And we're going to need every ounce of patience we can muster if we hope to bear this boy and his mother."

Bear this boy? And his mother? Barbara wondered why Yata had ever volunteered for Grannies R Us. The woman wasn't the altruistic type.

Yata looked down her nose at Barbara. "So, what's the mother's story? Drug addict? Alcoholic? Prostitute?"

"What? No. None of those things. She's a very sweet woman."

Yata chuckled. "Oh, they all are, aren't they? Don't worry, Barbie. I'm going to ask her some tough questions. We're going to figure out what she's hiding."

"Please don't," Barbara said. "The woman's under enormous stress. Her son is sick."

"So she claims," Carol said, butting in. "No one's been able to confirm it. And I, myself, find it quite suspicious that the hospital won't even confirm he's a patient."

Barbara's mouth fell open. "You called the hospital?"

"Of course, I called the hospital," Carol said before turning towards Yata. "It is suspicious, ain't it?"

Yata shrugged. "There are a lot of stupid laws, Carol. Everyone thinks they're the CIA now, neither confirming nor denying. The whole county is going down the tubes."

"Don't tell me about privacy rules," Carol said. "I know all about them. That's why I pretended to be the boy's mother. Still, they wouldn't tell me anything because I couldn't remember his birthday." Carol paused, shook her head in disgust. "Some people are so distrusting."

Yata nodded. "Yep. No argument there."

A moment later, the deadbolt snapped back, and the door opened.

Garrett's mother stood inside. She looked like death. Dressed in an old gray sweatshirt and plaid pajama pants, the woman's hair was tousled, and there were dark lines under her eyes. She was sick or hungover, or both.

"Oh, Barbara," Heather said, zeroing in on her. The woman's voice was full of regret. "I'm so sorry. I meant to call."

"Is everything all right?" Barbara asked.

"Hellooo," Yata said, stepping forward and extending a hand. "I'm Yata Miller. Barbara Becker's supervisor. And this is Carol, a concerned citizen."

Heather shook Yata's hand. Then Carol's too.

"That's not my permanent title," Carol said. "We're still negotiating."

Heather glanced back and forth between Yata and Carol, appearing confused.

"Ignore them," Barbara said. "What's going on?"

"Did someone party a little too hard last night?" Yata asked, leaning to the side and looking inside the house, presumably searching for empty liquor bottles.

Heather forced a laugh. "I wish. Garrett had a little trouble breathing. I almost had to take him to the ER."

"Oh, I'm sorry," Barbara said.

"We'll see who's sorry," Carol said, butting in and holding up a finger like a bulldog attorney cross-examining a witness. "I have but one question, ma'am. A simple yes or no. You don't deny not taking the boy to any hospital, such that no record can be found to prove this supposed claim, which is not really a claim at all because it's not supported by any evidence, except for things which cannot be proven, because you didn't do them. Have I got it right?"

Heather's face soured, her eyes narrowed. "I don't care for your question."

Yata agreed. "Neither do I, Carol. It's very difficult to understand. It's excruciatingly long and peppered with passive voice. I think you should wait in the car. We'll talk about sentence construction on the way home."

"Fine," Carol grumbled. She turned, went down the steps, followed the path back towards the Subaru Wagon on the street. Over her shoulder, she said, "In *The War and the Peace*, the sentences were even longer!"

Yata shook her head. "Please forgive the woman's behavior. She isn't affiliated with Grannies R Us. She only came along to test drive the Subaru."

Heather looked confused.

"Listen," Yata said, "I see the oxygen tank. The IV pole. I gather your son really is sick."

"Was there ever a doubt?" Heather asked.

"No, not with me," Yata said. "Though, people tell me I'm too trusting."

Heather looked at Barbara. "We're going to have to reschedule. Garrett's resting."

"Of course, I understand," Barbara said. She reached into her purse, pulled out a small jewelry box. "Could you give this to him for me?"

Heather took the box, opened it. "A rock?"

Barbara shook her head. "He'll know what it is. We've talked about it."

"Okay. Say, that reminds me. Garrett left something for you, too. Let me grab it."

The woman disappeared inside the house. She returned a moment later, carrying a sealed manila envelope. She handed it to Barbara.

58

When they were back in Yata's Subaru, Carol racing them down the freeway, Yata in the front seat, Barbara in the back, Barbara tore open the envelope.

"What is it?" Carol said, glancing back over her shoulder.

Barbara reached inside, pulled out the contents. There was a wallet-sized school picture of Garrett and a short handwritten note. Beneath that was a sheet of copy paper, on which, in big block letters colored in red, yellow, and blue crayons, Garrett had written the phrase, "World's Greatest Grandmother."

"Oh, how sweet," Barbara said.

"Give it to Yata," Carol demanded.

Barbara shook her head. "No, it's private."

"Private? What are you? His girlfriend now? Pass it up."

"No."

"I swear to God, Barbara Becker, if you don't hand it up right now, I'm pulling this car over and prying it out of your fingers. I ain't gonna be gentle either."

"You're out of control, Carol," Barbara said.

Yata cleared her throat, then joined the conversation, using her snotty, patronizing voice. "Actually, Barbie, I do need to see it. As your supervisor, I must know everything."

Barbara hummed. She didn't want to show them the note, but she didn't think she had a choice. Yata could report her to Veronica, claim she was uncooperative. Plus, holding it back would only pique Yata's interest, making it seem worse when she read it later.

Reluctantly, Barbara handed the papers forward.

Yata glanced at the picture, then scanned the World's Greatest Grandmother certificate before taking the time to read the note.

"What does it say?" Carol said, her eyes alternating between the road and the papers in Yata's lap.

Yata shrugged. "It's innocent, Carol. Pathetic, but innocent. The boy says she should put the drawing on her refrigerator like a 'real grandma.' Then he talks about drinking hot chocolate with marshmallows. It's quite sad. I think the kid's a little slow, if you know what I mean."

"He's not slow," Barbara said.

"He might be. Look at this." Yata held up the note so Carol could see it. She pointed at a postscript. "He wants a copy of *Dorothy Rides Again*. Need I say more?"

For a second, Barbara thought she was the only one who didn't understand the reference. But then she glanced at Carol and saw her squirming in her seat. It was clear she didn't understand it either and was trying to decide whether to pretend that she did, in order to preserve some phony sense of being well read, or admitting she didn't, so Yata would explain it.

After a long pause, Carol opted to get dirt on the boy.

"I've never heard of it," Carol said.

"Of course, you haven't," Yata said. "Only people in the biz know it. Some people say it's the worst novel ever published in English. Personally, I think that's idiotic because how can a New York book be worse than self-published trash? I mean, seriously, people?"

"Why is it so bad?" Barbara asked.

"Why is it so bad?" Yata shuttered. "How much time do you have? The simple answer is a guy at the publisher figured out he was going to be fired before he was supposed to know. So, in an act of revenge, he screwed with the book. Laid it out all wrong. Moved chapters around. Rearranged paragraphs. Even cut full sentences. And let me assure you, the author was no writer before this artistic rendering. The entire thing is incomprehensible."

"How did it still get printed?" Barbara asked.

Yata raised an eyebrow. "Um, because few people read books before they're printed. And this guy was the last stop on the line."

Carol waved a hand at them. "Okay, we get it. The book is awful. No one cares why. Tell me this, Yata. Why would the boy, who's a bit of a schemer, ask Barbie to get it for him?"

"Oh, well, that part's easy," Yata said. "After the publisher spotted the error, they tried to corral all the books. But you can't put the genie back in the bottle. They've become a collector's item now. They sell for a few grand online."

"See, I told you," Carol said, her voice growing more animated. "The kid's a bad seed. First, he asks you to buy him that expensive syrup. Then he asks for a five hundred dollar piece of jewelry. Now, he wants a thousand dollar book. When is it going to end?"

Barbara felt her face turn red. She knew Carol wasn't totally off base. The kid's requests were bordering on too much, and she couldn't afford it anyway, not without asking her daughters for help, which was something she wasn't prepared to do. But Carol also believed Garrett was faking cancer, so Barbara didn't give her twisted theories too much weight.

Barbara said, "Did it ever occur to you that maybe he just wants to read it?"

Carol laughed. "No, Barbie. It did not."

"Maybe it should have."

"Don't be silly, Barbie," Yata said, "No one reads *Dorothy Rides Again*. It's a moot point, though, because you're not buying it for him. As your supervisor, I forbid it."

"Forbid it?"

"Yes."

Barbara scoffed. "You can't forbid me from doing something."

"I can," Yata said. "And I did."

Barbara rolled her eyes. "I think I'm old enough to make my own decisions, thank you. And while I don't plan on buying Garrett a thousand dollar book, if I were to find one at an estate sale-"

"No," Yata said, shaking her head. "This is about more than money, Barbie. When we became volunteer grandmothers, we take an oath—"

"I never took an oath."

"—to be faithful and honest and true. To impart wisdom. To correct for bad parenting. To maximize a child's limited potential, as hindered by genetics."

"That's offensive," Barbara said.

"But it's our oath all the same. Our sacred duty, Barbie. We must resist the urge to be clown grandmothers, dallying around as personal shoppers or circus acts, existing only to entertain the children. We must hold the line against the darkness. For no less than the fate of humanity rests upon our shoulders."

Carol jerked the Subaru to a stop at the curb outside Barbara's building.

When she was out of the car, Carol rolled down the window and called to her.

"We're watching you, Barbie Becker!"

59

A strip mall with a liquor store and a weight loss center was not the sort of place Matt Simpson expected to find a mediator's office. But it made him respect the man more. Say what you wanted about his ridiculous name. Bhagavan Om Shanti was obviously an expert at twisting arms. The proof was in The Problem Solving Center's continued existence. People didn't pay three hundred dollars an hour to visit a storefront that could have been a cell phone store or a Karate studio unless they got value somehow.

Matt's plan was to ambush Kate Becker in the parking lot as she left Bhagavan's office after the mediation session. It was the only way he could think of to make contact with her. He had already tried calling her office, but the receptionist who answered referred him to a PR person named Patricia Vulcan. Susan Wilson Law didn't like its attorneys talking to reporters.

The upside of the plan, if you called it an upside, was that it complied with Bowers's ambush recommendation.

At nine thirty-five, the door to Bhagavan's storefront flung open. A man stormed out. He stopped in the first row of parking spaces, glanced back over his shoulder, then turned to face a woman who followed behind him. She stopped close to him but not so close that he could hit her.

The two argued loudly. The man waved his hands in the air. The woman appeared not to be fazed by his theatrics. Matt couldn't hear what they said, but he knew the woman had won the argument when the man slammed the car door and squealed his tires on the way out of the lot.

The woman was Tina Black. He knew this from a picture he saw online. She wasn't as pretty as her glamour shot, her hair was tied high in a bun, and she wore glasses and no smile. Even so, she was attractive. More so to him, since she didn't seem bothered by what had transpired.

A few minutes later, the door to the suite opened again. This time, a smug-looking woman in a yellow sundress came out, flanked by a teenage boy wearing a white button-down shirt and black slacks. The boy seemed to be an assistant, as he was carrying the woman's purse and careful to stay a step behind her.

They stopped near the driver's side door of a black BMW. The woman motioned for the boy to hand her something. He reached inside the purse and pulled out what appeared to be a silver lipstick container. She twisted it open, then wrote a single word in big block letters across the BMW's front windshield. Then the two climbed into a beat-up old pickup truck and drove away laughing.

A moment later, Kate Becker came out of the office. Matt approached her as she reached the BMW.

"You got to be kidding," Kate said, shaking her head in disgust.

The word sellout was written in big letters across her windshield.

"It's only lipstick," Matt said. "The woman in the white pickup did it."

"Yeah, I know who did it."

"I'm Matt Simpson," he said. "I'm an investigative reporter with The Austin Free Press. I was hoping to ask you a few questions about a story I'm working on."

"Does it involve Susan Wilson Law?"

"In a way."

Kate shook her head. "Then I can't talk. Firm policy requires—"

"Media go through PR. Yeah, I know. Your receptionist gave me the same line. I hung up on her."

"You hung up on her?"

Matt shrugged. "Listen, I'm going to be straight with you. I don't have time for games. I have a source, a well-placed source, who's helping me with a story about Tina Black and Judge McDaniel."

This piqued her interest.

"What story?" Kate asked.

"So, I can assume you don't know anything about it then?" he asked.

It was a gamble to put her on the spot that way, but he needed to find out what she knew without swaying her.

"No," she said. "Of course, I've heard things."

"Things you can share with me?"

She studied him for a moment. "Why are you here, Mr. Simpson? There are a hundred lawyers in the city who know Tina Black and Judge McDaniel better than me."

"Could we talk someplace more private?" he asked. "I'd rather not go into it in the middle of a parking lot."

"Fine," Kate said. "Meet me at five o'clock this afternoon. At a place called Driscoll's. Have you ever heard of it?"

For a second, Matt thought he heard wrong. Driscoll's? He wondered what the odds were of a sophisticated lawyer like Kate Becker randomly picking the same dive bar where he met The Eagle?

"The place on El Dorado?"

Kate nodded. "You do know it. Don't be late, Mr. Simpson."

He wanted to ask her if she'd be wearing a helmet party mask, but he bit his tongue. It didn't seem like a smart move.

60

If Kate hadn't seen it with her own eyes, she never would have believed it. Driscoll's Bar was less appealing at five in the afternoon than at nine o'clock at night. The ambiance was the same. Jukebox tunes and sticky tables. But there was no popcorn to mask the stale beer or normal people to soften the edges of the regulars.

She had arrived early to pick a booth in the back, away from the door, so no one would overhear them, though it turned out they could have sat anywhere and gone unnoticed. The place was deserted. The worn-out men at the bar looked like zombies. She doubted they would have even glanced over if she started dancing on the table.

Not that she would ever do that again.

"I'll have a club soda," Kate said to the bartender as he wandered over, polishing water spots from a glass with a checkered dishtowel.

He rolled his eyes. "We're not doing it again, are we?"

"I don't know what you're talking about," Kate lied.

She had been to Driscoll's only once before. A recruitment event her sister had organized for The Austin Chess Club. It was a disaster. The intern who had managed it confused Driscoll's on El

Dorado with Driscell on State Street. The two bars were not similar; their patrons were not equally interested in chess. In fact, the only person at Driscoll's who bothered to pick up a brochure that night was a one-armed lumberjack who tossed it back after he heard the monthly dues. "I play for free on the 'puter," he said, stumbling back to the bar. Of course, this was all before Willa. Willa would never have made such a mistake.

Kate couldn't remember who suggested they stay and drink, only that it wasn't her or Jessica, which left Terry Eide or Sergei Petrov. Or both. Terry had been crushing on her for weeks. Sergei flirted with Jessica incessantly. It was why the two men had volunteered to be co-ambassadors.

Her memory of what happened next was hazier. There were shots of vodka. Beer. More vodka, rum, and a round of Long Island Ice Teas to commemorate her time in the Northeast.

Then someone suggested a game of truth or dare.

As her sister retold it the following day, Kate climbed on top of the table wearing only a mismatched bra and panties and surfed a wave all the way back to shore. When she heard this, she pulled the covers up over her head and resolved to become a homesteader in Alaska to hide her shame. Fortunately, this proved unnecessary because Jessica said Terry Eide and Sergei Petrov had drunk more and remembered less than she did.

This was months ago, and word of her surfing still hadn't reached polite society, so when she needed to pick a place to meet the reporter where no one would know her, she traded a few minutes of uncomfortable memories for the privacy Driscoll's offered.

The door to the bar swung open. Matt Simpson came inside, glanced around, then made his way past the high-top tables to the booth where she was sitting.

"I'm not kidding," the bartender said before Matt got close enough to hear, "keep it low key, all right? My boss chewed me out last time."

Kate nodded to get the man to leave.

"One club soda, and one Chivas," the bartender said as he walked away.

Matt Simpson slid onto the bench across from her. For a second, Kate wondered how the bartender knew his drink order, then thought better of it and let it go.

"Tell me about this story," Kate said.

Matt Simpson shook his head. "First, tell me what you've heard about Judge McDaniel."

"What do you mean?"

"Are women lawyers talking about him?"

She raised an eyebrow. "Talking about him? Please tell me you mean what in some unconventional way."

"Have you heard he's harassing women?"

Kate forced a laugh. "Judge McDaniel? Are you joking?"

"You're sure?"

Kate nodded. "A hundred percent. McDaniel is the world's last boy scout. They don't make arrows straighter than him."

The reporter's face fell. He tried to hide his disappointment, but she saw it anyway. A person didn't get hired by Susan Wilson if they weren't good at reading people.

"What can you tell me about Tina Black?" he asked.

Kate shrugged. "How much time do you have? The woman's a snake." Her flippant answer didn't amuse him. "She's the anti-McDaniel. Does that help? Not the slightest bit straight."

"Do you think she'd do something unethical to advance her career?"

"Yes."

He leaned forward, rested his elbows on the table. "Did you see the article about her in The Austin Times?"

Kate shrugged. "Maybe."

He summarized the article, getting most of it right. The guy wouldn't have lasted a week at Susan Wilson Law with his sloppiness, but he worked for The Austin Free Press, which wasn't a paper to write home about, so she let it slide, figuring he was doing his best. She only started paying attention when he explained the relationship between The Austin Times reporter and Judge McDaniel's law clerk. When he finished, he leaned back and crossed his arms, acting like he had confided a great secret to her.

She was trying, very much wanting, to believe the worst about Tina Black, but even she was having trouble connecting the dots the reporter was drawing.

"What are you implying?" Kate asked.

"Isn't it obvious?" Matt Simpson looked annoyed. "Tina Black and Judge McDaniel are having a sexual relationship. He ruled against your client and arranged for The Times article to advance her career."

The bartender saved her from having to hide her reaction by returning and clanking down their drinks.

The idea that Tina Black was sleeping with Judge McDaniel was mind-boggling. Judge McDaniel was a white-haired geriatric with bushy eyebrows, hearing aids, yellow teeth, and a stomach so big he had to put his hands on his lower back for balance every time he stood up. He had suffered two massive heart attacks on the bench, and Kate always assumed he was impotent.

"Are you sure?" she asked when the bartender was gone.

"You're saying my source is wrong?"

"No, but— We're talking about Chief Judge Randolph McDaniel, right?"

"Do you know of any other McDaniels?" Matt Simpson said.

"No, but I was hoping there might be."

"You just told me that Tina Black was a woman who'd do anything to advance her career."

"Yes, but I'm not sure anything stretches that far."

"It does," Matt Simpson said. "No one's saying she's in love. It's purely transactional."

"I suppose."

"Listen," he said. "I'm the last person who's interested in sex gossip. But the story isn't about that. It's about McDaniel misusing his office. Ruling for Tina Black's clients in exchange for sexual favors."

Kate hummed.

"Can you think of anything in your case with Tina Black that proves Judge McDaniel shouldn't have awarded the father custody during that first hearing?"

Kate glanced away for a moment. She stared off towards the bartender across the room. The man was hunched forward, rinsing glasses in a tiny sink under the bar.

The truth was McDaniel hadn't done anything wrong. Of course, Eide's prompting to reverse the order made it seem like he screwed up, but if that morning's mediation proved anything, it was that McDaniel's instincts about Ruth were right.

She looked back at him. "I can't point to anything, specifically. The law's very discretionary."

"Think," he said, snapping at her.

She didn't appreciate the tone.

"Look, I'd love to expose Tina more than anyone, but I can't give you what I don't have. Go back to your source. Ask for more."

"You think I haven't tried that already? They can't get in the middle of the story. They're too close."

The explanation made no sense to her. Weren't whistle-blowers always in the middle of a story?

"So what, then?" Kate asked.

"I guess he gets away with it."

"You're just giving up?"

"I don't have a choice. There's nowhere for me to go."

Kate scoffed. "What percentage of my cases do you think seem like losers at first? No guess? Okay, I'll tell you. All of them. Every. Single. One. And do you know why? Because if they didn't seem like losers, a partner would have stolen them from me. To get ahead, you need to learn how to turn a frog into a prince."

"Thanks for the Cinderella metaphor. Unfortunately, I don't have a frog if no one will go on the record."

Kate shook her head. "There's always a frog. It just might not be the one you think."

"What I think is our jobs are very different."

"Maybe. But we're both searching for things others don't want us to find. Perhaps you can't write a story about McDaniel's misconduct. Not yet. But you could write a story about how his decision was reversed after my client hired a lawyer. Let the implication hang in the wind awhile. It might shake something lose."

"Even if I wanted to, I couldn't. The paper doesn't run stories about custody cases. Not unless they involve a celebrity."

Kate pursed her lips. "What if it weren't a straight piece?"

"I don't understand."

"Why not write a story about how The Austin Times profile of Tina Black was fake news. You could interview me. Use the article as cover to lob shots at Tina Black and Judge McDaniel."

Matt Simpson hummed. "I don't know."

"Think about it. You never know what will happen if you pull the right thread."

Kate dropped a five-dollar bill on the table and left. She glanced back when she reached the door and saw him flash a funny look that made her wish a different reporter had found the story.

61

At noon on the day after the meeting at Driscoll's Bar, Kate met Matt Simpson in a downtown park surrounded by skyscrapers.

It was a suitable spot for an interview. The concrete table where they sat was in the shade and set back far enough from the street to provide some privacy, but not so far it was a pain to reach. There was grass and mature trees and in the distance a pond where a person was kayaking. During the moments in between his meandering questions, she could hear the faint sounds of children playing. It was the type of place that made you want to stay and keep talking just to avoid going back to your real life.

But even an oasis becomes a prison, eventually. Kate's coffee had turned cold, her lower back ached, and she needed to use the bathroom.

"So," Kate said, nudging him forward, "do you have everything you need?"

"Um, one second."

He was looking down at a spiral, flip-style notebook scanning the notes he had taken. Ninety-nine percent of them were worthless answers to questions he shouldn't have asked. No one cared why she went to law school or if she had always been interested in chess. If she had been interviewing him, she would have finished thirty minutes ago. Even Riley would be done by now.

But Matt Simpson was a moron.

The few reasonable questions he had asked didn't come from good preparation. They resulted from the law of large numbers. Ask enough stuff, and you'll stumble on something.

She tried not to let him see these thoughts. Instead, she focused on being pleasant and professional and helpful. She pinched her thigh when he asked her about her favorite food. She restrained herself because Matt Simpson had agreed to run the puff piece she suggested. An hour of stupid questions was a small price for getting her picture on the paper's front page.

"Give me another minute," he said. "I want to be sure I can read everything."

Kate sighed, then reached across the table and tapped the red microphone icon on Matt's cell phone. The recording app stopped blinking.

"The benefit of recording a meeting is you don't need to worry about the notes." He blushed. "At least, that's how I see it. I record so I can listen to the answers. Ask smart follow-up questions. But you should do whatever works for you."

"They make us do both," Matt Simpson said.

"Okay," Kate said, not believing it for a second. People got so defensive when you tried to help them.

"I think the only thing left is the pictures," Matt said.

Kate frowned. She wouldn't mind sitting for a few photos with a professional photographer, but Matt had insisted the pictures be taken in the park, which made her worried she'd wind up standing in front of a tree looking like a do-it-yourself high school glamor shot.

"You checked with your editor, right?" Kate asked. "You're sure we can't use a picture from our website? I could email you a high resolution file."

Matt Simpson shook his head. "Don't worry. It won't take long.

My photographer's waiting in the car. Have you heard from Ruth? We can start as soon as she gets here."

Kate hummed. *We're going to be waiting a long time*, she thought. Because I didn't invite her. Nor will you ever speak to her, if I can help it.

"Let me check my phone," Kate said. "Maybe she left me a message."

She grabbed her phone off the table and pretended to scroll through messages.

"Sorry. Nothing."

"But she is coming, right?" Matt Simpson asked.

Kate shrugged. "I think she said she'd try. Something must have come up. She's not a person who makes people wait."

"Then let's give her a little more time. I'd hate to miss her."

"Sure, of course." Kate squirmed on the bench. She needed to use the bathroom, and she would not sit on a public toilet. "I can wait a few minutes, but then we should take the pictures. I have a one-thirty."

She didn't have a one-thirty, but she wasn't going to waste an entire afternoon waiting for someone who wasn't coming.

"If you need to go, go," Matt Simpson said. "I can wait. I have nothing today."

"Oh, how wonderful."

Five minutes later, he said, "You could give me her number. I'll call her myself."

Kate shook her head. "I wish I could. But, you know, rules."

A woman's voice called out to them. "I'm here. I'm here. Sorry, I'm late. Traffic was horrible."

Ruth Jacobs rushed over to the table and dropped a gigantic faux leather purse on top of it. Dressed in her ever-present yellow sundress uniform, she smiled and extended a hand towards Matt. Her hair was shiny and full of volume like she had come from the salon. She wore bright red lipstick, dark eyeliner, and enough blush to tell Kate she knew about the photographs.

"Kate's told me so many nice things about you," Ruth said to him.

"It's good to meet you, Ms. Jacobs. I was just telling Kate how I hoped you'd come. There's no story without you."

Ruth smiled. "Oh, aren't you a sweetie? I almost didn't make it. There was a mix-up. If I hadn't called Kate's office, I never would have known."

Kate smiled. "I would have called to remind you, but I can only talk to Elwood."

Matt Simpson raised an eyebrow. "Who's Elwood?"

"My number one lawyer," Ruth said.

Matt looked confused. "I thought Kate was your lawyer."

"I am."

Ruth shook her head. "Kate's my number two lawyer. Elwood is my number one."

"Is he at your firm, Kate?"

"No," Kate said. "He's at Alameda Community College."

The answer seemed to confuse Matt Simpson, but that was how it was dealing with Ruth.

Kate said, "It's nothing that affects the story, Matt. I say we take the pictures and move on."

"I had to hire Elwood to monitor Kate," Ruth said. "To double check she was telling me the whole truth."

Matt glanced at Kate, and she saw a flash of distrust in his eyes. Maybe he will grow up to be a real reporter someday.

"Let's take the pictures," he said.

Matt called the photographer. They walked over to a group of trees and waited as a burly man in an untucked black t-shirt and slacks pulled a rolling suitcase up a path from the parking lot.

"Is the baby here?" Matt asked.

Ruth laughed. "Oh, heavens, no. Did you think I left it in the truck?"

"Is she close by? Could someone bring her over?"

Ruth frowned. "Bring it over? Why?"

"It would look good if you held her."

"It's just a baby. Everyone's seen plenty. Plus, I'm not holding anything. It'll make me look fat."

The photographer worked fast, taking pictures first of Kate, then of Ruth, then of the two of them together. Kate left as soon as he was done. All things considered, it could have gone worse.

62

Matt Simpson waited until Kate and Ruth were gone before reaching into his pocket and pulling out a wad of twenty-dollar bills. He handed them to the photographer.

He was forced to hire his own photographer, a discount wedding guy he found online, because none of the newspaper's editors knew he was writing the story. And he needed to keep it that way until he nailed down the facts a little more.

When he left the park and was on the sidewalk by the street, a woman called out to him.

"That photographer seemed real good."

He turned and saw Ruth Jacobs coming towards him.

"I wish Kate were that good," Ruth said.

The photographer was not good at all. The man had snapped pictures like a machine gunner fearing for his life. The entire affair took less than ten minutes, and not once did he give any indication of skill or art or craft.

"I'm sure Kate's much better," Matt said.

Ruth shrugged. "Maybe sometimes. But not with me. You know she's a volunteer, right?"

"So?"

"So? It means she's getting paid another way."

"Another way? I don't follow."

"This story you're writing," Ruth said. "It's about her, ain't it?"

There had been no talk of the story during the photoshoot. Matt assumed Kate had already explained it all to Ruth, but apparently not.

"An element is, yes."

"See," Ruth said. "She's gettin' paid another way. How much does a big story cost, anyway?"

He didn't like her tone.

"You can't buy a story, Ruth," Matt said.

"Sure, you can. I bet this whole thing was her idea. Tell me I'm wrong."

"I need to get going. It was nice meeting you, Ms. Jacobs."

He turned away from her and began walking in the opposite direction from where he wanted to go. It was better to cut back in a block or two than continue conversing with her. As his feet kept moving, he sensed her following behind.

"Ain't it fishy that she keeps making the story about herself? Instead of her client?"

If I don't acknowledge her, eventually she'll go away, he thought.

But she didn't.

She stayed behind him for a long block before hustling up alongside and keeping a step in front so he couldn't help but see her.

"You know she sold me out, right?" Ruth said. "Some super lawyer she is."

"I've seen the court file, Ms. Jacobs. You agreed to joint custody." He regretted speaking the instant the words left his mouth. Encouraging her only made it worse.

"Because she didn't tell me the judge wanted me to have one hundred percent custody. Did you know that, Mr. Reporter?"

He stopped at the curb by a crosswalk and waited for the signal to change. A stream of cars whizzed down the one-way street. He kept his eyes focused forward, but she stared at him hard, giving him no choice but to answer.

"Nothing in the file suggests Judge Eide wanted you to have sole custody."

Ruth leaned forward an inch, her head hanging over the curb so she could look back at him. "Of course, they don't put it in the file. Lawyers don't write the bad stuff down."

The light changed. Matt crossed the street quickly, hoping to put some distance between them. It didn't work. By the time he reached the sidewalk, she was at his side again.

"You know Kate's boss don't like her, right?" Ruth said.

Matt stopped. He turned to face her as people streamed past them.

"She didn't tell you that part, did she?" Ruth reached into her purse, rummaged around for a moment, then pulled out a business card and handed it to him. "Her boss gave me her personal cell number."

The card was for a person called Patricia Vulcan. Matt knew the name from somewhere, but he couldn't place it. He glanced at the handwritten telephone number, then handed the card back to her.

"It proves nothing."

"It proves they don't trust her," Ruth said. "And neither should you. She's got her own agenda."

"And you don't?"

Ruth smiled. "Of course I do. It's my case. But you know what my agenda is. To protect my baby."

He wondered if she actually believed what she had said.

"Why are you telling me this?"

"Because I want you to write the real story. Tell people what's happening."

"That's what I'm trying to do," he said.

"Then why aren't you doing it?" Ruth shot back, raising her voice.

"Because I don't have a source who will confirm Tina Black's relationship with Judge McDaniel!"

She had provoked him, made him yell, lose his cool.

A woman passing on the sidewalk glanced at him, then quickly looked away. Ruth had flinched when he yelled. Her reaction lasted only an instant, but he saw it all the same.

"I'm sorry," Matt said. "I shouldn't have yelled."

"It's all right."

"No. It was unprofessional."

"In my book, honesty beats phony every time."

"Thanks."

"If you have a minute, maybe I can help your story."

He wanted to tell her no, but he had just yelled at her on the street.

Ten minutes later, they were sitting at a small round table in a chain coffee shop. The place was deserted. He offered to buy her coffee to apologize, and she ordered a six-dollar blended drink with whipped cream on top.

"What did you want to tell me?" he asked.

She glanced down at her drink, then back up at him. "On the street, you mentioned Tina Black and the other judge."

"Yes. Do you know anything about that?"

She looked down at her drink again. "Forget it."

"Ruth, if you know something, you need to say it."

"It's probably not true."

"Tell me."

"Just pretend I never mentioned it, okay? Write the story about Kate. I'm sure it will be real good."

Matt leaned forward, rested his elbows on the table. "Ruth, the judge we're talking about, is it the chief judge of Travis County? Because if he's doing something wrong, people need to know."

She bit her lower lip, hesitated for a moment. "But if anyone finds out I'm the one who talked, I'd be ruined."

"No one will find out, Ruth. I won't tell a soul."

She gazed over his shoulder. He could tell from the pained look on her face she wanted to talk but was afraid.

"You could remain anonymous," he said.

"That's possible?"

"Sure. Happens all the time."

"I guess that'd be okay."

He nodded. "Go ahead. Tell me what you know."

She took a deep breath, then paused so long he thought she might changed her mind. Then, suddenly, she blurted it out.

"They're doing it, Mr. Simpson. Tina Black and that judge. Nasty sex."

Matt's heart skipped a beat. Her words were exactly what he hoped to hear. Finally, someone had confirmed it. He had himself a real story.

63

It was a week after Barbara argued with Yata before she could arrange another visit to Garrett's house. Partly, this was because she was playing phone tag with the boy's mother, whose voicemail box was full and refusing messages, and partly because she was waiting for the book to arrive in the mail.

At first, Barbara planned to visit estate sales to find a copy of *Dorothy Rides Again*. But midway through the first day, after spending over a hundred dollars in rideshare fees, she realized how foolish that idea was. It could take years, decades even to stumble on the book.

Instead, she used the emergency credit card Kate had given her to buy the book online from a guy in Ohio. It cost fifteen hundred bucks, but she negotiated free shipping, so she didn't feel too bad. Plus, it wasn't all that much money if you compared it to how much a real grandparent spent on their grandchild over sixteen years. And didn't the boy deserve at least that much? He had cancer, after all.

With the back of her hand, she knocked on Garrett's bedroom door, then went inside. He was on the bed again, lying on his back on top of the covers, his head propped up with pillows, his ankles crossed. His face was hidden behind a yellowed paperback. He was wearing the same t-shirt and jeans she had seen the last time.

He lowered the book, smiled at her.

"Grandma Becker, what a treat. Come sit down. Listen to this." He waited for her to sit beside the bed before reading from the book in his hands. "Did you know that Babe Ruth hugged Lou Gehrig after his famous speech at Yankee Stadium?"

Barbara recognized the name Babe Ruth, but that was far as her baseball knowledge went. She wasn't a fan of the game, finding it only slightly more exciting than chess.

"Wow. Very interesting," she said.

"It is interesting, isn't it? My mom doesn't like it when I read baseball facts."

Barbara didn't like it either, but if Garrett loved baseball, she'd learn to like it, at least a little, for him. She couldn't understand why his mom hadn't done the same.

"So you love the game, huh?"

"Nope," Garrett said, shaking his head. "I just like reading baseball facts to people. Did you know that Lou Gehrig played in 2,130 straight games?"

Did he just say he only enjoyed reading facts to people? That he didn't care about the game itself? She wasn't sure she could pretend to listen to random trivia, which meant nothing to anyone. Even grandmothers had limits.

She smiled. "I did not know that."

"Guess how many years that was?"

"Years? I don't know. Six?"

"Six?" He lowered the book and frowned at her. "How many games do you think they play every year? Four hundred?"

"I don't know."

"Come on. Guess again. This time, for real."

"I don't know, Garrett."

He sighed. "We're talking about facts, Grandma Becker. Interesting facts. The answer is fourteen, all right?"

"Okay."

"Here's another one. In the middle of his career, a pitch once hit Lou Gehrig in the eye and knocked him unconscious for a full five minutes. Five minutes! Has anyone has ever knocked you unconscious, Grandma Becker?"

"No."

"That's good. How many games do you think he missed because of it?"

Barbara fidgeted in the chair. Listening to him read facts and doing this little back and forth was excruciatingly painful. She didn't know how much longer she could stand it.

"I don't know," Barbara said. "Five? Ten?"

Garrett frowned. "It was a trick question, Grandma Becker. He didn't miss any games since he played 2,130 in a row. Are you even listening? I thought you said these facts were interesting."

Barbara leaned forward, snatched the book from his hand.

"Hey," he whined. "What'd you do that for?"

"I'm taking it with me so I can learn facts. We'll read more later. In the meantime, I got a present for you. Something you'll like even better."

She reached into her purse and pulled out a thick paperback. She handed it to him.

Garrett's eyes went wide when he saw the title on the cover.

"I can't believe it," he said, stammering. "You actually found a copy of *Dorothy Rides Again*?"

She nodded, trying not to smile. She had never felt more proud of herself than she did at that moment. Carol and Yata were idiots. The boy's reaction was worth all the money she paid.

"You like it?" she asked.

"Of course, I like it," Garrett said. "But it's too much. I can't accept it."

He tried to hand the book back to her, but she refused to take it.

"I want you to have it, Garrett. You deserve it. Why don't you read me a few pages?"

Garrett paused, appearing to think it over, then exhaled an

exaggeratingly slow breath. "I want to, I do, but I don't have the energy."

Barbara flashed him a puzzled look. He didn't seem the least bit tired when he was quizzing her on baseball facts.

"Then give me the book," she said. "I'll read it to you."

He shook his head. "Could we cut our visit short today? Just this once. I don't feel good."

He was lying. She almost called him on it too, but she caught herself. If he wanted her to leave, she should go. It didn't matter why. She had only come to help him.

"Of course," Barbara said. "Whatever you think is best."

"Can you put the book in my special spot? Along with all my other treasures?"

She took the book to the dresser, pulled open the bottom drawer. Her heart sunk when she saw the unopened bottle of pomegranate molasses next to the jewelry box with the Mexican Fire Opal.

She put the book inside and closed it. It's not about you, she reminded herself. You're doing this for him.

"Grandma Becker," he said over her shoulder, as she was leaving the room.

"Yes, Garrett."

"I love you, Grandma. I feel like the luckiest boy on the face of the Earth."

She thanked him, then hurried out of the house, preferring to wait by the curb for her rideshare car so she could be alone with her thoughts.

The kid was messing with her, right? He didn't actually love her. They had only spoken twice. Plus, there was no way he could think he was the luckiest boy on the face of the Earth. He had cancer. She shook her head in disgust.

But as she waited, she wondered if she was being too hard on him. Was it possible he did believe it? Could she be effecting his life more than she realized? Could her very presence somehow be transformative?

Because if so, then she was an outstanding grandmother. And maybe he kept those presents in a drawer because they were treasures.

64

The day after Kate spoke to her Certified Online Internet Protector, the guy she paid to vacation in Panama, she sat with her back to the wall at a tiny two-seat table inside Café Noir, scanning discovery responses for one of Susan's cases. A Fortune 500 company Susan was battling on a hostile work environment claim had dumped fifty thousand pages of emails on them, trying to bury the evidence in a sea of paper. Susan assigned each associate a thousand pages to review and summarize by the end of the week.

Kate was hiding at Cafe Noir because she knew the place would be deserted on a weekday afternoon.

Her plan to blaze through the pile worked for an hour until a glare from the sun caused her to look up and see Jessica stroll inside the coffee shop, carrying a black binder under her arm.

Kate sighed. She knew her sister's presence wasn't a coincidence. Jessica hated coffee in the afternoon. She said it gave her indigestion.

Kate looked back at the papers and tried to hide her face with her hand.

"Kate? Is that you?" Jessica said, after ordering a drink at the counter. "What luck."

Kate marked the end of the paragraph she was scanning, then looked up at her sister.

"Yeah. What luck. I thought you swore off coffee in the afternoon."

"Oh, I did." Jessica set the binder on the table, then pulled out a chair across from her and sat down. "It's mint tea. An English thing. I wasn't sure about it at first, but I rather like it. Ever tried it?"

Kate shook her head. "I don't have time to chat, Jess. Susan's given me a rush assignment."

The mention of Susan's name caused Jessica to perk up. She leaned forward and surveyed the stack of papers. After recognizing the formatting, she leaned back in the chair and frowned.

"Please tell me you're not doing document review."

"It's all hands on deck. Opposing counsel dropped off two U-Haul trucks full of paper. He's trying to overwhelm Susan."

"I see." Jessica paused for a moment. "Even Kathleen's helping?"

"No," Kate said, "Of course, not Kathleen. She's got the Spencer trial next week."

Jessica hummed. "What about Heather? Did Susan give her a stack?"

Kate scoffed. "No. I mean, I don't know. What does that have to do with anything?"

"Come on, Katie, wake up. Don't you know what this means? Senior associates don't do doc review. That's a. . ."

Jessica's voice trailed off as if she couldn't say it.

"A what?"

"A newbie job, Kate. There, I said it. Are you happy? Goldman doesn't even let our first-years do it anymore. He farms it out to zombies in Cleveland."

Kate winced. She had thought the same thing when she read the email from Susan's paralegal assigning the work. When she asked the woman about it, she learned Susan had specifically added her name to the worklist.

"Well, it's not a newbie job in our office," Kate said. "I think Susan wants me up to speed in case I have to sub-in and take a deposition."

Jessica laughed. "That's funny, Katie."

Kate flashed her a hard look.

"Anyway, I come with news. I spoke to Wayne this morning."

"Has he done it? Has he napalmed Asha?"

Jessica shook her head. "He's close. He determined Asha used a DTS protocol."

Kate shrugged. "I don't know what that means."

"Neither to do I. But he made it sound important. To be honest, sometimes I worry he's making things up to impress us."

Kate raised an eyebrow. "You only sometimes worry about that?"

"Hey!" Jessica scolded her. "So, the guy's not perfect. Who is? Willa trusts him. I think you should cut him some slack. He's doing his best to help us."

"Who are you? And what did you do to my sister?"

Jessica shook her head. "I'm just saying that maybe we misjudged him. He seems to really care about you. Did you know that?"

"The only reason he cares about me is because I keep funding his tropical adventures."

"That's not fair, Katie. During our call this morning, he said he's worried you might have lost confidence in him."

"Lost confidence? I never had confidence in him. The man's a disaster. I need to get back to work."

"Well. . ." Jessica sounded put out at being brushed off. "Wayne wants to win back your trust."

"Tell him to finish the job."

"Yes, of course. But he wondered if there was something he could do for you in the meantime." *In the meantime?* Kate thought. The Asha project was supposed to be wrapped up ASAP. "He wondered if maybe he could find us sperm donors."

Kate scoffed. "No. Absolutely not."

Jessica held up a hand. "He said that to find Asha, he's been reading a lot about sperm donors."

"Why?"

"He said the reason we didn't have better luck with applicants was because we were looking in the wrong place. He said he could design a computer program to find us the perfect man. It'd only take about two hours."

"Right," Kate said. "And I suppose he wants to be paid to do it."

"Of course. You didn't expect him to do it for free, did you? It's his job. Do you handle cases for free?"

"Yes. Let me guess. I bet he wants another two grand. Plus, a trip to Tahiti. Because everyone knows you can't write code in Panama."

Jessica squirmed in her chair.

"Good Lord!" Kate said. "I'm right, aren't I?"

"He estimates it would cost around ten thousand dollars."

Kate's eyes went wide. "Ten thousand dollars! For two hours of computer work?"

"It'd be a bespoke program."

"I don't care if it's gold plated. I'm not paying him another cent."

The strength of her response seemed to catch Jessica by surprise.

"Well, I don't know what to say, Katie. I thought you were serious about having a baby."

"I am serious, but I've lost the ability for rational thought."

"Ten thousand is nothing if it gets you a child."

Jessica was leaning on her favorite crutch. What's an extra few thousand dollars if it solves a problem. The trouble was a few thousand here and a few thousand there added up to a lot of thousands everywhere.

"I'm not paying him, Jess. And nothing you can say will change it."

Jessica bit her bottom lip, and Kate watched the thinking in her eyes.

After a moment, her sister changed gears. "How about this?

What if he works on contingency? Only gets paid if he finds you a great guy."

Kate shook her head. "I don't think so. I don't want him—"

"Please, Kate. Do it for me."

She didn't understand why her sister was insisting on giving him another job. Especially since Jessica didn't really want a baby. In the past, she'd gone to great lengths to copy Kate, but this was a new low.

"Fine," Kate said, sensing Jessica wouldn't leave until she got what she wanted. "Contingency. But I'm only paying half. And only if I like the guy he finds."

65

"What the hell are you doing here, kid?" Bowers said.

Matt Simpson was standing in the hallway outside the door to Bowers's apartment. The veteran reporter's eyes were bloodshot. He was dressed in a t-shirt, plaid boxers, and crew cut black socks that bunched up at his ankles. He held the door open with one hand and a tumbler of whiskey in the other. He sounded a little drunk but not too drunk to help.

"You weren't answering your phone," Matt said.

"So you show up at my apartment?"

"It's an emergency."

"Then you should call 911."

"Are you going to invite me inside?" Matt asked.

"Hadn't planned on it. It might encourage you."

After Bowers's divorce, he moved to a rundown motel turned extended stay apartment building. People sat on the concrete steps out front in tank tops and smoked cigarettes and drank forties from paper bags.

"This is serious, Bowers. I've got a story."

"No, you don't. I listened to all your messages, kid. What you got is gossip. Gossip you should ignore."

"There's more I haven't told you."

"Okay, fine. So you don't want my advice. Good luck, kid."

Bowers stepped back and tried to swing the door shut. Matt reached out, stopped it with his hand.

"Just give me ten minutes," Matt said. "Then I promise I'll leave you alone."

Bowers forced a laugh. "You couldn't, even if you wanted to."

Still holding the door open, Matt raised his other hand. In it was a white paper bag with a cellophane square on the front.

Bowers sighed, then snatched the bag from him.

"Only two?"

"You're lucky I could find any donuts at this time of night."

Matt went into the apartment. The short hallway led to a living room. On the left, there was a small kitchen with Formica countertops and avocado-colored appliances. Directly in front, across the living space, there was another hallway that presumably led to a bedroom and bathroom. The place was utilitarian, depressing, and void of any personal touches.

He sat on a couch in the living room, a rough, maroon beast that felt like it came third hand from a secondhand store. The furnishings looked original to the building.

"This place isn't bad," Matt said.

Bowers frowned. "Watch the sarcasm, kid. A guy who lives in a place like this doesn't have much to lose."

Bowers went to the kitchen and switched off a portable radio that was playing a baseball game. He grabbed a whiskey bottle by the neck and came over to sit in the armchair next to Matt.

"What do you want, kid?"

"I need your help convincing Arthur to run my story."

"Can you say waste of time?"

"I don't think so. Once he hears what's happening in the courts, he'll come along."

"If you believe that you're drunker than me," Bowers said. "Arthur doesn't have an ounce of altruism in his body. And he'll never cross your grandfather just to print libel."

"It's not libel."

"Have you found anyone willing to go on the record?"

Matt hesitated. "I don't need anyone on record. I've got other proof."

Bowers laughed. "This isn't cable news, kid. We try to get it right around here."

"You use unnamed sources all the time."

"Yes, but we are not the same. I know what I'm doing."

"So do I."

"Come on, kid. You're shattering my illusion that the Ivies are good schools. Did you ever think there might be a reason no one will put their name on this anchor?"

Matt shook his head. "My source wants to go public. She just can't yet."

"Oh, I see." Bowers stretched out the words to mock him. After staring at Matt for a moment, he glanced down at his watch. "Time's up. Good luck with the story. If I were you, I'd run the other way as fast as my rich little legs could carry me."

Matt stayed seated on the couch.

"I'm not leaving until you help me."

"I did help. I told you to run away."

"Is this about money?" Matt said. "Because I can pay you."

"I don't want your money."

"I'll give you five hundred bucks."

"No."

"A thousand."

"No."

"Five thousand."

Bowers hesitated. Matt could tell the number was working on him. He went higher.

"Ten thousand. Cash. Your ex never has to know. You'd be a fool to say no."

Matt would have gone as high as a hundred thousand, if that's what it took to get the story printed. Money was of no consequence to him. He had more of it than he'd ever need. The fact that it all came from his grandfather made it sort of ironic.

Bowers shifted in the chair, then poured himself another drink. He did not offer one to Matt.

"Fine," Bowers said at last. "Torch your career. But don't say I didn't warn you."

"Thank you."

"The only way to get Arthur to run your story is to make it impossible for him not to do so."

"I don't follow."

"If it were me, I'd send out advance copies of the article to all the local media outlets. Tell them its running on the front page. Say there's been some national buzz. Then offer to do an exclusive interview with one TV station. If you drum up enough interest and say the words Austin Free Press enough times, he'll have to print it."

Matt raised an eyebrow. The idea was nuts.

"Or fire me," Matt said.

"Yes, there's that possibility, too. Which is why I said you should walk away."

Matt couldn't imagine Bowers or any reputable journalist doing what he suggested. But they didn't have to do it, did they? The newspapers where they worked wanted to print their stories. They didn't have a grandfather trying to sabotage them.

Maybe it would work, he thought. The story was compelling. People deserved to know their justice system was corrupt.

"Do you have contact info for people at the TV stations?" Matt asked.

"I have a woman's cell."

66

Four days after Kate agreed to let Wayne play matchmaker, she still hadn't heard a word about the sperm donor project. Or the mission to napalm Asha. The four messages she left on his mobile all went unreturned.

Usually, she would have seized on Wayne's evasiveness as proof of his incompetence. People avoided you for a reason, she believed. And none of them were good.

But at that moment, she could only wonder about Wayne's progress because she was stuck in her office, reviewing even more stacks of discovery. Her sleek, private oasis had been transformed into a stale file room filled with rows of waist-high banker's boxes. A skinny path along the side wall was now the only route from her desk to the door. "Ms. Wilson wants you to finish it yourself. By Monday. K thanks!" Susan's paralegal said before spinning on her heel and giving way to a squadron of goons who stacked boxes around Kate until she began to feel claustrophobic.

The paralegal's voice had been so sassy it felt personal. The woman could have just as easily said, "Get it done by Monday. Or you're fired. K thanks!"

After a moment of disbelief, Kate realized what was happening.

Susan was punishing her for hiring Riley. Assigning an impossible amount of work in hopes she'd fail. Kate shook her head. Becker women never fail, never quit.

She recognized the pivotal moment this was in her career. If she could finish the assignment and accomplish the impossible, it'd go a long way to winning back the woman's respect. Because above all else, Susan wanted winners.

Winning would transform her hiring Riley from office joke to act of extraordinary courage. She'd be a visionary. A breath of fresh air. "Why can't y'all be more like Kate Becker," she imagined Susan saying at an all-firm meeting. "She's got killer instincts."

That Riley wasn't RBG 2.0 proved nothing. It didn't mean she made a mistake. There were plenty of reasons a person might hire him. Like—

She paused.

Her mind was blank. Of course, Riley was pleasant and charismatic. But she couldn't think of anything that would warrant him breaking the glass ceiling at Susan Wilson Law. Except for his looks. He was hot. But even at an all-woman firm, you can't use that reason. She made a note on her phone to come up with a good reason for hiring him as soon as she finished the discovery.

She ordered Riley to her office, then conscripted him into twenty-four-hour service. "Welcome to the practice of law," she said, thrusting a box at him. "Cancel everything. We're not leaving until we've scanned every page."

To his credit, he nodded and got straight to work.

After hour twenty-six, Kate realized there wasn't enough time before Monday to finish the job, even if they cut out showers and limited bathroom breaks. She needed more help.

To buy herself space to think, she made a production of checking her email, then announced that Susan needed her help on an "important matter." Before leaving her office, she admonished him to work faster and not slack off while she was gone.

She rode the elevator down to the lobby, then made her way outside to the sidewalk. It was a little after eight o'clock in the evening, and darkness was about to snuff out the last of the light. Not wanting to wander the streets alone, she made her way to Jessica's condo building, a quick ten-minute walk from her office.

When the elevator doors opened on Jessica's floor, Kate's nose was hit by the skunk-like odor of marijuana. Every time she visited, it disgusted her. She couldn't understand why all the air quality advocates who had fought so hard to stomp out cigarette smoking abandoned the fight on marijuana. Who cared if it was medicinal, or addictive, or a gateway drug? None of that meant a person should be able to light up in a communal building and poison the air. Period. Full stop.

Plus, it made everything else stink, too.

Kate stopped at her sister's door and knocked.

"Oh, hi, Kate," Jessica said. She had opened the door only an inch and was looking at Kate through the crack. "What are you doing here?"

"Susan's hazing me. I needed a break. Can I use your bathroom? Maybe grab a snack?"

Jessica hummed. "You know, I'm going to decline."

Kate wrinkled her nose. "Decline? Is that supposed to be a joke? Let me in. It's not funny."

"I, I—"

Kate pushed open the door. Jessica gave way. A moment later, Kate found herself face to face with a man dressed in a black t-shirt and jeans.

"What are you doing here?" Kate said.

67

Wayne looked as surprised to see her as she was to see him. The grungy, mullet-cut moron had a glass of red wine in his hand and a buzzed look on his face.

"Katie," he roared. "My favorite person."

"If I'm your favorite person, why don't you return any of my calls?"

"You called?" He acted confused, grabbing his mobile phone off the coffee table and scanning it. "I never got a message. If I had gotten a message..."

Kate hummed, then glanced around the condo. A second glass of wine was on the kitchen counter beside a jug-like bottle. Classical music danced in the air. She looked at her sister.

"What are you celebrating, Jess?" Kate asked.

"Celebrating? What gives you that idea?"

Kate pointed at the bottle on the counter. "That's the Rodney Donald I gave you for your birthday."

Jessica shrugged. "When you give someone a present, Kate, they can use it however they want."

"It cost three thousand dollars," Kate said. "You said you were saving it for when Susan hired you."

"Well," Jessica hesitated, "after the Asha incident, it seems pretty far off."

Kate glared at Wayne. "What's going on?"

"I, we, your sister—"

He looked away. For all his bravado, the guy didn't hold up well under the lights. She had him on the ropes. One more quick jab ought to finish him off.

"I'm your client, Wayne," Kate said. "Remember your ethics."

Wayne glanced at Jessica, who shot him a hard.

"All right, all right," he said. "I'll tell you."

Jessica threw up her hands. "You idiot. We talked about this."

"She's going to find out, anyway."

"No, she wouldn't."

Realizing she couldn't stop it, Jessica went to the kitchen and began drinking her wine while Wayne explained what had happened.

"My program works," he said. "Jessica got a match."

Kate raised an eyebrow. "Oh, really? And who is our lucky suitor?"

"His name is Thorton Andrews. He runs a hedge fund in New York. He has ten billion dollars under management."

Kate gagged. "So, he's rich. So what. We're not looking for child support."

"He went to Harvard," Jessica said, rejoining them in the living room. "Twice. Undergrad and B School. He also played lacrosse. Former All-American. Isn't that right, Wayne?"

He nodded.

"Okay," Kate said. "The Harvard connection is a plus."

"It's more than a plus, Kate," Jessica said. "His IQ is 180."

"Not terrible."

"And he plays chess. Competitively. He won the Northeast regional when he was only fourteen years old."

"What's wrong with him, then?" Kate asked. "Does he have ears like an elf?"

"No. He's quite sexy, actually. Wayne, show her the picture on your phone."

She waited for Wayne to pull up the image. When he handed her the phone, her biology took over. The guy was hot, like heartthrob movie star hot. He had short brown hair, a square jaw, and piercing blue eyes. If a sperm donor clinic were dreaming up guys to put on a poster, he'd be at the front of the line.

"Good job, Wayne," Kate said, doing her best to sound like she never doubted him. "How did you convince him to apply?"

"Wayne doesn't believe in applications," Jessica said.

"What?"

Wayne swallowed the last of his wine. "It's not that I don't believe. It's more a structural problem. Asking people to apply means you're sorting through the same group of self-selected losers. I thought it would be a better if we started with qualifications, then worked backward to donors."

Kate laughed. "Wonderful idea. Except for one little problem."

"He might be married," Jessica said.

"Exactly."

Jessica continued, "Or in a relationship. Or against sperm donation."

"Yes, yes."

"We talked about those things," Jessica said. "But then I realized they didn't matter."

Kate raised an eyebrow. "I'm sorry. Did you just say you don't care if he's married or in a relationship?"

Jessica nodded. "Don't give me that face. I'm not trying to seduce the man. I just want a dollop of his sperm."

"Oh, well, if it's only a dollop."

"Even if he is married," Jessica said, "and we don't know that, why would his wife care? I'd be honored if another woman wanted my husband's sperm."

Kate could hardly believe her ears. Her sister had gone mad.

"Maybe when you have dinner with this man's wife, you could

ask for a natural insemination. You know, to make the process more... organic."

Jessica crossed her arms, glared at Wayne. "This is why I didn't want to tell her. I told you she'd pick it to death."

"Me," Kate said. "You think this is my fault?"

Wayne spoke over their voices. "He's not married, all right. I checked. Even I thought that might go too far."

"Well," Jessica said in a huff, "once you see my perfect little girl, you'll be sorry Wayne couldn't find you a match!"

The room went silent. A flash of regret passed in Jessica's eyes. She began rambling trying to cover up what she had said, but Kate didn't hear any of it. She just kept replaying her sister's words over and over.

Kate looked at Wayne.

"What did she mean? You didn't find me a match."

Wayne bit his lip. "You know I think you're beautiful, Ms. Becker? I'd knock you up, if you asked."

"Thank you, Wayne," Kate said. "But please, tell me what she meant."

"I entered your criteria into the computer. Age, IQ, beliefs, charitable giving. All of it." Kate nodded. "It came back... undefined."

"Undefined? What does that mean?"

"Technically, it means there is no answer."

"As in, there's no person on the planet who matches me?"

Wayne shook his head. "More like, never in history has a person ever met your criteria. I thought it was a mistake at first. I call my mentor. He called his mentor at MIT. We searched every public database and a few not so public. I'm sorry to tell you, Ms. Becker, there's no one for you."

68

In Kate's mind, it was perfectly acceptable for certain life events to ruin your day. Or week. Or even month. For example, a psychologically healthy person might feel down after losing a job. Another might scream in rage after finding their partner in bed with a stranger. These things made sense to her. They were normal.

What did not make sense, however, was to let an idiot like Wayne dominate your thoughts. Why was she surprised that he couldn't find her a match? It was a miracle the man could even turn on a computer. The only reason she had even agreed to let him try was to get Jessica off her back. She never thought he'd actually succeed.

Yet, in the days following her visit to Jessica's condo, she couldn't stop feeling blue. Maybe her standards were too high. Maybe she should have settled for Dr. Lotus's medical gang bang. The thought of raising a frat boy still made her sick to her stomach, but she also really didn't like cats.

The worst part of Wayne's news was that it had destroyed the imaginary wall she built around the baby issue. Before that night, she compartmentalized her thoughts. Pushed babies to the side when she needed to focus on work. Now, every time she found a quiet moment, Willa's voice crept back into her head. "How can a woman be so clueless about biology? It's like, duh. Obviously, geezers can't have kids."

She looked up from a stack of papers she was reviewing and glanced off towards the line stretching out the front door of Cafe Noir.

It was Saturday morning. She was sitting alone at a table near the back, having opted to work there in hopes the noise from the cappuccino machine might drown out the Willa soundtrack. It didn't. She had been there an hour already and only made it through twenty pages of emails.

Through a large plate-glass window, she saw a commotion in the line outside. She couldn't make out what was happening, but she heard a man yell, "Hey, she's cutting. Someone stop her." A moment later, Jessica barreled through the door, pulling a small suitcase on wheels.

"I told you," Jessica yelled back over her shoulder, "I ordered already."

Her sister scanned the coffee shop. When she found Kate, she walked over to the table, pulled out a chair, and sat down.

"Good Lord," Jessica said. "When did people become so rude?"

Jessica looked bundled up and ready for winter, even though it was fifty degrees and sunny outside. She was dressed in a white ski jacket and a fuzzy pink stocking cap.

"Headed to the North Pole?" Kate asked.

She pulled off her hat, fixed her hair. "I mean, what does he think I should do? Stand in line even though I've already ordered?"

Kate raised an eyebrow. "You haven't ordered."

"He doesn't know that," Jessica said. She raised a hand in the direction of a pink-haired barista, who nodded back at her.

Jessica had an arrangement with the baristas whereby she got to skip the line on busy days and order from a table. In exchange, she left them a ten dollar tip.

"Did you know it's only going to be forty degrees in New York today?"

"What's with the sudden interest in New York weather?"

"I'm flying there. This morning. To meet Thorton."

Kate rolled her eyes. "You're seriously going through with that?"

"Why wouldn't I?" Jessica used a hand to fan herself. "I'm burning up in here."

"Maybe take off your parka."

Jessica continued to fan herself. "Have you decided if you're going to drop some of your outrageous criteria so Wayne can find you a man?"

Kate shrugged. "Haven't given it much thought. I've been so busy with work. I think I'm off the baby thing."

Jessica's eyes went wide. "What?"

"I mean, it's like you said before. It's never been a priority for me."

Jessica shifted uncomfortably in the chair. "Priorities change, Kate."

"You heard Wayne. He said—"

"Wayne's an idiot. Don't give up."

"I don't know."

"Look." Jessica leaned forward in the chair as if she were trying to convince a jury. "We've put too much effort in to quit now. I'm flying to New York for goodness' sake."

"We?"

"When I get back, we're going to sit down and brainstorm a way to get you pregnant, okay?"

"I don't know."

"We're doing it, Katie."

Deep down, a part of her was glad her sister wouldn't let her give up. Even if Jessica was doing it selfishly and for all the wrong reasons.

"All right."

The barista delivered Jessica's latte, and she stood up. "I need to go. I don't want to miss the free cocktail before takeoff."

"You're flying first class again?"

"What? You'd rather I get bitten by another dog?"

The dog didn't actually bite her. It only nibbled on her finger after Jessica shoved it back across the invisible line separating her seat from the woman who was supposed to be holding it. There was very little blood.

Kate shook her head. "I give you credit for convincing Thorton to meet you."

Jessica pursed her lips. "I wouldn't say he agreed exactly."

"What?"

"You know how it is these days, Kate. People love chance encounters. Kismet and stuff."

"Kismet? I don't think it's kismet if you fly across country and scheme to meet someone."

"Says you." Jessica had an edge to her voice now. "If we hit it off, we hit it off. Who cares how it happened?"

"I think Thorton might care. If he ever found out."

Jessica's eyes narrowed. "But he won't find out, will he? Because only you and me and Wayne know. And Wayne will never tell."

"Okay."

"I'm not joking around, Katie. If you tell him, I will never forgive you."

"I said okay. But I'm warning you. This isn't a good idea."

69

Barbara was in the kitchen at the condo wiping up the last of the dinner crumbs, when she heard a knock at the front door. Kate called her name in a curious voice. Clutching a dishrag in her hand, she went to the living room to find Yata Miller standing beside the couch.

In all the years they had lived in the same building, Yata had never stepped foot inside the condo, which was how Kate liked it. And, truth be told, how Barbara preferred it too.

Despite Yata and Kate having both gone to Harvard, the two women couldn't stand each other. Yata was baffled by how her beloved alma mater, a place that stood for diversity, inclusion, integrity, and fair-dealing, allowed such a cold-hearted, competitive monster like Kate to walk its halls. And Kate saw Yata as proof that even the Ivies sometimes screw up and admit scattered, bird brains, who belong at big state schools. "If you're going to write smut," Kate said to Barbara one Sunday, after finishing Yata's first novel in her vampire in space series, "at least have the decency to use a pseudonym. And for goodness sake, delete all reference to Harvard. It's embarrassing." Kate was the only person Barbara knew who had actually read one of Yata's books.

"What are you wearing?" Kate said, shaking her head at Yata in disgust. "That is not University-sanctioned apparel."

Yata was dressed in a hideous denim onesie with button snaps on the front, and the word Harvard embroidered across the chest. The getup made her look like a giant baby. She had her long hair pulled back in a ponytail and was holding a bottle of champagne.

"You can't get one, Katie," Yata said. "It's bespoke. Made by a dressmaker who owed me a favor."

"I don't want one. And neither should you. You look ridiculous."

"Envy is not a good color, Katie." Yata held up the bottle of champagne. "I refuse to let your bad attitude ruin your mother's big night."

"Big night? What are you talking about?" Barbara asked.

Yata smiled. "So, you haven't heard? Wonderful. I was hoping I'd get to break the news. Congratulations, Barbie! You've been shorted list for a GOTY."

"What's a GOTY?" Kate asked.

This time, Yata was the one who turned up her nose.

"Only the most prestigious award for seniors in the state. It stands for Grandparent of the Year, silly."

It took Kate a second, but then she snapped the pieces together. She looked at Barbara and said, "Please tell me this isn't connected to that Grannies R Us scam."

"Scam?" Yata said. "Who says it's a scam?"

"Everyone."

Yata laughed. "Katie, Katie, Katie. Grannies is an official 501. As a lawyer, I trust you know what that means. The IRS doesn't just handout those certifications."

"Yes, they do," Kate said, "As long as you file the right paperwork."

Yata waved a dismissive hand. "Barbie, be a dear, will you? Grab us some glasses. The hot air in here is drying out my throat."

Barbara grabbed three glasses from the kitchen and returned just as Yata popped the cork. She filled them, then raised hers for a toast.

"To the best mentee I've ever had," Yata said.

"There must be some mistake," Barbara said.

"I thought so, too," Yata said, "so I checked the list of nominees on the Texas Senior Council's website. Your name is there. Crazy as it is."

"How could this happen?" Barbara asked.

"Only one way, dear. Your teenage stink bomb nominated you."

Garrett? Nominated her for an award? He wouldn't do that, would he?

"It must have been his mother," Barbara said. "Heather and I get along well."

"Doubtful," Yata replied. "When I spoke to Veronica, she mentioned the boy's essay. What were her words again? Oh, yes. She said it was the most moving piece of writing she's ever read. Now, personally, I don't think that means squat since Veronica stopped reading books back when they took out the pictures, but she says the people at TSC believe you're a shoo-in."

Kate laughed. "My mother? A shoo-in to win Grandmother of the Year? I don't think so."

Barbara's face turned red. "You don't think so?"

"Come on, Mother. Be serious. You don't even like children."

Barbara had expected some razzing from Kate, but to say she didn't like kids? That took it too far.

"I did in-home daycare for fifteen years."

"I know, but–"

"Do you think I would have done it for so long, if I didn't like kids?"

"Then why were you always telling Jessica and me that you didn't want to be a grandmother?"

Yata pressed forward, ignoring Kate's question. "Let me just say, Barbie. Better you than me. Better you than me. I couldn't stomach giving a speech at that banquet."

"Speech?"

"I'm not saying I couldn't do it," Yata said. "Of course, I could do it. I've done sci-fi conventions ten times bigger. But that sort of speech?" Yata shivered. "No, thank you."

"What sort of speech does she have to give?" Kate asked.

"Every year, the GOTY winner does a big multimedia presentation. Pictures, video clips, you name it. It'd be half-way interesting if TSC didn't make the winner focus on how the kid changed them. Changed them? The kids don't change us. We change the kids."

Yata's phone rang from somewhere inside her onesie. She unsnapped the top button and pulled the phone out of her bra. After pressing it to her ear, she barked at the person on the other end and hurried out of the condo without saying goodbye.

70

Standing at her dining room table, Kate glanced back over her shoulder towards the living room to make sure no one was watching. When the coast was clear, she picked up the little container of pomegranate juice and hid it behind a carafe of decaf coffee. Kate had only put out the expensive juice because she wanted the continental breakfast spread to seem like it had a juice option. She didn't want people to actually drink it.

"Smart. Very smart," Jessica said, sidling up beside her, holding a plastic cup filled to the rim with pomegranate juice. "If it were my party, I'd put it away altogether. These people don't appreciate fine things."

These people were their mother, Riley, Willa, and a few close friends Kate knew from the chess club. She had purposely kept the guest list small because she needed to go to work in an hour and no one liked breakfast parties.

"So," Jessica said, using a fork to pick through the big bowl of cut fruit on the table then opting not to take any, "they're really putting you on the front page?"

Kate huffed. "Why do you keep asking me that?"

"I mean, I know it's only The Austin Free Press, but..."

"Haha," Kate said. "Let me know when anyone, anywhere, runs a story about you on the front page."

"It's not a story. You know that, right? Puff pieces aren't stories."

"Call it what you want. Susan's going to love it, and it demolishes Tina Black. I thought you'd be happy, since your future at the firm is looking up."

Jessica pressed her lips together, swallowed her pride. "Touche, Katie. Congrats on the story."

Kate waved a hand at her. "No worries. It's hard being left behind. I get it. But I meant what I said. I'll talk to Susan about a job for you. Soon."

"Please do."

In the living room, Barbara called out to everyone.

"It's coming on. Right after the commercials."

Kate and Jessica walked over to where the others stood by the TV.

The Channel 8 logo spun on the screen. The camera cut to a close-up of a woman called Sunny Skies. She was blond and thin and pretty and dumb. When she started at Channel 8, her name was Sunny Streets because she did the traffic report. Then she moved to weather and became Sunny Skies. Now she hosted the morning news program, and there was talk she might become Sunny Stories. She was sitting in an armchair on a set resembling a fake living room.

"We're back at eight thirty-five," Sunny said.

The camera pulled back to reveal her sitting beside Matt Simpson. He looked good in the blue blazer, white button-down shirt, and khakis.

"And we're joined by investigative reporter Matt Simpson. He's with The Austin Free Press. He has a new series starting tomorrow exposing corruption in Texas government. Matt, good morning to you."

"Good morning. Thanks for having me, Sunny."

Kate felt a lump in her throat. The story was part of a series? Matt hadn't mentioned a series.

"Tell us where this story begins?" Sunny said, leaning forward like she was genuinely interested.

"Well, it starts with an extraordinary attorney named Kate Becker."

Matt summarized Ruth's case and how Kate had reversed the first custody order and got Ruth's daughter back. To that point, everything he said was true.

"Do we know why this first judge, Judge Randolph McDaniel, got it so wrong?"

Matt nodded. "We do. And unfortunately, it wasn't a mistake. Multiple sources have confirmed that Chief Judge Randolph McDaniel and the father's lawyer, a woman named Tina Black, were involved in a sexual relationship at the time he ruled for her client."

Kate's eyes went wide. Multiple sources? Who were they?

Sunny Skies shook her head. "It gets even worse, doesn't it? I understand that in your piece, which hits newsstands tomorrow, you say Judge McDaniel ruled for the father despite the father abusing the mother."

"He did. Kate Becker filed photographs with the court documenting the abuse. They're pretty graphic. Black eyes, swollen lips, even marks on the baby. The disturbing thing is that this wasn't the only case Chief Judge McDaniel and Tina Black had together. So, there are potentially many more victims out there. We're setting up a tip line people can call if they believe McDaniel has wronged them."

"Wow. I hope the authorities read your piece and take some action."

"Me too," Matt said.

"So, where does the story go from here? You haven't given away the ending, have you?"

Matt forced a laugh. "No, no. Trust me. It gets even crazier. Your viewers are going to have to buy the paper to find out. New installments in the series come out every week. If I can, though, I'd like to give a big shout out to our publisher, Arthur Spalding. Without his unwavering support and guidance, none of this would be possible."

"Way to go Arthur," Sunny said. "Speaking truth to power is never easy. But before you go, Matt, you must give our viewers at least a teaser of what's on the horizon. You've got half of Austin hanging on the edge of their seats."

Matt smiled. "Okay, Sunny. For you." He paused a moment to build the tension. "During her investigation, Kate Becker stumbled onto something bigger."

Kate's mouth fell open. *No, I didn't.*

"What did she find?" Sunny asked.

"You'll have to read the story. But, I can say it involves sex. A church. And a high-ranking politician."

"Oh, my," Sunny said, sounding intrigued. "We're going to get Ms. Becker on the show. Matt Simpson, thanks so much for all your hard work. We can't wait to read it."

Matt nodded.

Sunny sat up straight and smiled into the camera. "Up next, Darla, the pet psychic, gives us a glimpse inside the wonderful world of birds. What do our feathered friends really want from us? You'll find out next. Stay tuned."

Barbara switched off the TV and looked back at Kate. "What a wonderful story, honey."

"Yeah, congratulations, Ms. Becker," Willa said. "You're amazing. Like a real life Clarence Darrow."

Barbara and Willa continued praising her, tossing out compliments that made her shutter, before veering off track and discussing Matt Simpson's symmetrical face. Riley stared at her. His silence felt like the loudest voice in the room.

Later, she rode the elevator down to the lobby with Jessica.

"What's going on, Kate?" Jessica said. "And don't lie. There's no way Tina Black is sleeping with Judge McDaniel."

Kate kept her eyes trained forward and watched the elevator's digital panel counted down the floors. After a moment, she said, "She could be."

Jessica frowned. "No. McDaniel is old and gross and impotent."

"You don't know he's impotent."

"All old, fat men are impotent, Kate. Plus, he's retiring soon. There's too much bang for Tina's buck, if you know what I mean."

"Ew."

"Tell me what's really going on."

Kate sighed. "I don't know. The story was supposed to be only my puff piece."

"Nothing about a sex church or politicians?"

She shook her head. "Ruth's mentioned it, but there's no evidence. It's just her being crazy."

"Then you need to say something."

"No."

"Yes. That airhead Sunny Skies asked the cops to investigate it."

"So? That's Matt Simpson's problem, not mine."

"I don't know, Kate. I have a bad feeling about this."

Kate's phone chirped a new text message. She fished it out of her pocket, glanced at the screen.

"Well, apparently, Susan isn't worried. She said she loved the interview. She invited me and my team to a party at her place."

71

Carol eased the white Buick Lucerne to a stop at the curb, across the street from Garrett's house, her tired brakes squealing from the effort. It was Monday, ten o'clock in the morning, and the humidity in the air was so thick it made you wish the bright blue sky was clouded gray.

"This car is dangerous," Yata said from the passenger seat.

"What do you want me to do?" Carol sounded defensive. "I offered to drive your Subaru. You said no."

"My wagon isn't a loaner, Carol. You need to buy your own. Randolph will treat you right. He'll get you almost dealer pricing."

Carol shook her head. "A lot of money fits in almost. Plus, I ain't buying a car from no one named Randy. He sounds like a gay porn star."

Yata sighed, then rolled her eyes. "It was a little funny the first time you said it, Carol. Now, it's just offensive."

"Offensive? Why? I have lots of porn star friends. I just don't buy cars from 'em."

Sitting in the back seat behind Carol, Barbara listened to the two women argue. They had been going at it the entire drive. It seemed the only things they agreed on were making Barbara's life harder and arguing in English.

The fact that two women spoke the same language did not mean they understood each other. Case in point: Carol's reluctance to buy a Subaru. Yata seemed to believe this was because of a lack of information. If Carol only appreciated the car's true value, she'd close the sale. But, of course, this was never going to happen because Carol wasn't buying a car. Not now. Not ever. She didn't have the money.

"Let me out," Barbara said.

They had trapped her in the back seat using the child safety locks.

"Don't let her out," Yata said. "Not until we have a plan."

"Plan?" Barbara said. "The plan is I'm going to meet Garrett, and you two are staying in the car."

Carol shook her head. "I don't like that plan."

"There is no other plan," Barbara said. "You're not coming near the house, Carol. You embarrassed yourself enough last time."

"Embarrassed myself? I don't know what you're talking about."

Yata cut in. "Barbie's right. Last time, you were a disaster, Carol. And we still haven't talked about that question you asked. Whoa. It was a doozy. Very poor sentence construction."

Barbara nodded. "Perhaps you could use this time to help her, Yata. Teach Carol to speak better. You know, share some tricks you learned at Harvard."

Yata hummed. "Maybe I could teach her a few things. But definitely not anything I learned at Harvard. That's far too advanced for her."

"Sounds good," Barbara said. "Let me out."

Yata hesitated for a moment, appearing to think it over, before pulling the door handle. She was standing on the grass next to the curb when her cell phone rang.

"Hello, this is Bestselling Author Yata Miller," she said, pressing the phone to her ear.

Barbara could only hear Yata's side of the conversation.

"Oh, that's too bad."

"Yes, of course."

"Well, that's how these things go, isn't it?"

"No, it's no trouble at all. Thanks for letting us know."

Yata ended the call, then put one hand on the roof and leaned inside the car.

"The damn stink bomb canceled again," Yata said. "Another excuse about a hard night."

Carol scoffed. "I knew it. I knew it. The kid's not sick at all."

"Shut up, Carol," Barbara said.

Yata motioned for Barbara to hand her the plastic shopping bag she was holding on her lap. "Give me the cookies. I'll bring them up to the door. Supposedly, his mother's awake."

Barbara tightened her grip on the bag. The cookies were Garrett's favorite, at least according to the questionnaire he filled out for Grannies R Us. She learned this when she called Veronica to find out more about the GOTY nomination. It was the first of many, many things she needed to know about him if she wanted to pull off the speech.

She had gone online and paid a hundred dollars for a tiny batch of Danish cookies hoping it'd encourage him to talk. The cookies arrived in a fire engine red tin box. Knowing Yata and Carol disapproved of her buying gifts, she put the box in a plastic grocery bag and said she got them at the dollar store.

"No," Barbara said. "I'll take them up myself."

"Don't be ridiculous. I'm already outside."

Barbara sighed, then loosened her grip on the bag. It felt like she had just flushed a hundred dollars down the toilet. What was the point of buying expensive cookies if she didn't get to deliver them?

Yata crossed the street and headed up the path to the front porch. Garrett's mother answered the door immediately. Yata was back in the car thirty seconds later.

"Let's go," Yata said. "I need to get home. I started writing a new book last night. The characters won't stop talking to me."

"Maybe you should go to the doctor instead," Carol said. "Get some medicine for those voices. Sounds a little cuckoo."

Yata frowned. "Stop pouting, Carol. Start the car. What I said before wasn't personal. Lots of people have poor sentence construction."

"Mm-hmm," Carol said, not giving the slightest sign she intended to comply.

"Start the car," Yata said again, firmer.

"No. This ain't your Subaru. And you're not my supervisor. So, we're going to wait here for a few minutes. I have a feeling something is going to happen."

Yata clenched her jaw. "I'll tell you what's going to happen, Carol. I'm going to scream so loud it will burst your eardrums."

"Then you'll burst yours too, won't you?"

Yata raised an eyebrow, appearing unsure of how to answer. Barbara wondered the same thing. Could a person scream so loud they'd hurt themselves? She thought probably not.

"This is your last warning," Yata said, her voice rising, bordering on yelling. "Either start the car or-"

"Be quiet," Carol hissed. "He'll hear you. Look."

She pointed towards the driveway along the side of the house. Garrett was standing near a large plastic trash bin. He must have come out a side door because Barbara hadn't seen him leave the house. He was dressed in his usual t-shirt and jeans and didn't look the least bit sick.

He lifted the trash can's lid, tossed something inside. Barbara recognized the fire engine red tin box as soon as it left his hand. Carol did too.

"Holy shit!" Carol said. "The little snot threw away your cookies!"

"It's probably only the tin," Barbara said, hoping, but not believing it.

Carol tugged on Yata's arm. "Get down. He'll see us."

They all slouched low in the seats, watching as Garrett strolled down the driveway. He turned left when he reached the sidewalk and moved away from them.

"Whew," Carol said. "I don't think he saw us."

Yata raised an eyebrow. "Of course, he saw us, Carol. We were only ten yards away. He just pretended not to."

"Why would he do that?" Carol said.

"Who knows why?" Yata said. "Hormones maybe? I stopped trying to understand that sex after my second husband passed, God bless his wretched soul."

"Start the car," Barbara said. "Let's follow him."

Carol turned the key, glanced over at Yata. "Weren't you married like three more times?"

"Yes," Yata said. "Each one richer than the last. It worked out. For me. Not them."

Carol shifted the car into drive, easing away from the curb, careful to stay far enough back not to draw his attention. But because the Buick was the only thing moving on the street, and because she was driving down the center of the road, if Garrett had even glanced over his shoulder, he would have seen them for sure.

Carol said, "I just want to repeat that he doesn't look sick."

Barbara hummed.

When Garrett reached the end of the block, he veered to the left, following a sidewalk west and disappearing behind a house. Carol gunned the engine. They quickly reached the intersection and spotted him up ahead. He was too close for them to keep moving. Carol pulled to the side of the road and stopped.

"What are you going to do now, genius?" Yata said. She was looking at Carol, but the comment was meant for Barbara, too.

Suddenly, Garrett cut to the right, ran across the street, and disappeared into a dense group of trees that seemed to mark the beginning of a wildlife area. There were no houses on that side of the road. It was all waist-high brush and weeds. The kid was gone.

72

When they stopped at the spot where Garrett went into the trees, Barbara yelled for Yata to let her out.

Once on her feet, she hurried to the edge of the thick brush, scanning the ground for an entry point. She found a narrow dirt path resembling a deer trail at the base of two tall trees whose trunks couldn't have been over fifteen inches apart. She sucked in her belly, turned to the side, then squeezed through the narrow space, feeling the bark rub against her shirt.

Keeping a hand extended in front of her, she pushed into the brush, swatting away the branches of weeds that had grown so tall they resembled trees themselves. Mosquitoes attacked her body: face, neck, arms, and legs. The only good thing was that when she found Garrett, she'd be able to talk to him alone. There was no way Carol or Yata would venture in that far.

It was thirty yards of thick brush before she reached a clearing, a rocky, dry riverbed. Garrett sat on a rock with his back to her, tossing pebbles into a rusted metal coffee can.

She had stopped at the edge of the trees and was trying to work out what to say when he called out to her.

"Are you waiting for an invitation, Barbara?"

She went over to him, feeling a bit foolish. She was no doctor, but nothing about the kid told her he was sick. Not his coloring or posture or the way he was tossing pebbles like he didn't have a care in the world. Maybe Carol was right. Maybe he was a faker.

"Do you have cancer, Garrett?" she asked.

He shot her a quick glance. It lasted only half a second, but it was long enough to send a clear rebuke. "You're really asking me that?"

Her face turned red.

"Why did you throw away my cookies?"

"Why did you buy them for me?" Garrett asked.

"Because they're your favorite."

"Nope. Never eaten one in my life."

"What? Why did you put it on your questionnaire?"

Garrett stopped tossing pebbles. He looked straight up at the sky, shook his head. "Jesus, Barbara. I mean, I half expected you to buy the pomegranate molasses. But the Fire Opal? And the book? And the cookies? I mean, seriously. Why are you wasting your money on that stuff when you know it ends up in my dresser?"

Barbara felt her blood pressure spike. "You said it was where you kept your treasures."

Garrett scoffed. "Do I need to spell it out for you? I don't want you to be my fake grandmother, okay? I tried to be nice, tried to push you away, tried to make you blame me. But you just kept coming back, over and over. I don't want to spend time with you. Do you understand?"

Tears clouded Barbara's vision. There was a lump in her throat. His words had cut deep.

"Listen," he said, sensing she was on the verge of a breakdown, "it's not personal. You seem nice enough. I'm sure you'll make a wonderful grandmother to someone else."

Barbara stared off at the dry riverbed and focused on her breathing, inhaling, exhaling, then starting the process anew, trying to lengthen the intervals each time and using the space to blink away her tears. How pathetic was she?

"If you didn't want me as a grandmother, why did you nominate me for Grandmother of the Year?"

Garrett hummed. "You heard about that?"

"Heard about it? It's all people are talking about. Apparently, I'm the first volunteer grandparent ever short-listed."

"Probably, it wasn't my best idea. But I only did it because I felt bad you wasted so much money on that book. You know the thing's unreadable, right? You should return it."

Barbara nodded, electing not to mention that the seller had been explicit: all sales were final.

"Regardless of why you did it, it's done now. And we have to stick out it. Until they pick a winner."

"I don't have to stick it out," Garrett said.

"Yes, you do. I'm not letting you turn Grannies R Us into a joke. It's a good organization. It helps many, many children. Plus, you owe me for all those 'treasures' I bought you."

He sighed. "Fine. I'll play nice until the banquet. But no more visits. Give me your phone."

"Why?"

"Because I'm giving you my email address. Anything you need, send me a message."

It would not be easy assembling a speech based on email, but she'd make it work. If the boy didn't want to see her, she didn't want to see him.

"What about pictures?" she asked.

"People email pictures, Barbara."

"Okay, but you're coming to the banquet. And you have to act adorable. Fool the people into thinking you're a good person."

He forced a laugh. "Me? Act adorable? No, I don't think so. Don't worry, though, Barbara. No one will see us. One of the other finalists is a paralyzed girl in a wheelchair who lives with her real grandfather. We're safe."

73

The thing Kate liked most about Riley was that he was a good soldier. Like all obedient soldiers, he'd grumble and complain when he thought you were making a mistake, but when it came down to it, he'd charge the hill. Take the beach. Or, as here, stop badgering you about Matt Simpson's reporting. At least for a while.

"My mom loved your picture in the paper," he said.

They were in her office. Kate was at her desk checking emails, and Riley was killing time in a straight chair across from her. Any moment, the receptionist was supposed to buzz and say Ruth was waiting in the conference room.

"That's sweet," Kate said, her eyes still focused on the screen.

Ever since Matt Simpson's TV interview, she averaged twenty new emails an hour from prospective clients. Most were family court losers looking for a free lawyer. But a few were genuine prospects, which meant she had to open all of them and scan each one.

"Did you hear about Judge McDaniel?" Riley asked.

Kate nodded. "Early retirement was a smart move. Why go

through the hell of an ethics investigation when you're hitting mandatory retirement in two years."

Riley raised an eyebrow. "Uh, to clear your name, perhaps? To preserve your legacy?"

"I guess. Unless you're guilty."

Kate could feel Riley's skepticism from across the desk. Not looking at him made it easier to ignore.

Riley said, "Did you hear Tina Black is out at Hansmeier too?"

She glanced up at him. She had not heard this.

"Of course, I've heard it, Riley. I hear everything first. How did you hear?"

"I know a guy who works there. Apparently, it was a big scene. Tina refused to leave her office. They had to call in two big goons who dragged her out kicking and screaming. She escaped when they reached the lobby. They cornered her again by that marble bust, you know, the one of the very first Hansmeier who's wearing the wig." Kate nodded. "Well, she pushed it over. Cracked the guy's head in half."

"No way."

"Yeah," Riley said, nodding. "Supposedly, the marble is super rare and they don't know if they can fix it."

Kate shook her head. "I told you that woman was crazy."

He frowned.

"Don't frown at me," Kate said. "You don't know the terrible things she's done."

"Maybe. But you can't say she deserved to lose her job over Simpson's stupid article."

"Don't put that on me. I didn't write it. Plus, if you recall, he said he had three sources for the story."

"No, Kate," Riley said, head shaking. "He said he had two. Both were unnamed. And one was Ruth."

"You don't know that for sure. And even if it's true, what do you want me to do about it? I don't work at the paper."

"Ruth is a liar, Kate. She shouldn't be anyone's unnamed source."

"Off the record, I agree with you. Our client has an aversion to the truth. But she's our client. And it's our job is to protect her. Tina Black and old man McDaniel can fend for themselves."

Riley crossed his arms, shot her a hard look.

"Make that pouty face, if you want, but you'll never guilt me into caring about Tina Black. She is a terrible person. Maybe she slept with McDaniel. Maybe she didn't. Who cares? She deserves everything that's happened and more."

"You're making a mistake, Kate."

Kate shook her head. "Thank you for your opinion. Your objection is noted. But remember: I'm the general in this relationship, and you're the private. We're going to do our duty to help Ruth."

Riley nodded like a good soldier did when an argument reached its end. She looked back at her computer, and they sat for a moment, the only noise coming from her clicking delete with the mouse.

"You know it's one-fifteen?" he said after a while.

Kate glanced at the clock on her laptop.

"Yes. Thanks for the update."

"She's late."

"I can tell time, Riley."

"It's a bad sign if she no-shows, right?"

Kate looked up at him. "Are you trying to drive me crazy?"

"No, I'm just worried."

Out of the corner of her eye, Kate saw a figure appear in the doorway.

It was The Hatchet. The woman stood with her hands laced together in front of her. As always, she wore her trademark black trench coat, black turtleneck, black slacks, and villain-like black latex gloves. Kate figured the outfit had to get really hot in the summer sun. She decided that if she ever became a comic book villain, she'd dress like wonder woman to stay cool. The new 1984 version. The one with the denim shorts and less revealing top. Not the old Lynda Carter style blue underwear look.

"Why are you worried, Mr. Anderson?" The Hatchet asked.

"He's not worried," Kate said. "We're talking case strategy. Is there something you need, Ms. Vulcan?"

The Hatchet stepped into the office. "Ms. Wilson is reassuming control of the Ruth Jacobs's case."

No, Kate thought. Susan would never say reassuming control. It sounded idiotic. She'd use a powerful word. Something like seizing or hijacking or commandeering.

But whatever Susan had said, it wasn't going to happen. Kate wouldn't let it.

"Of course," Kate said. "Would Susan like me to stay on as second chair? Continue handling the day-to-day work?"

The Hatchet frowned. "No, Ms. Wilson would not. Where is Ruth anyway? She's not in the conference room."

"Yeah, she had to reschedule. Last minute deal. She's coming in tomorrow."

The Hatchet hummed. "Very well. Gather up your notes, Ms. Becker. I want everything in my office immediately."

The Hatchet left, and Kate got to her feet.

"We're taking a field trip," she said. "Right now."

74

In law schools across America, professors speak of law as a profession, not a business. They repeat it over and over so many times, new students believe it's true. It's not until a year or two later that most discover these Pollyanna types know nothing of the real world. Had they ever bothered to climb down from their endowed chairs, they might realize that student loans and mortgages and doctor bills don't get paid by professional membership. Business pays the bills. Always has. Always will.

Kate had never lost sight of this. To her, practicing law meant bill, bill, bill. Win, win, win.

But there was one sense in which the uppity professors had gotten it right. Lawyers weren't fungible goods. Clients tended not to like it when a new person took over their case suddenly. It was like when you're sitting half-naked at the doctor's office waiting for your longtime physician and some new guy comes in, starts peeking under the sheet.

At least, that's what Kate planned to tell Ruth when she saw her.

As long as Ruth demanded to keep Kate as her lawyer, Susan Wilson or The Hatchet could do nothing to stop it.

Kate signaled her turn and made a left onto a narrow street in a trailer park on the outskirts of Austin. It was trash day. Plastic bins with overflowing garbage lined the curb on both sides of the road.

She didn't need to check the address to know Ruth's trailer was the one at the end of the block. The TV truck with the satellite on top gave it away.

"This can't be good," Kate said to Riley. He was in the passenger seat beside her, making faces.

"With her, it never is."

She parked behind the news truck. They got out and made their way up a dirt path to the trailer. In a brown patch of grass that was the front yard, a man was setting up a camera on a tripod. He appeared to be trying to find an angle in which the background wasn't a beat-up trailer or a rusted car on cinder blocks.

There was a handwritten sign tied to the handrail by the trailer's front door. It read, "International Headquarters of Chicks Against Dicks, Inc."

"I hope you didn't know about that," Riley said.

"Shut up."

She knocked on the flimsy front door. A moment later, a twenty-something woman with spiky purple hair and a nose ring answered it.

"What?" The woman spoke as if it were the middle of the night, and they had disturbed her sleep.

"We're here to see Ruth."

"Ruth ain't here."

Kate leaned to the right and looked past the woman. At a booth-like kitchen table, she saw the outline of someone who looked like Ruth.

"She's right there."

"That's not her."

Kate scoffed. "Ruth, it's Kate Becker. We need to talk about your case."

"Tell 'em I'm busy," Ruth hollered, not bothering to look back.

"She's busy," the woman repeated.

"Ruth, do you think I would have driven all the way out here if it wasn't important?"

"Tell 'em to call Elwood," Ruth said.

"You need to—"

"Susan Wilson wants to take over your case," Kate said.

Ruth cursed, tossed something down onto the table, then stood up and walked over to the door.

"Thanks for nothing, Crystal," Ruth said, nudging the woman aside. "How am I supposed to think with all these interruptions? Now go ask the guy how much longer 'til he's ready."

Kate stepped to the side to let the woman pass.

"Ain't Susan Wilson your boss?" Ruth said after Crystal had sulked across the yard.

"Technically."

Ruth raised an eyebrow? "Don't bullshit me. We both know she is. Seems to me I'm trading up."

"You're not."

"Oh, yeah? Why?"

Kate glanced at Riley. "Could you give us a minute?"

"Seriously?" Riley said.

"Trust me," Kate said. "You want deniability."

He rolled his eyes.

She waited for him to walk halfway down the path back to the street before continuing. "If Susan takes over your case, she'll figure out you're lying. Then she'll drop you. Fast."

"You didn't."

Kate hummed. "If she drops you, Judge Eide will know you're lying. Susan doesn't quit cases she's winning."

Ruth shrugged. "Maybe. Or maybe you're selling me out again. Either way, I don't care. The case is a waste of time. I got bigger things cooking now. See that news van? They want to hear all about the sex church."

"Ruth." Kate was exasperated. She couldn't believe her future depended on this idiot. "Do you think they'll still want to interview you if they find out you were lying in the custody case?"

Ruth tilted her head to the side. It seemed she might be beginning to understand.

"If I wanted to keep you," Ruth said, a moment later, "what would I need to do?"

Kate felt the tension in her chest begin to ease.

"It's easy. Tell Susan you want to stick with me."

"Oh, that's it?" Ruth said. "Just pick you over her."

Kate sighed. "Why do you hate me so much, Ruth?"

"You mean besides forcing me into fifty-fifty?"

"We've been over that a hundred times. One hundred percent custody wasn't realistic."

"Elwood says it is."

"Elwood goes to community college."

"He predicted you'd make fun of his school."

"I'm not making fun of it," Kate said. "It is a community college."

Ruth crossed her arms, shook her head. "Some of the smartest people in history went to community college."

Kate wanted to scream.

At that moment, Crystal marched across the yard and came up to them, holding a cell phone.

"Lori needs to talk to you," Crystal said to Ruth. "The baby won't stop crying. She doesn't know what to do."

Ruth put a hand out, refused to take the phone. "Can't you see I'm in a meeting, Crystal. If your sister can't do the job, find someone who can. Otherwise, I'm taking your name off the website."

Crystal mumbled an apology, then turned around and yelled into the phone as she went back to supervising the cameraman.

"Fine," Ruth said. "I'll take you back. Under one condition."

"What's that?"

"That you respect me. And do what I say."

"You mean like arguing for one hundred percent custody?" Kate said.

Ruth nodded. "And I don't want Damion to have parenting time.

I'm sick of driving across town so he can play daddy for a few hours."

"He's the child's father, Ruth."

"Then he can do Zoom calls like all the other criminals."

"There's no basis for that. Even if Judge Eide ordered it, the Court of Appeals would reverse."

Ruth huffed. "Well, those are my conditions. Either take 'em or leave 'em."

"I'm only trying to help you."

"No, you're not. You're trying to save your own butt. But I don't have time for games. This is war, Kate Becker. A revolution. Chicks fightin' dicks. And I'm the new Ladyham Lincoln. So step up or step off."

Kate hesitated, then nodded slowly.

"If you need evidence, call Elwood. He'll get whatever it takes to win."

75

The text message Kate received said Susan Wilson's party started at three o'clock in the afternoon, which was why it was a little after four when she and Riley turned into Susan's epically long driveway.

The driveway was a private road that snaked for half a mile between two wood-fenced prairies that seemed to stretch out and touch the horizon. Not a single tree obstructed the three hundred sixty-degree view. Far ahead, off to the left of where the road ended at the mansion, Kate saw a red barn. A group of white horses was clustered in front of it, seeming not to understand how much freedom they really had. The horses could have galloped for five minutes before encountering a fence at the county highway.

A part of Kate understood why Susan had chosen this place, a monster of a horse ranch thirty minutes from downtown Austin. It smelled like old money. The kind of country estate respectable Southern families had been passing down for generations. Kate remembered the opening image from the TV show Dallas. The part where a helicopter flies over the property. It could have been filmed here. At Susan's ranch. Except Susan wouldn't have owned it back then. It would have been owned by a respectable family.

"I told you we were going to be late," Riley said.

She had picked him up outside his apartment building on her way out of town. To convince him to be her plus one (technically, Susan had invited only her), she offered to buy him a pizza on the way home. He countered with a steak dinner. They settled on pizza, beer, and wings. Although, given how much he had been whining on the drive out, she was considering not buying him anything at all. She had invited him to avoid making small talk with work people. But awkward small talk was seeming better by the second compared to his constant complaining.

"If you would have let me drive," he said, "we wouldn't be late."

She wrinkled her nose. "What sexist BS! My driving is fine. And we're not late. No one shows up when a party starts."

This was true of every party Kate had ever attended. Although, as they got closer, the mansion fifty yards in front of them now, she had doubts. There were cars parked on both sides of the road all the way up to the house.

"We should probably back up," he said. "Find a place to park."

She slowed so her eyes could scan the spaces between the cars, searching for a spot big enough they could squeeze into. There was nothing.

"I thought this was supposed to be a small affair," Kate said.

"Maybe it is for Ms. Wilson. Or maybe everybody brought an unauthorized plus one."

She flashed him a weak smile. Seeing all the cars depressed her. When she had gotten Susan's text message inviting her to a party at The Ranch, she assumed it meant something special, intimate. A gathering of the firm's most valued employees. A special thank you for her splendid work on Ruth's case. But the sheer magnitude of this giant bash made the invitation feel... generic.

They stopped in the center of a large circular driveway in front of the mansion. There was no place to park. Even if she could have squeezed between the pair of Ferraris, she wouldn't have done it because her measly three series BMW looked silly next to the six-figure gems. She shifted into reverse, looked over her shoulder, and was about to back up when a man in a black vest jogged up to them.

"Hi, ma'am," he said after she rolled down her window. "Welcome to Shady Acres Ranch. I'll take your car."

She stepped out and watched as the man flipped through a stack of paper tickets, looking for an empty sheet. After a few seconds, he found one.

"Can I get your name, please?" he asked.

"Kate Becker."

The words seemed to mean something to him. He became more engaged, expressive. He scribbled her name on a ticket, then ripped off the stub and handed it to her.

"Tell them your name at the door. They'll take you to Ms. Wilson. She's expecting you."

Kate nodded. Maybe Susan's invitation was special after all. Surely, the valet didn't say that to everyone.

When they reached the enormous front door, Riley said, "What's the best-case scenario when the boss is waiting and you're an hour late?"

She was spared from having to answer when the door opened. A distinguished-looking man dressed in a tuxedo greeted them with a cold, "Good Afternoon." His posture was perfectly erect, as if someone had fused his spine.

"I'm Kate Becker. This is my plus-one, Riley Anderson. Susan is expecting us."

The man frowned. She couldn't tell if it was because they were late or because she had used Ms. Wilson's first name or because she had brought a plus-one.

He motioned them inside a marble lobby with forty-foot ceilings, then led them down a corridor buzzing with the sounds of a party. In rooms along the right side, she saw people in fancy clothes, the kind of getup rich people wear to a 1920s flapper-style theme party. They were laughing and slurping brightly colored drinks from martini glasses. Jazz music came from speakers in the ceiling.

In one of the rooms, a woman about her age, who was wearing a black sequined dress with a white feathered boa around her neck, briefly locked eyes with Kate, then looked away as if to say, "We're not friends."

Standing beside the woman was a man in a black tux. He had close-cropped brown hair, a clean-shaven face, and a body that belonged in a magazine. When he glanced in Kate's direction, he smiled and winked. Before she could even process what it meant, a wall blocked him from view.

They continued on for another twenty yards until the butler stopped in front of a closed door. Using a key from his pocket, he opened it and ushered them into a gorgeous, gilded-age style library. The room was two stories high. Bookshelves filled with hardbacks in shades of browns and reds occupied every inch of the perimeter. A wooden ladder on wheels attached to the wall granted access to a catwalk above.

"Ms. Wilson will be in shortly," the butler said before backing out of the room and closing the door.

A moment later, there was a soft metal click.

Riley flashed her a puzzled look. "Did he just lock us in the library?"

76

Kate had wondered the same thing when she heard the noise.

She went to the door, tried the handle. It wouldn't budge.

Riley shook his head. "I told you she'd be pissed if we were late. You know Ms. Wilson. She hates being disrespected."

Kate glanced across the library towards a pair of stained glass windows smeared with reds and blues and greens. What was the point of locking them in a space that cost more than her condo? If she had really wanted to escape, she could have simply hurled one of the bronzed busts at a window and climbed out onto the lawn. But why would she want to leave? Susan had invited her to the party.

She tried the handle again, then swore under her breath.

"I'm telling you. She's punishing us," Riley said.

"For being late to a party? You think she's that petty?"

"Yes, I do. Or maybe she found out you're calling her Susan."

Kate shook her head.

The lock on the door clicked again.

It swung open to reveal the dashing man she saw in the other room. The one who had winked at her.

"Quick," he said mischievously, with the aurora of a teenage boy who had sneaked into his girlfriend's room after dark. "We should go. Before someone sees us."

Although she didn't know the first thing about him, something deep inside made her want to follow him. Out of the room. Anywhere.

"Leave?" Kate said. "I don't want to leave. I'm waiting for Susan."

The man frowned. "Sorry to tell you, but she left. Forty minutes ago. Now, if you'd rather not spend the evening being suffocated by Russian novels, we should go."

Riley moved towards the door. When the two men were side by side, she couldn't help but see the similarities. In broad brush strokes, they were about the same size. Both were clean-shaven. Both had close-cropped brown hair and powerful jaws. From a distance, a person might even confuse them.

But, she could easily tell them apart. Riley didn't have an ounce of dashing in his body.

"Ms. Wilson left because we were late, right?" Riley said.

The man shrugged. "I don't know. Were you late?" Riley nodded. "I guess, maybe. All I know is locking you in here wasn't my aunt's idea. I overheard Vulcan ordering Burrows to grab you as soon as you showed up."

"The Hatchet's here?"

The man smiled. "Good nickname. She is sort of hatchet-like, the way she splits people in half."

They followed him down the hall, away from the rooms where the partiers were gathered. She didn't like sneaking out, but with Susan gone, there was no reason for her to stay.

He opened a door to a storage room lined with metal shelving units packed full of trinkets and home furnishings, which, despite probably costing a fortune, still weren't good enough for Susan to display.

At the back of the room, a steel door led them outside to a concrete walk bordered on both sides by ten-foot-tall hedges. All she could see was the sky above and fifty feet straight ahead where the path jutted ninety degrees to the right. It felt like she was in a secret garden maze.

"This way," he said. "The garage isn't far. Give me your ticket. I'll get your keys from the valet."

She pulled out the folded slip of paper and handed it to him.

"You're Susan's nephew?" she asked.

He nodded, then extended a hand to her. "My name's Braxton Wilson."

"Kate Becker," she said. The instant their hands touched, her heart raced. His grip was firm but not hard. His skin was warm but not clammy.

"Nice to meet you." He nodded in Riley's direction, then refocused on her. "Now, Ms. Becker, you must tell me, because I'm dying to know. What did you do to provoke The Hatchet into locking you in our library? And don't say it's because you were late."

Kate flashed Riley a quick I-told-you-so look.

"I don't know," she said. "The woman has disliked me from the beginning."

"I don't believe that. You seem very likable to me."

Kate blushed. She tried to think of a cleaver, witty response that said she also found him likable (and attractive) without sounding pathetic, but she couldn't think of a single thing. She wondered if she had always been so bad at flirting or if she was just rusty.

"The Hatchet doesn't like her because Kate won't be bullied," Riley said.

"Bullied?" Braxton looked confused. "The Hatchet's a bully?"

"Um, yes."

Braxton looked at Kate, then at Riley, then back at her again. "Why doesn't anyone call her out?"

"Because they're sheep," Riley said.

Kate scoffed. *I should never have invited him as my plus one*, she thought. *He doesn't know when to shut up.*

"No one's a sheep," Kate said. "It's capitalism that keeps us quiet. Women lawyers are a dime a dozen these days. Susan could replace any of us, or all of us, at a whim."

"I doubt that's true," Braxton said as they approached a t-intersection in the sidewalk. In front of them was a large brick building that looked like an airplane hanger. He pointed to the right, where the path turned back towards the driveway and the front of the house. "Go that way. I'll send the valet with your keys."

He went left. But just before he disappeared from view, Kate saw him glancing back at her.

77

On the drive home, Kate couldn't stop thinking about the man who rescued her. Okay, maybe rescued was a bit strong, but he had saved her from an unpleasant evening with The Hatchet.

Back at her condo, she grabbed her laptop and went to sit on the couch. She opened an internet browser and typed Braxton Wilson's name in the search box.

The first result was a Wikipedia page. According to the bio, Braxton was a single, thirty-seven-year-old American businessman, socialite, and former college lacrosse player. After graduating summa cum laude from Dartmouth, he switched coasts, went to Stanford for an MBA. He didn't finish, though, because he was scooped up by a Silicon Valley start-up and made head of sales since no one else at the company could schmooze without sounding like a nerd.

His decision to leave school turned out to be quite wise. Six months and one day after he started work, the company's little app was swallowed by an even bigger app that burped oodles of money. He quickly sold his stock, which was a good thing because soon after, the big app was diagnosed with an eating disorder and died.

He paid the millions he owed in taxes and moved back to his aunt's ranch in Austin to retire.

Kate deduced this last part by reading between the lines of a puff piece profile The Austin Times Sunday Magazine had run the previous year. Braxton claimed he moved home to pursue community advocacy, but the reporter noted it was widely believed he harbored political ambitions. First for the governor's mansion. Then, perhaps, the White House.

Kate clicked back to the results page as the front door of the condo opened. Her mother marched inside, yelling back over her shoulder.

"Yeah, yeah, yeah," Barbara said. "It's not open for discussion. We're stopping at Carol's. Deal with it."

Her mother passed by without even glancing at Kate. She went down the hall to her bedroom.

Jessica shuffled inside a moment later, her head hung low, her shoulders slumped forward. She dragged a rollie suitcase behind her like a pouty six-year-old girl.

"But I don't want to go to Carol's. I want to go home."

"Stop arguing!" her mother yelled from back in the bedroom.

When Jessica looked up, her eyes met Kate's.

"You're here," Jessica said.

"Yes, I live here."

"Mom said you were at Susan Wilson's party."

"I was, but she cut it short. A client emergency."

Jessica nodded, readily accepting the idea that Susan might bolt from her own party to attend a client problem on a Sunday night. She came to sit on the couch beside her.

"I wish I had known," Jessica said. "I would have had you pick me up at the airport. Mom said Sally could do it, but guess who subbed in her place?"

Kate shook her head.

"And now, the woman's holding me hostage. Refusing to take me home until after we have coffee. Do I look like I can survive coffee at Carol's?"

Jessica's hair was flat and snarled. She had large dark circles under her eyes, and she was wearing a child-sized tourist sweatshirt with the words "I love NYC" stamped across her chest.

"I'll drive you home," Kate said.

"God bless you. It's been a hellish weekend."

Kate set her laptop on the couch, then stood up and went to the kitchen to grab her keys.

"I take it kismet didn't go as planned?"

"That's the understatement of the century." Jessica leaned back against the cushions, dramatically draped an arm across her face. "All weekend, Wayne had me crisscrossing the city in a taxi, always claiming he had a new lead on Thorton, but the guy's an idiot. This afternoon, I gave up. The only way I could get home was riding coach. A middle seat back by the toilet."

"At least you got a nice sweatshirt."

Jessica laughed, brought her arm down. "Oh, yeah. This gem. I got it courtesy of the airline. This is what they give you when the guy who's been breathing on you for hours finally vomits on your shirt."

Kate wrinkled her nose. "I thought you smelled funky."

"Yeah, that's me. Oh, before I forget. Wayne wanted me to give you a message. He says Asha is being quite a spitfire. But, he still thinks he can get her."

He thinks he can get her? Kate thought. What happened to the confident Certified Online Internet Protector, who keeps demanding more money?

"Have you ever heard of a guy named Braxton Wilson?" Kate asked.

"Um, of course. Why?"

"I met him today."

Jessica sat up, suddenly very interested. "Met him how? Like you saw him across the room? Or like Susan introduced you?"

"More like he rescued me from The Hatchet. We talked for a bit."

"Tell me everything."

When Kate finished explaining it, beat by beat, Jessica's mouth hung open and she gawked at her.

"What?" Kate said after awhile when the silence became awkward.

"I'm speechless."

"Yes, I can see that."

Jessica leaned forward, pulled a leg up underneath her on the couch. "And you think he likes you?"

"I mean, I don't know. Maybe. I felt like there was chemistry."

"Wow." Jessica shook her head. "He's the real deal, Kate. There's talk he's going to run for senator."

"Governor," Kate corrected.

"Whatever. So, what are you going to do?"

"Do?" Kate asked. "There's nothing to do. We talked at a party. It's over."

Jessica scoffed. "Tell me you're joking. Otherwise, I'm losing respect for you."

"What do you want me to do? March up to Susan? Ask for his telephone number? Maybe a dollop of his sperm, too?"

Jessica forced a laugh. "Don't be silly. Men like Braxton live for the chase. You need to make him come to you."

"Oh, I don't like the sound of that."

"Come on, Katie. You know I'm right. The guy's obviously got a savior complex. You wouldn't have met him, otherwise."

Jessica had a point. Braxton had gone beyond what an average person would do after only a few seconds of eye contact. Usually, she found overt displays of chivalry to be a turn off. But not this time. This time, she liked it. Maybe it wasn't the chivalry she detested. Maybe it was the men doing the saving.

"I'm not doing anything crazy."

Jessica smiled. "Define crazy."

78

One week after Barbara met Garrett at the dry riverbed, she sat alone in the condo, camped out at the dining room table, a cold cup of coffee beside her, trying to make sense of Garrett's answers to her questions.

She had spent an entire day drafting them, brainstorming, revising, and typing the best fifteen. They were questions she thought a real grandmother ought to know, questions which revealed the boy's character, personality, traits. She was so proud of her work that after pressing send, she nearly showed it to Kate before realizing that nothing she could ever write would impress her Ivy League daughter.

She had expected it to take several days for him to respond. Even if he saw the email right away, which wasn't guaranteed, the questions weren't the sort you could answer quickly. They were too detailed, required too much thought, demanded too much introspection.

But ten minutes after she sent the message, Garrett's first volley of replies came back. She felt like she was on the beach at Normandy being shelled by enemy fire. Boom, boom, boom. The speed of his messages caused her tablet to ping uncontrollably. She wondered if a computer could overheat from too much email.

When the pinging stopped, she opened the first message. From margin to margin, her screen filled with text. One giant paragraph, a never-ending sentence, no punctuation or capital letters. It was like reading a voice-typed stream of consciousness in which the boy added stories and thoughts and ideas at random. She tried to connect his answers to a question, but gave up when she got a headache.

She squeezed her eyes shut and was pinching the bridge of her nose when the doorbell rang.

"Oh, good, you're home," Veronica said, breezing into the condo the moment Barbara opened the door. "I was afraid you'd be at the grocery. Isn't today double coupon day?"

It was double coupon day for seniors at Devon's Discount Foods. Barbara would have been there too, standing in the line with the feisty crew who rode the bus from the assisted living facility, if Carol hadn't canceled with the flu: the bottle kind, not the viral one.

"Is everything all right?" Barbara said.

Veronica's eyes were big and wild. She glanced around the room. "Are we alone?"

"Yes. Why?"

"This is top-secret, Barbara. You can't tell anyone. And I mean no one. Especially not that gossip, Yata Miller."

"Veronica, you're scaring me. Is something wrong?"

"If they find out we know, they'll take it away."

"Take what away?"

Veronica studied her for a moment. "No, I can't. I'm sorry. I shouldn't have come, Barbara."

Veronica headed for the door. Barbara followed close behind. She didn't know what the woman was talking about, but suddenly, she very much wanted to.

"Tell me," Barbara begged.

Veronica stopped when she reached the door. She turned, looked Barbara in the eyes.

"You promise?"

"I already have."

It was clear the woman wanted to share but was holding back. Barbara stood quietly, hoping silence would dislodge the information.

After a moment, Veronica said, "So, I have this friend, whose daughter, is dating a man, whose mother, works at the Texas Senior Counsel."

"All right."

"I can't explain it, Barbara. I don't even know how it's possible. But you're going to win. You're going to be Grandmother of the Year."

"What?"

"They picked us, Barbara. You and me. Grannies R Us is going to be listed as a Class A charity in TSC's annual report. Can you believe it?"

"No, not really," Barbara said. "What about the paralyzed girl? I thought she was a shoo-in?"

Veronica nodded. "Everyone did. The Board picked her first, but it turns out she's a snot. When they sent a film crew to her grandfather's house to shoot b-roll, she said she only applied to be ironic."

"What does that mean?"

Veronica shrugged. "They have her on tape saying her grandfather is a big phony. She says the only TSC group he belongs in is the Texas Satanic Council. It was all very embarrassing. So, they went with us. Isn't it great?"

"Oh, yes."

"It gets even better. The Board decided it needs to increase visibility, something about losing the war to the Cancer Society, so it's hired a famous filmmaker to make a documentary about you and the boy."

Barbara's eyes went wide. "A documentary?"

Veronica nodded. "They want to screen the movie at senior centers across the country, hoping to encourage people to volunteer as grandparents. Do you know how big this could get?"

"I'm thinking about that, yes."

Veronica nodded. "Good. The reason they're keeping it a secret is because they want to capture your authentic reaction when they tell you. But obviously, we need your authentic reaction to be well-rehearsed. You know, for the good of the organization."

"Of course," Barbara said, feeling a little offended.

"Do you think we ought to tell Garrett? My inclination is yes."

Barbara nodded. Catching him off guard would be very bad.

"I'll tell him," Barbara said.

"Are you sure? Maybe it would be better if his mother heard it from me."

Barbara shook her head. "No, Garrett and I have a tight bond."

As Veronica pulled open the front door, she said, "This goes without saying, but I'm going to say it, anyway. This is a once-in-a-lifetime opportunity for us. If it goes well, I think we might franchise our model across the country. Do you know how many kids we'd be able to help?"

"We'll do everything we can to make you look good."

"It's not about looking good," Veronica said. "People love family drama. All we need is for the camera to capture the warmth you and Garrett have for each other. If you do that, everything will work out fine."

When Veronica was gone, Barbara leaned back against the closed door. If there was one thing no one could see, it was the way they actually felt about each other.

79

Within an hour of Veronica leaving the condo, Barbara hailed a car using a rideshare app on her phone and traveled across the city to Garrett's house. After a quick chat with his mother, she knocked on his door and pushed it open before being invited in.

Garrett was lying supine on the bed, ankles crossed, a book covering his face. He was dressed in his favorite sweatshirt and jeans and looked at ease.

He lowered the book as she entered the room. A flash of anger crossed his face.

"Grandma Becker," he said. "I thought you were going to be away for a long, long time."

"Yeah, well, things change."

"How wonderful."

She went and sat down on a wooden chair beside his bed and told him about Veronica and Grandmother of The Year and the documentary film crew.

"Absolutely not," he said when she was done.

"The film crew will be here the day after tomorrow. They're going to film your spontaneous reaction to the news."

"No, they aren't."

"Garrett, this is important."

"Not to me."

"Think about how it will look if you refuse. People will assume bad things about Grannies R Us."

He shrugged. "The truth always comes out in the end, Grandma Becker."

"It's not truth, Garrett. Grannies R Us is a wonderful organization. It has helped many kids."

"Not me." Barbara flashed him a hard look. "All right, all right. I'll have my Mom tell them I'm too sick to participate. No one can complain about that."

Barbara threw up her hands. "But you're not too sick. You need to stop using your illness as a crux."

"A crux? You do remember I have cancer, right?"

"Cancer, cancer, cancer," Barbara said, shaking her head. "How many times are you going to trot out that tired, old excuse? A minute ago, you were fine."

Garrett sat up in the bed. "Fine? What part of fine spends five straight days in bed because you're too weak to stand up."

Barbara scoffed. "I wish I could spend five straight days in bed. Listen, no one's asking you to run a marathon, all right. We'll prop you up with some big pillows. They'll record you talking about how close we are. How much you love me. How much of a difference Grannies has made in your life. It'll take fifteen, twenty minutes, tops. And Grannies can use the clip to pitch franchises."

"Franchises?"

"Veronica thinks it's the future."

"I'm not doing it."

"Fine," Barbara said. "I didn't want to call in this chip, but you've left me no choice. You're going to do it because you owe me for all that stuff I bought."

Garrett paused. "I'm not trying to be a jerk, Barbara." It was the first time he had ever used her first name. It felt awkward, inappropriate. "But there's no way I'm starring in a documentary as the cancer kid. For all eternity, people will see me as sick Garrett. Girls will see me as sick Garrett."

"I think you're overestimating the reach of this film. They want to show it in senior centers."

"They'll put a trailer on YouTube, Barbara. It'll never go away."

What little she knew about the internet suggested he was right. Still, she couldn't just give up. People were depending on her.

"Do this," Barbara said, "and I'll buy you whatever you want. Another book? A box of Danish cookies? Anything."

He raised an eyebrow. "Anything?"

She sighed. "No, Garrett, not anything. Good Lord, I'm your grandmother."

He looked away for a moment, appeared to think it over. When their eyes met again, his glistened.

"I'll do it," he said. "Under one condition."

Her pulse quickened. "What's the condition."

"It's nothing big. I just want you to help me feel... normal."

She swallowed hard. "Normal? What does that mean?"

He shrugged. "Whatever I say it means for as long as they keep filming us."

She shook her head. "No way. You'll turn it into something crazy."

"I'm not talking about crazy. Barbara, I'm sixteen years old. For as long as I can remember, I've been the sick kid whose Mom won't let him do this or that because she's afraid it might make me worse. Well, that ends now. If you want my help, then you're going to help me do the things I've never gotten to do. You know, rites of passage, so to speak."

Rites of passage? Barbara didn't like that phrase. It sounded like they'd be smoking a joint or–she didn't even want to think about what else it sounded like.

"I won't contribute to the delinquency of a minor," she said.

He forced a laugh. "Delinquency? Who said anything about delinquency? I'm talking about normal stuff."

"Give me an example."

"Okay." He paused for a moment. "Driving a car. I'm sixteen. I've passed all the written tests for my learner's permit, but my Mom still won't let me drive. You could teach me."

"Me?" Barbara's voice rose in disbelief. "I don't think I'm qualified for that job."

"You have a license, right?"

"Technically."

"Then it's fine. The rules say you're a qualified adult supervisor."

She doubted the person who created the rules intended to include people who had promised their daughters not to drive after bumping police cars.

"I want to help, Garrett. I do. But, I don't have a car. Or insurance."

"You can rent a car with insurance."

She hummed. It wasn't the worst thing he could have asked her to do. He was sixteen, and he had passed all the written tests. Plus, there was nothing wrong with teaching a kid to drive. It was the sort of rite of passage most kids do, cancer or not.

"All right," she said. "I'll do it. After your first interview."

He shook his head. "Nope. We're doing it tomorrow, at noon, come ready to have fun."

80

Kate lifted her fingers off the keyboard and swiveled her office chair ninety degrees to stare out the wall of windows behind her. An hour before, her writing had swerved off the road, sending her plunging headfirst into a ditch the size of the Grand Canyon. She had tried to climb out by shifting her focus to a different section of Ruth's affidavit. Still, every sentence she wrote came out sounding hollow, disjointed, like a bald-faced lie.

Which, of course, it was.

The best thing you could say about the custody argument Kate crafted for Ruth was that from afar, it seemed plausible. But up close, under the hood, it wasn't good.

There were two quick raps on her door. She glanced over to see Braxton Wilson poke his head into the office. He flashed her a big smile that made her heart flutter.

"Quick," he said, in the same playful voice she had heard at Susan's ranch. "We need to go. Before The Hatchet catches us."

She laughed, got to her feet.

"What are you doing here?"

Despite Jessica's insistence that they do something to pique his interest, they hadn't agreed on anything yet. This visit was entirely his doing.

Braxton slipped into the office and closed the door behind him. As he crossed the carpet, she pushed a strand of hair behind her ear. If she had thought there was even a one percent chance he might do a "pop in" like this today, she would have never worn the maroon blouse or baggy gray slacks. She only picked them because today was supposed to be a writing day. A day she didn't see anyone.

He stopped by the desk.

"Jeez, this place is colder than an art museum."

A part of her wanted to take a bow. Those were the feelings she hoped to invoke. Cold. Hard. Intimidating. But she sensed he hadn't meant it as a compliment.

"I could talk to my aunt," he said. "Usually, she lets new hires redecorate. I can't imagine she'd force you to keep it this way."

Kate smiled away what she wanted to say. "I'd rather just tough it out."

"I get it. When I started at Tickex, everyone treated me funny because I was friends with the founder. But I kept my head down, worked hard. By the end, at least three people accepted me."

She laughed. He was cute when he was being humble.

"I'm sure more than three people liked you."

He walked around the desk to the windows, looked down at the city below.

"At least you got a good view," he said.

"I think your aunt made sure everyone has a good view."

He glanced back at her. "I'm sure she thinks so, but it's not true. Come here. I'll show you what I mean."

She went to him, standing so close her shoulder brushed against his. The smell of his cologne made her skin tingle. A peppery lemon mix with a hint of orange and—She couldn't quite place the last bit. Was it cedar?

He pointed down at the bank of the Colorado River.

"See the boathouse?" he said. "The one behind the group of trees?"

She tried to look, but kept getting distracted by her desire to sniff him.

"Oh, yeah. I see it. The little building with the tin roof."

He nodded. "Now, look to the right, out towards the end of the dock. Do you see the boat?"

"Yeah."

"It's mine," Braxton said. "You can't see it from the other offices. The trees block the view." He looked at her. Her heart skipped a beat. "Like I said, yours is special."

The words hung in the air between them for a moment.

She swallowed, stared back at him. "I guess I am lucky."

"You know what would make you even luckier?"

"What?"

"If you got to ride on my boat. No one at the firm has ever ridden on my boat. Not even my aunt."

Kate's face lit up. She playfully hit him on the chest.

"Well, maybe we should make that happen."

"Let's go."

"Now?" All the playfulness had disappeared from her voice. "In the middle of a work day?"

"Sure. Ditching work would make it even more memorable, right?"

It was true. She had never ditched work before. Not once. Her mother joked that she was a better version of the postal service. Neither snow nor rain nor heat nor gloom of night stays Kate from billing of clients.

"I wish I could." She reached out and touched his hand. "But, I have to finish a brief."

"My aunt's paralegal could handle it. She owes me a favor. I got her kid a plum job in San Francisco."

"No," Kate said sharply. She hadn't intended to snap at him, but she couldn't afford to let another lawyer near Ruth's case. "I'm sorry. It's just, this client is special to me. I don't want to pawn her off."

"I get it. And don't apologize for caring about your work. I love that about you."

She had spent less than forty minutes with this man, knew virtually nothing about him, and yet she was fantasizing about a life with him. She saw a version of her future where she had more than one child. Two. No, maybe four. A big family would be fun around the holidays.

"How about tomorrow?" she said. "We could ditch then."

He laughed. "I don't think it's ditching if you plan in advance."

"It is at Susan Wilson Law. I can show you the handbook, if you don't believe me. Leaving before eight o'clock at night for any reason is ditching."

He smiled. "Tomorrow, then. It actually works out better for me, anyway. I'm have to meet a lawyer this afternoon."

"Really? Why?"

"Oh, it's nothing," he said. "I'm helping a friend find local counsel. Do you know a woman named, Tina Black?"

Kate's eyes went wide. "Tina Black?"

Braxton nodded. "Yeah. Supposedly, she's going to be a big star. The Austin Times ran an article about her a while back."

Kate struggled to keep her face neutral. "I don't know. Maybe, I've met her."

"Well, if I end up recommending her, I'll tell her she owes you big time. Because if you hadn't turned me down, I was going to cancel my meeting with her. Go with a different guy. But now, she gets a chance to woo me over. And it's all because of you."

Kate's heart thumped in her chest.

"You know, on second thought, I could ditch today."

He waved her off. "Don't worry about it. We have tomorrow. It will be just as good."

"But what if it rains?"

"It's not going to rain tomorrow."

"It might."

"Not supposed to."

"But it could."

Braxton raised an eyebrow. "Then I guess we'd go the day after that."

"You guess?" Kate's eyes were wild. Tina Black's name had sent her into a frenzy. "But it could rain then too. A thick wall of black clouds could blow in off the Gulf. Soak us for an entire week."

He wrinkled his nose. "A week? Probably not a week."

"It's rained for a week before, Braxton. Don't be so naïve."

He seemed confused by the comment. A moment later, he laughed. "I think you're the first woman who's ever called me naïve. Did I say something wrong? Because you seem upset."

"I'm not upset," she said. "I'm just explaining why we can't wait. A week is forever. Anything can happen in a week. I could die. You could sell your boat. You could be wooed to the cult of conservatism."

"One, I hope you don't die. Two, I don't plan to sell my boat. And three, I'm only open to cults that woo me with women in skimpy bikinis."

"Stop joking around," Kate said. "Let's go now."

"All right, all right. But what about your client?"

Ruth's case had dropped from her thoughts for the first time in a long time.

"I'll have Riley do it. He's good enough. My client's not a real winner, anyway."

As she guided Braxton out the door, she held out her hand.

"Give me your phone. I'll text Tina Black. Cancel for you."

81

As Garrett's suggestion, Barbara set out to rent a car with insurance. She went to the airport and stood in a big line at the rental center. When she reached the front, the teenage girl working the counter, who was smacking her gum and twirling her hair with a pen, said they didn't accept cash.

Having never rented a car before, the need to use a credit card struck Barbara as blatantly un-American. "You're discriminating against the poor," she said, raising her voice and glancing around as if she were performing some kind of public service. When the girl didn't answer, Barbara whipped out her wallet and slapped down a hundred-dollar bill on the counter.

"This Note is legal tender for all debts, public and private," Barbara said.

The teenage girl stayed quiet, pointing to the spot in Barbara's wallet where the emergency credit card was kept.

Using the card wasn't an option. She was close to the limit already. Going over would trigger an investigation by Kate Becker, Esq., and she had no plausible reason why she needed to rent a car when she wasn't supposed to be driving. So, she swallowed her pride and went back to the condo and rode the elevator to the penthouse.

"I knew this day would come," Yata Miller said, standing in the doorway, smiling and rubbing her hands together like a movie villain. "Trust me, Barbie. Once you go Subaru, you won't go back."

Convincing Yata to give her a test drive was the easy part. Convincing Yata to let her do it alone, without dealership trained supervision, was nearly impossible. Barbara only succeeded by promising to bring both Kate and Jessica to an all-day prospective owner's seminar at Yata's nephew's dealership next month. "They'll have a blast," Yata said. "There'll be a snow cone machine, balloon twisters, and people to testify about how Subaru has changed their lives."

She met Garrett at a small park near his house. Through the windshield, she watched him hop off a swing and jog over to her.

"Get in," Barbara said, rolling down the driver's side window. "Let's talk first."

"We can talk while I drive."

She shook her head. "There will be no talking while you're driving. This car is very expensive, Garrett. You need to be extra careful."

"It's a Subaru, not a Lamborghini."

"It might as well be a Lamborghini to you, mister, because my friend loves this car more than life itself."

"This isn't Yata Miller's car, is it?"

"Do you know her?"

"Oh, this is going to be so fun," he said. "Come on. Get out. I'll tell you."

Barbara got out reluctantly and went around to the passenger seat. The instant she sat down, Garrett's foot was on the gas, revving the engine with the car in park.

"Stop that!"

"Relax. The engine likes it."

"What? Who told you that?" Barbara said.

He shifted the car into drive, then punched the gas, sending them screaming out of the parking lot and down the neighborhood street.

"Whoa, whoa," she said. "Slow down. Slow down."

Instead of slowing down, he made the car go even faster. If a person had poked their head outside of one of the cars parked along the tree-lined residential street, it would have been chopped clean off. Barbara's heart raced. She grabbed the handle above the door.

"The speed limit is twenty-five," she said.

He turned to look at her. "My mom says you can go ten over."

"You're going fifty over."

"Don't be ridiculous. Hold on, Barbara. This is going to be cool."

He slowed a little but was still going way too fast as they approached a t-intersection. Yanking the wheel to the left, they blew through a stop sign and skidded across the pavement up onto the lawn of a house on the other side. When the car stopped, he hit the gas again, tearing up the grass and sending them racing back down the road.

"Pull over!" she yelled.

"Why?"

"Because you're done!"

"Done? We're just getting started." Garrett began jabbing at the buttons on the center console. "Do you know how to work the Bluetooth? I want to hook-up my phone, so we can listen to music."

"Stop."

"Relax."

"No, stop!"

She pointed out the windshield. A block in front of them, there was a stoplight at a major cross street. It had changed from green to yellow.

By the time Garrett looked up, it was too late. The light was bright red when they flew through the intersection. Fortunately, none of the waiting drivers were too quick on the draw.

"Well, that's lucky for us," he said as they continued on, his eyes drifting back to the center console. "So, do you know how to work the Bluetooth or what?"

Before Barbara could find her voice, she heard a police phaser behind them. She glanced back to see red and blue flashing lights.

82

Garrett pulled over to the side of the road and switched off the Subaru. They waited for the cop to approach them.

Barbara said, "Keep your mouth shut, your hands on the wheel, and don't do anything stupid."

He made a face at her. "What am I going to do? Grab my oxygen tank and make a run for it?"

"I don't know. Are you?"

"I might, if you wouldn't rat me out."

Barbara scoffed. "Stop screwing around, Garrett. This is serious."

"Serious? Come on, Barbara. We're not bank robbers. So, I made a little boo-boo? Ran a red light? We're not criminals."

"You raced through a neighborhood. Chewed up that lawn."

Garrett rolled his eyes. "He doesn't know that. And no one is going to tell him, right?"

Barbara hummed.

He said, "Listen, let me handle it. I know how to talk to these cowboys. There's only one thing they understand."

Barbara saw the police officer walk up from behind the car. He was a big, burly, bald man, dressed in a dark uniform with mirror sunglasses and a scowl on his face. He didn't seem like the type of person who had much patience for a lippy teenager.

A part of her wanted to let Garrett handle it. He was the one who blew the stoplight. He was the one who should suffer the consequences.

But she knew that wasn't fair. He had cancer. She didn't want him to spend his last days worrying about a traffic citation.

"Be quiet. Follow my lead," Barbara said.

They gave the officer Garrett's paper permit, her driver's license, and Yata's insurance card. Then Barbara asked to speak to the man alone. After studying them for a second and deciding they didn't pose a threat, he told her to meet him back by the trunk.

"Let me just say I'm so sorry," Barbara said. "This whole situation is my fault."

The officer glanced at her license. "You're Barbara Becker?"

"Yes. I was only trying to teach my grandson to drive. This is like a make-a-wish thing. Some people go to Disney. Others to Hawaii. My Garrett wanted to learn to drive. He's got the cancer, you see. Terrible cancer. Anyway, when the light turned yellow, I froze. My life passed before my eyes."

"Your life passed before your eyes?"

"It's a figure of speech. So, I'm almost catatonic, not knowing what to do, when suddenly I'm floating outside my body, looking down at the car and the street and the light from way up above."

"Have you been drinking, ma'am?"

"What? No, of course, not."

"Have you taken any drugs or other medications today?"

"No. It's not like that, officer. I'm trying to explain. As I'm floating above the car, I have this moment of ultimate clarity. I can see truth with a capital T. Do you know what I realize is the safest option?"

"Running the red light?"

"Yes. You do get it."

The officer grunted a negative sound. It was somewhere

between a hum and a scoff. He glanced at Garrett's permit, then the insurance card.

"This is Yata Miller's car?" he said, sounding surprised.

"Don't tell me you know her, too."

"Did Ms. Miller give permission for this boy to be driving her wagon?"

She wanted to ask if everyone in the city knew Yata Miller, but she stopped herself before it came out.

"Of course, Yata knows," she lied.

The man studied her for a moment. "I think I should call her. Have a seat, ma'am."

He pointed at the cement curb and waited for Barbara to sit down before going back to his car.

Standing behind an open driver's side door, he made the call on his cell phone. Barbara wondered if Yata might report the car stolen. It wasn't out of the realm of possibility. She had promised to bring it back more than an hour ago.

After a short conversation, the officer came over to her, handed her the phone.

"Hello, Yata," Barbara said, trying to sound light.

"You're in deep trouble, Barbara Becker. How dare you let Stink Bomb drive my wagon!"

83

Kate turned to the side and studied her reflection in a mirror on the floor of her bedroom. Standing five feet back, she could see down to the top of her shins, and she didn't like it one bit. She tried in vain to smooth out a crease on her left thigh, then gave up.

"You really don't think it makes me look fat?"

Jessica rolled her eyes. "For the hundredth time, no."

Her sister had offered to help her choose an outfit for her date with Braxton but had grown bored with how long it was taking and began saying everything looked fine.

Kate hummed. "I don't know. I feel like it draws the eye here." She pinched an inch of fat on her belly. "Look how disgusting this is."

"If you were any skinner, your organs would start shrinking."

"Oh, really? Why don't you come a little closer. I'll squeeze out of this spandex and jiggle my flab in your face."

Jessica winced. "Please don't. The last thing I need is nightmares from seeing my sister naked."

"So you do think my body is scary!"

"What's scary is how neurotic you've become. Braxton doesn't care about your little pouch." Kate gasped. "Oh, relax, Malibu Barbie. We both know you don't have a pouch. A bump, maybe. But I bet he thinks it's cute."

"That's it," Kate said, tugging at the dress's zipper. "I should never have agreed to try this one on."

Jessica groaned, then went to the foot of Kate's bed and fell back onto it. She stared up at the ceiling like a turtle flipped on its shell.

Back in her closet, Kate whipped through a series of hangers before finding the dress she wanted. "I'm wearing the floral patterned one."

"Really?" Her sister's voice was full of surprise. "The tight one?"

"Argh!" Kate slammed the hanger back onto the bar, then grabbed a blue dress Jessica had set aside during their first pass.

"If I were you, I'd go with the blue one," Jessica said.

Kate didn't answer.

"So, what number date is this, anyway? Five? Six?"

"Seven," Kate said as she stepped in the blue dress and yanked it up over her shoulder. "But, if you count our first boat ride, it's number eight."

There was a pause.

"Eight dates," Jessica said. "In seven days?"

Kate zipped the dress, then stuck her head out of the closet. Jessica was sitting up on the bed.

"Yeah, so?"

"Sounds pretty fast," Jessica said.

Kate went to the mirror, studied herself. She hated to admit it, but her sister was right. The blue dress was better.

"It's not fast."

"Look," Jessica said, "I like a fling as much as the next girl, but if you want a future with this guy, you need to slow it down. Connect emotionally. He can't see you as some floozy who gets naked after a few drinks."

Kate glanced back over her shoulder. "Thanks for that. But no one has gotten naked. We've spent most of our time talking. In fact, yesterday, he told me he thinks I'm his soul mate. I think he might be mine too."

"After a week?"

Kate shrugged. "When you know, you know."

"Uh-huh. And what did your soul mate say about your need to get pregnant ASAP?"

Kate hesitated, looked away. Jessica leaped to her feet and went to Kate's side.

"What did he say, Kate?"

"Well, he," Kate paused. "He believes family is very important."

"Oh. My. God," Jessica shook her head. "You haven't told him."

"Don't act like it's some big secret. I've only known him a week. And it hasn't been the right time yet. I'm going to tell him. Soon."

"How about tonight? At dinner."

"At The Austin Club?"

Jessica shrugged. "Why not? People discuss important things there all the time. Isn't that how Ms. Wilson uses it?"

Susan did use the club that way. Whenever she had to wine and dine a person, she took them there. Even made sure they sat at the same table. The one in the center, by the windows, with the best view of the formal garden outside.

"If I can, I will."

"Good," Jessica said, reading more into her words than she intended. "And maybe ask for a sample, too. One we could analyze."

Kate's eyes went wide, her mouth fell open. "Have you lost your mind? I'm not asking him for a sample."

"Why not?"

"Because it's crazy."

Jessica shook her head. "Actually, it's quite sane. Do all wines age equally well? Of course, not. After five years, most have oxidized to overpriced vinegar. Almost all will have, if you store them in a warm, moist place. What makes you think sperm is any different?"

Kate didn't know what to say.

"I'm confident his sperm hasn't turned to vinegar."

"For your sake, I hope so," Jessica said. "But are you willing to bet your future on it? Suppose he spends hours each day on a stationary bike. That would be bad for his little swimmers, right?"

"He doesn't bike."

"All right. What if he caries a gene that gives a child three nipples? You'd want to know that, right?"

Kate raised an eyebrow. "That's not a real thing."

"Oh, it's real. I watched a documentary about it last week. You can't imagine the hell these children endure at public swimming pools."

Kate glanced across the room at the clock on her nightstand.

"I have to go. Good talk, as always, sis."

84

Although it was Kate's second visit to The Austin Club, you wouldn't have known it from how differently she was received this time. Strolling in through the wood-paneled lobby, her arm wrapped around Braxton's elbow, she even got a smile from the snotty front desk clerk. The last time she had been there, when she met Susan, the man made her sit in a straight-backed wooden chair and wait for an escort.

Braxton led her up a grand staircase to the main dining room. They stopped at an empty hostess stand, and she surveyed the crowd in front of her.

The room, which was about the size of a small ballroom, buzzed with energy. Every chair at the round, white-clothed tables was occupied by someone in a dark suit or fancy dress. People laughed and talked loudly, the way some do after two or three drinks. It felt like a wedding reception where everyone was old friends instead of a private club where you could drop five hundred dollars without drinks.

A short, bald man, who reminded her of a used car salesman, grabbed two menus from the hostess stand before doing a quick submissive bow to Braxton. Then he paraded them around the room in a circuitous route that could only have been designed to let everyone see her from all angles. By the time they reached their table, which would have taken less than fifteen seconds had he walked in a straight line, Kate's face was bright red. The entire room was leering at her.

The used car salesman pulled out her chair and she sat down.

Kate leaned forward, whispered across the table. "Why is everyone looking at me?"

Braxton smiled. "Maybe because you're the first woman I've ever brought to dinner here."

The words made her heart flutter but did nothing to slow its frantic pace.

"Really?"

He nodded. "Half the ladies here have set me up with their daughters. The other half have made passes themselves. But you're my first honest to goodness date."

The used car salesman returned, carrying two glasses of champagne. The moment he set hers on the table, she grabbed it and guzzled it down in a series of quick gulps.

The man flashed her a surprised look. "Would the lady like another glass of Dom Pérignon?"

"Yes," Kate said. "The lady would like."

"Relax," Braxton said. "In a minute, none of them will even remember you."

"Ouch."

"What I mean is they're all histrionic attention seekers. They can't stand being out of the spotlight for more than a second. By the time we order our food, they'll be climbing over each other trying to turn heads back in their direction."

Kate took a deep breath, steadied herself.

The used car salesman came up from behind and set a martini down on the table beside her plate. Then he leaned in close to her ear. "In case the lady requires something stronger."

"Thank you," Kate said before taking a sip of the clear liquid. Whoa. It was strong.

They looked down at the menus. A single placard with four main course options. Beef, chicken, fish, and vegetarian. When the server stopped by, Braxton ordered blackened swordfish with roasted potatoes. She opted for a bacon-wrapped filet mignon with pommes frites (at least it sounded better than saying French fries).

For twenty minutes, he peppered her with random questions about her life. Did she play sports in high school? No. Did she always want to be a lawyer? Yes. What was her favorite pizza? Pepperoni. Did she like chocolate? Of course. Her favorite type of coffee? Whole milk vanilla latte. No, what kind of real coffee? Dark roast. If she could pick only one movie to describe her life, what would it be? Little Women.

She turned the last question around, asked him for his movie. His face turned serious. He deadpanned the answer.

"Ferris. Ferris Bueller."

She laughed.

The rapid-fire questioning left her feeling like a participant at a speed dating event. Still, by the time their food arrived, she had forgotten all about the people watching her. She wondered if this had been his plan all along.

She savored the first two bites of steak before nudging the conversation away from personal preferences.

"Do they ever let kids in here?" she asked, stabbing a French fry with her fork.

"Sure," he nodded. "Sundays. Holidays. And some Mondays too. You should see how it looks at Christmas. They go all out for the kids. They have a Santa come for the family party."

"Nice."

"Last year, they did a live action role play of A Christmas Carol. I ended up playing Tiny Tim's father because the kid's real dad got a sudden case of the stomach flu."

She smiled. "I bet you were a brilliant father."

"No," Braxton said. "I was the worst father ever. No one bothered to tell me that the planning committee had rewritten the play. Given all the characters the same number of lines. And of course, I never saw the script."

With her mouth full of food, Kate burst out laughing. She covered it with her hand. "That sounds horrible."

"What's even worse is my aunt told me it was my best performance ever. Including the time I had the lead in my high school musical."

"Oh, my. Dare I ask how you got the lead in a musical?"

"No," Braxton said. "I have repressed the memory. What I will tell you, however, is that ditching school in real life rarely works out like it did for Ferris Bueller."

Kate raised an eyebrow. "And yet, you convinced me to ditch work, anyway."

"I never said I was reformed."

Kate rolled her eyes, then stabbed another fry. "Well, I'm sure you'd be a much better father in real life than you were to Tiny Tim."

Braxton shrugged. "Sometimes, I wonder."

"Don't be silly. You'd be a great dad. You care about the planet, education, equal opportunity. And you appreciate the dangers of skipping school."

"Ha. It's actually the time trade-off that worries me. You can't be everything to everyone."

"Of course, not. But people have kids and careers."

He pressed his lips together. "I'm not sure they do."

"Be serious, Braxton."

"I am serious," he said. "Sure, people have kids and jobs. But few I've met with careers are functioning parents. Simply creating a child doesn't make you a parent in my book. Only a genetic donor."

She scrunched up her face. "So what? Are you saying people shouldn't use daycare?"

"No," he said, shaking his head. "I'm not talking about daycare. I'm talking about nannies and cooks and chauffeurs. I'm talking about people who send their kids to boarding schools and summer camps that stretch until Labor Day Weekend. I lived that kind of life, Kate. And I can assure you, it's neglect. Even when your parents pay fifty thousand dollars a year in tuition."

"But you don't have to send them away."

He let out a long exhale. "You do, if you want to accomplish extraordinary things. Come on, Kate. You know this. Can you even imagine my aunt making someone a partner if they left the office every day at five to pick up their kids? No way. Not in a million years."

Kate clanked her fork down against her plate. "It sounds like you've already made up your mind."

He must have sensed her frustration went deeper than their conversation because he reached out and tried to take her hand. She pulled it back before he could touch it.

"Look, I'm sorry if I was too harsh," he said. "I was just spinning out the argument. I didn't think it would upset you."

Her face softened. "So you're not set against kids?"

"No. I'm not set against anything. Except maybe discrimination and injustice."

She smiled, put her hand back on the table. He took it.

"I was only being direct with you because I adore you, Kate. You're smart. Pretty. Quick on your feet. And I knew you'd push back, make me see it from another angle."

"You adore me?"

He tilted his head to the side. "Do you think I'd make you my first date at the Club if I didn't?"

"I don't know," she said coyly.

"I guess the reason I'm so anti-kids right now is because I don't want you to miss anything." He paused, let the words sink in. "I've decided to run for governor, Kate. And I want you on the stage with me. Holding my hand."

To say she swooned over his words was like saying kids on Christmas got a little excited about presents. Her heart raced.

Dopamine surged through her veins. She felt like she had finally found her person. Someone who understood her.

"I want to be there, too," she said. "How about this? You agree to keep an open mind about kids. And I'll figure out a way we can be parents and change the world."

"Deal," he said, smiling.

85

The only thing Kate would have changed about her magical first night with Braxton was her mother. She wished the woman hadn't been sleeping across the hall. Although to be fair, it wouldn't have changed much. Her mother was in a deep, Ambien-induced haze when they returned from The Austin Club, and the instant Kate began unzipping Braxton's pants, she forgot about the woman, anyway. Plus, Kate wasn't big into noises. This gave her an excuse to be extra quiet.

Braxton had suggested they go to his place (*i.e.*, Susan's ranch), but Kate decided the only thing worse than having her mother walk in during sex was having Susan Wilson walk in during sex. He offered to pay for a hotel room, but that seemed sleazy. They weren't sneaking around, after all. They had just come out to high society.

She woke up the next morning to him caressing her face, which would have weirded her out if it had been anyone else. They made love again in the bed, showered together, then returned to the bed for the last time before getting dressed and venturing to the kitchen for coffee.

Instinctively, she grabbed a package of bacon from the freezer and began frying it in a pan on the stove. She made coffee, handed him a steaming mug.

"You really do like bacon, huh?" he said, peering at her over the rim of his cup.

She shrugged. "I don't know. I'm craving meat today."

He flashed her a mischievous smile. "I think I know the reason."

Before she could shush him, her mother marched into the kitchen, grabbed a mug from the cabinet, and poured herself coffee.

"You know the reason for what?" Barbara asked.

Kate glanced at Braxton. "It's nothing, Mother. Just a private joke."

"Uh-huh," her mother said. "Is it the same private joke that caused all the noise in your room last night?"

Kate's face turned red. "Mother!"

"I heard so much grunting I thought maybe you were hosting a weightlifting competition."

"Stop. You're embarrassing, Braxton."

Barbara raised an eyebrow. "Why would he be embarrassed? He wasn't the one grunting."

Kate gasped.

From behind her, a voice said, "Who was grunting?"

Kate turned to see her sister. Somehow, Jessica had managed to slip into the condo and make her way across the living room without anyone noticing.

"Good Lord," Kate said. "Why don't we just invite the whole building over?"

"Kate was the grunter," Barbara said to Jessica. "At one point, it got so bad I took two of my pills. Do you think it helped? Nope. Every time I was about to drift off to sleep, I was jolted awake."

Jessica shook her head. "I know what you mean. Last week, I fell asleep watching the women's tennis tour. I was jolted awake by this tank of a woman who made me think I was having a heart attack."

Braxton glanced at his watch.

"This is fun," he said, "but I have to go. I'm late for a meeting."

"On a Saturday?" Barbara asked.

"Yes," Braxton said.

He set his coffee down beside the sink, then went over to Kate and kissed her cheek. In her ear, he whispered, "Have a nice day, grunty."

She swatted him on the arm.

When he was gone, Jessica began rifling through the kitchen cabinets.

"I didn't appreciate that, Mother," Kate said, hastily flipping the bacon and splattering grease across the stovetop.

"Neither did I," Barbara shot back. "But I've told you that I don't like you doing that sort of thing when I'm sleeping across the hall."

"Oh, excuse me for bringing my soul mate back to my condo!"

"Found it," Jessica said, swinging the cabinet closed.

"What are you doing?" Kate asked.

"Back in a minute."

Jessica raced out of the kitchen.

Barbara said, "How could he be your soul mate? You've only known him for a month."

Kate sighed. She was sick of people putting a timeline on love.

"It doesn't matter how long I've known him." Kate said. "Love is love. It can happen in an instant. You of all people should know that."

"Lust isn't love."

Kate scoffed. "You know, I thought you'd be happy for me. Since I met him in a normal, coincidental sort of way."

"I am happy for you, Katie."

"It doesn't seem like it."

"I just don't want you to get hurt."

Kate shook her head. "I won't get hurt. Braxton is everything I've ever wanted in a man. Do you know he's running for governor? People say he'll win in a landslide."

"Is that good a thing?"

Kate squeezed her eyes shut. Sometimes, talking to her mother made her brain hurt.

"Of course, it's a good thing. He asked me to stand by his side."

"Does that mean marriage?"

"No. No one said anything about marriage. We've got too many decisions to make already. The campaign kicks off in less than a year."

Barbara took a long sip of coffee, then studied Kate for a moment.

"How will it work with your job?"

Kate took a plate from the cabinet, lined it with paper towels, then used a tongs to take the bacon out of the pan.

"Good question," Kate said. "I asked Braxton the same thing. He said he'd talk to Susan. Apparently, once she hears we're together, things will be very different."

"I see. Did you tell him about your computer troubles? About the girl in India?"

"No," Kate said, sounding annoyed. "There's nothing to tell. Wayne said it's over. We're in the clear."

In fact, she had not spoken to Wayne recently. The last update she received came from Jessica. But her mother didn't need to know. It was all under control.

Barbara hummed. "And what about your plans to have a baby? Is Braxton on board with being an insta dad?"

Kate was spared from having to lie when Jessica swaggered back into the kitchen. Her face beaming with pride, she went to the counter and, in an overly theatric manner, raised her hand above her head, then slammed it down onto the surface. Pulling her hand back, she revealed a sandwich-sized plastic bag stuffed with what looked like rolled-up toilet paper.

"Oh. My. God." Kate's eyes went wide. "Please tell me that's not what I think it is."

Jessica smiled. "It is. I'll admit I gagged a few times getting it into the bag, but it was worth it. Do you have any shea butter hand cream? I had to wash my hands like six times."

Barbara seemed to realize what was inside the bag because she winced, took a step back. "Get that off the counter. We put food on there."

"It's in a sealed bag, Mom," Jessica said.

"I don't care if it's in a lead container. It doesn't belong in the kitchen." Barbara glared at Kate. "This is why I didn't want you doing that when I'm around."

Kate raised an eyebrow. "Because Jessica might rummage through my bathroom trash and toss a used condom on the counter?"

"Why did you bring that in here?" Barbara said.

"Because I knew Kate lacked the courage."

Barbara shook her head in disbelief.

"Frankly," Jessica said, "I expected a little more gratitude from both of you. If I hadn't risked an STD, we wouldn't be able to run his sample. Who knows what horrors lurk in Braxton's DNA."

"That's what this is about?" Barbara asked.

"Jessica's worried our baby might have two heads. Or three nipples."

"Keep on joking about the nipples, sis," Jessica said. "Because Karma can be a real bitch."

Kate rolled her eyes. "Ooh, I'm scared."

Jessica looked at Barbara. "You agree with me, right, Mom? It makes sense to analyze a sample. Check for problems before she gets pregnant."

Barbara hummed. "I'm not sure, honey. You do make some good points, but—"

"But what?"

"Usually, if you love someone, you take the good with the bad."

"That's insane," Jessica said. "You're saying that if she loves Braxton, who she's known for only a week,—"

"More than a week," Kate said.

"—that she should risk a three-nippled child?"

"Does this nipple thing run in his family?" Barbara asked.

"It could," Jessica said. "Or maybe he carries the recessive trait for attached earlobes. Or lacks the ability to roll his tongue. A test would tell us these things and more."

Barbara looked at Kate. "Would you really leave him? Not have his baby? Because of the ear lobe or tongue rolling thing?"

"No," Kate said.

"Good." Barbara went to the sink and grabbed the dirty tongs. She used them to pick up the plastic bag and carried it to the trash. She dropped it inside. "Now, that's over. Jessica, we need to go. Carol's probably already hot because we're late again."

Later, when Kate was alone in the condo, she peered into the garbage can. The plastic sandwich bag was still perched on top of the bacon packaging. She bit her lower lip, did a quick pro-con list in her head, before sticking her hand inside and snatching the bag like someone was watching.

It can't hurt to know, she thought.

86

The website said Dr. Lotus's office was open until noon on Saturdays, which gave Kate enough time to stop for coffee before making the trip across town.

She parked in a space marked "Patients Only," then walked through the medical building's empty lobby to suite thirteen. She shook her head at Lotus's lack of PR skills. How could an intelligent, professional woman decide to base her practice in such an unlucky place? Especially when she worked with high-risk fertility cases. Kate guessed more than few women had turned around and gone back to their cars rather than jinx their pregnancy to a doctor in suite thirteen.

When Kate entered Dr. Lotus's small waiting room, two things struck her. First, there were no patients or staff. Second, all the guest chairs were stacked in four columns and pushed against the back wall.

She went to the counter and tapped a chrome call bell. Behind the reception desk, two cardboard boxes waited open on the floor, half-packed with office supplies.

A woman dressed in pink medical scrubs came out from a back room. She had tight, curly brown hair, a plump middle-aged face, and red eyes that looked like she had been crying. She flashed Kate a weak smile, then sat down behind the desk and woke up the computer as if everything were normal.

"Hello," the woman said. "Do you have an appointment with Dr. Lotus?"

A part of Kate wanted to ask if the woman was okay, but she thought it might be inappropriate.

"Um, no, I don't. But I am one of her patients."

She gave her name and watched as the woman scanned what Kate assumed was an electronic database.

"Here you are," the woman said. "Are you here for the charged injection?"

Kate forced a laughed. "Good Lord, no. I don't plan on doing that soon."

"Are you sure? Because our inventory is very low. Dr. Lotus says it could be years before she offers injections again."

Kate never thought there could be supply chain problems in the sperm business. Didn't it replenish itself every few days?

"Why is it out of stock?"

The woman motioned towards the waiting area. "Dr. Lotus is moving, for one. And the way she combines donor samples to maximize potency— Well, it's more of an art than a science."

Kate nodded. "I always thought of it as art, not science."

The woman's eyes narrowed. She didn't appreciate the attempt at humor.

Kate reached into her purse, pulled out the plastic sandwich bag, and set it on the counter.

"I was hoping Dr. Lotus might analyze my boyfriend's semen."

The woman looked at the bag, then wrinkled her nose.

"Is there a sterile collection container in there?"

Kate shook her head. "No, but there is a used condom I pulled from the trash."

The woman winced. "I see. Well, I'm very sorry, ma'am, but we're not allowed to accept samples from home. There's a procedure."

"I figured. However, I was hoping Dr. Lotus might make an exception."

"For you?"

"Yes, for me."

The woman looked confused. "Why would she make an exception for you?"

"Because I would pay her money. Cash, if she wants."

The receptionist seemed offended by the crass offer. Kate assumed most medical doctors would have been offended, too. But, something told her Dr. Lotus was not among them.

"It is unethical. We cannot analyze a specimen without a donor's consent."

"He consents," Kate said, nudging the plastic bag forward an inch. "I'll sign whatever you need."

"You can't sign for him."

Kate titled her head to the side. "How about I talk to Dr. Lotus? We'll work it out."

"She'll tell you the same thing."

"This is important," Kate said. "Either go find her, or I'll grab one of those chairs and we can wait together, staring at my sample, until you do."

The woman scoffed, then stood up and went into the back.

A moment later, an angry-looking Dr. Lotus appeared.

"Why are you disrespecting my staff, Ms. Becker?"

While pretending to yell at Kate, Lotus stepped to the counter and used her body as a shield to block the receptionist's view. Then she pointed at the plastic bag and mouthed the words, "Is this it?"

Kate nodded. "Your staff refused to analyze my boyfriend's semen. I am very angry."

The exchange was so stilted, Kate struggled not to laugh.

Dr. Lotus picked up the bag, studied the contents. "They refused for good reason. Analyzing a specimen from a used condom is a waste of money."

"I'll take the risk."

"Lab tests are expensive without insurance," Dr. Lotus said.

"I would pay two thousand dollars for results in a week."

"Impossible. As my staff said, it is unethical to analyze genetic material without permission from the donor." Dr. Lotus held out the bag like she wanted Kate to take it, then quickly pulled it back. "No, I will not return this to you. You'll just attempt to have it analyzed elsewhere. I will dispose of it properly. Nurse, please escort Ms. Becker out."

Then Dr. Lotus mouthed, "I'll call you."

87

Kate stood five feet behind the tuxedo-wearing butler in an interior hallway at Susan Wilson's ranch and watched as the man knocked on a closed wooden door. It was the same man who had escorted her to the library during her last visit. But what a difference two weeks made. Now, he was grimacing and promising to be "at her service" should she need anything during her stay.

She had never had a butler before, but the thought seemed almost as intoxicating as what she planned to do that night with Braxton. More actually, since the butler appeared displeased by her presence.

She wondered how the man had reacted when he learned Braxton invited her to stay the weekend. *Probably pretty pissed*, she thought.

Braxton had called as she left Dr. Lotus's office and said he couldn't bear to be away from her for another moment. He asked her to come to the ranch. Bring a nice dress for dinner and then plan to wear nothing else until Sunday afternoon. She agreed but packed a small overnight bag with her three favorite outfits.

"You won't lock me inside again, will you, Jeeves?"

The butler frowned. "The name's Burrows, ma'am. And that was a most unfortunate misunderstanding."

"Which part? That you locked me in the library? Or that I escaped?"

"I've apologized already, ma'am. I regret any inconvenience."

It was one of the least sincere apologies she had ever heard. But she wasn't going to push it. If he hadn't locked her in the library, she would never have met Braxton.

The butler opened the door to a billiard room full of masculine energy. It reminded her of a room in a fancy hunting lodge, except there were oil paintings on the walls instead of big game heads. There was a pool table in the middle of the room, balls scattered mid-game.

The instant she stepped inside, she smelled Braxton's cologne. It made her heart throb.

She saw him at one end of the table. Dressed in a navy blazer with a white button-down shirt and jeans, he held a pool cue in one hand and a tumbler of whiskey in the other.

He smiled and winked at her. She smiled back.

Figuring he wasn't playing pool alone, she glanced down the table at the other end. A short, stocky, bald man in a wrinkled gray suit, white shirt, and a loosened tie nodded at her. She guessed he was about fifty, although it was hard to tell from the lines on his face.

"Kate, meet Eric Arnold," Braxton said. "He's Governor Richard's Chief of Staff."

"Hello," she said. "It's a pleasure to meet you, Mr. Arnold."

"Call me Eric, please. And the pleasure is mine. I've heard great things about you."

She blushed. "Well, I hope at least some of it's true."

"Grab a drink." Braxton motioned towards a beverage cart on the sidewall. "I asked Burrows to premix you a Cosmo. Eric was just bringing me up to speed on a few house races."

She grabbed the metal shaker off the cart and shook it a few times to make sure the alcohol hadn't settled on the bottom, then poured the contents into a martini glass. It was good having a man like Burrows around.

She stood next to a high-top table and listened as Eric described a vulnerable Republican incumbent in House District 14A. Apparently, the guy had sexted his wife's sister. When he refused to get a divorce and marry her, the sister took the messages to the local Democratic precinct office. A volunteer gave Eric Arnold her number.

"And you think she'll stay quiet until after the filing deadline?" Braxton asked.

"Yes," Eric said. "She wants to run for city council. I promised her the Governor's support, if she did what I said."

"He'd do that?" Braxton asked.

Eric shook his head. "No."

They moved from the billiard room to a formal dining room with a white-clothed rectangular table that had seating for twenty. Sitting at one end, they used ivory china with Susan Wilson's initials engraved around the edges.

Braxton had preordered Kate a bacon-wrapped filet mignon with French fries. She thought it was sweet that he remembered but immediately resolved to stop eating so much bacon. Three times in two days wasn't healthy.

"If we flip 14A and 17B, we could take back the house," Braxton said.

"If we flip 'em both, we will take back the house. No question."

"What's going on with 17B?" Kate asked. Thus far, no one had mentioned it.

Eric glanced at Braxton and waited for his approval before explaining.

"For twenty years, 17B has been a cakewalk for Republicans. Less so recently, though, because of the twenty-something professional crowd that's taken over Grover Square. It's Tom DeVot's district. He's been there forever. Even liberals like him because he smiles and waves and wanders around main street like a deranged Santa Claus. I don't think he even votes on bills anymore. At one point, he started voting present because he didn't want to discourage the free exchange of ideas."

Kate raised an eyebrow. "Really?"

Eric nodded. "He's so sickeningly nice we stopped running people against him a while back because it was demoralizing. Everyone thought he'd die in his seat. But last month, fate smiled at us. It turns out Tom's wife, Hildreth, is sick. Her doctor recommended moving to a drier climate."

"Where are they going?"

Eric twisted up his face. "Who cares? The only thing that matters is that it's not in Texas. We're running Chief Justice Wilkerson for the seat." Eric must have read the surprise on her face because he said, "Wilkerson hits mandatory retirement next year, so he's making a move. Isn't it ironic that the law says he's too old to decide cases but not too old to make new laws."

Chief Justice Wilkerson was the last judge Kate would have guessed might run for political office. Jessica was going to go crazy when she heard.

"Has the Governor decided on a new Chief?" Kate asked.

Eric looked at Braxton.

"We were hoping you might take the job," Braxton said.

88

At first, she thought she misheard him. But after a comical back and forth that went on too long, it sunk in.

"Why would the Governor choose me?" she asked. "I mean, of course, I'm flattered. But I don't think it's a stretch to say I wasn't on anyone's short list."

"You were," Braxton said. "Mine."

Eric rolled his eyes. "So you weren't on a pimple-faced staffer's short list? So what? The Governor will to nominate you. And the Senate will confirm you. If I ask them to."

She looked at Braxton, then back at Eric.

"And why would you do that?"

"Because Braxton assures me you're loyal. That you see the big picture."

She didn't like how that sounded.

"I think maybe there's been a misunderstanding," Kate said. "I'm not a political person."

Braxton leaned forward, took her hand. "What he means is that you share our commitment to progressive values."

"Is that right?"

Eric waved her off like the seasoned pro he was. "Of course.

Listen, half the job of the Chief Justice is running the judicial branch. Handing out money. We're looking for someone who aligns with Braxton's vision on reshaping the courts."

Kate raised an eyebrow. "We?"

"Eric has agreed to become my chief of staff."

"I see."

"Look," Eric said, "We don't care how you decide cases that don't effect the administration. Be independent. Follow your heart. Make Texas the next San Francisco, if you want. But, you need to promise us you'll work twenty-four-seven. This is a once in a generation opportunity. There's much to be done."

"This is our chance, Kate," Braxton said.

"What do you say?" Eric asked. "Can we count on you?"

She hesitated. "Um, Braxton, can I talk to you for a moment?"

89

"What's the matter?" he said. "I thought you'd be excited."

They were standing outside the dining room on a large concrete veranda near a waist-high stone pillar wall. Below them, there was a pool area worthy of a magazine cover. A tiki bar, a hot tub, and twenty chaise lounge chairs, all lit up by little white lights on a string.

She looked up at him. "I am excited. It's just... I don't want to be the woman whose boyfriend appoints her chief justice. If I get it, I want to deserve it."

"You don't think you deserve it?"

"Come on, Braxton. There are hundreds of people more qualified than me."

"Why? Because they've written articles or practiced longer."

"Amongst other things."

He shook his head. "It's all phony crap, Kate. You graduated from Harvard, right?"

"Yes."

"And you practiced some?"

"Yes."

"I assume you won a few cases."

"More than a few."

"My aunt hasn't fired you yet, right?"

Kate shook her head. "Not yet."

"Then you're more than qualified. You deserve it because you have more heart and energy and passion than anyone else I've ever met."

Her eyes lit up. "You believe that?"

"I wouldn't have convinced Governor Richard, if I didn't."

She smiled.

"You were made for this job, Katie. And I know you'll spend every second working to make Texas better for ordinary people. That's the qualification I want in a Chief Justice."

She had never, not once, ever given less than her very best. Her unwavering commitment to the law had cost her friends, lovers, and, for a time, even a relationship with her mother. The idea of giving the job of chief justice any less was unthinkable.

But suddenly, it was all she could think about.

"What about us?" Kate asked.

Braxton shrugged. "What about us? I've spoken to Eric. It will raise some eyebrows, and the Republicans will complain. But he assures there's no rule against it. Plus, it's not like we'd be keeping our relationship a secret. If people don't want the Chief Justice dating the future Governor, then they can vote against me."

"But we'd never get to see each other."

He smiled. "Kate Becker: are you searching for a reason to say no?"

"I just—"

She stopped herself.

"Talk to me, Katie."

"We're just finding our way, Braxton. I don't want this to screw it up."

He smiled. "Taking the job will only make things better. Imagine the press coverage if we get married someday. We'd be like a modern day Camelot. The Kennedys, only better."

"I don't know," Kate said. "The Kennedys had cute kids."

He cocked his head to the side. "Are you saying our kids wouldn't be cute?"

"I'm saying you don't want them."

Braxton hummed. "Maybe I've changed my mind."

She perked up. If he were open to kids, maybe it could work.

"Have you? Have you changed your mind?"

He glanced off over her shoulder for a moment.

"I suppose I have. Look, the first term will be crazy. We have hundreds of things to fix. People are depending on us. But by the second term, things will slow down. At least enough for us to talk about family."

"Second term?" Kate did the math in her head. That was five or six years into the future. "I'd be forty-one. Almost forty-two."

"The perfect age."

"No," she said. "Not the perfect age. Too old."

He waved a hand at her. "Don't worry about it. They have many ways to extend fertility these days."

"Those things don't work for everyone."

He frowned. "Then we'll adopt. It's better anyway. Environmentally cleaner. Plus, if got a pair of siblings from Africa like that movie star couple, we could shore up our support in the minority community."

Kate cringed. He sounded horrible when he talked that way.

"I don't want to adopt," she said.

He shrugged. "Then we won't." He stepped forward, wrapped his arms around her. "Just say yes. As long as we're together, we'll figure it out."

90

By mid-afternoon, there was no one in the grandstand at Golden Acres Racetrack, except for Barbara, Yata, Garrett, and a handful of sad-looking middle-aged men who couldn't afford to leave until the last race was lost.

"I'm dying out here," Yata said.

Yata was leaning back in a plastic stadium seat, her feet propped up on the row in front of her, her eyes closed, an arm draped over her face, sipping sugar-free iced tea through a reusable straw she had brought from home. Her big, floppy straw hat, which she had worn with sunglasses, a white blouse, and khaki shorts, was now on her knees, shielding her legs from the powerful sun.

"If I catch skin cancer and die, it's your fault, kid."

"Yata!" Barbara said, rebuking her.

"What? Is the boy so delicate we can't even say cancer now?"

"Stop it."

"Just ignore her," Garrett said. "I've been doing it all afternoon."

Yata lowered her arm, shot him a hard look. "Be respectful, kid. As Barbara's supervisor, I'm in charge here."

"So you keep saying," Garrett said.

Yata took her feet down, sat up straight in the chair. "One more. I dare you. One more wise crack, and I'm telling your mother."

"Go ahead," Garrett said. "I doubt she'll care after I tell her you lied about taking me to an art museum."

Yata looked at Barbara. "You said his mother approved of the racetrack."

"Did I say that?" Barbara said.

Yata stood up. "That's it. We're leaving. Now."

Garrett and Barbara stayed seated.

"Get up!"

"Actually," Garrett said, "we're going to stay until the end. But you can go. We'll catch a rideshare home. It will be more comfortable than that old Subaru, anyway."

Yata's eyes narrowed. She clenched her jaw and made fists with her hands, which were hanging down at her side, crumpling the edge of her floppy hat. Yata wasn't one normally stymied for words, but what could she do when she invited herself along to "supervise" and wound up being an accessory to a lie.

"Barbara," Yata said, "tell your grandchild we're leaving."

She shook her head. "What's the harm in a few more races? No one's gambling."

This was the great compromise Barbara reached with Garrett. After a morning of tense, pressure-filled negotiations, she drew a line in the sand: either accept money for the snack stand and agree not to gamble or go to the museum like planned. The boy sighed, then nodded. Barbara had felt a little bad about winning the argument because, like Garrett, she agreed watching horse racing without gambling was a lot less fun, but she had to set an example. As his grandmother, she needed to model good behavior.

Yata huffed, then sat back down and crossed her arms over her chest.

Across the dirt track, a horse with the number twelve on its back was resisting the starting gate. Several men were trying to force it inside when the announcer said it was scratched.

"Was he the one you liked?" Barbara asked Garrett.

"She. And no. My money is on Dizzie Dangle. She's a killer on hard tracks."

Yata snorted. "Hard tracks? Will you finally admit you lied about never coming to the races before?"

"No," Garrett said. "I've never been. I did know a guy once who was kind of a lifer, though. He used to show me clips of old races, explain why a horse won. It was real boring."

The bell rang, and the horses shot out of the gate. Dizzy Dangle lagged behind for half a lap before the jockey hit the afterburner and whizzed him past the others, winning by a nose in a photo finish.

"Jeez," Barbara said. "You won again. How many is that for you?"

"Five. But only three in a row."

"Good job."

The payouts on a two-dollar bet flashed on the jumbotron. The announcer said the horses for the next race were showing in the circle out back.

"I'm getting another popcorn," Garrett said to Barbara. "Do you want anything?"

"Another popcorn!" Yata whined. "Good God! What are you doing? Starting your own stand?"

Three giant tubs of popcorn sat untouched on the ground beside Garrett's chair.

"The deal was I get to buy food every race."

"Yeah, yeah. I know the deal," Yata said. "Get me another tea. Mega size. And make sure no sugar."

"Because you're too so sweet already, right?"

"Haha," Yata said.

Garrett stood up and extended a hand towards Yata, his palm facing up.

"What?"

"Give him some money," Barbara said.

Yata shook her head.

"Then no tea for you," Garrett said.

Yata sighed, then reached into the front pocket of her shorts and pulled out a twenty-dollar bill. She held it up in the air, refusing to drop it into Garrett's hand as a kind of little protest. He snatched it before she could pull it back.

"I want the change, mister. And don't give that girl a tip, either. She doesn't deserve it." He turned and started off down the concrete steps. "I'm serious."

Garrett kept going, acknowledging her only with a back hand wave.

Yata shook her head. "You need to get control of that boy, Barbie. Before things spin out."

"You know what, Yata? I think you've finally lost it. Become even crazier than Carol."

"Oh, really? Then tell me this: name one thing you've taught the boy all afternoon."

"No, I'm not playing that game."

"Because you can't. We've been sitting here for three hours, broiling in the sun, smelling horse crap. And for what? So you can prance around like the kid's best friend?"

"Trust me, I'm not his best friend."

"Well, you're not much of a grandmother either."

Barbara looked away. Earlier that morning, when she had slid into the passenger seat of Yata's Subaru, she had promised herself she wouldn't let the woman ruin her day.

"You do understand why you need to teach him, right?" Yata said a moment later.

"To counter the poor parenting?"

"And the genetics. Don't forget about the genetics."

"Uh-huh."

"Now, realize, there's only so much we can do for the boy. But that doesn't mean we give up. Maybe with a little luck, he can become a half-way decent tradesman or a dishwasher."

"I can't believe Veronica lets you around the kids."

"Oh, I never say these things around her. She's just as messed up as them."

An announcement came over the public address system. "Paging Barbara Becker. Barbara Becker, please come to the administrative suite on the first floor for an important message. Barbara Becker to the administrative suite."

Yata raised an eyebrow. "How much do you want to bet he's in trouble?"

91

"What do you mean, you're not sure?" Jessica asked, furrowing her brow in disbelief.

It was late afternoon on Sunday. Kate had just returned from her weekend with Braxton. They were sitting at a wrought-iron table on the patio at Cafe Noir. The sun had slipped behind the building, throwing the area into shade and dropping the temperature ten degrees.

"I want to accept, but—"

"But you're too afraid?" Jessica said. "Too weak?"

"No, no."

"Too worried you're not smart enough?"

Kate scoffed. "Clearly, not."

"Have you posted naked pictures online somewhere I don't know about?"

"Stop it."

"Then tell me why you're hesitating at a once in a lifetime opportunity. And don't say it's because you lack experience. I'm almost out of patience."

Kate sighed. "I'm not hesitating. I'm trying to be responsible. You know, thinking through the implications."

Jessica squeezed her eyes shut. "Oh. My. God."

"Don't act like I'm being crazy," Kate said. "This job would take over my life. They expect me to eat, sleep, and breathe judicial administration."

"Oh, poor you," Jessica said. "You might have to work to change Texas."

"This is serious, Jess."

"I sure hope so. There's thirty years of damage to fix and not much time to do it. The state house could flip back again in two years. The time is now."

"I realize that," Kate said, sounding annoyed. "But who's going to take care of Mother, if I'm not around?"

Jessica laughed. "The same person who takes care of her now."

Kate's face turned red. "Don't worry about it. She'll be fine."

"And you? Who's going to take care of you?"

Jessica frowned. "What's really going on, Katie?"

She looked away, not sure she could bring herself to say it.

"He doesn't want kids. At least, not for five years."

"Which is never, for you."

Kate nodded.

"I bet he'd change his mind, if you explained things."

"He might," Kate said, "which is why I would never tell."

Jessica hummed.

"He doesn't want to be an absentee dad, Jess. And if I become Chief Justice, neither of us will have time for kids until after his first term."

"He sounds like a perfect ten."

"He is," Kate said.

They sat quietly for a moment. Six months ago, Kate would have sold both ovaries for a lower court judgeship. Now, she was thinking about turning down the best law job in the state to change diapers and arrange playdates. She wondered if there was something wrong with her brain.

"I think all your swooning has caused you to lose touch with reason," Jessica said. "This career/baby decision is a false choice.

You can be Chief Justice and have babies. Look at Amy Coney Barrett. She's got seven, and it worked out fine for her. Plus, when does a guy have a say, anyway? It's your body."

Kate raised an eyebrow. "I think you're confusing pregnancy with abortion."

"If he has sex with you, he loses all say."

"What are you saying? That I should trick him?"

"Jeez, no. What kind of person do you think I am? Just make sure he loves you, then inseminate yourself. Tell him the condom broke."

Kate closed her eyes, hoping that when she reopened them, her sister would have disappeared. "No."

"Fine. I figured you'd balk at that one. How about this? Strip down. Get him really excited by—"

Kate put her fingers in her ears. "I'm not listening to any play-by-play accounts."

"Whatever," Jessica said. "Just get him excited and then, at the last minute, convince him to ditch the condom."

"He won't. He's serious about being elected governor."

"He will," Jessica said, "They always do."

Kate shook her head.

"Why not? He's your soul mate. He assumes the risk of unprotected sex. Plus, you'd actually be helping him. Politicians without kids are weird."

Kate lingered in her chair for a while after her sister left. As much as she hated to admit it, she sort of liked the idea of leaving it to fate. At least then, she wouldn't have to decide what to give up.

92

The administrative offices at Golden Acres Racetrack were tucked away in the back corner of the building, past the concession stands, near the restrooms. With linoleum floors, buzzing overhead fluorescent lights, and cheap furniture, the reception area could not have been more different from the elegant winner's circle outside. The red and white roses were the only thing that connected the two places. Out by the track, the flowers were alive, vibrant, blooming strong. In the office, they were cut and stuffed in plastic vases, losing their color, withering, dropping petals as they died.

Barbara saw Garrett as soon as she opened the door. He was sitting on a straight-back chair, handcuffed to the metal frame.

"What's going on," Barbara said.

A security guard glanced up at her from behind the desk. He had white hair, a weathered face, and wore a cowboy hat that made him look like a small town sheriff.

"Are you Barbara Becker?" he asked.

"Yes. Why is he handcuffed to the chair?"

Yata Miller, who had trailed in Barbara's wake since leaving the grandstand, stepped forward and shook her head disapprovingly at the boy. "I can guess why he's chained up."

"Ma'am," the security guard sheriff said, "are you the boy's parent or guardian?"

"I'm his grandmother."

"Not a good one, though," Yata said out of the corner of her mouth.

"Ma'am, the boy's being held for underage gambling."

Barbara's eyes went wide.

"He's a lying prick," Garrett said.

Barbara glared at him. "Show some respect."

"He only grabbed me because I won the trifecta. He's trying to steal my money."

"Be careful, boy," the man said. "That sort of accusation gets people hurt."

Barbara didn't know what to make of the man's comment. It sounded a lot like a threat, but that was ridiculous, right? He was a security guard at a horse track.

"Garrett," she said, "apologize to the man so we can leave. Your mother will be worried sick if we don't get back soon."

"I'm not apologizing."

Barbara raised her voice. "Garrett, you're embarrassing yourself. And me, too."

"And me, too," Yata said. "All day long he's been embarrassing me."

The security guard sheriff waved a hand at her. "Don't waste the effort, ma'am. It won't make any difference. I have to call the police."

"You're calling the police?" Barbara asked.

"I have to. We're obligated to prosecute all underage offenders. Otherwise, the track could lose its gaming license."

Barbara's mind raced. She thought of what people would say when they found out Garrett was arrested while with her at the racetrack. She imagined the documentarian spinning it to make it seem like it was all her fault. The scandal would destroy Grannies R Us. Erase any hope of franchises.

While Barbara was busy catastrophizing, Yata's lips were moving. "Well, I, for one, think you're doing the right thing, Sheriff. For weeks, I've been warning Barbie about this kid. Getting scared straight is exactly what he needs."

The security guard smiled, then tipped his hat at Yata. "Thank you, kind lady. Do I know you from somewhere?"

"He can't be arrested," Barbara said. "He's got cancer."

"Come again?"

"He's got cancer," Barbara said, louder, more forcefully.

The man raised an eyebrow. "I'm sorry about that, but I'm not sure what that has to do with this."

"Yeah, Barbie," Yata said. "Who's embarrassing whom, now?"

Barbara huffed, then looked at Yata. "You do realize that I'm not the only one who looks bad here, right?"

Being predisposed to always think the worst of Garrett, and to always put herself high above him, it took Yata a moment to realize what Barbara meant. As the boy's "supervisor," she was going down, too. Barbara saw the exact moment this occurred because the smugness instantly disappeared from Yata's face.

"Mr. Sheriff," Yata said, summoning what little flirtatious charm remained after five marriages, "are you a fan of great literature?"

"Oh, yeah," he said.

She strutted over to the desk, leaned forward, and did her best to show off her droopy breasts like she was Marilyn Monroe. The sight caused Barbara's stomach to churn and Garrett to recoil, but the man seemed to be enjoying it. He rolled the chair close to her. Yata bent down, whispered in his ear.

The man looked stunned. His eyes were as big as saucers, and his mouth fell open.

"No way!" he said.

"Yes." Yata held up her palms. "It's me. In the flesh."

"I can't believe it. I thought you retired to California."

"I did. But the taxes were killing me. So, I had to move back.

What I tell people is that my body may be trapped in a red state six months a year, but my mind is blue all the time."

"That's a good way to say it. I'm going to say it like that."

Barbara doubted it. Of all the low effort flirtatious responses a man could give, his was at the front of the line.

"I hate to ask," Yata said, "but is there any way you could help the boy? It sure would mean a lot to me."

The man hummed. "We're not supposed to."

"Of course," Yata said. "I'm sorry. Forget I asked."

"No worries. I just can't believe it's you. I mean, I thought maybe it was, but then I said, 'Billy, you've gone bananas. She's too famous to be at Golden.' And then, here you are."

"Here I am."

"My wife's an even bigger fan. She's got all your books. She made a display case for our living room. We keep the hardbacks behind the glass, you know, to protect them from the UV light."

"That's an excellent idea. More people should do that."

"I wish she was here to meet you," he said. "She'd talk your ear off about books. She sent your agent an email a while back, but we never heard anything. I know she'd still be willing to do a fifty-fifty deal, if you two worked together. Provided you did all the writing. She's more of a big picture gal, you see."

Yata shrugged. "Too bad I missed her."

"You could hang around," Barbara said.

Yata pressed her lips together. "No, I don't think I can."

"Yes, you could. I could take Garrett home in the Subaru. Then I'd come back later and pick you up." Barbara glanced at the man. "If you'd be willing to let him go."

The man thought for a moment. "If Ms. Miller agrees to talk shop with my wife, I think we could work something out."

The man uncuffed Garrett, and Barbara pushed him out the door before he could say anything stupid.

As she was leaving, Yata raced up to her, grabbed her arm.

"What have you done, Barbie!" Yata's eyes were filled with fear. "The woman's crazy. She's built a shrine to me in her house."

93

By the time Kate made it back to the condo after coffee with her sister, she had fallen in love with the idea of gambling on fate. If she got pregnant, she got pregnant. Braxton couldn't blame her. At least, as long as he didn't know she was sabotaging the birth control methods. Plus, leaving it to chance meant she could accept the job, keep Braxton in her life, and maybe have a baby, too.

She was still smiling when she answered the doorbell and saw a disheveled-looking Dr. Lotus staring back at her.

Lotus looked nothing like the hard-nosed professional from the clinic. Dressed in a beige trench coat and jeans, her eyes were red and bloodshot and she had the kind of thousand-mile stare new lawyers got when they stayed up for three days straight trying to finish a brief.

"Dr. Lotus, are you okay?"

The woman held out a manila envelope. "Your semen analysis."

There had been no discussion about how she'd get the test results. But, she never expected Lotus to show up at her door and deliver them.

"Ah, great," Kate said.

She reached for the envelope. Before she could get it, Dr. Lotus pulled it back.

"First, you must pay."

"Okay... Can I write you a check?"

"Of course."

Dr. Lotus came inside to wait, and Kate grabbed her checkbook from a dresser drawer.

"If it's not too much trouble, could you make it out to cash?"

Kate raised an eyebrow. "All right."

They exchanged the check for the envelope.

"I heard you're moving," Kate said.

Dr. Lotus nodded. "They've finally driven me out. I'm heading south."

"South? Where? Like San Antonio?"

"Panama."

Kate laughed. "Panama? Are you joking?"

"No."

"Isn't that place a dictatorship?"

"Since 9/11, it's actually freer than here. Very little bureaucracy. And the government understands there are always hiccups on the road to progress."

Kate cringed. Of course, she knew progress wasn't an upward sloping line. In every endeavor, there were peaks and valleys. Advances and set backs. Still, it was unnerving hearing your own doctor talk about problematic hiccups.

"There've been hiccups?" Kate asked.

"Not with you, dear," Dr. Lotus said. "I don't even believe it was my fault. The woman likely contracted it elsewhere. She wasn't exactly chaste, if you know what I mean. But of course, the Medical Board took her side."

"They're disciplining you?"

"Revoked my license," Dr. Lotus said. "You're a lawyer. Tell me what you think. How can they blame my injections for her STD, if she's the only one who got sick? Fishy, isn't it?"

Kate bit her lip. She wasn't sure what to say, but she was glad she hadn't done the injection.

"Never mind," Dr. Lotus said, waving a hand. "It doesn't matter. I'm not appealing. They're not squeezing another dime out of me."

Kate couldn't believe she had hired this woman as her doctor.

Dr. Lotus continued, "Do you know that in Panama they pay American doctors a stipend to open an office. Good people, the Panamanians."

Kate ushered Lotus towards the door.

"Yes, well, good luck with that."

"You should check it out," Dr. Lotus said. "Maybe they have a similar program for lawyers."

"Yeah, I'll think about it."

She pulled open the door and waited for Lotus to leave. The woman stopped in the hall, looked back at her.

"Panamanian men are very attractive, you know."

"Yes, I'm sure they are," Kate said, slowly closing the door. "Goodbye."

"And potent too. Most of my samples came from there."

"Wow." Kate shook her head in disbelief. "I did not know that."

"No one did. It's a legal gray area. I'm only telling you because of your condition. Extra potency matters."

"Thank you," Kate said. "But I've met someone. In fact, you analyzed his sample. We're going to trust our future to fate."

"Oh... I see."

Dr. Lotus pulled out a business card from her coat pocket and handed it to Kate. Unlike the one Kate had gotten before, this one only had Lotus's name and telephone number on it.

"My office in Panama opens in three days. Call me if you change your mind. The weather is marvelous this time of year."

Kate closed the door. Alone again in the condo, she tore open the manila envelope.

The single sheet of paper inside was a standard lab test result. Medical terms ran down a column on the left side. Across from them were measured values. All the results were in red. There was a handwritten note at the bottom.

"Has this man had a vasectomy?" Dr. Lotus wrote. "Because he's sterile."

94

The moment Barbara's eyes flicked open, she grabbed her cell phone off the nightstand and checked her messages. She was worried she had missed Yata's call, somehow slept through the ringer. But she hadn't.

Yata had never called.

This was a bad sign.

Sitting up in the bed, the morning sun streaming through cheap curtains Kate had bought for a room she never intended to be occupied, Barbara feared the worst. In the pit of her stomach, she was sure the security guard sheriff had done something terrible to Yata. There was no other explanation. Yata wouldn't have voluntarily stayed overnight at the man's house, not if she had been free to leave.

Barbara put on a robe and made her way to the kitchen. Kate was sitting at the dining room table, eating avocado toast.

"Why are you up so early?" Kate asked.

"Is it early? I never know since my room is like a tanning bed after four am."

Kate rolled her eyes. "What am I supposed to do, Mother? I've already ordered the room darkening shades."

"Oh, I don't know. Maybe pick a style that's in stock. After a year, I think I've given it the old college try."

Kate shook her head, "I'm not compromising quality just because you're being impatient."

"Impatient? I could end-up in assisted living before those shades arrive."

"Yes, Mother. You could. In fact, if you keeping nagging me, I'd say—"

Barbara turned away and stopped listening when the doorbell rang. It was followed quickly by three hard knocks.

"Are you expecting someone?" Kate asked.

"No. You should get it. If it's the police, tell them I'm not here."

"The police? Why would it be the police?"

"Who knows why? They're always harassing people, aren't they?"

Kate made a face, then reluctantly stood up and went to answer it. On the way to the door, she glanced back at Barbara.

"I'm calling the old folks' home today, Mother."

Barbara held her breath as Kate pulled it open. If it was the police, she didn't know what to say. Should she admit to having been at the horse track? Should she mention Garrett's gambling? Or was it better to leave that stuff out? In her mind, it really didn't seem pertinent to Yata's disappearance.

Before she could decide, the door opened wide and she saw Yata. The woman had a crazed look in her eyes. Her hair was wild and her clothes were ripped and torn. Yata pointed a finger at her and screamed.

Barbara turned and ran. She made it to the guest bathroom and locked herself inside as Yata began pounding on the door.

"Come out, you coward. You're going to see what they did to me."

"No, Yata. No," Barbara begged. "Can't you see I was worried sick. Thank God, you're alive."

"You aren't going to be alive much longer, woman!"

Barbara heard Kate outside the door.

"Stop banging on my door," Kate said in her no-nonsense, lawyer voice. "What are you doing here, Yata?"

"I'm going to kill your mother because she pimped me out yesterday."

Kate laughed. "Pimped you out? I'd hate to see what the guy looked like."

"Haha," Yata said. "Not my body, Katie. My mind. She tried to pimp out my mind to a wannabe writer."

Kate rolled her eyes. "Good Lord. So, you weren't assaulted, then?"

"That depends on your definition of assault. If it includes being forced to endure eight hours of inane observations, pointless memoir, and stories with no action or appreciable value change, then yes, I was assaulted."

Kate scoffed.

"You didn't see the woman's prose, Katie. It was horrible. Even you could have done better."

"If you weren't assaulted, what's with the wild hair? Torn clothes?"

"My cell phone died. I had to take the bus home. A word of advice: never pay extra for a ticket on the seventy-eight thinking it will get you home faster. It won't. It goes the wrong way, all night, northwest towards New Mexico. Thank God, I saw the sign for Odessa before it was too late."

Kate shook her head. "You kids behave yourself today while I'm at work. And if you break anything, I'm holding you both responsible. Understand?"

"Yes, Mommy," Yata said.

After Kate left, Barbara spoke to Yata through the door.

"She can be so bossy."

"Yes," Yata said, "but it's not the worst thing a woman can be."

"I guess." Barbara was silent for a moment. "I'm sorry about pimping you out. I never thought you'd be forced to ride a bus."

"Well, I suppose it's not all your fault. Sheriff Billy offered to drive me home, but I didn't want his wife knowing where I lived, so

I told them you were meeting me at the bus station. Who knew the city had so many buses?"

"There are a lot of them."

"And they all go different ways."

"Yes," Barbara said. "I believe that's how it works."

"You know I'm a big supporter of public transit. Always have been. But we have to get rid of these buses. They're unusable. What we need is more light rail, with defined routes, and stations where people can see a map."

Barbara detected a change in Yata's voice. No longer fearing for her life, she unlocked the bathroom door.

In the kitchen, she made them coffee using Kate's special reserve beans and pour-over device. They stood across the counter from each other, sipping the strong liquid.

"We have to do something about the boy, Barbie," Yata said.

"What do you mean?"

"He's out of control. First, he takes my wagon for a joyride. Then he lies, and gets caught gambling at the track."

"He made a couple of mistakes," Barbara said. "I spoke to him about it. Made clear it mustn't happen again."

"Yes, well, forgive me if I don't trust your judgment. You're not the model authoritarian parent."

"Authoritarian? Don't you mean authoritative. I think that's what psychologists say is best."

Yata turned up her nose. "Who knows more about words, Barbie? You or me? Of course, I mean authoritarian. I don't care what some two-bit shrink says. I'm talking about the real world. This kid needs discipline. He needs to know that if he doesn't follow rules, there will swift, harsh, unforgiving consequences."

"I don't know."

"That's why I'm your supervisor, Barbie. It's my job to make the hard calls."

"But he has cancer."

Yata shook her head. "That's the root of the problem. Everyone's walking around on eggshells, treating him special, letting him skate by because they think they're being nice. But they aren't. They're hurting him. The nice thing is to bring the hammer down, hard. Hit him into place."

Barbara cringed. Nothing about what Yata said sounded nice.

"What are you proposing?" Barbara asked.

"Let's summon him to your condo. Give him a lecture he'll never forget."

95

It took several days after Kate's talk with Ladyham Lincoln (a/k/a Ruth Jacobs) for Elwood to "find" the evidence needed to support a motion for one hundred percent custody.

He came into her office with his head down, looking embarrassed about the manila envelope he handed across the desk. Inside were more of Ruth's favorite shoe-polished black eye pictures. Six new shots from different angles. Kate didn't ask how the woman kept finding new pictures of an old injury. There was also a close-up of the bumper on Ruth's pickup truck. Apparently, Damion had caused a tiny dent that wasn't visible in the photos.

When Kate reached the last few pictures in the stack, she paused and looked up at Elwood.

"I think these were included by mistake."

Elwood shook his head. "Ms. Jacobs says they're the most important."

Kate hummed. The shots were PG-13 porn. Ruth was dressed in provocative black lingerie, kneeling on a bed, making a come-hither motion towards the camera.

"Did she say why?"

"She believes they show Damion's deviance."

Kate glanced back at the pictures. "Deviance, huh?"

"Yeah. This morning, she lectured me about how men objectify women."

"And she thinks these prove that?"

Elwood nodded. "It's best not to argue with her, Ms. Becker. She's the client."

"I heard once lawyers are supposed to give advice."

"I'm not a real lawyer, ma'am. You know that."

"Yes, Elwood. I do know. However, maybe you could remind Ruth, because she seems to forget." Kate slid the lingerie photographs back into the manila envelope. "Tell her I won't be using these."

He glanced down at the floor, refused to take the envelope. A moment later, he looked back up at her.

"I don't think that's a smart move, Ms. Becker."

"You won't advise a client, but you'll advise her lawyer?"

"It's my job, ma'am. As your supervisor, I must oversee your performance."

"Uh-huh."

"Ms. Jacobs told me that if you didn't agree to file all the pictures with the court, I was to find Ms. Vulcan. Tell her you're fired."

After Elwood left, Kate spent three hours stringing sentences together using the words abuse, danger, deviant, and sole custody. It was if the more she repeated them, the more likely they were to be believed. When she finished, she had a thirty-page motion that passed grammatical muster but said nothing apart from, "Give me sole custody."

She would never have filed such garbage before Ruth. Even now, even with Judge Eide on the case, it still made her stomach churn.

As she was uploading the pictures as exhibits in the court's electronic filing system, there was a knock on her open door. She looked up to see Matt Simpson. He was dressed in a blue button shirt and khakis.

"Ms. Becker, do you have a minute?"

"Actually, it's not a great time," she said with a tight smile.

He nodded. "I understand. I can wait."

He walked into her office and sat down in the chair across from her. She wasn't sure how he managed to get back there. The interior hallways at Susan Wilson Law were locked. A person couldn't just wander around unescorted. It violated client confidentiality.

She clicked the button on the court's web portal and waited for a confirmation screen to appear before looking over at him.

"Okay," she said. "How can I help you, Mr. Simpson?"

"Have you spoken to your client recently?"

"Define recently."

"Today." She shook her head. "Because I've left her several messages, but she isn't returning my calls."

Kate shrugged. "I don't know what to tell you. If I talk to her, I'll pass along the message."

"Please do. Did you see her on the McDougall News Hour last night?"

Kate shook her head. She had never even heard of the McDougall News Hour. There were so many cable news shows these days one couldn't keep track. It seemed like every political hack was doing a show out of his basement now.

"You'll want to check it out," Matt said.

"How about you give me a recap instead?"

"Ah, I think you'll want to watch it. It got pretty wild."

"Just tell me."

"Okay. Ruth claims Damion was having sex with Senator Waylon Jackson."

Kate's eyes got big. "What?"

"Oh, it gets better. She says they did at that church she's always railing against. The Apostle of the Disciple. Apparently, they did it on the altar. While Damion was holding the baby over his head."

Kate's face turned red. She shifted in her chair.

Before then, she had always rationalized Ruth's lying as relationship crap. It didn't matter to her that the woman's lies had hurt

Damion, Tina Black, or even Judge McDaniel. All of them had it coming. Besides, it was he-said-she-said nonsense. If Judge McDaniel hadn't been such a pansy and quit, he would have been cleared, eventually.

But this new claim, the claim about Senator Jackson, it was different. Kate was pretty sure neither Damion nor Senator Jackson was gay. She was equally confident the two probably had never even met. Because Senator Jackson was something of a national celebrity, she also worried he might have an alibi that put him a thousand miles away at the moment Ruth said he was on the altar with Damion.

"Interesting," Kate said. "I don't know anything about it. I'm only representing Ruth on the custody case."

"Sure. That makes sense." Matt paused for a moment. "Although, maybe I'm off base here, but isn't this the sort of thing you would raise in a custody case? I mean, it involves the baby."

"Yep, you said it. You're off base, Mr. Simpson. Now, if you'll excuse me, I need to get back to work."

"Okay," Matt said, getting to his feet. "For what it's worth, Senator Jackson's people put out a statement saying she's lying. They claim he's never heard of that church. I guess he's Catholic and not gay."

"Thanks for the heads up."

Matt stopped a few feet short of the door, turned and looked back at her.

"The next installment in my series goes to press in a few days. I really do need to talk to your client ASAP."

"I already said I'd pass along a message."

He nodded. "But if I don't hear from her by then, I'll need to write a different story. One with two villains. A lawyer and a client."

When Matt Simpson was gone, Kate picked up the phone and dialed Ruth's number. It went straight to voicemail. She dialed Elwood's number next and left a message instructing him to call her back immediately.

Her phone rang a minute later.

"This is Kate Becker."

"Hi, Ms. Becker," a bubbly young female voice said. "This is Alexi from Judge Edie's chambers. I'm calling on the Ruth Jacobs matter. The Judge wanted to let you know that we've received your motion paperwork. However, you're going to have to wait a few days to schedule the hearing. The case is being reassigned to a new judge."

96

Barbara took a wide stance, shifting her weight from right to left, trying to wobble the wooden platform Yata had assembled in the corner of the living room. The last thing she needed was for Garrett to get hurt on his first visit to the condo.

"This thing is dangerous," Barbara said. "You need to take it back upstairs."

Yata shook her head, waved a dismissive hand.

Ever since Yata poured her third glass of wine, everything about her (body language, facial expressions, gestures) had become more dismissive.

"Relax, Barbie," Yata said. "My nephew uses it at the dealership all the time. If the grease monkeys can stand on it, I think your Stink Bomb can sit on it."

Barbara pressed her lips into a fine line and hummed to herself.

When she had agreed to invite Garrett to the condo for Yata's lecture, she never imagined the evening would turn into a circus. In hindsight, she knew she should have.

Barbara stepped off the platform and walked over to the dining room table.

"Remind me again how shaming him will make him a better person?"

Yata sighed. "First, we're not shaming him."

"Then why is there only one chair on the stage and all the others are facing it like a theater?"

"So we can see him, Barbie," Yata said. "Everyone must be able to see him."

"Everyone?" Barbara raised an eyebrow. "There are only three of us. And that includes Carol, who isn't even supposed to be here."

Carol scoffed. "I was invited."

"By who?"

Yata cringed. "Whom, Barbie. How many times do I have to tell you that a pronoun, which is the object of a preposition, is always whom, never who. It's like fingernails across a chalkboard."

"Yeah," Carol said. "You should take some English classes. Learn to talk right."

Barbara flashed Carol a hard look, which immediately shut her mouth.

"Oh, Lordy," Yata said. "I think your poor grammar has triggered another migraine." Yata closed her eyes, pretended to wince.

I'm sure it was my grammar, Barbara thought. It has nothing to do with you chugging all that wine.

"I need to lie down," Yata said. She looked at Carol. "Let me know when we have a quorum. I'll be in Barbie's bed."

"What? No! You're not going in my bed."

"Well, I have to go in someone's bed. And obviously, I can't go in Kate's. Who knows what lurks in there."

"Lie down on the couch," Barbara said, patting her hand on a cushion. "It's very comfortable. Kate paid twenty thousand dollars for it at an outlet center."

"Aren't you sweet," Yata said, flashing her a patronizing smile, before heading off down the hall towards her bedroom. "Call me when it's time, Carol."

When Yata was gone, Barbara looked at Carol. "Who else was

invited? Because we need to cancel. We can't have all kinds of people watching this, if we want to win GOTY."

Carol shook her head. "Yata and I already discussed it. Conventional wisdom is upside down on this one."

"Oh, you discussed it, did you?"

"Yes. Yata had a series of vivid dreams about it. She believes a public lecture will improve your standing, since people will see you as a strong disciplinarian. A person who's unafraid to tackle marginal parenting head on."

"That's the dumbest thing I've ever heard. Who's coming?"

Carol shrugged. "I don't know. Yata sent out the emails. She wasn't thrilled about the RSVP numbers, though."

The doorbell rang. Barbara went to answer it.

Garrett was in the hallway, standing with his thumbs looped through the straps of a backpack worn over both shoulders. He was dressed in jeans and a gray hoodie that had the word Princeton stamped across the front.

"Hey, Barbara," Garrett said, his eyes looking past her, deeper into the condo. He turned up his nose when he saw the folding chair on the wooden platform. "Are you hosting a speaker?"

She stepped into the hall, closed the door behind her.

"You know how Yata got us out of the jam at the racetrack?" Garrett nodded. "Well, as my 'grandparenting supervisor,' she's not happy. She thinks I'm failing you, claims I'm not holding you accountable for your inappropriate behavior."

"Seriously?" Garrett's face turned hard. "She's such a conniving b----"

"Hey, no cursing."

"Sorry. It's just, you know, none of it is my fault. The man stole my ticket."

Barbara held up her palms, tried to get him to lower his voice. "I know, I know. But Yata thinks, and this is only her opinion, that maybe you shouldn't have been gambling."

Garrett scoffed. "She's blaming the victim? How progressive."

Barbara raised an eyebrow. "I'm not sure it's fair to call yourself a victim, Garrett. I mean, you are underage."

"The track didn't have a problem with my age when they took my money."

"Still... You promised me you wouldn't gamble."

"And I didn't. Gambling is about chance. Slot machines, roulette. What I did was skill. How do you think I got the hundred dollars I used for the trifecta?"

"I'm just saying—"

"She's not my grandmother, Barbara. I won't let her bully me."

"No one's bullying you."

"Whose side are you on? Mine or hers?"

Barbara sighed. She didn't enjoy defending Yata, but she also didn't want to be on his side for this either.

"There are no sides, Garrett. She just wants to talk. Help you make better choices in the future."

He forced a laugh. "Right. Well, tell her thanks, but no thanks. After the day I've had, I can't stand more talking. I came over to relax, to quiet my mind."

"Is everything all right?"

"Sure. Of course."

She studied him for a moment. There was something off about him tonight, something she couldn't quite put her finger on. Maybe it was his eyes. They were duller, not as vibrant as usual.

He turned, started back towards the elevator.

"Where are you going?" she asked.

"Anywhere but here. And home."

"I'll come with you."

"Stay. They need you."

"They don't need me," Barbara said. "Give me a second. I have to get my purse."

There was a rooftop deck on the fifty-fifth floor of Barbara's condo building. It had a small rectangular pool, a warm porcelain tile floor, a gas fireplace, elegant nighttime lighting, and wicker furniture arranged in multiple seating areas with cushions that felt new to the touch. It's kept pristine, being constantly swept, vacuumed, and polished by a small army of staff. The maintenance costs a quarter of the association dues residents pay each month.

These dues, which are higher than any other building in town, are the result of five pages of research, which is tucked away behind a plastic cover like the kind a middle schooler uses when they're trying to distract a teacher from shoddy work. The research says the rooftop deck is the number one thing people admire about The Filtmore Condo Building.

Whether this is true and whether admiring a deck has ever caused anyone to buy a condo is a matter of great debate among the building's residents, especially since the research was done by Yata's nephew, who, before finishing, quit to follow his passion for selling Japanese cars.

Hoping to avoid yet another scandal under her leadership, Yata finished the research herself and proclaimed the results "neutral, professional, and transformative." Channeling her inner Nancy Pelosi, she declared the issue of the deck expenses settled, now and forever. Amen.

While Yata managed to preserve the deck's obscene level of funding, something her idol would have been proud of, she could not, despite her best efforts, convince the residents of the building to actually use it. This was because of a problem she herself caused years earlier as chair of the Condo Association's Labor Committee.

Spearheading what she later called "the fairest labor negotiation in the history of the world," Yata signed a twenty-year deal with the building's unionized staff, which, among other things, designated a corner of the rooftop deck as the employees' smoking area. This seemed a reasonable accommodation at the time since only two employees smoked, and both were old and sickly and likely to die soon.

But as so often happens with smokers, these two lived long enough to tell their smoking friends about this smoke-friendly employer. When The Filtmore sought to hire new staff, every applicant, for every position, smoked like a chimney. And as the smokers increased, their behavior grew more brazen, banning together like a pack of wild hyenas, traveling in groups of three or four, first seizing the couches by the corner, then engulfing the entire deck in smoke so thick people on the ground thought the building was on fire.

Barbara wasn't sure this last part of the story was true. The occupation smoke-out had occurred before she moved into the building. However, when she went up to the deck to look around, the local union boss came over to her, a cigarette dangling from his lips, and said residents *technically* could still use the deck, provided they behaved themselves and treated others with respect.

Barbara had never gone up there again, not until tonight, when she brought up Garrett so they could talk alone.

"This place is amazing," he said, collapsing into a couch and putting his feet up on a glass-topped coffee table. "Do all these people live in the building?"

There was no one within one hundred feet of them. Garrett was referring to the crowd gathered by the pool. People were squeezed together so tight it looked like a cross between a family reunion and group swimming lessons for four-year-olds.

"If you work here, you can bring family and friends to swim. Whenever you want."

"Seriously?"

"Yes. Why are you surprised?"

"Because it must cost a fortune to fix all the stuff they break," he said.

"Why would they break anything?"

Garrett laughed. "See those two guys over there." He pointed towards a small deck area between the pool and a glass wall at the edge of the building. "They just flicked cigarette butts into the water."

"No, they didn't."

"Okay," he said sarcastically.

He grabbed his backpack, unzipped the front compartment, and pulled out a small rectangular container.

"What's that?" Barbara asked.

"My water bottle."

"No, it's not. It's a flask."

He unscrewed the cap and took a long, slow drink. Then he held it out to her.

"Want some?"

"No. And you're not having any more either."

"How about we agree to disagree?"

"I can't condone you breaking the law, Garrett."

"I didn't think you were. Plus, technically, I'm not. In Texas, minors can drink, if they're in a private residence, and accompanied by a parent or guardian."

"This isn't a private residence, and I'm not your guardian."

"You say potato I say pot-ah-to."

Barbara didn't know what to do. Should she stay silent? Try to preserve his trust? Or should she rip the flask from his hands? Ultimately, she did nothing, telling herself it didn't matter because of the cancer.

"Do you think there's a point to all this?" Garrett asked. "Life, I mean."

She shifted uncomfortably in the chair, crossing, then uncrossing her legs. He hadn't asked it with his usual glib.

"Of course, there's a point."

She said it hoping he wouldn't ask her to explain what that point was because she couldn't.

He nodded, looked away.

"Did something happen, Garrett?"

"Something always happens, Barbara."

"Do you want to talk about it?"

"No."

They sat for a moment and watched as a teenage girl in a bikini dipped her toe into the pool, then shrieked because the water was too cold. Barbara had read somewhere that sometimes the best thing you can do for a person is to just sit with them. Say nothing.

He took another sip from the flask. After a while, he said, "Do you know I've never seen a girl naked?"

Barbara's ears turned red. She felt a lump in her throat.

"Oh?"

"I mean, sure, I've seen a little porn. But it's not real. You can't touch them or anything."

"Mm-hmm," Barbara said, grimacing, hoping the comment was a random observation that would go no further. She couldn't handle discussing anything more graphic.

"I want to see a girl naked, Grandma Becker."

"Oh, I see."

She felt light-headed. She had never considered herself a prude before. Now, she did. A great big one.

Garrett saw the change in her face. "I'm sorry. I shouldn't have shared."

"No, no, no. I'm very open-minded."

"It's just, I feel like I can talk to you. That you're a safe person."

"I am a safe person."

He looked away.

"Please, Garrett," she said. "Don't shut me out. Tell me. Never be ashamed of yourself."

He looked back at her, pausing for a moment as if thinking it over. "Could you get me a girl, Grandma Becker? Someone I could see. Someone I could touch."

Barbara's mouth fell open. Her eyes got as big as saucers.

He abruptly stood up. "I'm sorry. I should go."

"Don't. We'll figure it out. Now, give me that flask. And don't ever say Grandma Becker and naked girl in the same sentence again."

98

There is a grand staircase at the front entrance of The Austin Chess Club that leads up to the second floor. The dark wood mahogany structure was hand-carved by a somewhat famous Bavarian immigrant in 1892. The story told to new members is that it was done by the same master carver who did the James J. Hill House in Minnesota and the Biltmore Estate in North Carolina. Although it's likely not true, because Biltmore was being constructed around the same time and Vanderbilt didn't like to share.

At the base of the stairs is a velvet rope and a small sign that says, "Closed. Staff Only." It is enough to keep most visitors away. Those who do climb the stairs rarely notice that the hallway is too short. Instead, they make an immediate left for the club manager's office or go right into a small conference room. No one without a key card goes straight ahead to the door marked janitorial.

Kate pressed her key card against a white electronic lock on the wall. A moment later, the janitorial door clicked open.

She remembered the first time she learned The Lounge existed. She had won a big contracts case, and her name appeared in the paper. The club's president, Ted Oak, invited her to a private reception in the conference room. When she arrived, he whisked her down the hall, through the locked door, and into a space the size of a small coffee shop. It had dark wood paneling on the walls and felt like an old-fashioned speakeasy. There was a bar to the left and small round tables with chessboards and leather armchairs positioned throughout the room.

There were three ways a person got invited to join The Lounge: (1) be a long time club member (ten years plus) in good standing; (2) be a FIDE ranked chess player; or (3) be someone who, because of wealth, status, or occupation, brought favor upon other Lounge members. This last prong was how Judge Eide got a key card after less than a year of membership.

"Judge Eide," Kate said. "Could we talk for a moment?"

She had raced up the stairs and stopped beside the table where he had just finished a game. From the smile on his opponent's face, it was clear Eide had lost.

"Sit here," Ted Oak said, pushing back his chair and getting to his feet. "We're taking a break. I need to visit the little boys' room, and the Judge needs another drink to ward off depression from all the money he's lost."

As far as the State of Texas knew, alcohol was not consumed at the club. Nor did any gambling or smoking occur on the premises. But these things happened all the time in The Lounge.

Kate sunk into the chair across from Eide.

"I should have warned you about Ted," she said. "He's a shark."

Eide waved a hand at her. "No worries. I let him win. Losing at first makes winning easier later."

She nodded, although she wasn't sure she agreed. Her strategy had always been win, win, win.

"I got a call from your clerk this afternoon. A girl named Alexi."

"Oh yeah. You should meet her. She's in your club."

Kate raised an eyebrow. "What club is that?"

"Perfect ten. You know, great booty, breasts, legs, eyes, lips, skin, hair, nails, smile. Wait. That's only nine. There's one more. I can't remember it, though."

"Intelligence?"

Eide shook his head. "Come on, Kate. You know we don't allow that talk in here."

She clenched her jaw.

Before Ted Oak had handed her a key card, he was explicit about the terms of membership. "This is not a safe space," he said. "The only trigger warning you'll get here is if you pull a gun on somebody. We picked you because you run like the boys. Don't go proving us wrong by acting like a PC Nazi, okay?" Over the years, Kate had lost count of all the offensive things she heard behind the locked door. However, she had never taken any of it personally, because she didn't want to change these men. She wanted to be one of their equals.

Eide snapped his fingers. "Hourglass shape. That's number ten. Hers is killer. Yours isn't bad, though."

Kate flashed him a terse smile. "Your clerk said Ruth Jacobs's case was being transferred to a new judge."

"Yep. Sorry about that. I tried to keep it. But apparently, it would raise eyebrows. Dumping cases is a perk of becoming chief judge."

Kate's eyes went wide. "You're the new chief judge?"

Eide nodded.

"How?"

"Through order of succession. It's all laid out in the district court rules."

"That's not what I meant. When did you become assistant chief?"

"Two weeks ago, when Llamas went back to private practice. It turns out she doesn't have the right judicial temperament."

Kate struggled to process what she heard. The only way a person could go from new judge to assistant chief to chief judge in less than a month was—

"You're the one who tipped off the reporter."

Eide smiled but didn't answer aloud. The confessional seal of The Lounge might have protected locker-room humor, but it didn't extend to taking down district judges.

"You're his source?"

Eide shook his head. "Of course not. Do you think I'm an idiot? I merely suggested the kid investigate the Tina Black-Judge McDaniel angle. I had no idea he'd print that garbage."

"But you wanted him to?"

"Sure. Same as you. I guess it proves what they say, though. Real journalism is dead. It's all hit pieces now."

"Why did you give him my name?" Kate asked.

"To help you." He stared at her for a moment. When she didn't seem to understand, he continued, "Wake up, Katie. Everyone knows Susan Wilson wants that comic book villain to fire you."

"You didn't help, Terry. You made things worse."

"Not true. The story saved your job. It got you invited to Susan's ranch. How was I supposed to know you'd let your screwball client go on national TV?"

"That wasn't my idea."

"I should hope not. The woman's crazier than a loon."

"Did Alexi show you the motion I filed today?" Kate asked.

He shook his head. "I wouldn't look at it after she told me you asked for one hundred percent custody. Have you lost your mind, too? No sane person says hundred percent custody."

"I know. That's why you can't let the case be reassigned. Any other judge will destroy us."

Eide turned up his nose. "Is that a compliment? Because it doesn't feel like a compliment."

"Please, Terry. This is serious."

"You know I love you, Katie. I'd do anything for you. Anything except this. This I cannot do. As chief judge, my ethics must be beyond reproach. People will ask questions if I poke my nose where it doesn't belong."

"Please," she begged. "Some of the evidence I submitted today might not be true."

He laughed. "Might not?"

"I could get disbarred."

He shook his head. "No way. Suspended, probably. But not disbarred."

"I'll lose my job."

"Personally, I'd see that a plus. Susan is turning you into one of her shapeless ogres."

Kate stood up, pushed her chair back. Her hands shook, and her heart raced.

"If you won't help me, Terry, I'll have to tell Simpson what's really going on."

His eyes narrowed. He spoke in a slow, calm, deliberate manner. "I'm going to pretend you didn't say that. Friends don't threaten friends. And we are still friends, right?"

Kate hurried out of The Lounge and threw up in the public restroom downstairs.

99

"Katie, it's time to go."

Barbara stood at the edge of the living room and peered down the hall towards Kate's bedroom door. Her daughter was supposed to have left an hour ago, but Jessica canceled their dinner reservations because of a last-minute work problem. Thankfully, the problem wasn't big enough to keep them from going to the fundraiser.

Kate came out of the bedroom, fastening a diamond-studded earring as she walked. Dressed in a black sequined ball gown and carrying a tiny purse under her arm, she had her head cocked to the side.

"Where's Jessica?" she asked as she reached the living room and didn't see her sister.

"She'll be here any second," Barbara said.

"Any second? Why did you call me if she wasn't here? I'm not done with my makeup."

"You don't need makeup, honey."

Kate frowned at her as the doorbell rang.

"See," Barbara said, walking over to answer it. "She's here now."

But instead of Jessica, it was Yata Miller.

Yata wore a rainbow-colored, long sleeve dress that ran from her chin all the way down to the top of her boots. Across her chest, in big, white, iron-on letters, was the word Harvard. She pushed inside the condo and glared at Kate.

"Don't bother asking, Katie," Yata said. "You can't get one. It's one of a kind."

"I should hope so. It's repulsive."

"You're jealous."

Kate scoffed. "No. The dress makes you look like the Wicked Witch of the West turned hippie."

"It's the style."

"Whatever," Kate said. "But this is your last warning. If you stamp Harvard on anything else, I'm reporting you to the school for trademark infringement."

"I'm not afraid of you."

"You should be. You can't use the school's name without their permission."

"I don't need their permission, Katie. I'm an alumna. Do you understand the word alumna?"

Kate raised an eyebrow.

"Alumnas own the school," Yata said. "And as owners, we can do whatever we want."

Kate squeezed her eyes shut and pinched the bridge of her nose. "Alumni don't own the school."

"Oh, really? Then who does, Katie? Who does? The students?"

Yata laughed in a way that Barbara thought made her sound a lot like the Wicked Witch of the West.

Kate looked at Barbara. "I told you I didn't want her down here anymore. I don't care if the boy is coming over. She's not welcome."

Barbara pressed her lips together.

"I knew it," Yata said. "I had a feeling you were up to something, Barbie."

Barbara sighed.

The doorbell rang, and Barbara answered it again. Still, it wasn't Jessica.

This time it was a tall, slender, big-busted woman dressed in a police uniform. She had her hair tucked up underneath a peaked service cap, and a baton slung over her shoulder.

"Is everything all right?" Kate said, coming to the door.

The officer widened her stance, hit the baton against an open palm. "I'm here because someone's been bad."

"What?" Kate said.

"Oh, yes, yes!" Yata rushed to the door, grabbed the officer by the elbow, and whisked her into the living room. "I'm so glad Detective Miranda let you come. I've been badgering him for a week. I was worried he might not send you." Yata glanced at Barbara. "It's lucky I stopped by tonight."

Oh yeah, real lucky, Barbara thought.

"Mom? What's going on?"

Barbara looked behind her and saw Jessica in the doorway. She was dressed in a red, sleeveless, v-neck ball gown with her hair tied high in a bun.

"Don't ask," Kate said. "We're leaving. It's Yata crazy, as usual."

Jessica took a long look at Yata's kaleidoscope dress, then nodded. "We should go, anyway. Willa told me a photographer from The Times will be taking candid shots by the fountain. Apparently, they're running an article in Sunday's society section on the renewed interest in opera by Gen Y."

Kate made a gagging sound as she passed Barbara on her way out the door. "Gen Y? I don't know why businesses pander to those slackers. They care nothing about opera. And not one has read a newspaper. Ever."

Jessica said, "I'm not sure they've ever read anything, apart from a tweet or status update."

Kate laughed. "Touche."

Barbara closed the door behind them and joined Yata in the living room, who was now sitting on the couch beside the officer.

"I assume you've done this before, Officer—" Yata leaned over and looked at the woman's name badge. She turned up her nose. "Officer Na-stey."

"The name's Nasty, ma'am. Officer Nasty. And of course, I've done this before. You're my second party tonight."

"Oh," Yata said. "Okay. So how does it work? Do you cuff him right away? Read him his rights?"

Officer Nasty shrugged. "If you want me to. Usually, I try to get them excited first. You know, take off my hat. Start unbuttoning my shirt."

Yata's eyes went wide. "Unbuttoning your shirt?"

"I don't have to do it that way, it just seems to work better. You know, guys are more cooperative if they get a little show first."

"My God," Yata said. "That's outrageous. They're using you as a sex object."

Officer Nasty nodded. "I know, but it's the job."

"It shouldn't be the job. Can you imagine a male officer having to do that?"

Officer Nasty shrugged. "I don't know what the guys do. We never see them. They keep us pretty separate."

Yata shook her head. "I can't believe this is still happening in the twenty-first century."

"It does sound bad," Barbara said. "Yata, perhaps you should go home and call a few of your contacts. Maybe with your influence you could fix it."

Yata stared blankly at her for a moment. "You know, Barbie, I think that's the wisest thing you've ever said. But I can't leave yet. Not until Officer Nasty teaches Garrett a lesson, without exploiting her body."

Officer Nasty tilted her head to the side. "So you don't want skin? Because I was told it was a full nude."

"Full nude?" Yata was aghast. "No, no, no."

The doorbell rang again.

Before Barbara could react, Yata was on her feet and headed to answer it. Never had Barbara seen the woman move so fast.

"If it's Garrett, maybe I should talk to him first," Barbara said.

Yata shook her head. "I'm taking the lead on this one, Barbie."

Garrett smiled when Yata opened the door.

"What the hell are you wearing?" Yata said.

She was talking about the gray hoodie he wore over a pair of faded blue jeans. In giant, red print, it said, "HAHVID." Then below, in smaller font, were the words, "Pretentiously Smaht."

"Hey, we're twinsies," he said, pointing at Yata.

"We are not twinsies. Where did you get that?"

"Do you want one?"

"I'm going to file a complaint."

"With who? Hahvid?"

Barbara motioned him inside. He came over to the couch.

"The proper grammar," Yata said, "is with whom. Not with who."

"Yeah, okay. I'll remember that for my application. The last thing I want is to get rejected on a technicality."

Yata laughed. "Oh, technicalities won't be the reason they reject you, son. They'll have many, many valid reasons."

"Wanna bet?"

"No one's gambling," Barbara said.

Garrett looked at Yata. "Tell me what you think of my application essay. The working title is Cancer and Me. I use the word cancer like fifty times in the first two pages. My guidance counselor cried when he read it, and he's the football coach. I'm getting in, baby. Money in the bank."

Yata scoffed, then flashed Barbara a hard look.

"What?" Barbara said.

"You're just going to let him get away with it? Not even pretend to grandparent?"

"Get away with what?"

"You seriously don't see it?" Yata looked on the verge of losing her mind. "Even Officer Nasty can see it."

"The kid's using his cancer to weasel into Harvard," Officer Nasty said.

"Exactly," Yata said. "And it's despicable, right?"

Officer Nasty shrugged. "Do you have cancer, kid?"

Garrett nodded.

"Then I think he can use it."

Garrett smiled. "Thank you. That means a lot, coming from a beautiful woman like yourself."

Nasty winked back.

"No," Yata yelled. "Cancer is random. Cancer is abnormal cell division. Cancer is not a spot at Harvard."

"Calm down, Yata," Barbara said.

"No, I will not calm down. Mark my words, Garrett. You're not weaseling into my school, even if I have to call-in every favor ever owed to me."

"Yata, you're taking this too far," Barbara said.

"It's okay, Grandma Becker. I know she's just loves our school. The Dean and I were talking about it on the phone today."

Yata's eyes got so big they nearly popped out of her head. She spun around on the balls of her feet and left the condo so fast Barbara swore she felt a gush of wind.

100

"I'm sorry Officer Nasty had to leave before she could do her thing," Barbara said, as Garrett walked gingerly back towards the living room.

His pain had started almost immediately after they were alone in the condo. He asked if he could to use her bathroom for more privacy. She consented.

She handed him a bottle of root beer, and he winced as he sunk into the couch.

"It's your back, isn't it?" He nodded. "I hate back pain. Two years ago, Kate convinced me to try tennis. She said it would be fun. Instead, I got a stress fracture and a bottle of pain pills."

He smiled weakly.

"Not that it's the same thing."

"Ow."

"Do you want me to call your Mom?"

He shook his head. "It's fine. I forgot to take my pain meds before coming over. It will pass. Ow, ow."

"We have medicine. Ibuprofen, Acetaminophen, name brands, generics. You name it, we got it. Kate's a virtual pharmacy."

"That stuff isn't strong enough."

Garrett squeezed his eyes shut, tensed the muscles in his face, then let out a long, labored breath. She wanted to call someone to help, but she also didn't want to seem like she couldn't handle it. Things were bound to get worse as time went on.

"What medicine do you take?" she asked.

"Percocet."

Percocet was the medicine Barbara's doctor had prescribed for back pain. She still had a bottle in her medicine cabinet. She wasn't supposed to have any extra pills, but the nice doctor said she had a pretty smile.

Barbara held up a finger. "Back in a minute."

She hurried to the bathroom and returned holding an amber-colored pill bottle. She handed it to Garrett.

"You have Percocet?"

His eyes lit up when he said the word. For an instant, he didn't seem like he was in pain anymore.

"I told you we had everything."

He popped off the cap, poured a few into his hand.

"Whoa, there, partner. Be careful. You can only take one."

"My mom always gives me two."

"Then you've got the smaller pills. These are five milligram tablets. You take one. Trust me. I learned the hard way."

He shrugged, poured all the pills back into the bottle, except for one.

"Could you get me some water?"

She went to the kitchen. When she returned, he was drinking the root beer.

"Sorry," he said. "I used the soda."

She felt a bit put out at having been sent on a pointless errand, but she reminded herself not to complain.

"No problem." She set the glass of water on the coffee table, then sat down next to him on the couch. "I'm sorry Yata ruined your evening. Next time, I'll get a hotel room."

She cringed at how it sounded.

"It's fine. I never thought you'd actually go through with it, anyway."

"You didn't?"

"No."

"Well, I did, didn't I? And let me tell you, I paid a high price for it. And I don't mean the five hundred bucks for Officer Nasty. One place I called added my number to an adult phone list. Now, I'm getting pornographic texts from someone called Gunther."

Garrett smiled. "I should have warned you about that."

She waved him off. "Not that I mind. In fact, between you and me, it's sort of exciting. No man has ever said those type of things to me. It's gets me so—" She stopped when Garrett pulled away. "Never mind. I just don't want Katie finding out. I'm on her family plan, and she can read my messages on her computer."

"My mom uses the same spyware on me."

"Technology," Barbara said, shaking her head. "Nothing is private anymore. I'm not giving up, though. Tonight, I'll send Gunther a message. Ask him if he knows any girls who want to do a show for a sixteen-year-old boy."

"Ah, maybe don't say it that way."

"Oh, right. Good point."

She hadn't considered it from that perspective. Hiring Officer Nasty felt awkward and sleazy, but she hadn't thought it might be wrong. All she wanted to do was help a sick kid have a normal teenage experience, an experience he undoubtedly would have had but for the cancer.

"You'll hold off then?" Garrett asked.

"No. This is a rite of passage. I'm not giving up because of what someone might say."

"But I'm not interested anymore."

"Uh-huh," Barbara said. "I might be old, but I'm not that old."

He sighed, looked away for a moment. "I didn't want to say anything because of all the work you did to find Officer Nasty, but I've met someone."

Barbara's eyes lit up. "Someone who's a girl?"

"Yes."

"And she's your age?"

He nodded again.

"Hallelujah! Praise Jesus!" Barbara clapped her hands.

Garrett laughed. "I suppose that means you're happy for me."

"Of course, I'm happy for you. And for me too. You can't tell, but I wasn't thrilled about venturing deeper into the world of sex workers."

He smiled. "I wish my mom felt that way."

Barbara flashed him a confused look. "She doesn't approve?"

"She thinks I'm too young, says Rainn is a bad influence."

Barbara waved him off. "No girl will ever be good enough for your mother. It's her job. So, have you been on a date yet?"

"People don't go on dates anymore, Barbara."

"Really? What do they do?"

"Hang out. Go to parties. And no, we haven't hung out yet. I've been trying to see her, but my mom won't drive me. Do you think you could—"

"Drive you?"

He nodded.

"I don't have a car, remember."

"You could borrow Yata's."

"Is that a joke?"

"What if I agreed not to go to Harvard? Do you think she'd let you borrow it, then?"

"Why would you do something stupid like that? Harvard is a great school."

"I'm sixteen, Barbara. Did you think I'm applying to colleges?"

Barbara hummed.

"College isn't really in my future, anyway, if you know what I mean."

She swallowed hard.

"I can ask her."

101

Kate pushed aside her bottle of everyday red and reached towards the back of the built-in shelf. She grabbed the neck of a bottle covered in dust.

"Yes, yes," Jessica said, sounding almost giddy. "I've been waiting forever to try this one."

It was twenty-four hours after Kate stumbled out of The Lounge in a daze. She had come home from work to find Jessica on her couch. Her sister had let herself in using a key Kate gave her for emergencies only. It was the second time in a month she had abused the privilege.

Kate opened the wine and poured them each a glass.

"Why so glum?" Jessica asked as Kate joined her on the couch.

"You don't want to know."

"Are you worried the hacker will destroy your life?"

"Not until you just mentioned it," Kate said.

"Well, you should be. That's why I'm here. Wayne called with an update."

"Can it wait until tomorrow? I need to get drunk."

Jessica shook her head. "Wayne claims he found Asha."

Kate lowered her glass. "Really? I didn't think he had it in him."

"He says we should negotiate. He thinks for a hundred and fifty grand—"

"He wants more money? No way. Why doesn't he just napalm her? Like we paid him to do!"

"He can't."

"Why not?"

"It doesn't matter why not. You don't have a choice, Katie. If people find out about your data breach, you'll never be confirmed as Chief Justice."

"I'm not going to be Chief Justice."

"What?"

Kate told Jessica about Matt Simpson's threat to turn the story back on her, about how she had filed a motion for one hundred percent custody, and about how Ruth's case was being transferred to a new judge. She didn't mention Braxton's vasectomy, however. A person could be only so honest with their younger sister.

A long period of silence ensued, during which they refilled their wineglasses, slouched deeper into the couch, and stared off at the ceiling.

"What are you going to do?" Jessica asked a while later.

"I was thinking of moving to Panama."

Jessica looked at her like she was crazy. "Wasn't Noriega from there?"

"Yes. But he's dead. It's more open now. Plus, I've read the Panamanian Supreme Court is quite respected."

"I don't think we're related."

They drank more wine. An hour later, halfway through an opera they were streaming on Kate's iPad, Jessica sat up.

"I won't let you throw it all away, big sister. We have to fight back. We must do whatever it takes to protect your reputation."

Kate had wondered how long it would take Jessica to realize that a burned last name would effect her future in Austin, too. She held up her wineglass, the fifth of the night, in a mock toast.

"Love the energy. But it's too late. My only hope now lies in the hospitality of the Central American people. You should come. We could bring Mother, too."

"You're drunk, Katie. You're not going to Panama. Think of all the good you'll do on the Texas Supreme Court."

"I would be good, wouldn't I?" Kate said, slurring her words a little.

"Pay Wayne, you fool. A hundred and fifty grand is nothing, if it saves your career."

"I could buy an entire city in Panama for a hundred and fifty grand."

"Maybe," Jessica said. "But then you'd have to live there. Habla español?"

"I already know half the language. Taco, burrito, jalapeno. Lotus could teach me."

Jessica shook her head. "Just pay Wayne. Let me worry about the rest."

"How are you going to fix it?" Kate spoke extra slow, careful to enunciate each word.

Jessica stood up and wobbled for a moment before finding her balance. She was on her sixth glass of wine.

"Call Riley." Jessica grabbed Kate's phone off the table and thrust it at her. "Tell him he's been promoted to first chair on Ruth's case. Then, when everything goes to hell, blame it all on him."

Kate looked up and to the right. Blame it all on Riley? My God. It was genius. Why hadn't she thought of it before? She couldn't think of a single reason it wouldn't work.

"You're so smart."

She stabbed twice at the call button before hitting it.

Riley answered on the fourth ring, sounding as if he had been sleeping.

"Listen up, boy," Kate said. "From now on, you're in charge of Ruth's case. Everything that goes wrong is your fault. Got it?"

"Capeesh?" Jessica yelled from across the couch.

"Yeah, capeesh," Kate said.

She set the phone back on the table but forgot to end the call when she laid down to rest her eyes.

102

Kate's head ached as she pulled open the door at Susan Wilson Law the morning after her wild night of drinking with Jessica. The last thing she remembered was something about Panama. She hoped she hadn't drunk-talked her way into blabbing about Dr. Lotus or how Braxton had been snipped.

She arrived at work an hour later than usual. As she made her way down the hall, she had the feeling people were watching her. She didn't understand why until she stepped into her office and saw a person sitting at her desk.

"Tisk, tisk, tisk," The Hatchet said, shaking her head. "Someone's tardy."

A manila file folder was open on the desktop. The Hatchet was flipping through a two-inch stack of papers.

"Why are you going through my client files?"

The Hatchet smiled. "The clients belong to Ms. Wilson. When you used to work here, she let you handle them."

Kate's chest tightened. She wondered if Matt Simpson had followed through on his threat to flip the story. She hadn't had time to scan the paper or catch the TV news before hurrying out the door.

"Did Susan tell you about my judgeship?"

The Hatchet laughed. "Good one. I'm here because I'm a nice person. I wanted to give you one last chance to redeem yourself."

"Oh, yeah?"

"Tell me the truth, Ms. Becker. It shall set you free!"

"Set me free, huh? Like it did for Lacey and that other woman?"

The Hatchet raised an eyebrow. "For someone so self-righteous, you'd think you'd remember their names. Her name was Azure, Sonia. And she's fine."

"I didn't know you two were so close."

"Last chance, Ms. Becker. Admit Ruth is a fraud. Admit you're a liar. Get down on your knees, crawl across the carpet to me, kiss my hand, and apologize for jeopardizing Ms. Wilson's reputation. If you do that, I will help you land on your feet. Like I did for the other women."

"Not going to happen."

The Hatchet shrugged. "So be it. Honestly, I'm relieved. I think a little comeuppance will do you good." She glanced down at the desk, tugged on a red sticky flag near the middle of the stack of papers, flipped to the spot, then spun around the folder so Kate could read it. She pointed at the Certificate of Representation Kate filed in Ruth's case. "Is this your signature, Ms. Becker?"

Kate exhaled a sigh of relief. If this was all The Hatchet had on her, there was nothing to worry about. She stepped forward, pretended to study the signature closely.

"That's me. I am her lawyer, you know."

The Hatchet slid her index finger two inches to the left and hovered over the date. "Is this date accurate?"

Kate shrugged. "I assume. Why?"

"Because it doesn't match the date Ruth Jacobs hired you."

Kate feigned surprise. "That's weird. Does it match the date on her Retainer Agreement?"

She wanted to answer for the woman. *Of course, it matches*, she thought. Do you think I'd be so dumb as to not use the same date on both documents?

"They match," The Hatchet said. "But neither is accurate. Kind of a problem, wouldn't you agree?"

Kate hummed. "I guess. I mean, I don't know. Sounds like someone accidently wrote the wrong date. Either on the papers or the calendar. Sloppy, but not a big deal."

"It was no accident, Ms. Becker. You did it intentionally, to defraud the court, to remove Judge Walter Isaacs."

"What? That's crazy."

"You did."

Kate's face turned serious. "Can I give you a little advice, Ms. Vulcan? I wouldn't go around saying that sort of thing, if I were you. People might think you're unbalanced. Especially since there's no way you can prove it."

The Hatchet nodded. "I had the same thought, at first. Then, this morning, I got a visit from your associate."

Kate swallowed hard. "Oh, yeah?"

"Oh, yeah," The Hatchet said, copying her tone. She pressed a button on the desk phone. "Please send us Mr. Anderson."

A moment later, Riley appeared. Standing in the doorway, fidgeting with his hands at his side, he glanced at Kate, then looked away. She could see it all over his face. He had told her everything.

"You fucking traitor!" she said. "After everything I've done for you. You ratted me out to her? To The Hatchet!"

Riley shook his head. "All you've done for me? Everything you do is about you. Only you. The only reason you even hired me is because you screwed up."

The Hatchet gasped. "No! Say it ain't so, Ms. Becker."

"None of that's true, Riley. You should know better than to trust her."

"Tina Black's the one who told me. On my second day here. She called because she was worried you'd rather ruin my career than admit you made a mistake."

"Tina Black? She's even a bigger liar."

"No, Kate. You're the bigger liar."

"Then why did you keep working for me?"

"Because I hoped she was wrong about you."

"She is wrong," Kate said.

"Then what about last night? When you drunk-dialed me? Told me I was responsible for Ruth's case."

Kate squeezed her eyes shut, pinched the bridge of her nose. "I was joking."

"I heard you and Jessica talking. Next time, maybe hang up before you plot behind someone's back."

Kate's eyes flicked open in horror.

From behind the desk, The Hatchet began to clap slowly.

"Bravo, Mr. Anderson. Well done. Ms. Wilson will give you an exemplary recommendation. You'll have no trouble finding a new job. One where they actually want you. As for you, Ms. Becker, I'd say clean out your office, but nothing here belongs to you. Please give me your key card and laptop. Then begone, forever."

103

Kate pushed back the dining room chair and went to the built-in shelf in the living room in search of more wine. It was becoming routine now. At her current pace, she'd blow through her entire collection in a matter of days.

When she returned to the table, she hit the spacebar on her laptop.

"What the hell? How can this thing be so slow?"

"It's a miracle it even works," Jessica said, sitting across from her. "It has to be what? Ten? Eleven years old?"

Kate scoffed. "Not even close."

As she stared at the screen, waiting for the internet browser to load, she thought maybe her sister was right. The laptop was close to a decade old. She wasn't going to admit it, though, because she was annoyed Jessica had popped over immediately after hearing Kate had been fired.

The little hourglass on the screen disappeared and was replaced by a wall of white.

"Damn it."

"Language, Katie!"

Barbara breezed past them with a phone pressed to her ear,

carrying a bowl of popcorn. She went to her bedroom and closed the door.

"Was she talking to Yata Miller?" Jessica said.

"Probably. Those two are joined at the hip nowadays."

"Maybe we should do an intervention."

Kate shrugged. "If you do, count me out. I'm jammed up. I don't have the time."

Jessica raised an eyebrow. "You don't have the time? Come on, Kate. I know everything."

"Good. So you're going to apologize?"

"Why would I apologize?"

"Because this is all your fault. If you hadn't insisted I drunk dial Riley, I'd still have a job and my judgeship."

"What does Braxton think?"

Kate shrugged. "I don't know. He won't answer my calls."

"I'm sorry. I'm sure he'll come around. Just give him some time."

"Well, if he doesn't, it's for the best."

Jessica frowned. "Don't say that."

"It's true. After I sue Susan, he'd break up with me, anyway."

Jessica's eyes went wide. Her mouth fell open.

"You can't sue Ms. Wilson."

"I can. And I am."

"For what?"

"Wrongful termination, for starters. Maybe defamation, too. I'll figure it out in discovery."

"You've lost your mind."

Kate shook her head. "On the contrary. I've never been more sane."

"Ms. Wilson had grounds to fire you. You backdated a Cert of Rep and struck a judge before the client hired you."

Kate waved a hand at her. "Semantics. No reasonable lawyer can second-guess my decision to strike Isaacs. It led us to Eide. Honestly, I should get a medal for representing Ruth. If you don't believe me, just watch how things implode now that I'm gone."

"It was unethical."

"It doesn't matter. The lawsuit is bigger than me. I'm filing a class action. On behalf of all the women The Hatchet fired."

Jessica gasped. "Sweet Jesus! Tell me you're joking!"

"No. I was trying to search the lawyer registration database for contact information for my other plaintiffs. But this damn computer is so slow."

Jessica glanced over her shoulder, back down the hallway towards the bedrooms. "Mom. Mom. Mom!" Her voice got louder with each word.

A moment later, Barbara came out, the phone still pressed to her ear.

"Family emergency," Jessica said.

"Let me call you back." Barbara clicked off the phone. "What's the matter?"

"Your eldest daughter needs to be hospitalized. On a seventy-two hour hold."

"Oh," Barbara said. "This is about the lawsuit?"

"You know?" Jessica said.

"She thinks it's a good idea," Kate said.

Barbara shook her head. "I never said that. I told you to follow your heart. I said I'd support whatever decision you make."

"And I've decided to sue," Kate said. "I already have two potential lead plaintiffs for the class. Both are skilled lawyers. Neither of them deserved to be fired by The Hatchet."

Jessica said, "Maybe not, but it doesn't make it unlawful. The firm is at-will employment, Kate. Susan can fire them for any reason or no reason at all. It's hornbook law."

"Unless." Kate held up a finger. "She fired them for a discriminatory purpose."

Jessica scoffed. "A discriminatory purpose? Now, you're just making stuff up. You told me Susan fired them because they weren't bringing in new business. Which is why you took Ruth's case."

"What?" Barbara sounded surprised. "I thought you took the girl's case because of Robert Frost Day."

Kate ignored her mother, answered Jessica. "Until I interview them and test their stories, we won't know if Susan had a discriminatory purpose lurking below the surface."

Jessica shook her head. "You're not going to give up, are you?"

"No."

Jessica sighed. "Fine. I'll help you locate them. A PI at my firm owes me a favor. But you have to promise. After we talk to them, if there's no there there, you'll let it go."

"If there's nothing there, of course, I'll let it go. I don't bring frivolous claims."

104

"Thank you for meeting me," Kate said, crackling the protective plastic cover on the 1960s sofa as she sat down.

They were in a tiny, pastel-colored living room in a post-World War II rambler. The couch and two patterned armchairs were arranged in front of a brick fireplace painted white. A boxy TV in the corner looked so old that Kate thought it only showed black and white movies.

"It's good to see you again," Lacey Abrams said, perched on the edge of an armchair, smiling at both Kate and Jessica. "Would either of you like something to drink? I made a new batch of iced tea this morning."

"Sure, I'll—"

"No, thank you," Kate said, cutting off Jessica. "We can't stay long."

Lacey nodded. "Of course. I know how busy Ms. Wilson keeps y'all."

"Kate doesn't work for Ms. Wilson anymore."

"Really?" Lacey said, sounding surprised. "What happened? I thought you were on fast track to partnership."

"Fake news," Jessica said.

Kate clenched her jaw. "I was on the fast track. Until The Hatchet screwed me. Like she did to you."

"The Hatchet? Do you mean Patricia Vulcan?"

"Yes," Kate said. "I'm here because I'm investigating filing a wrongful termination class action against Susan, on behalf of all the women The Hatchet fired. I was hoping you might be one of my named plaintiffs."

Lacey laughed. "Me?"

Kate nodded. "I know it might seem overwhelming, going up against a powerhouse like Susan, but there's safety in numbers. If we stick together, she can't accuse us all of sour grapes."

Lacey paused a moment. "I'm no expert, but I thought commonality was a central component in these cases. You know, that all the plaintiffs had to suffer the same basic wrong."

Jessica leaned forward. "Did you hear that, Katie? She's also concerned about commonality."

Kate pressed her lips together. "Obviously, we have to prove commonality. It's why we're here. To gather evidence."

"I don't see how it'd even be possible," Lacey said. "When I think of employment class actions, I think of the overtime cases. Or the ride share drivers called independent contractors. I don't think of associate lawyers at law firms."

"Me neither," Jessica said.

Kate scoffed. "Well, like you said before, you're not an expert in these matters, are you?"

Lacey shrugged. "I suppose not. But even so, you wouldn't want me as a lead plaintiff."

"Why?"

"Because I'm glad she fired me. It was the best thing that could have happened."

"What?"

"Before I was fired, the firm was my life. I out-billed everyone, including Ms. Wilson, who pads her numbers. My life was unbalanced."

"It's that way for everybody, at first," Kate said. "It gets better."

"Did it get better for you?"

Kate's face turned red. "This isn't about me."

"I wasn't trying to be snide, Kate. After being away from practice for a couple of weeks, I realized I had lost part of myself. A part I'm glad to have back again."

Kate resisted the urge to make a loud gagging sound. The woman was rationalizing away the shame she felt from being kicked to the curb by a firm she had devoted her life to. It was pathetic.

"You would agree, though," Kate said, "that it wasn't right for them to fire you?"

"Right? I thought we were talking about what was legal."

"Surely, you'd agree that getting fired hurt your career."

"I don't know," Lacey said. "I haven't applied for comparable positions."

"Because they won't interview you, right?"

Lacey shook her head. Before she answered, a woman's voice called out through a cheap walkie-talkie clipped to her belt.

"Lacey," the voice wobbled, "I need my pills."

Lacey got to her feet. "I'll be there in a minute," she said into the walkie-talkie before looking back at Kate. "I'm afraid we're going to have to cut this short. Sometimes, she fights me on the pills. They're suppositories."

Kate winced. "Is that your mother?"

"Mother-in-law," Lacey said.

Jessica's mouth fell open. "You're the best wife ever."

Lacey smiled. "I don't know about ever. But I am pretty good. And I earn a little money, too."

"Money?" Kate asked.

"Yeah, that's why I haven't applied to any firms. I'm working as a PCA. Personal care assistant. Who would have guessed Ms. English Lit should have been a nurse?"

105

On Friday night, a week after the Officer Nasty debacle, Barbara sat in the passenger seat of Yata's Subaru at the curb outside Garrett's house, watching as the boy made his way down the concrete walk.

He was dressed in dark blue jeans and a plain black t-shirt. Not the outfit she would have recommended for a first date, but he looked fine. A little skinny, perhaps. Had he always been so thin? She wasn't sure because she had never seen him in anything other than a baggy sweatshirt.

"What a pleasant surprise," Garrett said, nodding at Yata, who was behind the wheel, as he slid into the backseat of the car behind Barbara.

Yata glanced back at him, wrinkled her nose. "What is that smell? Did you bathe in sandalwood?"

"It's a new high definition body spray. Do you like it?"

"No, not even a little," Yata said.

"I wasn't sure if I did either until now. Now, I'm sure. I like it a lot."

Yata scoffed. "Roll down the window before your stink infests my leather seats."

Garrett laughed, then hit the button on the door console, cracking the window an inch.

"More," Yata said.

"Jeez, is someone PMSing today?"

Yata's eyes bulged, her nostrils flared. "What did you say?"

"Garrett, that's inappropriate," Barbara said.

He shrugged. "Why don't you just hit the button on your door?"

Yata clenched her jaw.

When it was clear she wouldn't answer, Barbara said, "The back window buttons don't work."

"You're joking!" Garrett said. "You're saying the Subaru has a defect?"

"It doesn't have a defect," Yata said. "Subaru doesn't make cars with defects. In fact, the president of the company assured me he'd rather shutdown production for a month than sell a single car that wasn't perfect."

Garrett raised an eyebrow. "You didn't believe him, do you?"

"What I believe is that this Subaru was a gem before you and Barbie drove it. Now, it's an old jalopy. I wonder why."

Garrett took a quick breath, put his fingers to his mouth. "Oh, no. She knows."

"Haha," Yata said. "We'll see who's laughing in a few years, when you're saddled with a degree from a second-rate state school."

Yata handed Garrett a manila envelope that had been resting on the center console. He tore it open, pulled out a sheet of paper from inside.

"A contract?"

"Did you think I'd trust you?" Yata said. "By the way, you should know that my attorney says the liquidated damages provision will hold up in court. If you even breathe on Harvard property, I'm going to squash you like a bug."

Garrett took a moment, read through it.

"I don't agree with this last paragraph. And I don't appreciate being called The Boy."

"What does it matter if you're barred from wearing university apparel? You don't have any connection to the school."

Garrett cleared his throat, began reading the disputed portion of the contract aloud.

The Boy is prohibited from wearing, owning, displaying, or causing to be worn or displayed, any item containing any derivation or alternate pronunciation or spelling of the University name, including, but not limited to, symbols or artifacts which a reasonable person might construe as relating to the school. In the event said issue is disputed, Yata Miller's subjective judgment of infringement shall be conclusive.

"What's the problem?" Yata said.

"It's ridiculous."

Yata shrugged. "Totally your call. I would never force you to sign anything. But, you might want to text your little hussy. Let her know you're going to be late. Since you'll have to ride your bicycle across town."

Garrett tugged on the door handle. "She won't mind. Especially when I tell her I'm opening the online store we talked about."

"Online store?" Barbara said. "What online store?"

"Oh, I didn't mention it? People have been hounding me about those HAHVID hoodies. So, I've been toying with selling them online. Wouldn't it be cool if my shirts became so popular they changed the name of the school?"

Yata clenched her jaw. A vein on the side of her neck became so engorged Barbara thought she might have a stroke.

"That's illegal," Yata said.

"No, it's satire."

Garrett stepped a foot out of the car.

"Wait!" Yata yelled.

He stopped, looked back at her.

"I'll remove the subjectivity clause," she said. "If there's a dispute, we'll litigate."

Garrett shook his head. "Either the entire apparel clause goes or I'm opening a store."

"But if the clause goes, you can open a store," Yata whined.

"Yep. I guess you'll just have to hope I'm too busy with my little hussy to care about selling shirts."

Yata hesitated a moment. "Fine. Cross it out. But you're signing now. Before I move the car."

Garrett scribbled his name, then handed the paper back to Yata. Barbara didn't understand why the woman had wasted money on a contract. Surely, her lawyer must have told her no court would enforce it against a minor.

"So where does the girl live?" Yata asked, after folding the contract and putting it in her pocket.

"I'm meeting her at a party. I'll text you the address."

Yata plugged the numbers into the GPS on her phone, then made a funny face. "North of the 183? Isn't that an industrial area?"

"Probably," Garrett said. "The parties are always moving around. Never in the same place twice. Isn't that the same trick you writers use to keep the audience interested?"

Yata flashed Barbara a concerned look, then started the car.

106

"Somebody's playing a trick on you, kid."

Yata eased the Subaru to a stop on a dark, deserted street in an industrial area near the train tracks in North Austin. The address Garrett had given led to an abandoned four-story warehouse with chipping paint, broken windows, and a parking lot encircled by an eight-foot-high chain-link fence with barbed wire on top.

"Go up a little," Garrett said. "Maybe there's a back entrance."

Yata shook her head, then shifted the car into reverse and began a three-point turn. "I never should have left that main road. We're going to get carjacked."

"I'm getting out," Garrett said.

"No, you're not."

When Yata stopped to shift the car into drive, Garrett pushed open the back door and got out. He was across the street, jogging towards the far end of the building, when Yata rolled down her window and yelled at him.

"Get back here!"

Barbara's heart raced in her chest. Yata was right. They needed to get off this street, out of the area, back to civilization, before something terrible happened. But she couldn't leave without Garrett.

"Stay here, Yata," Barbara said, pushing open her door.

"What?" Yata's eyes went wide.

Barbara climbed out of the car, her legs feeling unsteady. "Don't go anywhere."

"No way. I'm not hanging out here by myself, in this flashy car, waiting for some gangbanger to attack me. If you get out, you're on your own, Barbie Becker."

Barbara figured as much. "Stay close, though, okay? We need a ride home."

Yata pressed her lips together. "You've got ten minutes. I'll be at the gas station a ways back. But then, I'm leaving. Never to return."

Barbara nodded. She crossed in front of the car and followed the same path Garrett had taken.

Within twenty yards, she was out of breath. But unlike the day she threw away Kate's newspaper, she pressed on, her thighs rubbing together, her breasts heaving up and down.

When the fence turned ninety degrees to the right, she followed around the side of the building. Garrett was up ahead, crouched down, his back to her, squeezing through a hole in the fence that led to the parking lot.

She called out to him. He stopped, waited for her to catch up.

"What are you doing, Barbara?"

"What am I doing? What are you doing? You shouldn't have gotten out of the car."

"The party's here," he said. "I know it. Rainn would have texted me if the address changed."

Barbara thread her foot through the hole in the fence, then sucked in her stomach and pushed. She stopped when the metal scraped against her belly.

"Pull it back."

"I can't just rip open the fence. I'm not a superhero."

"Do it."

He grabbed the part of the fence that was touching her belly and pulled it back. It moved a little, just enough for her to squeeze through.

"See," Barbara said. "I knew you could do it."

"Uh-huh. So, you're through the fence. What are you going to do now? Because you're not coming to the party with me."

"Oh, yes, I am."

He shook his head. "The deal was you'd drop me off, then go to a movie."

"That was when the party was at a house. When the party's at an abandoned building, I must tag along. It's the grandparent code."

"I don't think so."

"You don't have a choice, Garrett. Either I'm coming with you or I'm calling your mother, telling her where you are."

He sighed. "Of all the times you could grow a backbone, why did it have to be now?"

She smiled. "I'm assuming that's a compliment. Plus, I want to meet this girl. I've never met anyone named Rainn."

"I swear to God, Barbara. If you—"

"Relax. When have I ever embarrassed you?"

He darted off across three rows of empty parking spaces headed towards the building. She tried to keep up, but settled for a brisk walk.

They climbed a set of cement stairs onto a loading dock. He tried the handle on a rusted door. It opened. Music came out from somewhere deep inside.

"This way," he said.

"It could be dangerous."

He frowned at her. "Where's your sense of adventure, Barbara?"

"Adventure? I don't want an adventure. Adventures are only fun when they're over."

He laughed. "That's from the Narnia books, right?"

"I don't know. What are the Narnia books?"

She pulled out her phone and switched on the light before following him inside.

The first thing she noticed about the space was its size. It was an old factory floor. Cement, bare walls, and large machines covered with drop cloths. The room spanned the entire width of the building. When she looked up, she could see all the way to the ceiling, four stories above. She wondered what they used to make here. Maybe airplane wings or those super big drills she saw on TV.

The second thing she noticed was the smell. The air was stale. Whatever used to happen in there hadn't happened in a long time.

She followed Garrett around to the left, staying close to the wall, moving deeper inside. The further they went, the louder the music got.

They passed through an open door, trading the factory floor for an administrative suite. The offices lining both sides of the hallway had metal desks, straight chairs, calendars, and even pencil holders. It looked like the employees had gone home for the night and never come back.

"This place gives me the willies," Barbara said.

"It does have a sort of zombie apocalypse vibe."

"We should go back."

"You should go back. I'll call when I'm ready to leave. Shouldn't be more than an hour."

Barbara grumbled but kept moving forward.

At the end of the hall, they stopped at a metal door that seemed to vibrate in tune with the music.

"Please don't embarrass me, Barbara,"

He pulled open the door, and the music engulfed them. Stepping inside, Barbara couldn't believe her eyes.

107

The door led to a three-story atrium packed with teenagers, hundreds squeezed close together, waving their arms in the air, jumping to music so loud it made Barbara's chest vibrate. Laser lights on the ceiling cast fat beams of color through a foggy haze. Across the room, on a makeshift stage, two fires in trash cans flanked a tattooed guy in a tank top, who was scrubbing a vinyl record on a turntable. It was exactly how Barbara imagined an underground rave would look, having seen one once on a TV.

She glanced to her right, intending to lecture Garrett about the inappropriateness of the party, when she realized he wasn't beside her anymore. He had kept walking.

She scanned the crowd. It took a moment for her to find him. He was off by the sidewall, with a group of kids sitting on desks and drinking from plastic cups. A girl stood in front of him. From how her head bobbed from side to side, it was clear she was unhappy.

Barbara assumed the girl was Rainn. She looked like a Rainn. She had long black hair, green eyes, and was dressed in a skimpy black tank top with fish netting over her stomach. Around her neck, there was a studded collar and heavy metal chains.

"I vouched for you, Gary," Rainn said as Barbara came up to

them. The girl frowned at her. "Please tell me Granny isn't with you?"

"She's cool," Garrett said. "Don't worry." He reached into the front pocket of his jeans and pulled out a sandwich-sized plastic bag. "I brought the pills."

Barbara recognized the pills. They were Percocets. Five-milligram tablets. The same kind she had given Garrett at the condo.

He pressed one into Rainn's palm.

"One? What the hell, Gary?"

"Rainn, we've talked about this. When you're drinking, you can't—"

"Wah wah WAH! Either give me the whole bag or go home. What it's going to be, Gary?"

"We should go," Barbara said, tugging on Garrett's arm.

He ignored her, looked at Rainn. "Fine. Take the bag. But promise me you won't take any more tonight."

The moment he loosened his grip, Rainn snatched the bag from his hand. She quickly counted the pills. Satisfied by the number, she turned into a different person.

Smiling, she wrapped her arms around his neck and hugged him like he was a long-lost lover returning from war.

"You're the greatest, Gary," she said. "Come. Meet my friends."

"Okay."

Rainn let go of him and turned back to the group, swaggering and holding up the bag of pills like she had earned them.

Barbara grabbed Garrett's arm. "How did you get those?"

He raised an eyebrow. "You're asking how I got pain pills?"

She paused a moment, feeling stupid. "You can't give them away. You might need them."

He shook his head. "It's a perk of cancer, Barbara. I can eat pain pills for breakfast, if I want. Nobody cares."

Her heart fell. So, it really was that bad, then.

"She's not interested in you, Garrett."

"Of course, she is."

"She calls you Gary."

He shrugged. "It's a fun nickname."

"Gary is not a fun nickname. She's using you."

He leaned in close, whispered in her ear. "We're using each other, Barbara. She wants pills. I want her body. It's a quid pro quo."

Over his shoulder, Rainn called out to him.

"Gary, come sit by me. I'm getting lonely."

He nodded at the girl, then looked back at Barbara. "See, she knows the deal."

"Garrett, please," Barbara said. "This isn't how it's supposed to be."

He laughed. "You're right. It's not. But it's how it is. Stay or go. I don't care."

He went over to Rainn and sat down. Her hands were all over him, running through his hair, across his chest, down his inner thigh. She kissed him frantically, like her tongue was hunting for something in his mouth. Then she moved to his neck, began sucking a hickey.

Barbara turned away, but not before Garrett met her eye and smiled.

108

Barbara moved away from Garrett and Rainn to a spot near the door where they had entered the room. Pressing her back flat against the wall, she smiled, pretending to enjoy the rave, acting as if she didn't care that Garrett had given away pain pills or that Rainn was sucking his neck and fondling his crotch.

Inside, she felt nauseated. What was she supposed to do? Getting mad wouldn't solve anything. Garrett wasn't leaving until he was ready, whenever that might be. And she couldn't force him to go. He was stronger and more detached. She hoped she could at least get him home safely.

A lanky boy with a greasy mullet, bad acne, and an adolescent mustache sidled up next to her. He was dressed in a plain black t-shirt and jeans and carried himself like a sixteen-year-old Don Juan.

"Hello, beautiful," he said to her.

Barbara raised an eyebrow. "What did you say?"

"Your skin. It's radiant."

"Radiant? Either you're stoned or blind, kid. Because I've got liver spots and a turkey neck."

He chomped at her with his teeth. "Gobble gobble."

"Gross," Barbara said. "Go away."

He shook his head. "I'm a cougar hunter, baby. Once I've locked onto a target, I never give up."

Out of the corner of her eye, she saw Rainn stand up and take Garrett's hand.

"Where are you two going?" Barbara asked as they passed in front of her.

Rainn pulled open the door to the back.

"We're going to have some private time," Garrett said, with a twinkle in his eye.

"No, you're not."

"Is someone feeling left out?" Rainn asked. "Because you could bring your boyfriend. We could do a quad."

"Sounds fun," the sixteen-year-old Don Juan said.

"Not going to happen," Barbara said.

Rainn reached into her pocket and pulled out another Percocet. She popped it into her mouth like it was a Tic Tac.

"Suit yourself, Grannie. Let's go, Gary."

"Garrett, please," Barbara said.

"We can leave when I'm done. Maybe find someplace comfortable to sit, because I've been told I have great stamina."

Rainn laughed as two disappeared behind the closed door. Barbara swatted away her teenage Don Juan, then spent a few minutes watching the DJ work the crowd, before pulling out her cell phone to check messages.

The first message was from Yata, a cursing, stream-of-consciousness rant about a homeless man at the gas station eyeing her. She believed he intended to ravish her or the Subaru or both. She said she was going to call the police if he came within ten yards of her.

The second message was from Kate, who claimed there was an emergency at home. She couldn't find the new carton of Almond milk Barbara had promised to buy at the store. Barbara deleted this message straight away because if her daughter had emptied the refrigerator like she claimed, she already knew where the Almond milk wasn't.

The third message was Yata again. Apparently, she had misjudged the homeless man. It turned out he wasn't homeless at all but rather an off-grid separatist type who had heard good things about Subaru. This changed her opinion of him, making him seem like a dreamy, sexy outlaw. She told the man that if he bought a new Ascent, loaded to the max, she'd consider letting him load her to the max. Then she told Barbara to call when she was ready to go, as she, Yata, planned to stick around a bit longer. "Mr. Off-Grid is taking me to his bunker to meet his friends, who also like Subaru. If I can sell four, I get a set of steak knives."

Barbara shook her head, then opened an app and began scrolling through social media feeds. She looked up when the metal door burst open, and Garrett came running out.

"Barbara," he yelled, his head turning from side to side, searching for her.

"I'm right here."

She went over to him. There was panic in his eyes.

"We need to go. Now."

"What happened? Is something wrong?"

"No, no." He tried to compose himself, but he was still speaking too fast. His hair was disheveled, and his face was blotchy. "I promised my mom we'd be home soon. I don't want her to get worried."

She knew he was lying, and she knew he knew that she knew, but it didn't matter. Not at that moment. Whatever happened, they could talk about it later. It obviously had something to do with that girl.

She followed as he led her out the front, instead of going back how they came.

109

The morning after Kate struck out with her first potential plaintiff, she spent ninety minutes driving north on the I-35 towards Wacko. She left right after breakfast, allowing only a quick call to Jessica, promising not to do exactly what she was doing. She had had enough of her sister's razzing and resolved to go alone.

She turned off the freeway ten miles past Waco and followed a rural road that led away from civilization. Out both sides of the car, stretching off towards the horizon, there was prairie land as far as the eye could see.

After a long time, she saw a wooden sign on the side of the road. It wasn't as big as a billboard, but it was close. A red arrow pointed left above the words Oswald Sanctuary. Two miles.

Kate turned and followed a gravel road all the way to the end. She stopped in a parking lot by a building with weathered-wood siding. It reminded her of an outbuilding a farmer might use to sell produce alongside the road.

She parked next to a handicapped bus, the only other vehicle in the lot, then got out and went inside. There was no one behind the counter or at the small tables in the lobby.

Through a large window at the back, she saw a group of people in motorized wheelchairs. They were on a blacktop path about two hundred feet behind the building, watching a woman, who was dressed in a black pantsuit, white blouse, and rubber boots, lay two-by-fours across a muddy stretch of ground leading to a wire-fenced field. Behind the fence were five of the biggest dinosaur-like birds Kate had ever seen in her life.

From the website, she knew the Oswald Sanctuary specialized in rescuing red-necked Maasai ostriches. The giant of the bird kingdom, Maasais can grow up to nine feet tall and weigh over three hundred pounds. But knowing it in theory, and seeing it in person, were two different things.

She went out the back door and made her way towards the group, stopping a few feet short to not interrupt.

"We won't know if we don't try," Sonia said, stepping out of the mud and onto the path. Grime covered her boots up to the ankle.

It had rained hard the previous night. Not hard enough to disturb Kate's sleep at her condo in Austin, but hard enough to turn a dirt path into a mud pit at the Oswald Sanctuary.

A middle-aged woman, standing off to the side, dressed in jeans and a purple sweatshirt, shook her head. "I want a refund."

"Because it's a little wet?"

"Because my clients can't get near the birds."

"They can," Sonia said, spreading her arms wide, "if we roll them down the boards, one at a time, very slowly."

The woman scoffed. "They'll get stuck."

"Not if we're careful."

"I would never have come out here, if I knew you weren't actually handicap accessible."

"We are handicap accessible. Why do you think we have the boards?"

The woman looked at the people in the wheelchairs. "Turn it around. We're going home."

Several of the people groaned.

"Please," Sonia said. "Can't you see how much they want to stay? We'll figure it out."

"What's the point? They need to touch 'em to get any benefit. Even the website says so."

"Not necessarily. Ostriches have been known to heal from great distances. Not that it's typical. Legally, I must add that my comments have not been evaluated by the Food and Drug Administration, and our ostriches do not diagnose, treat, cure, or prevent any disease."

As the woman helped her clients navigate their way back to the building, Kate stepped forward and introduced herself.

"If this is about the Blakely case," Sonia said, "I don't want to hear it. I washed my hands of that woman when I left the firm."

Kate didn't know what Sonia was talking about.

"It's not that. I was hoping to speak to you about the circumstances surrounding your leaving."

"The circumstances are I got fired. Weren't you in there?"

"Um, yes. The thing is, The Hatchet has fired many skilled lawyers over the past few weeks. Me included. I'm investigating bringing a class action against Susan. To get people some compensation."

Sonia raised an eyebrow. "Is this a prank? Did Lacey put you up to this?"

"Lacey? Do you mean Lacey Abrams?"

"Is there another Lacey?"

Kate hummed. "I didn't know you two were friends."

"We weren't at first. But now, we're part of the BOFs."

"BOFs?"

"Better Off Fired," Sonia said. "We video chat once a week. I could add you to the group, if you want."

"Fine. But you don't actually believe that nonsense, right? I mean, Susan Wilson Law is one of the best firms in the country. And this," Kate gestured towards the mud path leading to the ostriches, "I'm not sure what this is."

"It's a sanctuary. A healing space."

"A healing space? You tried to scam that group of quadriplegics into believing ostriches could heal them in the parking lot."

Sonia's eyes narrowed. "I'm disappointed in you, Kate. I never took you for an ethnocentrist."

"I'm not."

"Many African cultures believe ostriches have healing properties. In parts of Somalia, they use the fat to cure AIDS and diabetes. Why wouldn't it work with quadriplegism?"

Kate stared at her blankly for a moment, looking for any sign Sonia knew what she was saying was absurd. There was nothing.

"Um, because of science and medicine and general common sense."

"Maybe in your culture, but—"

"This isn't a culture thing. It's a facts thing. Ostriches don't heal people."

"At the Oswald Sanctuary, we believe in all forms of hope."

"Provided people pay admission."

"The animals can't eat hope, Kate."

Kate scoffed. "Look, I know you were only at the firm a few weeks, and things have obviously gotten pretty dire for you, but you had a successful career before The Hatchet derailed it."

"Maybe. But I'm part of something bigger now."

Back by the building, the woman in charge of the wheelchair group yelled out to them. "We're not leaving until we get a full refund."

Sonia sighed, then made her way over to them. Kate followed.

"Are you the only one working here?" Kate asked.

"For now. But next year, if our projections hold, we might be able to hire a few part-time staff. If I can stop refunding money."

Sonia disappeared into the building. A while later, she returned and handed the woman a check.

They watched as the bus kicked up mud as it sped away.

Sonia said, "I bet she calls next week to apologize. One of her clients will get healed. They always do."

"From quadriplegism?"

"Yes."

Kate thanked Sonia, then got into her car and drove away before the woman could spew any other falsehoods. It wasn't until she was back on the county road that she cried.

110

Three days after the rave party, Barbara was in the kitchen at the condo, sipping the last of her lukewarm coffee, when the doorbell rang. She rinsed out the slate-colored ceramic mug and put it back in the cupboard so Kate wouldn't know she had used it.

Officially, Barbara was banned from using Kate's favorite coffee mug because of an unfortunate incident involving an unwashable stain caked to the bottom. Kate called this stain "a foreseeable consequence of Barbara's reckless, self-centered behavior." She scoffed at her daughter's overreaction and swore never to use any of Kate's mugs again. And she hadn't. At least, not as far as Kate knew.

Barbara took her time crossing the living room. She had agreed to spend the morning with Carol, helping the woman pick out a new mattress for her guest bedroom, but it was all going to be a giant waste of time. Carol wouldn't buy a mattress. She never bought anything. The woman was such an indecisive penny-pincher all they'd do is wander from store to store, Carol complaining about this and that. She wondered why she had agreed to go.

When she pulled open the front door, it was Yata Miller instead of Carol.

Yata looked frazzled. She had the same wild look in her eyes as the morning after the racetrack.

"I swear to God, Barbara Becker." Yata pushed past her into the condo, heading straight for the living room couch, collapsing back into it and draping an arm over her eyes. "If my name makes the paper, I'm going to kill you. With my own hands."

It was the first time Barbara had ever seen Yata out of uniform. She was dressed in business-like attire (black slacks, white button-down shirt, green duster) with no visible collegiate logos. Seeing her that way was strange, sort of like seeing the president in a short-sleeve shirt and jeans.

"What's going on Yata?"

"I take it they haven't been here yet?"

Barbara closed the door and went over to Yata.

"Who?"

"Don't you watch the news, Barbie?"

"Not today. What's going on?"

"Your Stink Bomb got us tangled up in a murder investigation."

Barbara's mouth fell open.

"A murder investigation?"

"That's what the police are calling it. Although, personally, it doesn't feel much like a murder to me. I mean, if a teenage girl gets naked and ODs on a bunch of pills, whose fault is that really? Even if he did give her the pills, which, who knows, it's still not murder."

Girl. Pills. Naked. Barbara's heart raced in her chest.

"That's terrible," Barbara said, trying to keep her voice steady. "Do you remember her name?"

"It was something stupid. Like Earth, wind, or fire. No, wait, that's a band."

"Rainn?"

"Yeah. That's it. The name that doubles as a weather forecast."

Suddenly, Barbara felt out of breath. Everything made sense now. The panicked look on Garrett's face. Why he insisted on leaving so fast. Why he led her out front instead of retracing their steps through the back.

Yata said, "Do you know another stupid name I heard once? This woman in Detroit. She wanted to call her daughter, Promiscuous."

Barbara didn't answer.

"Hello? Barbie? Are you listening? I said promiscuous."

"Yes, I heard. It's a very unusual name."

"No, it's not unusual. It's absurd. You can't call your daughter a slut before she actually deserves it."

"I guess that's true."

"Tell me this: let's say the woman did name her daughter, Promiscuous. Then, the girl grows up to be a prostitute who's killed by her pimp. Whose at fault, Barbie? The mother or the pimp?"

"I don't know."

Yata lifted her arm off her eyes. "You're not even trying. Obviously, it's both. They should cut off the man's balls and burn the mother at the stake. What's gotten into you, woman? Are you worried your name will be in the paper? Because no one even knows who you are."

"So you didn't mention me then?"

"Are you asking if I ratted you out to the cops?"

"Did you?"

"Hell yes, I did. I sang like a canary."

"Oh, great. Thanks."

"Don't blame me. You're the one who made me drive Stink Bomb to the party."

"How did the police even find you?" Barbara asked.

"A building on the street has cameras on the roof. They got my license plate."

Barbara shook her head.

Yata said, "I'm a little surprised they haven't been here yet. I thought they'd come straight over after I left the station."

Barbara hummed. "Maybe they don't need to talk to me."

"Or maybe you're a person of interest."

"What? Why would I be a person of interest?"

Yata's eyes narrowed. "Yes, Barbie. Why would you be?"

She grabbed Yata's arm and pulled her to her feet. "Get up. You need to leave. I'm late for an appointment."

In the hallway, they met Carol coming towards them.

"It's about time, Carol," Barbara said. "We're going to be late."

"We are?" Carol looked confused.

"We need to make a quick stop before we go to the store."

Yata shook her head. "You better not be going where I think you're going."

111

Barbara knocked on the closed bedroom door, then turned the handle and pushed it open.

"I said I wanted to be alone," Garrett said.

The boy was curled up on the bed with his back to the door. The floor creaked as she entered the room, causing him to turn and look.

"What the hell are you doing here, Barbara?" he said, sitting up.

She stopped in the middle of the room.

"What happened to Rainn?"

"Nothing."

"Don't lie to me. Yata's already spoken to the police."

He sighed. "Stay out of it, Barbara."

"I saw you give her the pills. Then you took her back into those offices. Now, she's dead."

"Be careful."

"Be careful? Is that a threat?"

"You need to think about the story you want to tell."

"The truth isn't a story, Garrett."

"All life is a story, Barbara. And if you're not careful, yours might turn into a nightmare."

"What?"

"You're the only person who could connect me to her."

Barbara tilted her head to the side, flashed him a puzzled look. "No, I'm not. Half the kids at the party saw you two together."

"None of them will talk."

"I hate to break it to you, Garrett, but people always talk. It's the moral of those newsmagazine shows."

"These kids don't watch TV."

"Well, I'm not lying to the police. And you shouldn't either. If you liked this girl, you owe it to her family to tell the truth, explain what happened."

Garrett teared up. He closed his eyes, took a deep breath, then exhaled, trying to not let himself be overcome by emotion.

"She's got no family. No one's even going to claim her body."

Barbara winced. "Still, it's not right to cover it up."

"But I did nothing wrong."

"Then you have nothing to worry about."

He forced a laugh. "Once they hear I gave her the pills, they'll stop listening, take me straight to jail."

"No one's going to jail."

"I tried to stop her. But she kept taking them. Then she passed out."

"I believe you, Garrett. I'll call Kate. She can help."

Barbara pulled out her phone, began to dial Kate's number.

"Wait," Garrett said, holding up a hand. She entered the last digit but stopped before pressing call. "Even if you're right, even if Kate can help me, I don't want to spend the little time I have left fighting with the police. I don't want my Mom to remember me that way."

Barbara took a quick breath. In the past, she had gone to great lengths to keep from thinking about how much time he had left. She didn't want to rob him of a peaceful ending, but she wasn't sure she could lie.

"I, I—"

"Just promise me you'll think about it, all right?" he said. "You don't have to decide now. We'll talk again tomorrow."

"And if the police come to my condo first?"

"Tell them you want to talk to a lawyer. It will push things off for a day or two. Once we're on the same page, it will be easy. They've got nothing on us, Barbara. We just have to stick to the story."

Barbara went to the kitchen and pulled Carol away from a heated discussion with Garrett's mother, then spent the rest of the afternoon shopping for a couch no one would buy.

112

On the drive back from Sonia's ranch, Kate's tears gave way to a wall of dark thunderheads. The woman on the radio said it might rain for three days straight, the clouds being the second front of a large, tropical storm coming in from somewhere in the Gulf.

Let it rain for years, Kate thought. The weather doesn't matter. Nothing matters anymore.

Jessica was right. There could be no class action. Suing Susan would only make things worse. Somehow, The Hatchet had managed to fire the women and turned them into friends at the same time. Kate would have admired the woman's craftiness if she hadn't destroyed her life.

On the outskirts of the city, she left the interstate and followed a county road to a suburban park. She parked on the street, then made her way down a concrete path towards a small amphitheater with a statue in the center. She walked slowly, without an umbrella, unconcerned about the rain flattening her hair and running down her face.

Climbing down the steps to the third row, she took a seat directly across from the big bronze lady on stage. She couldn't help but think how different things were from the first time she sat in the amphitheater, a year ago, on that sunny day, watching as they unveiled the statue to the public, still believing anything was possible.

The statue had been her idea or Jessica's idea, or maybe both of their ideas together. She couldn't remember. What was undeniable, however, was that without Kate's dogged persistence, the old man would not have changed his will and donated the proceeds of his life insurance policy to the RBG Memorial Conservation Fund.

"What will my children think?" the old man said two weeks before he died, as she set the revised paperwork on the swing arm hospital tray.

"They should say thank you," Kate answered. "For all eternity, their names will be etched alongside a legal icon. What better legacy could you give them?"

The man's hand shook as he signed his name. "Do you think it's all right? Building an even bigger statue than the one in her hometown?"

"Everything's bigger in Texas, Arvin. Plus, if it's not bigger, we won't get the publicity. People need to know she's here. Otherwise, they can't pay their respects, be inspired to do good work."

When the statue was erected, it measured over twenty feet high. It was three times the size of the Ruth Bader Ginsburg memorial in Brooklyn, New York. People came from all across the South to see it. There were news vans, photographers, and, for the first week, even a pizza food truck. Those were the glory days.

Three months later, it all crashed down when a group of tech nerds from Bend, Oregon, unveiled their own statues. Fifty-foot replicas of RBG, Sotomayor, and Kagan holding hands and dancing under a rainbow of conflict-free gemstones. The only people who took pictures in Austin now were social media pranksters who posed with RBG inappropriately.

Kate closed her eyes, tried to think.

"You're imagining what she'd do, aren't you?"

The woman's voice came from behind her. She recognized it immediately. She didn't turn to look.

A moment later, The Hatchet stepped down two more stairs and turned to face Kate. She was holding a black umbrella over her head.

"Why are you here?" Kate said.

"To be inspired by the best judge of all time."

"She was a justice, not a judge. And I don't believe you."

The Hatchet shrugged. "Whatever. I'll confess I'm not big into statue worship. What the hell's wrong with you, Kate Becker?"

Kate's heart pounded. Her body tensed. "What?"

"How can you be so smart and so stupid at the same time?"

Kate clenched her jaw. "If you came here to fight, please leave. I'm not in the mood."

"Do you think I enjoy standing in the rain? Listen up. I'm only saying this once. Stop trying to be a second rate Wilson or Ginsburg or whoever else you fantasize about at night. It makes you pathetic."

Kate scoffed. "You have no right to—"

"My God, woman, you are stubborn. You lose everything. Yet, still, you're too proud to accept my help."

"Your help?"

"Yes, my help. Don't you wonder why Abrams and Azure respect me, even though I fired them?"

"Because they're crazy," Kate said.

"They're not crazy."

"Sonia's nonprofit is peddling ostriches as a cure for quadriplegism."

This seemed to surprise The Hatchet. "Sonia only worked for us for a short time. The point is, they respect me because I helped them see the truth. Neither wanted to practice law. Neither had the courage to admit it. I saved them."

Kate forced a laugh. "Right. But just so we're clear, I loved my job. And you stole it from me."

"Loved your job? Even though your boss hired you by mistake? Even though she ordered me to fire you?"

"That was before."

"Before what? Before you hired Mr. Anderson to work at an all-woman firm? Or before you lied about Ruth Jacobs's case, submitted false evidence to the court?"

"I had a plan."

"Sweet Jesus, let's hope not. Blame me, if you want. But when you grow tired of this," The Hatchet gestured at the surrounding emptiness, "I suggest you take a look at yourself in the mirror. Try to see who you are, not who you think you ought to be. If you do that, maybe you can chart a path forward. And it won't be the path of Ms. Wilson or Justice Ginsburg."

The Hatchet turned and walked away, leaving Kate alone again in the rain.

113

Barbara took a deep breath, then sighed as she looked down at the plate in the bottom of the double basin sink. It was coated with dried tomato sauce and basil. It was new since she had scrubbed the dishes the night before.

"Did you stop at Rossi's again?" Barbara asked, picking up the plate and scrubbing it.

Kate was at the dining room table, drinking coffee, eating toast, and reading the newspaper. She got up and came into the kitchen.

"No. My chef was from a can."

"Oh. . . ."

"You know, you don't have to do that anymore. Prewashing the dishes actually makes them dirtier."

"Don't be silly."

"I'm serious. Consumer Nation did a whole series on it. Apparently, there are enzymes in the soap that attack the food."

Barbara used a thumb to scratch at a clump of dried tomato sauce. It took ten cycles before it disappeared.

"Maybe if people rinse their dishes."

Kate shook her head. "The experiment used dried-on food. It worked perfectly."

Barbara hummed, then moved her thumb to another patch of dried sauce. "It must have been a fancy dishwasher."

"What's that supposed to mean? Ours is cheap?"

"No. Our dishwasher works fine. As long as I scrub the dishes."

Kate rolled her eyes. "I'll tell you what. Tonight, we're testing it."

Barbara twisted the plate and picked at a new spot. It felt like someone had taken liquid cement and glued down a tiny pebble.

"What did you eat, Katie? Spaghetti with caramel sauce?"

"Yes, Mother. That's what I ate."

She was about to tell Kate to cut the sarcasm when her thumbnail bent back. She cried, dropping the plate into the sink.

"What happened?"

"My nail."

Kate watched her for a moment, then said, "What's really going on, Mother? And don't say it's the plate. Because you're not using the scrub brush, and you've been acting weird for two days."

So, Kate had noticed.

She had tried to hide her feelings but was never very good at it. Ever since leaving Garrett's bedroom, Barbara had been on edge. At first, he called her non-stop, trying to make sure she wouldn't talk. She dodged him, not sure what to say. Then, when she told him they needed to tell the truth, he stopped calling.

"Everything's fine," Barbara said.

"Okay." Kate's voice made clear she didn't believe her. "Let me know if there's anything I can do to help."

As Kate poured the last of her morning coffee down the sink, there were three hard knocks at the front door. The unexpectedness of the sound caused Barbara to flinch.

"I take it you're not expecting anyone."

Barbara shook her head.

By the time Kate answered the door, there were three more knocks. Hard raps that were closer to banging.

Barbara watched from the edge of the kitchen.

"Is Barbara Becker here?" a man said. His voice was gruff.

Kate stepped to the side, glanced back at her. "Mother, it's for you."

There were two of them, a man, fiftyish, dressed in khakis and a brown sport coat, balding but trying to cover it with a bad comb-over, and a woman, about thirty, also dressed in khakis, with spiky hair, a hard face, and enough muscles to beat up most guys. The woman had a badge clipped to her belt.

"Are you Barbara Becker?" the woman asked, pushing past Kate and coming towards her.

Barbara felt a sudden rush of panic. Without thinking, she turned and bolted for the kitchen.

Before she had taken two steps, the hulk-like woman was on her, clenching her bicep, squeezing like an out-of-control blood pressure cuff.

"Let go of me. You're hurting me," Barbara said.

"Stop resisting," the woman cop said. She grabbed Barbara's left arm and twisted it behind her so hard Barbara thought she might dislocate her shoulder.

"Stop! Stop!" Barbara yelled.

The female cop did not stop. Barbara winced when she felt the cold, hard steel of the handcuffs smack her wrists and lock into place tightly. There was definitely going to be a bruise.

"Ow!" Barbara said.

The male cop came around in front of her. "Barbara Becker, you're under arrest for the murder of Rainn Peterson. You have the right—"

Barbara stopped listening. She looked at Kate. Her daughter's eyes were wide with disbelief.

"Murder?" Kate said. "You must be kidding."

Kate went over to the male cop, who told her to take a step back, not to interfere. He wasn't joking.

"Show me the warrant," Kate said. "And you'd better have one, because no one invited you inside."

"Are you her lawyer?" the man asked.

Kate glared at Barbara, who nodded.

He pulled a folded sheet of papers out of the breast pocket of his sport coat, handed them to Kate.

"We're taking her to the Second Precinct," he said. "You can meet her there."

Kate scanned the paperwork as the female cop led Barbara towards the door.

"I'm not dressed," Barbara said. "These are my pajamas."

"Don't worry," the woman said. "We'll get you a new set of clothes. A nice orange jumpsuit. Courtesy of the State of Texas."

Barbara glanced back at Kate. "Do something! Stop them."

Kate shook her head. "Pain pills, Mother? A rave party? Have you lost your mind?"

"I didn't—"

Kate held up a finger "Don't say anything. I'll meet you at the station."

Barbara nodded, then let the officers whisk her out of the building as tears filled her eyes.

114

Kate met Barbara in a small, windowless interview room at the back of the station. The room was narrow and bare, with only a table, two plastic chairs, and a ticking clock on the wall that looked like it had done time in an elementary school before joining the force.

She glanced up at the corner of the ceiling, confirmed the red light on the circa 1990s closed-circuit camera was off, then sat down across from her mother.

If there was anything positive about the situation, and seeing the glass as half full was a real struggle when your mother was hauled to jail on a murder charge, it was that she was still wearing her pajamas, having not been forced to don the standard jail-issued jumpsuit yet.

"I called Jessica," Kate said. "She's on her way."

"You shouldn't have done that. She's very busy this week."

Kate curled up her nose. Somewhere on the drive from the condo to police station, her mother had calmed down and traded being frantic for delusional.

"Uh-huh. Well, I figured she might make time. Considering your situation."

Barbara waved a hand at her. "You're blowing this out of proportion, Katie. I didn't murder anyone. They'll let me go as soon as they realize they've made a mistake."

The Kubler-Ross stages of grief popped into Kate's mind. Her mother was in stage one, denial.

"I hope you're right, Mother. But from what I've seen, I wouldn't be making dinner plans just yet."

"What's that supposed to mean?"

"Jessica told Willa, who called her father, who called— I don't know who he called. Long story short, one of the detectives let me peek at the file. The girl OD'd on Percocet—"

"Her name was Rainn, Katie."

"I don't think knowing her name helps you."

Barbara paused, seeming to understand. "I only know her name because Garrett introduced me. Before he gave her the bag of pills."

Kate raised an eyebrow. "He gave her the bag of pills?"

"That's what I said. Why are you looking at me that way?"

"Because yesterday, he told the cops you gave her the pills."

"Me?" The information frazzled her. "That's absurd. Why would I give the girl pills?"

"I don't know. Why did you give him pills last week?"

"You're making it sound like I'm a drug dealer."

"Are you?"

"No!"

Kate leaned forward, rested her elbows on the table. "You're saying it's all a big lie. That you didn't give either of them Percocet."

"I, I—"

"Sweet mother of God!" Kate pushed the chair back, stood up like a shot.

"I only gave him one pill."

Kate shook her head, began pacing on her side of the table.

"Why would you do such a stupid thing?"

"He was in pain. From the cancer."

She stopped. "Are you a doctor now, too? In addition to the fake grandmother thing?"

"He forgot his medicine. You know he's dying, right?"

"Dying? Who told you he's dying?"

"Everyone knows it."

"Think, Mother. Hard. Who told you? It's important."

Barbara looked away for a moment, appeared to think it over, then met her eye again. "It doesn't matter who."

"He's not dying."

"Yes, he is."

"No. The file said he's in full remission. There's a ninety percent chance he'll have a normal life."

"That must be a mistake."

"The same kind of mistake the police made arresting you for murder?"

Barbara ignored the jab. "If he's not dying, then why would his doctor prescribe Percocet?"

Kate shook her head. "His doctor never prescribed it! He told the police the first time he ever took any pills was that night at our condo. When you hired him a hooker!"

"I never hired him a hooker."

"You might want to reconsider your answer. Officer Nasty told them you paid her five hundred bucks to have sex with the boy."

Barbara gasped. "I did not. I only paid her to strip, Katie. Just to strip."

"Oh, if that's all. . ."

"I admit hiring Officer Nasty was a momentary lapse in judgment."

"Momentary lapse? Did you also have a momentary lapse when you took him to the racetrack to gamble on the ponies?"

"He promised not to gamble."

Kate shook her heard again.

"Tell the police to check my medicine cabinet. My bottle of Percocet is full. Only three pills should be missing. The two I took on the first day, and one I gave Garrett."

"They took the bottle, Mother. Moments after hauling you away."

"Good."

"No, not good. According to the cops, the bottle had only two pills in it."

"What?"

"Please don't say that's a mistake too."

The magnitude of what was happening seemed to hit Barbara all at once. The color drained from her face. Tears formed in the corner of her eyes. Her lower lip quivered.

"Help me, Katie. I think I'm in big trouble."

"Oh, yeah. I think you're right about that."

115

Kate stepped outside the police precinct and used a hand to shield her eyes from the sun. Scanning the plaza, she looked for her sister but didn't see her.

A moment later, her phone buzzed.

"Where are you?" Kate asked, pressing the phone to her ear. "We don't have much time. They could transfer Mother to the jail any minute."

"Look left. I'm in my car, on the street."

Kate turned and saw Jessica's silver BMW parked at the curb in a no-parking zone.

"Get out. We need to go back inside."

"I'm not going inside, Katie."

"What? Why not?"

"Because it won't help."

"I'm not in the mood for games, Jess."

"Neither am I."

Kate clenched her jaw. "If you're not out here in twenty seconds, I'm coming over there, grabbing you by the hair, and dragging you across the concrete."

Jessica huffed. "With those skinny arms? I'd like to see you try."

"That's it. I'm done."

Kate ended the call, then briskly crossed the plaza, not hesitating as she rounded the front of the car. She yanked on the driver's side door handle. It didn't budge.

"Get out!"

Jessica shook her head, then lowered the window an eighth of an inch. "You know this is a lease. If you damage it, I'm sending you inside. With Mom."

Kate swung an open palm at the glass. When her hand hit, pain rocketed up her wrist. She winced, then shook it out, trying to get the feeling back.

"What wrong with you?" Kate said.

"If you calm down, I'll let you in. Then we can talk like adults."

Kate flashed her sister a hard look, then sighed and went around and got in the passenger seat.

"I want to help Mom," Jessica said. "But we need to be smart."

"Smart how?" Kate asked.

"On the drive over, I heard about Mom's arrest on the radio. They went through all the evidence. It sounds pretty bad, Kate."

"Which is why we need to get inside and start planning her defense."

"No. She needs a criminal defense lawyer."

"And we'll get her one. The best we can find. Just as soon as we get her out on bail."

"Out on bail? We can't be her lawyers."

Kate tilted her head to the side and studied her sister. This was the first time Kate had ever heard Jessica say she wasn't qualified to handle a case. Normally, the woman was so overconfident in her legal ability it was a liability. Jessica had made tons of bail arguments over the years, freeing corporate clients accused of everything from embezzlement to domestic battery.

"Tell me what's really going on."

"I told you. She needs an expert."

"This isn't about Mother. It's about you."

Jessica gasped. "Me?"

"You don't want your name on this case, do you?"

"Don't be ridiculous."

"I can see the guilt all over your face," Kate said.

Jessica paused. "Fine! Maybe I am a little concerned. Maybe I don't want to be the next Becker dragged through the mud."

Kate pushed open the car door, got out.

Jessica said, "You're too emotionally involved. You're not seeing things straight."

Kate ignored the comment and headed back towards the police station.

116

It wasn't until Barbara had been in jail for two days that Kate admitted to herself Jessica was right.

She was too close to the situation to see clearly, too emotionally invested to help.

While she believed her mother's story, none of the criminal defense lawyers she interviewed agreed with her after she told them about the gambling and the drinking and the prostitute. And none would point the finger at a boy with cancer, without rock-solid proof he was lying.

She dumped the last of her wine in the sink and started off down the hall towards her bedroom. In the morning, she would visit her mother in jail and destroy any remaining hope.

Standing by her bed, she heard the doorbell. For a moment, she considered ignoring it. But out of a sense of duty and social obligation, she answered it anyway.

"Good Lord!" Yata Miller said, breezing into the condo's living room. "You look terrible. One would think you'd been in jail."

Yata was dressed in a hideous baby blue onesie with the word Harvard embroidered across her chest. She looked excited, ready for action. Carol trailed close behind her, carrying a clipboard and a pen. She had a black coach's whistle hanging around her neck.

"Not a good time, Yata," Kate said.

"Obviously. Do you think I enjoy coming down here at nine o'clock at night? We're only here because it's serious."

"Yeah, we're going to whip you into shape, solider," Carol said.

"Excuse me?"

Carol put the whistle in her mouth and blew hard. "Now, get down and give me twenty!"

Kate winced at the high-pitched noise two feet from her ear. "Stop it!"

Carol blew the whistle again. "Not until you shape up, woman!"

Yata reached out and yanked the whistle from Carol's mouth. "Really, Carol? You need to dial it back a few notches. This isn't a high school gym class."

Carol nodded, then glared at Kate, menacing, like an angry attack dog being held back by its owner.

Yata said, "What Carol is trying to say is you need to step up. Help your mother."

"Trust me. I am trying. I've done everything possible. All the lawyers agree. The best thing for her to do is take a plea."

Yata raised an eyebrow. "A plea? As in, admit guilt?"

Kate nodded. "It's not good, I know. But legally, we're out of options."

"Then we need to think illegally," Carol said.

Kate frowned. "No."

"It's not the worst idea," Yata said. "Even if sloppily expressed."

"No," Kate repeated. "If the DA were to even catch wind of what you just said, he'd refuse to deal and have both of you arrested for obstruction."

"He'd never catch us," Carol said.

"She's right," Yata said. "I have experience in these matters. I wrote a short story once about a similar situation."

"This isn't one of your stupid stories, Yata."

"Stupid stories? That little gem was nominated for a Sleuthing Award."

"Sleuthing Awards are real good," Carol said.

Kate shook her head.

Yata said, "What if I got the boy to admit he stole the pills? On tape. That would be good enough to free Barbie, right?"

"Please, Yata."

"Just tell me, Katie. Would it be enough?"

She sighed. "Probably. I mean, if you had him on tape. But he's never going to admit it on tape."

"Leave that to me."

Yata started towards the door. Carol followed her.

"What are you going to do?" Kate said.

"Nothing Barbie wouldn't have done for me. Or for you."

Kate sighed. She knew she was going to regret this, but something told her to go with them.

"Wait for me."

Carol smiled. "See, I told you she'd do the right thing."

117

Kate crouched in the backseat of Yata's Subaru, staring across the street at the green and tan Craftsman-style house. It was dark, and the road was empty. The only light came from a single bulb beside the front door.

"So, what's your brilliant plan?" Kate asked. "And please tell me we're not waltzing up to the front door and asking his mother for permission to see him."

Carol glanced back at her from the passenger seat. "If you're this negative at work, I can see why they fired you."

Kate scoffed. "I was being sarcastic, Carol."

"I'm not sure you were," Yata said, switching off the car. "We're waiting for his mother to leave."

There was nothing Kate could see out the window that suggested anyone might be leaving the house any time soon. In fact, apart from an old, four-door Civic in the driveway, it wasn't even clear anyone was at home.

"What makes you think—"

Yata shushed her, then pointed at the house. "Wait."

As if on cue, the front door opened, and a woman who Kate

assumed was Garrett's mother came out. She was dressed in tight blue jeans and a pink t-shirt that clung to her chest. Her hair was pulled back in a ponytail, and she seemed to have a spring in her step. She got in the car and started it.

"How did you know that was going to happen?" Kate asked.

"Carol's been watching the house," Yata said. "Just in case."

"In case what?"

"In case you didn't do your job," Carol said. "Do you think we'd leave Barbie's future in your hands?"

Kate ignored the jab. "Do you know where she's going?"

"A house four blocks over," Yata said. "There's a man, with a beard, and a gut, and a— Let's just say she's not thinking straight."

The instant the mother's taillights disappeared around the corner, they hurried across the street. When they reached the porch, Yata tried the front door. It opened.

"See," Yata said. "I told you she wasn't in her right mind."

They went inside the house.

There was a light in the kitchen at the back. Light also slipped out from underneath a closed door on the left. Kate heard music. A man singing in Italian. It sounded like Ave Maria.

Carol pointed towards the closed door. "That's his bedroom."

"All right," Yata said. "When we go in, you two be quiet. I'll do the talking."

"But if he resists—"

"No, Carol," Yata said. "Focus on your job."

Carol sighed, nodded reluctantly.

They assembled outside the door and waited for Yata's signal. On the count of three, they moved as one, bursting inside the room, fanning out like commandos hunting a terrorist.

But instead of a well-armed fugitive, they saw a boy lying supine on the bed, his head propped up by pillows, an IV coming out of his arm. He looked at them with irritation as if they were interrupting an opera.

Yata went to the wireless speaker on the dresser and switched off the music. Then she grabbed a straight chair by the wall and dragged it over to the bed. She sat down, crossed her legs, and folded her hands in her lap like she was about to give a book talk.

Carol reached into the pocket of her jeans, fumbled around with something, then nodded at Yata.

"You know why we're here, right?" Yata said.

"I can guess."

"Good boy. There are two ways this can go down. The easy way, and the fun way."

Kate fought the urge to roll her eyes. The fun way? Who did Yata think she was? Some sort of gangster?

"It's your choice," Yata said. "But we're not leaving until you admit it."

Garrett shrugged. "Fine. I admit it. Please leave, now. And turn my music back on."

Yata hummed. In all her brilliant planning sessions, she apparently had not considered the possibility he might agree to her demands right away. She seemed unsure of what to do next.

"No, no," Yata said a moment later. "You're not scurrying away that easily. Admit you lied."

"I lied," Garrett said.

"Not in a two-word answer. Explain it. In detail."

There was a noise out in the main room. It sounded as if someone had entered the house. Yata either hadn't heard it or didn't care.

"Admit you lied to the police about the pills. Admit Barbie never gave them to you. Admit you stole the pills from her."

"Admit, admit, admit," Garrett said. "Now, will you please leave me alone?"

There was more noise, the sound of keys jingling.

"I'm back early, Garrett," a woman's voice called out. "Tony had to work. Do you need anything?"

Yata flashed the boy a hard look, shook her head slowly.

Before he could answer, the door swung inward. Garrett's

mother poked her head inside the room. Her eyes went wide when she saw Kate and the two others.

"Carol?" Garrett's mother said. "What are you doing here?"

118

It was comical how fast they bolted from the house, Yata, Carol, and Kate, whizzing past Garrett's mother like kids caught stealing candy from a store.

Kate knew running wouldn't accomplish anything. Not long-term anyway. Garrett's mother had recognized them. Soon enough, they'd all be arrested for witness tampering or intimidation or anything else the DA could shoehorn the facts to mean.

Their only hope was that whatever harebrained scheme Yata had concocted would play out before they were caught.

Back inside the car, a mile away from Garrett's house, Yata glanced at Carol.

"Tell me you got it," Yata said.

"Of course, I got it." Carol sounded annoyed at the question as she pulled the voice recorder from the pocket of her jeans. "Do I need to play it back for you?"

"Yes, please do," Yata said.

"Fine."

Carol flicked a switch on the side of the device.

"Well, that's strange."

"What? What's strange?" Yata took her eyes off the road, glared at Carol.

"Don't snap at me. It's probably nothing. See this red light here. It's supposed to come on when I flip the switch."

Yata's eyes went wide, her mouth fell open. "Carol, please tell me you—"

"Changed the batteries? Of course, I did." Carol flipped over the device and slid off the battery cover. "I pulled out the old ones, even though they weren't old, and—"

She stopped mid-sentence.

"There're no batteries!" Yata yelled.

119

No one spoke for the rest of the car ride back to the condo. Yata was so angry her knuckles turned white from squeezing the steering wheel so hard. Carol stared out the passenger side window, pretending what had happened wasn't a big deal, but Kate saw her wipe away a tear when she thought no one was looking.

For Kate, Carol's mistake wasn't a big deal. The recording would have been useless, anyway. No judge would dismiss the case based on a few comments a kid made while under duress. If anything, the recording would have been Exhibit A against them in a criminal prosecution.

Yet, as much of a circus as the affair turned out to be, Kate was still glad she tagged along because hidden inside Yata's ridiculous plan was a kernel of brilliance. She realized that the answer to saving her mother did lie in Garrett's words. Just not the spoken kind.

Back at the condo, she logged into her email and clicked on a link. She wasn't sure it would work. A minute later, the video conference started.

"What do you want?" the woman said.

"I want to apologize. I should never have treated you that way." The woman stared back at her blankly. "I'm sorry."

"Words are cheap."

"I'm not offering only words."

"Good. Then you know what to do."

"Yes, but—"

"If you're worried about me keeping my end of the deal, you needn't be. I'm a person who always keeps her word."

The insult stung a little.

"It's not that. I was wondering if you might handle another job for me."

The woman raised an eyebrow. "Is that a joke?"

Kate shook her head. "It's not for me. It's my mother. She's in trouble."

The woman sighed. "What is it?"

Kate explained the situation and what she needed.

"Do you think it's possible?" Kate said.

"Of course, it's possible. Give me four hours."

120

Kate closed the video chat, then let out a sigh of relief. She followed another link and transferred two hundred thousand dollars from her investment account to a numbered account in a foreign bank. The sum was outrageous, but she wasn't in a position to negotiate.

Staring at the screen, trying to make peace with how little money she had left to her name, she heard a knock at the door.

"So much for paying extra for a secured building," Kate said, shaking her head at the man in the hallway.

Matt Simpson held a cell phone out towards her. On the screen, a red microphone pulsated in unison with her heartbeat.

"Susan Wilson says you knew Ruth Jacobs was lying. She says you falsified evidence to advance your career. Care to comment?"

"No. You're trespassing, Mr. Simpson. Please leave, or I'll call the police."

"Ms. Wilson says she's referred you to the Bar Association. She predicts you'll lose your license." His eyes twinkled as he spoke.

Kate shrugged. "Susan attacks to deflect. It's her MO."

"Ruth Jacobs sat down with me. Interested in hearing what she said?"

"Not really. The woman's a liar. Haven't you figured that out yet?"

"She says it was all your idea. Claims you told her that if she didn't cry abuse, she'd never see her kid again."

Kate raised an eyebrow. "Maybe you should call Senator Jackson. Ask him about her credibility."

"She's not the only one, Kate. Tina Black says the same thing. She claims you admitted to her the allegations were false. Judge Eide says he was also worried, but you settled the case before he could rule."

With so many knives in her back, it was hard for Kate to stay standing up.

She stepped back, started to close the door.

Matt Simpson put out his hand.

"Move your hand, Simpson," Kate said.

"Seriously? You're giving up? Just like that? No fight at all?"

Kate frowned at him. "You're not getting a freak-out quote, if that's what you're after."

He shook his head. "I want to hear your side of the story."

"My side? What's the point? No one's going to believe me."

"They will, if you give me a bigger fish."

"You're not making sense, Simpson," Kate said.

"The Eagle. Tell me his name."

"How would I know The Eagle's name?"

He scoffed. "Come on, Kate. I know you know. I saw it on your face the first time we met in the bar."

"You've read too many Watergate conspiracy books."

"Tell me what's going on, and I'll rewrite the story. Make you a footnote people won't remember."

She hesitated.

"Trust me, Kate. I can help you."

She swallowed hard. If she talked, life as she knew it would be over. Getting fired by Susan Wilson, being accused of falsifying evidence, being arrested for witness tampering. Those were bad things. No doubt. But in the rough and tumble law biz, where today's friend was yesterday's enemy, they were understandable bads. Maybe even admirable bads. She could hold her head high and say she had done it for her client.

But tattling to Simpson was different. It wouldn't matter if she was right or wrong. No one in the legal community would ever trust her again.

She thought for a moment, then opened the door and motioned him inside.

"Get out your pen, Mr. Simpson. I'm going to tell you a tale about a man named Terry Eide."

121

The morning after she told Matt Simpson everything, there was still one thing she needed to do.

Hire her mother a brilliant lawyer.

She stepped off the elevator into a windowless hallway, her stomach queasy, her mouth dry. She was afraid of what he would say when he saw her, but she needed to do it for her mother.

After rechecking the apartment number against what she had written on a sheet of scrap paper, she raised her hand and knocked three times.

The wait for someone to answer was excruciating. It took all her courage not to turn and run.

"Kate?" Riley said, opening the door. "What are you doing here?"

"I'm sorry," she blurted before her ego had time to reconsider.

"About what?"

Can the man really be so dense? she thought. A moment later, she saw the hint of a smile in his eyes. He was toying with her.

"You know what," she said.

He continued the charade. "No, Kate, I don't. You're going to have to spell it out for me. In detail."

"I'm not spelling it out for you, Riley. I said I was sorry, which is more than anyone's ever done for me."

"Did someone get you fired, Kate?"

She rolled her eyes. "I didn't get you fired."

"Yes, well, thanks for stopping by. I need to get to work."

"You found a new job?"

He nodded.

"Which firm?"

"Not a firm. I'm doing doc review for a litigation support company."

Kate winced. Litigation support companies preyed on unemployed lawyers. They were the legal equivalent of a black hole, sucking things in, never letting anything out. Not once had she ever met a person who got a real law job after doing time there.

"Why don't you hang your shingle? Susan did it."

Riley turned up his nose. "What do you really want, Kate?"

"I need your help."

"What?"

She told him about her mother and Yata and Ruth and Matt Simpson.

"My God," Riley said when she finished. "I'm sorry about your mom. She was always very nice to me."

"Which is why I'm hoping you'll represent her."

"Me? I don't do criminal law."

She waved a hand at him. "You can learn. Plus, your experience working at Susan Wilson is far more valuable."

"Remind me. What sort of experience is that again?"

She reached into her purse, pulled out two stapled sheets of paper.

"This is proof Garrett is lying. An investigator I hired, a woman named Asha, she did some digging for me."

Riley's eyes went wide. "Asha? As in Indian VA Asha who ransomwared Susan's computer?"

"You know about that?"

"Yes. Willa thought I deserved to know."

"I see." Kate made a mental note to smack her sister upside the head when this was over for being such a gossip. "Flip to the second page. Near the bottom. See where Garrett is texting the girl who OD'ed. Read the last exchange."

She watched his eyes move as he read.

"Wow. You couldn't have written this better yourself. He actually says the words 'stole the pills.'"

Kate nodded. "I know. It's great, right?"

"For sure." He tried to hand the papers back to her, but she refused to take them. "You don't need me, Kate. Any lawyer in town can get your mom released now."

She hesitated, trying to come up with a reason he'd believe.

"Oh, I get it," Riley said a moment later. "When you said Asha did some digging, you meant she did some hacking. You're afraid an ethical lawyer might not use it."

"No. I want you because you're good."

"Uh-huh. And because I'm trained in the art of Kate Becker Kung Fu litigation."

She smiled. "Well, that isn't a bad thing, is it?"

"It's not good, Kate."

"It means I respect you. You know I don't respect many people."

He pursed his lips. "True."

"So, you'll do it?"

"Under one condition."

"Anything."

"You need to apologize. For real. For everything."

"That's not one thing," she said, pushing past him into his apartment. "That's a lot of things. But we'll talk about it later. After you get my mother released. What do you think we should call our firm? Becker & Associates or just Becker Law?"

Riley chuckled as he closed the door. "I'm pretty sure it won't be either."

EPILOGUE

Six Months Later

It was Tuesday, at one o'clock in the afternoon, when Kate heard the bell above the front door jingle. She was crouched down near a filing cabinet, alphabetizing manila folders. She glanced over her shoulder, out the open door of the small office, back towards the lobby.

"He's early," Riley said, looking up from the file he was reading at a desk behind her. The desk was an old tanker-style beast the landlord had thrown in for free when he signed a two-year lease for the space.

"Better to get it over with," Kate said.

"If you want, I can sit in."

"No, it's fine."

She didn't feel fine, though. For days, she had been dreading this follow-up interview. Every time her mind drifted back to what her life used to be like, she got a little depressed. Not in need of counseling depressed. More like, I went from big-time lawyer to part-time paralegal at Riley's solo law practice depressed. But having your license suspended does that to a person sometimes.

"You don't owe him this," Riley said. "Simpson's already won a Pulitzer from his stories. And he didn't keep his word about making you look good."

He was right. Despite promising to make Kate forgettable, Simpson had cast her as a main character in his series of articles. Although, in fairness, everything he had written was true. And she did kind of deserve it since she egged him on with Ruth.

She stood up straight, took a deep breath, then went out to the lobby.

Her eyes lit up when she saw Bhagavan Om Shanti standing by the reception desk.

"Today's the day, right?" Kate nodded. "I have a few minutes before my afternoon session. Can I convince you to try a quick meditation? It will soothe that." He pointed at the tension in her face.

Ever since Riley rented the storefront office two doors down from Shanti's Problem Solving Center, the man had been trying to get her to meditate. Her first impressions of him were all wrong. He was a kind, sweet, ethical man. The proof of which was that he didn't get swept up in the Eide purges.

Still, none of that made Kate interested in his new-age nonsense.

"Another time," she said.

Out of the corner of her eye, through a big plate glass window that looked out to the parking lot, she saw a Subaru wagon swerve into a spot near the door. Yata Miller got out, followed by her mother. They made their way inside as Shanti left.

"I still don't see why I need to update my will," Yata said.

"We've talked about it a hundred times," Barbara said. "To account for changes. They recommend updating every year."

"Who's they? The lawyer groups?"

Barbara rolled her eyes. "Didn't you just option another novel?"

"Well, yes. That's quite a story. A guy from—"

"You got like a hundred grand, right?" Barbara said.

A hundred grand? Kate almost choked on her own spit. What idiot would pay a hundred grand for one of Yata's stupid stories?

"Actually, the deal was in yen. But I see your point, Barbie."

Kate laughed. "Yen? What's the exchange rate there? Like a hundred to one? So you got what? A thousand bucks?"

"Nine seventy," Yata said. "But that's nine seventy more than you make in a week, Missie."

"You don't know what I make."

"I know that if I hire Riley to update my will, I'll be a client of this firm. Which would make me your boss."

"You'll never be my boss, Yata."

"We'll see about that." Yata turned towards Barbara. "Have you told your daughter about our business idea?"

Barbara looked down at the ground. "Not yet."

"Good Lord, Mother," Kate said. "Please tell me you're not starting your own grandparents' organization."

After Matt Simpson's article went viral, Grannies R Us went bust. It was all her mother talked about for months.

"We are," Yata said. "In a manner of speaking. Except instead of grandparenting little Stink Bombs, we're grandparenting cats."

"Cats?" Riley said, coming out of his office. "Did someone say cats? I love cats."

In fact, Riley did not love cats. This was his new sales technique. He pretended to like whatever his clients liked in order to win their business. Kate told him being a sycophant was a long-term losing strategy, but he was too wound up trying not to lose money each month to relax, be himself.

The three of them went into Riley's office and closed the door. Kate stayed behind at the reception desk. Matt Simpson breezed into the office five minutes later, smiling, looking relaxed and light on his feet. Success had been good to him.

"Thanks for emailing," he said, reaching into a leather satchel and pulling out a notepad. "This won't take long. I only have a few follow-up questions."

"Okay."

"Has Eide tried to contact you from prison?"

Kate shook her head. "No, and I don't expect him to."

"I wouldn't be so sure. When I spoke to him, he still seemed pretty upset." Simpson glanced down at his notepad. "How about Garrett? Or his mother? Have you heard from either of them?"

"Last I heard, they moved west. Isn't that what it said in the paper?"

"Yep. What's going on with your Indian PI? The one who found Garrett's texts. I've sent her a few messages, but she never responds."

"I don't know. Maybe she doesn't like reporters."

"Yeah, well, can you try to make contact? I really want to talk to her? My gut says she's got some interesting stories."

She does, Kate thought. Too bad you'll never hear them.

Since that day she came clean to him, she resolved to tell the truth. More often. But that didn't mean he needed to know everything about her life. Asha and Wayne and the ransomware and her search for a sperm donor were off limits.

"I'll see what I can do," Kate said.

"Great." Simpson checked his notepad one last time, then shoved it back into his satchel. "Take care, Kate. I hope you get your license back, soon."

He turned to leave, and she called out to him.

"That's it? You're not even going to ask about the other thing?"

Simpson flashed her a confused look. "Are you will to talk about it?"

"Maybe I've changed my mind?"

"Have you, Kate?"

She hesitated.

"No."

He smiled. "You're one of the good ones, you know. Even if you do sometimes misstep, mislead, lie, submit false evi—"

"Thanks, Simpson."

"If you do change your mind, decide to talk about it, you know how to reach me. I promise you front page. The appetite for gossip about our future governor is insatiable. And now that your sister is with him," he shook his head. "It's despicable."

"We were over. Plus, he wasn't the man I thought he was."

Matt Simpson nodded, then turned and walked out the door.

He didn't believe it.

Neither did she.

THE BECKER FAMILY RETURNS!

Kate, Jessica, Barbara, Yata, and all the gang are back for another adventure. The second book in the series has a launch date in early 2022. Stay up to date on the latest news, including when preordering is available, by joining my VIP Club.

Robert Gadkey
Edina, Fall 2021

JOIN MY VIP CLUB

Join my exclusive VIP Club and be the first to hear about my new books. Plus, you'll get two of my short stories–absolutely free.

The first is *The Best Job Ever*. It's loosely based on a short story I wrote and published in The Carolina Quarterly in 2019. It's one of my all-time favorites.

> *Otis Covington loved his unusual job. And the six-figures it paid him.*
>
> *But as he approached mandatory retirement age, he needed to find a family member to take his place if he wanted to get a special pension his employer offered.*
>
> *However, when his twenty-year-old nephew turns him down, things begin to spiral out of control.*
>
> *How far will Otis go for money?*

The second story is *Making Partner*. It's a prequel to my book *Operation Snitch*. It's a suspenseful thriller about a young lawyer.

> *Young attorney Beau Campbell is three days away from his dream of making partner at the small boutique law firm of Morgan, Peterson, and Addison.*
>
> *All he wants is to cross the finish line without making waves.*

But late one night, he gets an urgent call from the firm's biggest client—a company he hardly knows. A simple assignment they give him turns his life upside down and forces him to question everything he thought was true.

Can Beau keep it together long enough to get the life he always wanted?

It's free to sign up. There's no obligation. You'll never be spammed, and you can opt-out at any time.

To join the VIP CLUB, go to:

www.robertgadkey.com/vip-club

ALSO BY ROBERT GADKEY

IN THE BEAU CAMPBELL THRILLER SERIES

Operation Snitch

Six years out of law school, Minneapolis attorney Beau Campbell was broke. No reputable firm would touch him because the FBI had shut down his last employer. Facing mountains of debt, he hung a shingle and started his own firm specializing in vengeful ex-spouses needing a divorce lawyer.

One night, while working late at the office, an unexpected female visitor appeared in his lobby. When she asked for his help, he felt powerless to say no.

Suddenly, he was thrust into the middle of a dangerous game with implications that stretched far beyond a simple court case.

Can Beau find a way back to a normal life before it's too late?

Also by Robert Gadkey

STANDALONE BOOKS

Hunting for Time

On a snowy afternoon in rural Minnesota, con artist Ronan Sullivan sat on a bus bench waiting to go back to civilization. At sixty-five years old, he had just finished his third stint at Rockville Prison. Broke and alone, his future looked bleak.

But when a car sent by his estranged brother arrives to take him home, his world is thrown upside down. Can Ronan seize the opportunity for a second chance? Or will he stay the man he has always been?

If you like fast-paced stories with a heart that keep you guessing, then this book is for you.

ACKNOWLEDGMENTS

As always, I am indebted beyond words to my wife, Angela, who is the best partner, friend, confidant, champion, and person I've ever known. Without her, none of this would be possible. She makes me better in every way.

I am also grateful to my parents, who've read every story I've written since the beginning. They are unwaveringly positive, even when a book isn't to their taste. My mother read a clunky, spiral-bound version of this book on an airplane. My father read it, cover to cover, some parts even twice, though he usually eschews books with no sex, violence, or action. I laughed at that last one.

My brother, Andrew, spent hours teaching me story and suggested numerous changes. He knows more about stories than anyone. Someday, he'll write a novel. When he does, please read it. Odds are it will be better than mine. He's smarter than me at everything.

To my writing colleagues, Krysta, Jake, and Tom. These three amazing people spent hours with me each week listening as I lamented about writing. They also read some pretty lousy prose and told me it was great so that I wouldn't give up. You all are very special.

My friend Meridith Wardle read an advance copy of the book and saved me from embarrassing mistakes. The mistakes that remain are mine.

My mentor and friend, Maureen Millea Smith, was incredibly generous with her time. I owe her a lot. More than will fit on this page.

Finally, years ago, when I started writing, I met Dean Wesley Smith. While Dean and I don't agree on everything (he'd probably say it's because I'm too inexperienced—he's written over a hundred novels), his guidance changed my life. Without him, I wouldn't have finished a single story. I had been starting and quitting for twenty years when he set me straight. Thanks, Dean. What you do matters.

ABOUT THE AUTHOR

Robert Gadkey graduated from Drake University and received a law degree from The University of Iowa College of Law. Prior to writing fiction, he spent more than a decade working as a divorce lawyer.

In 2018, he was a runner-up in Gotham Writers Workshop Goodnight New York contest. In 2019, his first short story, The White Room, was published by The Carolina Quarterly. In 2020, he published *Operation Snitch* and *Hunting for Time*.

He and his wife, Angela, have two children and reside in the Twin Cities metropolitan area.

For more information:
    www.robertgadkey.com
    Robert@robertgadkey.com

Made in the USA
Monee, IL
18 December 2021